Play the Game

Also by Doug Dixon

THE JUMP OFF

Play the Game

Doug Dixon

KENSINGTON PUBLISHING CORP.
http://www.kensingtonbooks.com

DAFINA BOOKS are published by

Kensington Publishing Corp.
850 Third Avenue
New York, NY 10022

All Kensington titles, imprints and distributed lines are available at special quantity discounts for bulk purchases for sales promotion, premiums, fund-raising, educational or institutional use.

Special book excerpts or customized printings can also be created to fit specific needs. For details, write or phone the office of the Kensington Special Sales Manager: Kensington Publishing Corp., 850 Third Avenue, New York, NY 10022. Attn. Special Sales Department. Phone: 1-800-221-2647.

Dafina Books and the Dafina logo Reg. U.S. Pat. & TM Off.

ISBN-13: 978-0-7582-1358-7
ISBN-10: 0-7582-1358-1

First Kensington Trade Paperback Printing: August 2007
10 9 8 7 6 5 4 3 2 1

Printed in the United States of America

This book is dedicated to my loving parents, Fred and Leola Dixon; my brother, Desmond Dixon; my sister, Deirdri Brown; and to the late Mrs. Cora Anderson, my spiritual adviser, who taught me how to walk in the confidence of God in troubled times.

ACKNOWLEDGMENTS

First and foremost, thank you God for every blessing you have put in my life.

Special thanks to Selena James and Rakia Clark for driving this project.

Thank you fellas: Tracey Clarke, Dwayne Butler, Kenneth Allen, Darryl Portis, Cedric Perryman, Gerald Westry, and Damian Collins.

Thank you nupes: Archie Wesley, Hampton Simmons, and Terrance Marshall for continued encouragement.

To the other nupes: Kenneth Ried and Eric Goshay.

Thanks to the fans who sent personal emails for *The Jump Off*.

Special dedication to the late Franck "Clyde" DuCloux (Rest In Peace).

PROLOGUE

"Excuse me. Do you have these boots in a size six?" Mya asked the clerk at Nordstrom's department store.

Mya LeVeaux was out doing her typical Saturday afternoon shopping to relieve stress. Lord knows that was what she needed right about now. Last night Mya had received word from her hometown of New Orleans that her ex-boyfriend, Marvin DuCloux, had just proposed marriage to a neurosurgeon, and asked Mya's own father, Bishop Franklyn LeVeaux, to do the service. Bishop LeVeaux had graciously accepted the honor, as Marvin's family had long been members at Greater Mount Olive Full Gospel Baptist Church.

Months earlier, Mya had left New Orleans after the annual church picnic. Marvin, her boyfriend of three years, had shown up two hours late but five minutes *before* Wendy Landreaux, the Church Hoe, arrived. Earlier that day, the church gossiper, Ms. Thibodaux, had left the two of them alone to finish loading refreshments into the church van for the picnic. No one had seen the two since then. When Wendy arrived she had what appeared to be semen scattered throughout the top of her hair and around her forehead.

"Let me check for you, ma'am," the clerk replied before walking off toward the storage area. A couple of minutes later the salesclerk appeared, holding the same burgundy boot Mya had given her.

"Ma'am, the only size six we have left is being tried on by those women over there." The salesclerk pointed out two strangers to

Mya—they were sitting in the corner of the shoe department. Stephanie Hall, a high-yella sista with her hair pulled back into a ponytail, was trying to talk her friend Tangie Jackson, a sista with shoulder-length hair and a shiny peanut-butter-color complexion, out of buying the boots that were actually too small for her size-seven foot.

Stephanie and Tangie had grown up together since middle school and were on their weekly girls' day out. For Stephanie it was a way for her just-out-of-jail boyfriend, Curtis Williams, to spend time with their two-year-old son, Brandon. But for Tangie it was a celebration, especially since her divorce from her second husband had just been finalized the day before. Tangie had very little patience when it came to what she considered a weak-ass man, and she was not afraid to express her opinion, whether it was about sex, the way he dressed, or if he was just getting on her nerves.

"We have a size five in stock. Would you like to try that one on?" the salesclerk asked Mya.

"Oh, no, that would be too small . . . Well, thanks, anyway," Mya replied, disappointed. "I'll just look around for something else," she added as she walked off, looking at other displays in the department.

Mya picked up another shoe but they didn't have that one in her size, either. She glanced back over at the two women who were still discussing the boots with their salesclerk. Curious as to what was being said, Mya walked toward them nonchalantly, pretending to browse other merchandise.

Tangie, still not convinced the boots were too small, opened the shoebox and pulled them out once again.

"Let me try them on one more time. They didn't feel that bad on my feet," Tangie said, taking off her shoes. Mya stood back and watched as Tangie forced each foot into the boots. As Tangie got up to walk around, she pressed her lips together as she took one step at a time, each one making her frown harder and harder. By the fourth or fifth step, she dropped to her knees in agony. "Girl, get these fucking boots off my feet," she shouted to Stephanie.

Mya turned her head to hide her laughter. It was obvious this girl wanted those boots at any cost.

As Stephanie struggled to get the left boot off, Tangie looked up at Mya as she tried to pull the right boot off. "Hey, don't just stand there. Help me get this damn boot off my foot," Tangie yelled at Mya.

Mya dropped her bags, then rushed over and grabbed the right boot and began pulling with all her might. People standing around were laughing as Tangie's body twisted and turned in all directions.

Stephanie and Mya struggled for two or three minutes, dragging Tangie's body down the aisle of the shoe department until they managed to get the boots off.

After more laughter, everyone managed to compose themselves while Tangie straightened her clothes and put her hair back in place before sitting down next to the empty shoebox.

Mya paused for a moment, admiring the size six that she so desperately wanted. "Do you mind if I try them on?" she asked politely.

"Hell, no. Be my guest," Tangie replied, wiping the beads of sweat that had formed on her forehead.

Mya took off her shoes and slipped both her feet into the boots with ease and walked in front of the mirror.

"Well, I'll be damned," Tangie said, disappointment in her voice.

"How do you think they look on me?" Mya asked.

"I hate to say it but they really look good on you," Tangie replied.

"Yeah, they do look nice," Stephanie said.

Then the salesclerk passed by and saw Mya walking in the boots. "Oh, so you *were* able to find the last pair of size six, huh?"

Mya smiled and turned toward Tangie, who was sitting with a look of disbelief on her face.

"Well, I guess she did," Tangie said dryly.

"Okay, well, when you're ready, I'll ring them up for you," the salesclerk replied as she walked off.

Mya smiled and sat down next to the two women, happy to get the boots, and began taking them off and placing them back into the shoebox.

"Thanks, you guys," Mya said as she stood up to walk to the register.

"Oh, you're quite welcome . . . Oh, I'm Stephanie Hall, by the way, and this nut over here is my friend, Tangie Jackson."

"Nice to meet you both. I'm Mya LeVeaux."

"LeVeaux?" Tangie repeated, sitting up in her chair. "Surely you're not from Atlanta?"

"No, I'm from New Orleans. Why?" Mya replied.

"Just never heard the name—"

"Anyway, Mya, so how long have you lived in Atlanta?" Stephanie interrupted.

"Oh, not quite a year yet," Mya replied. "I teach fourth grade at Austell Middle School near Six Flags."

"Oh, you teach school, too?" Tangie replied, surprised. "So do Stephanie and me. We teach at Stephenson Middle School in Stone Mountain."

"Oh, really? That's a coincidence," Mya replied.

"Well, Tangie and I are about to grab some lunch and drinks at the Cheesecake Factory down the street. You're welcome to join us," Stephanie said.

Surprised at the invitation, Mya agreed, and after paying for her boots, they all exited the store.

From that day on, the three of them found that they all had a lot in common and established a loving friendship.

CHAPTER I

Mya

At three o'clock the school bell rang, ending my last class for the week. I put my books in my desk drawers and placed all of the papers from the day's lessons in my briefcase to take home and grade over the weekend. I watched as my fourth-grade students rushed out the door with big smiles and filtered into the hallway with the other students.

Tangie put in a good word for me at Stephenson Middle School after the fourth-grade teacher moved out of state. I was glad to get out of Austell Middle School, being that my commute was about seventy miles round-trip. Stephanie teaches second grade, while Tangie teaches third.

After straightening up my classroom, I locked the door behind me and walked down to the teachers' lounge near the front entrance. When I opened the door I saw Tangie and Stephanie sitting on the couch, looking exhausted.

"Girl, I'm so glad it's Friday, I don't know what to *do*," Tangie said, pressing her palms against her temples.

"Girl, I'm ready to go home, take a hot bath, and sip on a nice, cool glass of wine," Stephanie said.

"Wine? Girl, I need some Grey Goose and cranberry juice right about now, with these bad-ass kids," Tangie said.

"I just want to go home and curl up with a good book," I said, my eyes closed in thought.

"A book?" Tangie mocked. "Girl, you *should* be trying to curl up with a man. When was the last time you got some?"

I opened my eyes as Tangie broke my train of thought. "What?"

"You heard me—*a man*. I know your dad is a big-time preacher and all, but c'mon. You'd better jump on one of these fine single brothers out there. What are you waiting for?"

"Tangie, you know Mya is waiting for Mr. Right. You'd better tell her—"

"Mr. Right, huh? Ain't no such thing," Tangie responded with assurance.

"Amen to that," Stephanie replied.

"One thing I do know is that I'm curling up with Mr. Todd Wilson tonight." Tangie continued.

Todd Wilson had been the quarterback of Tangie and Stephanie's high-school football team. According to Stephanie it was merely a sexual relationship that lasted throughout their high-school years. After graduation, Todd went to Alabama State University in Montgomery on an athletic scholarship, and never looked back.

"What? Todd Wilson?" Stephanie replied in disbelief. "Last I heard he was married with kids and living in Tennessee."

"He *was* living in Tennessee but they moved back to Atlanta about a year ago. We ran into each other at the club this past weekend and exchanged numbers."

"You mean after all these years you're just going to spread your legs for this man?" I asked in a shocked tone.

"Hell, yes. Girl, you don't understand. Todd was my first. Every time we did it, my fucking toes curled. It's rare that you meet a man that can do all that."

"Girl, where is your respect for yourself? That man is married with a family," Stephanie exclaimed.

"Look, I've been married twice, and me and those bastards got on each other's nerves. Hell, if you ask me, I'm doing his wife a favor by getting his ass out of the house every now and then. After all, it's just sex."

"Anyway," Stephanie replied dryly.

"Yeah, Tangie, you can't trust a man who cheats on his wife," I said.

"You two just don't understand. It's not trust that I want . . . It's that ten-inch dick." Caught off guard, Stephanie and I laughed out loud.

"Now, if you two don't mind, I will see you later. I have to get ready for my weekend." Tangie winked at us.

Outside the window from the teachers' lounge you could see the rain beginning to come down in drizzles. I gathered the rest of my things as Stephanie and I walked outside under the covered walkway.

"I'll call you later!" I shouted as I ran to my car. Stephanie trotted alongside me as she ran toward hers.

After struggling to get my car door open, I managed to get inside. Heading toward my town house in Lawrenceville, I hit horrible traffic. I sat there for about twenty minutes on I-85, staring at the back of this SUV that blocked my view of the traffic ahead. I turned up the radio to hear my favorite song. During the course of a ten-minute music marathon, a commercial came on about ladies' night at the newly opened club Nsomnia this Saturday night. *Hmm, this might be a good chance to meet some really nice brothers*, I thought. Still sitting in traffic, I grabbed a pen from my purse and wrote down the details of the event. *I'm going to call the girls and see if they are down for it*, I thought.

When I made it home I read through my mail, ate dinner, then headed upstairs and put on some shorts and a tee-shirt before lying across my bed. *Another lonely weekend*, I thought. I turned on the TV and watched the evening news before checking my answering machine. I had one call, from my Grandma LeVeaux. She's my paternal grandmother and the grandparent I'm closest to. When I was little, I used to spend the weekends at her house and we would stay up all night talking about her childhood. Grandma LeVeaux lives in Metairic, an outskirt of New Orleans. She's a mixture of French and Creole with a really thick New Orleans drawl. Grandma LeVeaux doesn't play, either. She keeps a 22-caliber pistol with her at all times and will pull it out in a heartbeat. She spends her day mostly sitting on the porch, drinking her table wine, gossiping with her friends that live down the street, or she sits in front of the TV, watching game shows and soaps. She's been on her own since my granddad passed ten years ago, but she's managed to stay strong despite her loss.

"Hey, Grandma. How are you?" I called.

"Mya? Girl, Don't 'hey, Grandma' me. Why haven't you called me lately, baby?"

"I'm sorry, Grandma, I—"

"I haven't heard from you in over two months. What are you doing out there?"

"Nothing much, just working . . . I like the new school where I'm teaching."

"When are you coming to see me? I see all of my grandchildren but you. You know Rodney is out of prison."

"What? Really?" I replied, surprised.

Rodney LeVeaux is my one cousin who is fucking insane. He is my dad's brother's son. We grew up really close until my dad banned him from coming over to the house with what my father called his "devilish ways." Rodney was in prison for robbing department stores in the malls around New Orleans. He would walk into a store about fifteen minutes before it closed, and hide underneath the clothes rack until the employees left for the night. Afterwards, he would walk around filling trash bags with clothes, then line them up near the fire exit. From there he would call his friends, who were waiting outside in their cars, and he would burst open the door, throwing everything in the trunk before driving off. Because he had prior offenses, the judge threw the book at him and sentenced him to four years in prison.

"Where is he now?" I asked.

"I don't know. He came by here one day for a while and ate dinner with me but I haven't seen him since. He asked about you."

"Really? Has he gone by to see Daddy?"

"You know better than that. You know how your daddy is."

My dad has a reputation for being a hard-nosed minister. I grew up in a very strict household. I couldn't wear makeup until I was a senior in high school. Couldn't talk on the telephone after seven o'clock until I was sixteen, and Marvin, my first love, had to join the choir and get involved in church activities before my father would even consider letting me go out with him. I was so afraid of my dad finding out, I was scared to let Marvin touch me whenever we'd go out on dates. Needless to say, he got tired of my excuses for not kissing him, and we finally broke up for a while until after my first year in college at Louisiana State University—which is where I saw a real, live penis for the first time, by the way. I actually lost my virginity to a basketball player named Lyndell Moody in the backseat of his Ford Mustang. He was so rough with me I was sore for about a week. Not to mention that fucker gave me crabs. The night before I was to go home for Christmas break, I was asleep and felt something crawling all over me between my legs. I jumped up and ran to the bathroom to check myself out. I freaked when I saw what looked to be little, tiny lobsters everywhere. They were on my pubic hairs, my arm, and even my eyelashes. I stayed up all night trying to kill them with rubbing alcohol but it felt like they were crawling all over my body.

I panicked and quickly called my Grandma LeVeaux, who laughed out loud when I told her what I was feeling. "Girl, you got the crabs, and alcohol ain't gonna do nothing but stir them up. I tell you what—instead of going home, come stay with me for a couple of days until we get you fixed up. Just tell your parents you're coming over to help me cook my Christmas dinner for the family. Oh, and bring all of the clothes and panties you wore for the week along with your sheets and pillowcases."

When I arrived at her house early that morning, Grandma LeVeaux was up waiting on me. She had me get into the bathtub and shave all of my pubic hair off, then had me rub this ointment all over my body. She took my clothes that were in this garbage bag and put them in a barrel in the backyard near her porch and set them on fire. When she came back inside, she looked over at me with a grin and cooked us some breakfast.

I love my grandma. I could tell her anything about my life and she would give me straight answers, whether it hurt my feelings or not. It's hard to believe how different she and my dad are.

In the midst of our conversation the rain started coming down really hard and lightning flashed through the window.

"Ohhh, Grandma, it's about to storm. I just saw lightning outside my window."

"Okay, baby, you'd better turn off your lights and get into bed so it won't strike you."

I smiled to myself. "Okay, Grandma. I love you and I'll call you later." I hung up the phone.

*　*　*

The rain continued to come down even harder as the daylight faded into darkness. It was the perfect evening to be curled up with the person you loved. I could hear the hard drops fall on my rooftop and along the leaves on the trees outside my bedroom window, like swishing waves in the ocean. My emotions were running wild as I began to get really horny lying balled in a knot with my pillow between my legs. I started thinking about old killer sex from back in the day with Marvin and how he used to get me right at my climax point before telling me he loved me softly in my ear, making me cum uncontrollably. And how he used to hold me afterwards, his soft, hairy chest pressed against my face. Just as my hand began to slowly move down toward my panties, the thunder suddenly exploded in the air like cannons going off, breaking everything that had a sexual appeal to it in my mind. I tensed up and grabbed the covers and pulled them over my head as my heart pounded from fear. *Marvin,* I thought to myself. *He should be the last person on my mind, the way he did me. Embarrassing me in front of my . . .* Before I knew it, the weight of my hectic day took over and I drifted off to sleep.

CHAPTER 2

Tangie

Todd called as I was getting out of the shower to let me know he was leaving for lunch. He worked the three-to-eleven shift at a telecommunications company not far from my apartment. By the time I put on something comfortable there was a knock at the door. As soon as I opened it, Todd walked in and we quickly kissed. Instantly it brought back memories from years ago when I would just melt when our tongues met. He moved his hand down the middle of my back and inside my panties, gripping my ass. I pulled back as he stared at me with his light green eyes.

"Damn, I missed those lips," Todd said, staring down at me.

"What lips are you referring to?" I replied with sarcasm.

Todd dragged his hand from around my ass to the front, feeling my moist kitty. I pulled his hand out and escorted him to my den.

"Would you like something to drink?" I asked, walking toward the kitchen.

"Look, baby. I only get an hour for lunch and I damn sure don't want to waste it with small talk."

That's the kind of man I like. Straight and to the point. I opened the refrigerator and got some bottled water. When I turned around, Todd was standing there with his shirt off, unbuckling his pants. His light-colored chest was still chiseled with rows of brown hair slightly covering his skin tone. I took a sip of my water and walked to my bedroom. By the time I pulled down my shorts, Todd was standing in the doorway butt-ass naked with his cell phone in hand. I scanned his body until my eyes stopped at the ten inches pointing right at me. You could put both my husbands' penises together and it couldn't compare to Todd's. His sex was in a class by itself. Not just because he was well endowed but because of the affection that came along with his sex. By the time I got into bed, Todd had placed his cell phone on my nightstand table and turned me over on my back.

"Is it as sweet as before?" he asked, kissing my breast and working his way down.

"Sweeter," I replied in a passionate tone.

Todd took his time kissing everything below my waist. His tongue action had me damn near drooling as he worked his magic. Minutes later he moved his kisses back up to my breast and tried to penetrate me.

"Uh-uh, aren't you forgetting something?" I asked, looking in his eyes.

"What? Oh, a condom? Baby, I'm sorry, but I forgot to bring some. It doesn't matter, anyway. The only woman I've been with is my wife."

"Fuck that! No glove, no love," I replied sternly.

There was a moment of silence as we stared at each other. "Wait. I just remembered I have one in my drawer." I got out of bed.

"Here you go. You better make this work 'cause I don't have any more." I handed Todd the condom. It was a Lifestyle condom, although Todd was probably used to wearing magnums. It didn't matter to me as long as the condom did its job.

When I got back in bed the mood changed quickly and I was more excited than before as Todd and I engaged in pure passion. He tossed my body around in different positions without missing a stroke. I moaned so long and hard that my mouth got extremely dry. His thrust was so powerful I felt it at the pit of my stomach, but enjoyed every minute of it. After climaxing twice, Todd finally reached his peak. His body collapsed on me as his heart pounded out of control. As he continued his soft kisses around my neck, his cell phone rang, interrupting our pleasure. He got out of bed and grabbed it on his way to the bathroom and closed the door behind him. I figured it was his wife, so I rolled over and pulled the covers over my naked body. Within seconds *my* phone rang. I got up and grabbed my cordless and walked into the den.

"What's up?" I answered—Burton Williams was on the other end. Burton was an older man who I often went out with from time to time. Burton owned a detail shop in Buckhead in downtown Atlanta. His clients include entertainers, athletes, and some wanna-be ballers. He was in his late forties and we met at a car show a few months previously. We'd fooled around a couple of times, hugging and squeezing, but had never had sex.

"Hi, Burt, what's going on?"

"Nothing much, baby, just had you on my mind and wanted to call and see what you were up to. Did I catch you at a bad time?"

"Uh, ooh—" I was interrupted by a pleasant sensation between my legs from the back.

I looked down and Todd was on all fours, licking me between the backs of my thighs. "Look, Burt, let me call you back." I hung up abruptly.

I was sizzling until I realized that we didn't have any more condoms. "Hey, wait, wait, wait. We don't have any more condoms. What happened to the old one?"

"Oh, I flushed it down the toilet. You didn't expect me to use the same one, did you?" Todd replied, looking up at me.

"Well, your chances of getting some more ass just went down the toilet with it," I replied, walking to my bedroom.

"Damn, Tangie. It never used to be like this," Todd reminded me.

"Yeah, and your ass never used to be married. Look, if we're going to do this, we're going to have to play by my rules, and the number one rule is a condom."

Todd chuckled. "A'ight, I hear what you're saying. Besides, I have to get back to work, anyway. When can we do this again?"

"Give me a call when you can get out and we'll go from there."

Todd got dressed and I walked him to the door. He gave me one last passionate kiss before leaving, then walked away as I closed the door behind him. Seconds later my phone rang again as I was about to take another shower.

"Hey, baby. What happened earlier? Are you all right?" It was Burt again, concerned about why I got off the phone so suddenly.

"No, I'm fine. I had some issues going on but I'm cool."

"You in the mood for some Burton Williams tonight?" he asked in a low tone. *Man, are you serious?* I thought. *After what I just got, ain't nothing an old-ass man like you can do for me tonight.*

"Burt, I'm going to have to pass. I'm really not in the mood right now."

"I hear you, baby. Maybe next time."

"Yeah," I replied before hanging up.

After my shower I sat in bed, reliving the evening. It had been years since I'd been with Todd, and he'd left me with the same feelings I'd had years before.

CHAPTER 3

Stephanie

I was awakened at the crack of dawn by Curtis as he staggered in, having been out all night. Curtis and I have been dating for over three years and living together for a year and a half, starting just after he got out of jail for doing a drug run for one of his cousins.

We first met at the wedding of mutual friends. I caught the bridal bouquet and he caught the garter and have been together ever since. When we first started dating, Curtis had a job working at an auto body shop repairing cars with the DeKalb County motor pool. Since his arrest he hasn't been able to keep a job for more than three months at a time. When he gets in his little moods, he escapes reality by hanging out at all hours of the night with his friends, drinking and smoking. The only reason I put up with his shit is because of our two-year-old son, Brandon, who thinks the world of Curtis. I, on the other hand, am losing patience daily with Curtis's irresponsible behavior.

Curtis took off his clothes and tossed them on the floor by his side of the bed and got under the covers. The smell of cheap alcohol and weed immediately filled the air. I turned over with my back facing him and pulled the covers over my face to filter the smell. As I drifted off to sleep I suddenly felt Curtis's manhood stabbing me in my back. I turned over again, this time facing the ceiling. Curtis reached over and rubbed his hand on my stomach, moving it downward and between my legs. I grabbed his hand and pushed it away.

Seconds later he tried the same move and again I pushed his hand away.

"What's up with that shit?" he said in a drunken slur.

"You're kidding, right?" I replied in disbelief.

"Oh, so I can't get any attention tonight?"

"Hell, no. I'm trying to sleep. You should have thought about that before you stayed out all night getting drunk."

"Oh, so that's what this is about? You know what—forget it," he replied before rolling over and falling asleep.

I slept for about three more hours before being awakened by Curtis's annoying snore. I jumped in the shower and went to the kitchen to prepare breakfast for Brandon. I walked into Brandon's bedroom as he lay in bed holding his stuffed teddy bear. When he heard me enter the room, his eyes slowly opened—then he got out of bed and walked toward me with his arms extended.

"Good morning, sweetie." I hugged him.

Brandon kissed me on my cheek as I picked him up, taking him in the hall bathroom to wash his face before giving him his bowl of cream of wheat. I made a cup of coffee and took a seat next to Brandon as I opened the morning paper that Curtis had left on the table. The first thing I did each morning was read my daily horoscope, applying what it said to my everyday life. It was sort of like a guide to help me through my day. My friends and family thought I was crazy for actually believing in it, but they don't know how much it helped me in getting my job and winning money at lotteries—even when Curtis was fighting his legal battles, I used our horoscope to guide us through the tough times.

Minutes later, Curtis woke up and walked into the bathroom. When Brandon heard this, he jumped from his chair and ran toward Curtis as he washed his hands.

"Brandon, come back here and finish your breakfast," I yelled in a polite tone.

Brandon ignored me and continued in the direction of Curtis. By the time Brandon got to the door, Curtis was coming out and they met outside the door.

"Good morning, son," Curtis said as he picked Brandon up.

Brandon just giggled as Curtis carried him back into the kitchen and sat him down at the table to finish his breakfast.

"Good morning," Curtis said, directing his attention to me.

I looked up at him as he walked over to the coffeepot with his do-rag tied around his braided hair. "Good morning," I replied dryly.

"What's for breakfast?" he asked.

"Oh, so you've got the munchies now?"

"What's that supposed to mean?" he replied.

"You know what I mean. Did you forget why you went to jail? You, coming in here at odd hours of the night, drinking and smoking with your friends—"

"I was drinking, yes. But I didn't touch drugs of any kind . . . Is that why you have an attitude this morning?"

"I don't have an attitude. I just want you to understand that what you do out there in those streets affects us," I replied.

"Well, being out in them streets last night landed me a job working on a couple of cars today."

I took a sip of my coffee.

"Can I please get a bacon and egg sandwich before I go to work?" He stared at me.

I looked up at him as I got up to make him a sandwich. After all, Curtis *was* doing all he could to keep a steady flow of money coming. I was doing just fine on my teacher's salary but I wanted more out of life than just getting by. Curtis had dreams of one day owning his own body shop, and I guess this was the way he had to build up his reputation. My horoscope said that I should have more patience with troubled situations, and I could see that if I kept going back and forth with him it could have escalated.

As I made Curtis a breakfast sandwich, Brandon sat in front of the TV while Curtis showered. By the time he got dressed I had his sandwich and had filled his thermos with coffee.

He walked over to me and kissed me on the lips. "Baby, I'm sorry for disrespecting you last night, okay?"

I smiled as the words wiped away the little anger I had inside of me. *My horoscope was right again*, I thought.

Curtis walked over to Brandon and kissed him on the cheek before going out the door. I began cleaning up the kitchen and parts of the other rooms before doing laundry. In the midst of this, Mya called.

"Hi, Mya," I said.

"Girl, what's up?" Mya asked.

"Nothing. Just doing my usual weekend cleaning."

"There's a ladies' night party at Club Nsomnia tonight. I don't want to go by myself. Are you down for it?"

"Have you talked to Tangie?" I asked.

"No, but let's call her on the three-way," Mya said as she clicked over to call.

"Hello?" Tangie answered in an exhausted tone.

"Girl, you still sleep?" Stephanie asked.

"No, I'm awake. What's up?"

"Hey, Tangie," Mya cut in. "There's a ladies' night at Club Nsomnia tonight. You down for hanging out?"

"Nsomnia? Hell, yeah. Saturday is when the ballers come out," Tangie replied, excited.

"What about you, Stephanie?" Mya asked.

"I don't know about that. You know how Curtis is about me going to a club."

"What?" Tangie shrieked. "As much as Curtis hangs his ass out in the streets, you deserve at least one night on the town. Make his ass stay home with Brandon for a change."

"Yeah, Stephanie. Just tell him we're having a ladies' night out tonight," Mya said.

I paused for a moment. "You know what? You're right. He dragged his ass in here this morning at around four o'clock. Yeah, count me in."

"Great," Mya replied. "Let's meet over to my house at around six o'clock and we can ride to the club together."

"That sounds like a plan. I'll see you guys later," Tangie said before hanging up.

"Okay, Mya. I'll see you then. I'm just going to finish doing laundry."

Curtis came in at around three o'clock with a look of exhaustion on his face. I was in the kitchen finishing up dinner as Brandon sat in the den watching cartoons. Curtis put his thermos on the kitchen counter and kissed me on the cheek.

"Hey, baby," he said as he continued past me.

"How was your day?" I asked. "Dinner will be ready in a few minutes."

"I'm beat. I'm going to take a shower and get into bed."

"How long are you planning on sleeping?" I asked as I dropped everything and followed him into the bedroom.

"'Til about ten o'clock and then I'm going out. Why?"

"Well, I had planned on going out with the girls tonight and I wanted to make sure you were home to watch Brandon."

"What? Going out where?" Curtis responded as he turned toward me.

"I'm going out to have some drinks—why?"

"Why tonight?" he asked.

"Why not tonight? Didn't you go out last night?" I replied defensively.

Curtis reached in his pocket and pulled out a wad of money. "Yeah, and look at what I made in doing so."

I looked at the hundreds and twenty-dollar bills he had in his hand. "What does that have to do with me going out with my girls?"

"Nothing, but I was going to meet Cedric tonight to try to get some more clients."

"Cedric? Is that who you're hanging out with?"

Cedric Nichols, Curtis's childhood buddy, has a reputation for being in all kinds of illegal shit.

"That's who's helping me get work. What's wrong with that?"

"Think about it, Curtis. What kind of brothers do legitimate business in a club?" I asked firmly.

"I'm not going to a damn club. I'm going to meet them at Cedric's body shop."

"Club, body shop—it doesn't matter where. Who does business with clients that late at night?"

"I'm just trying to help Cedric with his workload until I can build up my client base to start my own business."

"You've been using that same line for the last year. But almost every night you come home smelling like liquor and weed."

He bit down on his teeth and gave me a hard look. "Look, I don't have a master's degree like you, so I'm doing what I have to do for my son."

I turned and walked away. "Yeah—whatever, Curtis. I'll just get a baby-sitter, then."

"A baby-sitter? You know how much that costs? How can we save money if you're always spending it on things like a baby-sitter. . . . Fuck it, do what you want—I'm going to bed."

I kept walking as I heard the bedroom door close behind me. *Have patience, have patience*, I repeated as I continued on into the den. I called Carol down the street, who is our regular baby-sitter—she agreed to come by at around seven o'clock.

By the time I gave Brandon his bath and got dressed, Carol was at my door. I put on my makeup and left for the night.

CHAPTER 4

Mya

I jumped in the shower before heading to the mall. Macy's-Rich's was having a sale, and since I hadn't been to a club in a while, I needed something more in line with today's fashion and appropriate for the cool night air.

The store was filled with people aggressively walking from rack to rack, picking out clothes. All I was trying to find was a pair of black pants to wear with my black leather boots.

For hours I went back and forth to the dressing room, trying on one pair of pants after the other, until I found a really nice pair that matched a pretty blouse on the rack directly across from it. *This would blend in well with my golden-colored hair hanging past my shoulders.*

I walked through the rest of the mall looking in stores to see if I could find a matching scarf or something that I could wear to accentuate my outfit. Finally, after the fourth store with no luck, I found myself near the food court. My stomach began to growl at the smell of the different foods being prepared by the fast-food restaurants. I walked over to the Chik-Fil-A, where the line wasn't as long, and stood to the side of the register looking at the menu. *Hmm, the grilled chicken sandwich looks good,* I thought.

"Excuse me, are you in line?" a deep voice sounded from behind.

"Well, no, I—"

As I turned around there was a small-framed, light-skinned

brother standing behind me with gold teeth that had the initials L.J. on the front two staring at me, smiling from ear-to-ear.

"No, you can go ahead—I'm still trying to decide," I replied with a slight frown.

"Still can't decide, huh? I get that way, too. The chicken salad samich is good."

I covered my mouth with my right hand. *Samich*, I thought. *Oh my God, no—he didn't just say "samich" in this day and age.* "Oh really," I frowned.

"Yeah, oh, uh. My name is Larry Jenkins, by the way. My peoples call me L.J.," he said with a smile.

I wanted to say, "I see," looking at his teeth. "Hi. I'm Mya," I said.

"Mya," he replied as his eyebrows arched. *"Uh-oh, my love is like woe, my touch is like woe,"* he said, snapping his fingers and laughing.

"Huh?" I replied with a confused look.

"You know—the song by Mya the singer."

"Oh, yeah, right," I replied as I turned toward the cashier at the register.

"Hi, ma'am. May I take your order, please?" she asked politely.

"Yes, can I get the grilled chicken sandwich with a small lemonade?"

L.J., or should I say Larry, walked to the next available cashier and placed his order.

I got my sandwich and walked to the table in the middle of the food court and sat down.

Before I began to eat, I could see Larry staring at me from the corner of my eye. I slowly turned my head away and began eating. Moments into it, Larry came to my table, still smiling and showing off his gold initials. "You mind if I sit wit ya, Mya?" he asked.

I didn't want to seem rude in a public place and besides, I only had a sandwich to finish and could take the lemonade with me. "Uh, no, not at all."

Out of all the chairs at the table he had to sit in the one closest to me. Instead of taking my time eating like I would normally do, I was stuffing my mouth with every bite. He sat down and got comfortable as he began eating what looked to be a chicken salad sandwich. I took another huge bite and began chewing faster, then took a gulp of lemonade. Larry smiled as the marinade from his chicken salad sandwich covered the "J" on the gold initials in his mouth.

Uhhh, I thought. I turned my head before I threw up or lost my appetite.

"So, what kind of work do you do?" he asked with a mouthful of food.

"I'm a schoolteacher," I replied with my head down.

"Do you have a biness card or something?"

"Huh?" I replied.

"A biness card—you know—wit all your numbers or something on it?" he repeated.

"Well, I'm a schoolteacher. I don't really have any use for business cards."

"Okay, the reason I was asking 'cause I'd like to call you sometime, you know what I'm sayin, maybe we could—"

"Well, look, Larry," I interrupted.

"No, its L.J.—call me L.J., sweetheart."

"Look, I don't mean to seem rude, but I'm kind of in the middle of something with someone right now and I don't think it would be a good idea to give you my number."

"I see," he smiled. "Say no more, say no more, I understand."

"Thanks—well, look," I replied as I crumpled the leftover sandwich and placed it in the bag. "It was really nice meeting you."

"Likewise, Mya. Uh, I do hope we meet again someday. Next time I hope you're single," he replied with his arm extended to shake my hand.

I reached over to touch his hand and his fingernails were filthy. He had dirt logged deep into the nail. I slightly closed my eyes and shook his hand. *Uhhh*, I thought. They were rough and sticky. When our hands touched I cringed as he firmly squeezed. I then gave him a hard smile and walked off, heading straight to the nearest bathroom to wash them. While inside I beat what looked to be an empty soap dispenser to get a drop out while waiting on the water to get piping hot to scrub my hands clean. When I walked outside the bathroom I saw Larry standing with a group of guys, talking. To avoid another encounter with him I walked away in the opposite direction, cutting through the north end of the mall before making it to my car and driving off.

When I got home, I ironed my new outfit and placed it on a hanger in my closet. I ran some hot bathwater and mixed it with scented gel beads and soaked while I listened to soft jazz. My mind drifted like it always does when I'm relaxed and thinking about being married with kids in a big house, or cuddled up on the floor near a fireplace with my toes rubbing together with my special someone.

Later that night, Tangie and Stephanie came over as I rushed to get ready for the club. Stephanie was in the bathroom getting her makeup together when Tangie walked into my bedroom with a glass of wine.

"I'll be ready in a minute—I just have to put on some lipstick," I said in a rush.

"Take your time," Tangie said as she took a seat on the bed. "It's only nine-thirty. I don't want to get there until eleven, anyway."

"Why so late?" Stephanie asked from the bathroom.

"Yeah, all the good men will be taken by then," I said.

"Girl, trust me. If you got it, you got it. The brothers will still be there. Besides, if they want you they will leave whoever they're with to be with you," Tangie replied before sipping her wine.

She did make a good point. I was just anxious to get there. "So did Todd come over last night?" I asked.

Tangie blushed. "Yeah, you know he did, and he put it down, too. I had an incredible orgasm that had me shaking like I was in the damn electric chair, girl."

"Really?" I replied, laughing.

"Then his cell phone rang—that kind of spoiled the mood. I think it was his wife or something," she continued.

"What's up with him and his wife?" I asked.

"I don't know, and don't care," Tangie replied.

"Why? I thought you two were cool like that. Don't you two discuss his wife?" Stephanie asked.

"No. When you're fucking another woman's man, rule number one is not to get caught up in family business."

"Why not? It doesn't hurt to listen," I said.

"When I only have him for an hour, all I want to do is fuck. I don't want to waste time listening to how bad things are at home. I know things are bad—otherwise, his ass wouldn't be here."

That's Tangie, rough and rugged. She sets her rules from the jump and doesn't want to compromise. In my opinion that's the reason she's single and has had two failed marriages. She's too stubborn.

We left the house at around ten-thirty. When we got to Nsomnia, it was packed. We parked, put our purses in the trunk, and went inside. I was a bit more anxious than Tangie and Stephanie because I was ready to meet a nice single man. Stephanie was along to be admired, and Tangie just wanted to have a good time.

We stood in the center of the club and pulled our jackets off and laid them across our arms. I turned around to get a better look at the place and saw a bunch of brothers standing in the back, checking us out and whispering to one another.

"Hey, don't look now but we're being checked out by some guys behind us," I said.

"Where?" Stephanie asked.

"Directly behind Tangie, against the wall," I described.

Tangie looked discreetly around the club. "Yeah, they're all right. We can do better, though. Let's walk around and see what the others look like," she said. We turned and walked toward the back near the restrooms and stood with our backs closest to the wall. This view was better. Instead of being watched by people, now we could see them as they came through the door.

"So what do you think?" I asked, looking at Tangie and Stephanie.

"There are more women than men in here," Stephanie replied.

"Soul brothers at that. Look at this brother with the red suit, matching red hat and shoes," Tangie said. We all giggled.

"Well, I didn't come in here to stand around," Tangie said.

"I know that's right," I replied.

"Are you ready to run the Decatur take'em or shake'em?" Tangie asked, looking over at Stephanie.

"Absolutely," she replied.

"Take'em or shake'em?" I replied, confused. "What's that?"

"Girl, as much as we hang out together, you don't know it yet?" Tangie said, looking at me.

I nodded.

"Watch this," Tangie said as she got the waitress's attention.

"Yes?" the waitress asked.

"What do you two want to drink?" Tangie asked, her eyes shifting to me and Stephanie.

"I'll have a glass of white wine," I replied.

"I'll have a glass of Remy XO," Stephanie said.

"Make that two glasses of Remy," Tangie replied.

"Wine?" Stephanie asked, looking at me. "You ain't at home in front of the fireplace."

"What? Girl, wine is what I want."

"Okay, well, wine is what you'll be drinking all night, then," Stephanie mocked. Tangie laughed as Stephanie continued. "See, Mya, the game is this. You order an expensive drink, right? You stand here and drink it until it's half empty, then walk around the club. By then, brothers will be checking you out and offering to buy you a drink. When they see you drinking that expensive shit, they will either buy you another one—and chances are they got a little money—or they will refuse when they see what you're drinking, at which time they can keep steppin' because they're probably broke as hell."

I laughed. "You two are some gold-digging hoes."

"It ain't that. It's just that I don't have time to sit here all night trying to feel a brother out. Show me what you're willing to do from the jump and we can work the rest out later."

I shook my head in disgust at this ghetto attempt to get a man.

The waitress came back with our drinks and Tangie paid for them with the money she kept in her jacket pocket.

We sipped on our drinks for several minutes, watching more guys come through the door. Moments later this guy came over, dressed in all black with a white Kangol hat. "Would any of you beautiful ladies like to dance with ole Roger?" he asked with a wide smile.

We looked at each other, waiting on the others to give him an answer. "I would," Tangie replied as she gave me her drink and put her coat on the empty chair next to us. His smile got even wider as they proceeded toward the dance floor.

Stephanie looked at me with a grin. "Tangie must be desperate to have fun tonight."

"Not me," I replied. "Where are all of the cute brothers sitting?" We looked around the room once more.

"Maybe if we walk around we might run into some nice guys to choose from," Stephanie said.

"Yeah, but let's wait on Tangie first," I replied.

Several minutes later Tangie came back to where we were, breathing heavily. "Whew, that old bastard can dance, but his breath smelled like shit."

"What?" Stephanie laughed loudly.

"Yeah, when I danced with my back toward him, he tried to hump me, and when I danced facing him, I had to hold my damn breath."

We laughed hysterically.

"So you guys aren't going to dance?" Tangie asked.

"Yeah, as soon as I find someone cute to dance with," I replied.

"Girl, you know cute guys can't dance. They're probably on the other side of the club, sitting at the table," Tangie continued.

"Well, that's where I need to be," I replied.

"Not me," Tangie said. "I'm gonna stay over here for a minute and dance some more. Besides, I didn't come here to find a man, I came here to party."

I looked over at Stephanie. "You want to go over there with me?"

"Sure, why not?" Stephanie replied.

"Well can you hold on to my jacket, 'cause I'm going back on the dance floor," Tangie said.

As Stephanie and I made our way toward the other side of the club, guys were smiling as we passed by, some even winking, trying to get our attention. They looked decent but none of them gave me that warm and fuzzy feeling enough for me to stop and have a conversation.

When we got to the back of the club, there were a couple of tables with empty chairs next to them near the emergency exit doors. We made our way through a narrow aisle and took a seat. Suddenly it was, like, all eyes on us. The brothers on this side looked a whole lot different. They were all dressed in sport coats as opposed to the zoot suits the brothers were wearing up front. As minutes passed, it seemed as though more cute guys were starting to filter in. Stephanie and I sat back and sipped our drinks, trying to look sophisticated to get some attention. At least I was, anyway. Stephanie was too busy looking at her watch, checking the time every ten minutes.

A few moments later two guys came over. One was walking toward Stephanie, and the other guy was walking toward me. They both wore really nice dark-colored suits with open-collared shirts. The one walking toward me was a light-brown-skinned brother with a neatly trimmed goatee who stood what looked to be over six feet, while the brother walking toward Stephanie was a little darker in complexion and stood maybe an inch shorter. I noticed Stephanie as she put her drink on the table—it was almost empty. The gentleman sat down next to her as he placed his Heineken next to her glass.

The brother in my direction walked up to me and leaned slightly over to my ear as I sat back in my chair. "Hi, you mind if I sit down for a minute or are you with someone?" he asked.

I smiled casually, looking at the chair directly in front of me. "No, that's fine," I replied.

He put his beer on the table before moving his chair closer to me, then sat down, looking at me. "Hi—I'm Darryl Cooper, by the way." He extended his hand.

"Nice to meet you, Darryl, I'm Mya LeVeaux."

"Mya—I like that name."

"You do? What's so special about it?" I asked.

"My great-grandmother's name is Mya."

"Oh, really? Then I guess it *is* special."

Darryl smiled, showing off his pretty white teeth as he reached for his beer. In the meantime, I glanced over at Stephanie, who was engaged in conversation with her newfound friend.

"So, are you enjoying yourself?" Darryl asked, getting my attention.

"Yeah, so far I'm having a pretty good time." I could smell a hint of his cologne as he leaned over to talk.

"So what do you do for fun?" he asked.

"Fun? Well, I read a lot. For me that's fun."

"What kind of books do you read?"

"They vary, but I'm mostly into romance."

"Oh, okay."

"And you?" I asked.

"Well, I'm mostly into the arts."

"Oh, do you paint?"

"No, not that kind of art, I was referring to martial arts." He smiled at me.

"Oh, really. When I was a kid I always wanted to take up karate."

"Yeah, well, it's not too late."

"Well, it's too late for me." I replied.

He smiled again, then said, "Maybe one day I can get you to change your mind."

"I doubt it, Darryl. If something goes down now, I'll just have to call my cousins out here to handle things for me."

He laughed out loud. "I hear that," he replied. "So, what kind of work do you do?"

"I'm a schoolteacher."

"Oh, a schoolteacher. That's interesting."

"Why?"

"Well, my first impression of you was something more, like, a lawyer or something corporate."

"Sorry to disappoint you."

"No, it was just my impression of you, that's all," he continued.

I chuckled. "No, I'm just a little ole schoolteacher."

I took the last sip of wine from my glass and placed it on the table. Seeing this, Darryl turned and gestured to a waitress walking passed us. "Can I get you another drink?"

"Uh, sure. Thanks," I replied.

When the waitress made it over to our table, Darryl stood up and handed her my empty glass. "Yes, can I get another—" He looked at me.

"Oh, any white wine is fine, thank you," I replied.

Darryl pointed at Stephanie, who was still talking. "Would your friend like another drink as well?"

I politely tapped Stephanie on the shoulder and got her attention as she turned around.

"Would you like another drink?"

"Oh, yeah," she replied, looking up at Darryl smiling.

"What were you drinking?" Darryl asked.

"Oh, I had a Remy XO."

I braced myself for a response from Darryl about her drink order, but without hesitation he turned toward the waitress and ordered both drinks, along with a beer for himself. Stephanie looked over at me and smiled.

As the waitress walked away, Darryl sat back down, looking into my eyes in silence.

"What?" I asked, confused by his stare.

"Nothing, just looking."

"So what kind of work do you do?" I asked.

"I'm a pharmaceutical sales rep."

"Really?"

"Yep," he replied proudly.

"I can't see a salesman in you," I said.

"Oh, really? Then what did you see?"

"I don't know, but not a salesman."

The waitress came back with our drinks and placed them on the table. I took a sip of wine as Darryl and I chatted for several more minutes. He chipped away at several topics until finally asking for my number. I thought he was cute and had enough good qualities to warrant a call, so I gave him my cell phone number before he left.

Stephanie couldn't shake her friend for nothing. She sipped her drink sarcastically in his face, pretty much ignoring most of his conversation. Finally, I got tired of just sitting there alone so I got up and gathered my things.

"Are you about to leave?" Stephanie asked desperately.

"Yeah, I'm going over to check on Tangie."

"Wait up—I'm going with you."

I leaned over to her right ear. "What about your friend?" I whispered.

"Who, Carlos? Girl, I ain't thinking 'bout him. I was just trying to be polite," she whispered back.

Carlos had a half-embarrassed look on his face as he watched us talk. I grabbed what was left of my wine and stood next to Stephanie. She got up, pushing her chair in as she straightened her blouse. Carlos gently touched Stephanie's arm, getting her attention. "Can't you stay for a little while longer? I was just getting a chance to know you," he said.

"No—besides, I told you I'm in the middle of a relationship." Carlos's half-embarrassed look turned to disappointment as he nodded before Stephanie and I walked off.

"So, what's up with your boy?" Stephanie asked.

"Who, Darryl? He seems nice."

"Yeah, he's a keeper," she continued.

"He's all right. What about Carlos?"

"What? Please. He was so boring I could barely keep my attention focused on what he was saying. Plus, if I *were* single, I wouldn't give him the time of day, because his cheap ass couldn't even buy me a drink."

I smiled, turning my head as we continued on to join Tangie. As we turned the corner by the bar, we saw Tangie sitting at a table with some real soul brothers. One wore all red, the other all white, and the third brother had on all green. I had to hide my laughter as we got closer. It looked as though Tangie was really having a good time as she sat there with a drink in hand and several empty glasses in front of her.

"There my girls are," Tangie said loudly, waving her hand. Stephanie and I smiled as we walked up to the table.

"Fellas, these are my girls. This is Stephanie," she said, touching Stephanie's arm. "And over here is Mya." She pulled me closer to her. "Girls, this is Wallace," she said, pointing to the gentleman in the white suit. "And this is uh, uh. Aw, hell. I forgot your names," she said, looking at the other two gentlemen at the table. "We'll just call you Red," she said, pointing to the guy in the red suit. "And we'll call you Green," she added as she looked at the guy in the green suit.

Stephanie pressed down on her bottom lip with her teeth to keep from laughing as I looked down at the floor, giggling inside.

"Nice meeting you," Stephanie and I said in unison.

They nodded, staring us up and down deviously.

"How about a drink?" Wallace asked.

"Oh, no, thank you. I think I've had enough to drink for one night," I replied.

"Yeah—me, too," Stephanie said.

"Well, let's dance, then," Red said as he got up and walked toward me.

"Let's all dance," Wallace suggested.

"Well, what about our jackets?" Stephanie asked.

"Just leave them right here—we'll keep an eye on them," Wallace replied as he reached for Tangie's hand.

Green got up and we all walked onto the dance floor. The dee-jay was hot! He played one great song after another as the people filled the dance floor. Those old dudes could dance, too. By now Tangie was feeling good off all those Remy X0s. She had to have been, because Wallace was all over her and not one time did she push him away. In fact, it looked like she was encouraging it. He was occasionally humping her from behind as she bent over, shaking her ass in rhythm. I played it safe by dancing an arm's length away from Red so he wouldn't get any ideas. Stephanie was dancing at a safe distance with Green, occasionally backing away before his hands could touch any part of her body.

Finally, after about five songs, my feet began to hurt so I signaled to Red that I was ready to sit down. Seeing this, Tangie and Stephanie both left the dance floor as the guys trailed them. When we got back to the table, I sat down and wiped the small beads of sweat that had formed on my forehead. Green grabbed a napkin, walked over to Stephanie, and began wiping the sides of her face. She smiled and politely took the napkin from him and wiped around her neck, looking over at me to see my reaction.

"I'm thirsty—does anyone need anything?" Wallace asked, then waited on everyone's response. We all declined.

"C'mon, the night's still young," he said.

Stephanie looked at her watch as her eyebrows rose in surprise. "Wow, it's almost three o'clock. I have to be in church in a few hours."

"Yeah, it *is* getting late. But, thank you, guys, for a good time," Tangie said as she hugged Wallace.

Wallace reached in his pocket and gave Tangie a slip of paper that she folded in her hand.

Stephanie and I grabbed our leather jackets and started toward the door. By now the crowd had thinned out a little. Outside there were groups of people standing around talking in the parking lot as we got in the car, heading toward my town house.

"That was fun," Tangie said. "Most of the brothers in there were fake, though."

"It was all right. I was tripping on how some of the brothers just stood there staring a hole in you like they wanted you to sweat them," Stephanie replied.

"What about you, Mya? Did you meet your Mr. Right?" Tangie joked.

"I met someone nice. We had good conversation and we seem to have a lot in common. I guess you can say we sorta connected visually before he approached me."

"What?" Stephanie interrupted. "That brother you met came out of the crowd over to your ass and you know it. Don't make that

shit seem like something out of a soap opera. 'Connection visually—'"

"Aw, damn, she had me going for a minute," Tangie replied,
laughing.

"And Tangie, what's up with you and the old man with the zoot
suit throwback?"

We laughed.

"Take'em or shake'em. They kept on buying the drinks and I
kept on drinking. Plus, they were cool. Wallace must be out of his
mind if he thinks I'm going to call his old ass, though."

"Yeah, and what's up with Green trying to wipe the sweat from
my face. I almost told his ass something," Stephanie said.

"He didn't mean no harm, girl. They were just out trying to hook
up with a little young thang, that's all. In fact, they actually made
my night," Tangie replied.

The ride home began to wear us down as we continued on in silence. My mind drifted to Darryl for a minute. Tangie was joking,
but what if he *was* my Mr. Right? *He seemed to have all the character-
istics. And damn, was he fine,* I smiled to myself. *So far so good,* I
thought, as a smile came over my face.

CHAPTER 5

Stephanie

"So you finally decided to bring your ass home, huh?" a voice sounded in the darkness as I walked through the front door. I paused, startled, before turning the light switch on. Curtis was sitting on the corner of the couch in his boxers and do-rag, frowning.

"You scared the shit out of me, Curtis. What are you doing home so early, anyway?" I said as I walked toward the kitchen.

"I've been here all night," he replied, getting up from the couch.

"Why? The baby-sitter was here when I left."

"As soon as you left I sent her home. We can't afford a baby-sitter for you to go out drinking with your girls, so I stayed home with Brandon and missed out on making money because of it."

"Who's fault is that, Curtis? The baby-sitter was hired for you to do what you needed to do while I went out with my girls."

"Well, why couldn't you all just meet over here and have some drinks?" Curtis said, standing in the middle of the kitchen.

"Be-*cause*, we wanted to go *out* for drinks."

"I bet it was that damn Tangie who suggested it. Just because she can't keep a relationship she wants to fuck up everyone else's. Besides, what kind of mother are you to be hanging out all times of night like uh, uh—"

"Curtis, you'd better go on to bed with that shit," I interrupted. "Besides, Tangie had nothing to do with me wanting to go out. It was my decision."

He twisted his mouth, about to respond, then turned in silence and walked toward the bedroom.

"Are you going to church with me in a few hours?" I asked.

Soon after I finished my statement, Curtis walked through the bedroom door without responding. *Well, fuck you, too,* I said under my breath before turning off the rest of the lights in the house.

My alarm sounded at around eight o'clock. I pulled myself from Curtis's hold and went to the bathroom before starting breakfast. Curtis came out of the bedroom a while later dressed in his jeans and sweatshirt. "Can you make me some coffee and put it in my thermos?" he asked as he grabbed a couple pieces of bacon.

"Aren't you going to church this morning?" I asked.

"I can't. I'm going down to the shop to see if I can get some work to make up for the money I missed last night."

The shop is an old, broken-down establishment where body shop repairmen from at least three generations hang out in downtown Atlanta, drinking while working on people's cars. Most of their clients are drug dealers because they pay in cash. The owner of the shop is Curtis's friend, Cedric Nichols. Cedric's father ran the shop for many years until he passed away, leaving it to Cedric. Since then it hadn't generated a lot of business, so Cedric opened it up to a list of wanna-be bailers, many of whom did time in jail at some point in their lives.

"Curtis, we're not *that* hard up for money that you have to work on a Sunday. Can't you just—"

"Can't," he interrupted, kissing my cheek while grabbing his thermos. "Gotta go, 'bye."

After Curtis rushed out the door, Brandon came running from his room and into my arms. "Good morning, baby," I said. "Sit down and eat your breakfast so I can get your clothes together for church."

By the time I got to New Birth Missionary Baptist Church, the choir was already singing. Brandon and I took a seat in the middle pews facing the front of the altar as we joined in on the praise and worship.

Moments later, the voice of the choir began to fade as Bishop Eddie Long appeared at the podium.

"Amen . . . amen," he shouted as he looked over the congregation.

It wasn't until he was about to get into his sermon that I realized I had walked off and forgotten my Bible. I looked around to see if there were extra ones in the pockets on the pew in front of me but there weren't any. Bishop Long began reading from the Book of John as I continued to search. When I looked over to my left, there was an older lady next to me with a fairly large Bible sitting open on her lap.

I leaned forward, narrowing my eyes to get a peek at the passage, when she looked over at me with a frown before shifting her body, placing her Bible out of my view. *You low-down old biddy*, I thought as I rolled my eyes at her. Seconds later, I felt a light tap on my right shoulder. When I turned toward the touch there was a slim gentleman sitting next to me with his Bible placed in between us, his finger pointing at the words being read by Bishop Long. I looked up and politely smiled before following his finger across the words.

As the service continued, the gentleman next to me managed to shift his body closer to me. I felt awkward at first but I focused my attention on the words and blocked him out. Shortly afterward, the service had ended and we were about to disperse. Brandon was asleep under my arm as I got up, carrying him against my shoulder. As I followed the crowd and made my way outside, I stopped and talked to a few of the members I knew.

"Excuse me, sister," a voice sounded.

I turned where I stood, facing the gentleman who had shared his Bible with me. "Hi," I replied. "Thank you for sharing your Bible with me today. I was rushing out this morning and completely forgot mine."

"Not a problem. I've seen you in and around church a few times and just wanted to introduce myself. I'm Reggie Gaines—nice to meet you." He extended his hand. I smiled and we shook hands. "I'm Stephanie Hall, Reggie—nice to meet you."

"Good to meet you, and feel free to share the word with me at any time, sister. Are you a member?"

"Well, not exactly. I'm looking for a church home and I think this is it."

"Is this your son?" He looked over at Brandon in my arms. "How old is he?"

I smiled. "This is Brandon, he's two."

"Two . . . Has he been baptized yet?"

"Well, no, but—"

"Oh sister, you must get him baptized as soon as possible. His soul depends on it."

I looked down, slightly embarrassed. "Uh, okay—what do I need to do?"

"Tell you what. Here's my card. I work at the church. Give me a call so I can talk to the bishop and make sure he gets baptized as soon as possible."

I was in a state of shock because I was so busy trying to get a feel for the church that I forgot to get my son baptized.

"I would also recommend coming to Bible study. We meet here every Wednesday at six o'clock. In the meantime, I'll make sure we get Brandon's paperwork together," Reggie continued.

"Thank you so much, Reggie. I'll do that." I put his card in my pocket.

Reggie smiled. "Okay, see you Wednesday."

"Have a good day," I said, walking off.

I got in my car, immediately upset at myself. I have time to go out and party but forgot to get my son baptized. What kind of mother am I to forget something as important as this? I took Reggie's card from my pocket and placed it in my cup holder to remind me to call later in the week.

When Curtis got home he smelled of alcohol again. He walked through the door and kissed me on my cheek before heading toward the kitchen. "Hey, baby? Guess what. I made seven hundred dollars today. Things are starting to look up for us."

"Curtis, we need to talk," I said firmly.

"Talk about what?" He took off his shirt.

"Do you know that Brandon hasn't been baptized and he's almost three?"

"Huh, so what? I didn't get baptized until I was five or six. It's no big deal."

"That's bullshit. It *is* a big deal, a big deal to me. I want my son to get baptized right away."

"Okay, then make the arrangements."

"I need to know that you're going to support me with this," I snapped.

"Sure, just set it up and let me know. What's for dinner?"

"What? I'm talking about our son and all you can do is worry about your appetite?"

"Damn, baby, I said okay. Just set it up and I'll be there. Now, are you going to fix me something to eat or not?"

I barely held my anger. "Yeah—go shower, Curtis, and I'll fix your plate," I replied, still annoyed.

Curtis came up behind me as I stood by the stove. "Baby, look. I'm sorry. Seriously, if you set it up, I'll be there," he replied, kissing the back of my neck. I felt relieved by the sound of his sincerity. My next move was to contact Reggie on Wednesday to get the information I needed.

CHAPTER 6

Mya

I had just gotten out of the shower and was about to do my nails when the phone rang. Still wrapped in a towel, I rushed to the phone on my nightstand.

"Hello."

"Hey, girl, do you know *A Mother's Revenge* is about to come on? Are you watching Lifetime?"

Lifetime was our little outing on Sundays. We would all sit on the phone for hours watching back-to-back movies. Tangie and I mostly argued during the commercials about how we would handle the situations in the movie, and Stephanie acted as the mediator. Seconds later, Tangie came back on the line. "Mya, hold on—that was Stephanie. I'm gonna three-way her in."

Suddenly, I heard my cell phone ringing downstairs. "Hey, hold on. Someone is calling me on my cell."

I ran downstairs, answering it on the third ring.

"Yes—Mya, please," the deep voice sounded.

"This is Mya. Who is—"

"This is Darryl—I met you last night at the club."

"Oh, hi, Darryl—yeah, I remember."

"Did I catch you at a bad time?" he asked.

"No, uh, I was just watching TV. What are you up to?"

"Not too much, I was about to throw some meat on the grill. In the meantime, I thought about you and decided to call."

I blushed at the thought of being on his mind. "Can you grill, man?" I joked.

He chuckled. "Can I grill? Can I grill? I can't see how you can fix your mouth to say that," he joked.

"Well, I don't know, so I thought I'd ask."

"Oh, yeah, if I can't do anything else, I can grill."

"I hear you," I replied.

"So how are you for getting together next weekend? I would really love to see you again. I'll be out of town most of next week and was wondering if we could meet for dinner or something."

"I don't know. You're still a stranger to me," I replied sarcastically.

"Oh, I see. Well, what—"

"I'm teasing. I would love to meet for dinner someplace. What day are you talking about?"

"Well, I'll be back in town on Friday. Let's say Saturday."

"Saturday's fine."

"You like Caribbean food?" he asked.

"Oooh, yeah."

"What about eight o'clock at Bahama Breeze?" he asked.

"Let's say three o'clock at Bahama Breeze," I replied.

"Three?"

"Yeah, I feel more comfortable that way," I said.

"Okay, I can respect that."

"I was thinking of the one in Alpharetta," he suggested.

"That sounds good to me," I replied.

"Well, let me get back to my grill. I just wanted to see what you were up to. I'll let you get back to your movie."

"Yeah—oh, shoot," I yelled. *I left Tangie and Stephanie on the phone.* "Okay, Darryl, I'll talk to you later."

I ran back upstairs and picked up the phone I had left on the bed. "Hello? Hello? Tangie, Stephanie?"

"Yeah, bitch, we're still here. Must've been a man," Tangie said.

"That was Darryl, the guy I met last night."

"Really? Details, please," Stephanie said.

"Well, there's nothing to tell. He seems cool. We're getting together next weekend for dinner."

"Really?" Stephanie replied with excitement.

"Yeah, we're gonna meet at Bahama Breeze."

"Oh that's a nice place," Stephanie said.

"Yeah," Tangie replied. "They make some good-ass drinks."

"They sure do, especially the tropical ones. They are *so* strong," I said.

"Don't drink too much on your first date," Stephanie added.

"For real," Tangie laughed. "You might wake up next to his ass with a strange taste in your mouth."

We all burst out laughing.

"Oh hell no, I won't. That's why I told him we'd meet at around three o'clock."

"Three o'clock?" Stephanie replied, surprised.

"Yeah, he might be cute, but I don't want his ass to get any ideas as the night goes on."

"That's smart," Tangie said with a slight yawn.

There was a moment of silence.

"Are you guys gonna watch another movie?" Tangie asked.

"No, I have to clean the kitchen before going to bed," Stephanie replied.

"Yeah, I'm going to do my toes," I said.

"Well, I'll talk to you guys later," Tangie said before hanging up.

I hung up the phone and changed into my nightclothes before polishing my toes.

CHAPTER 7

Tangie

After school, I had a parent-teacher meeting with the parents of one of my newest students, Tina Washington. Tina is a straight-A student and very well behaved, so I was confused as to why her parents wanted to meet outside of the normal PTA process. Nevertheless, I waited while reading my *Essence* magazine and sipping a Pepsi. Minutes later there was a knock at my door. When I looked up I saw a short, huskily built woman walking toward me. I got up and smiled as I greeted her.

"Hi, I'm Ms. Jackson. You must be Tina's mother."

She smiled with her hand extended. "Hi, nice to finally meet you. I'm Gloria Washington."

"Have a seat, Mrs. Washington. What can I do for you?" I asked as I put my magazine away.

"You mind if we wait on my husband? He should be coming in any minute."

"No problem," I replied as I pulled out my grade book. "Can I get you anything to drink while we wait?"

"No, thank you," she replied.

I heard loud footsteps coming down the hall. Mrs. Washington and I both looked in the direction of the noise as it got louder and louder. Appearing through the door was a tall, light-skinned gentleman with thick, black curly hair and drop-dead gorgeous looks. He was dressed in a long-sleeved, golf-style shirt that showed off his muscular physique. I was about to jump into club mode and scan the rest of his physical attributes but caught myself.

"Uh, hi. I'm Tangie Jackson." I extended my hand.

"Good to meet you—I'm Walter Washington," he replied.

"Have a seat, Mr. Washington. Okay, what can I do for you guys today?"

"Well, we just wanted to get an update on how Tina is doing. Since this is her first year at Stephenson, we just want to make sure she's adjusting," Mr. Washington said.

"I see, and indeed she is," I replied. "As you can see, her grades are very good and her conduct is equally good," I said as I handed them both samples of Tina's work.

Tina's mother smiled. "See? I told you she was fine," she said, looking at her husband.

I smiled.

"Tina talks about you all the time, so my husband thought it'd be a good idea to meet with you personally," Mrs. Washington continued.

"I completely understand," I replied.

"So, is she getting along well with the other students?" Mr. Washington asked.

"As far as I can see, things are fine. She works well with other students and she participates in all of the class activities. To sum it up, she's one of my best students."

I noticed Mr. Washington's eyes scan downward toward my breasts as he nodded in response to my comments about Tina.

When I got up to show them Tina's work that was displayed around the classroom, I felt Mr. Washington's eyes on my ass. When I turned around, my intuition was correct. He wasn't paying any attention to a word I was saying. He was too busy watching me.

When our eyes met, he gave me a cunning smile while Mrs. Washington looked at Tina's drawings. Instead of turning my head I stared directly at him, determined not to be intimidated. I get hit on by many of my students' fathers but this situation was different. The guy was fucking cute. When he turned his head I quickly looked him over, my eyes stopping at his midsection. It was obvious he had on boxers by the way his penis hung down on the right side. As he took a step forward, I could see how his pants clung to it, showing its thickness. The situation began to feel weird.

My heart began to race and I felt a hot flash on the back of my neck. While they continued to look over Tina's other work, I walked back over and grabbed my Pepsi off my desk and took a sip to cool off.

"Did my daughter do all this?" Mr. Washington asked as he walked toward me. I nodded as I took another sip. By the time I swallowed, he was standing in front of me holding one of Tina's projects. "Are you guys going on any field trips anytime soon? If so, I'd love to chaperone," he said.

"I don't think we're going to have anything going on until after the Christmas holidays."

"Well, if you do, give me a call. My wife works rotating shifts at the hospital so one of us should be able to help out," he said as he gave me a business card.

I wanted to reach for it but hesitated and composed myself. "We normally send slips home with the kids asking the parents if they want to volunteer," I replied.

He nodded as he put his business card away but still kept his eyes on me. Mrs. Washington, who was still standing in the back of the classroom, came over and grabbed her purse out of the chair.

"Are you about ready, Walter? I think things here are fine," she said, looking at her husband.

He nodded, placing one hand in his pocket.

"Thank you so much for taking the time to see us, Ms. Jackson," she said.

"No problem. If you have any questions in the future, just let me know."

Mr. Washington gave me a long stare before they both turned and walked toward the doorway and into the hall. With a slight grin, I turned and walked back to my desk to gather my things. *Tina's dad definitely has it going on*, I thought as I headed out the door.

I got home and found a message from Todd to call him at work. We made plans to meet on his lunch break and I couldn't wait. When he got to my apartment he pissed me off because he forgot the fucking condoms. No matter how much he begged, I still didn't give in to giving him any without protection. He was so desperate he went into the kitchen and grabbed a sandwich bag and tried to penetrate me. I was so frustrated at that shit that I basically put his ass out. Seeing him naked, though, only made matters worse for my sexual hunger. So if Todd couldn't get me off, B.O.B., my battery-operated buddy, had to take his place. I went to my closet and pulled out the box that I kept hidden underneath my clothes and pulled him out.

CHAPTER 8

Stephanie

I met Reggie at Bible study and he introduced me to several other members of the church. He took me into one of the offices in the back and had me fill out a membership form and a request for baptism for Brandon. Afterwards, we talked about other church activities that I could get involved in once I became a member. Reggie seemed very spiritual, often quoting scripture at the right moment to help me understand more of what my purpose should be as a child of God. It was comforting being in his presence because he was so positive. Before leaving, I took an extra application for Curtis. Since his arrest, the church he grew up in pretty much had turned its back on him and I thought this would be a way to get our family on the right track.

It was late by the time I finished my meeting with Reggie, so he insisted on walking me to my car. We continued our casual conversation until we reached my car.

"So, sister, you're all set. I'll make sure we get your papers processed as soon as possible. Someone from the church should contact you by the end of the week."

"Thanks, Reggie. I wish my boyfriend had been able to come with me, but he had to work," I said, slightly embarrassed by the lie I'd just told.

"I'm looking forward to meeting him. I hope we can get him involved in our mentor program," he replied.

I nodded.

"Well, have a safe drive home, sister, and if you need anything, just give me a call," he said.

I made it home, and Curtis was sitting on the couch watching TV, drinking a beer as Brandon played with his blocks on the floor.

"What's up, baby?" he said as I walked through the door.

Brandon dropped what he was doing and followed me to the kitchen.

"Has Brandon had dinner?" I asked.

"I gave him a piece of my sandwich about an hour ago."

"Damn, Curtis, that's not dinner. Why didn't you heat up the spaghetti in the refrigerator?" I asked.

"I didn't know if that's what you wanted him to eat for dinner," he replied.

Frustrated, I heated the spaghetti and fed Brandon before giving him his bath and putting him to bed. I got the church membership application and sat next to Curtis, who by now was lying on the couch with about three empty beer bottles on the coffee table in front of him.

"I got everything set for Brandon to be baptized and I also brought you a membership application to fill out."

"A membership application for what? Besides, I'm already a member at a church," he replied.

"Yeah, but you never go. You said yourself that they treat you like shit."

"So what? My mother is still a member, my grandparents are members, and so are all my cousins."

"I'm saying do this for Brandon," I insisted.

"Do what for Brandon? This is about him being baptized, not me becoming a member."

"I thought maybe we could do this together as a family. Then maybe we could become more involved in other things. Maybe you could mentor other kids or something."

"What?" Curtis laughed. "A mentor? Girl, please. I ain't got time for no shit like that. I'm trying to get paid. Besides, I got problems of my own to deal with."

"So, you're saying you're not going to join?" I asked.

"Hell, no, I'm not joining."

I tossed the application on the table in front of him and walked away. "I give up, Curtis."

I got in bed at around nine o'clock and watched a movie. Curtis turned off the TV, got in bed next to me, and pulled me close to him.

"You still mad at me?" he asked.

"You know what, Curtis? I don't give a shit anymore. I'm trying to do the right thing and all you do is shoot me down, so I give up. From now on, do what you want, but I'm going to do what I think is right for me and Brandon."

"C'mon, baby. Don't act like that. Trust me, we'll be okay," he whispered as he kissed my neck. "I know you want what's best for Brandon, but I want what's best for all of us. You handle that end and trust me, and we'll be okay. Give me a few more months to get my business affairs together and I'll show you," he continued as he caressed my body. His words had no meaning but his touch turned me on. He somehow knew the right buttons to push when I was pissed off at him.

CHAPTER 9

Mya

The temperature dropped to about thirty-five degrees. I lit my fireplace as I sat in front of the TV sipping herbal tea. Minutes later my cell phone rang.

"Hey," the voice said. It was Darryl. "How are you?" he asked.

"I'm fine, just relaxing after a long day. What about you?"

"I'm sitting in the hotel just finishing up some work for my presentation tomorrow."

"Oh, where are you?" I asked.

"I just arrived in Memphis from Nashville. I'm driving back to Atlanta on Friday."

"Wow, that's a lot of traveling. So what's the weather like in Memphis?"

"About fifty-four degrees and raining. I just wish I was at home in my own bed."

"I know, there's nothing like home. It's cold nights like this that make you appreciate that."

"Yeah, here I am, lying on a bed that strangers lie on every night. God knows what's on it."

I laughed. "Oh, poor baby. I'm chilling in front of my fireplace sipping some tea."

"See there?" he replied, laughing. "You had to go there . . . So how was your day, by the way?"

"Ugh, I don't even want to begin to talk about my day. Let's say I earned my money as a teacher, as little as it is." I replied.

"That tough, huh?" he said.

"Yeah,"

There was silence.

"Are we still on for Saturday?" he asked.

"Yeah,"

"Still at three o'clock, huh?"

"Yep." I sipped my tea.

He laughed.

"Are you laughing at me, Darryl?"

"No, I'm just tripping. I feel like a high-school kid getting ready for his first date."

"A high-school kid?" I was confused by his comment.

"Well, yeah. Not because of the time we're meeting. I'm not trippin' about that. I think you're different, that's all. You're pleasant to talk to, you have a good sense of humor, and you have standards. Most women aren't like that. For that reason alone, I'm just anxious to get to know more about you."

"I don't know about all *that*," I replied.

"No, I'm just saying—"

"Well, Darryl, thank you for the compliment," I interrupted. "I'm still not going to change my mind about the time," I replied, giggling.

He laughed along with me.

Several minutes later, we ended our conversation for the night. I was really feeling him—the things he said were so comforting. Not one time did he try to slip in a perverted line or bring up materialistic things. He was sort of laid-back and smooth.

I got up to shower before bed. When I looked in the mirror, I realized that I had to do something about my hair before my date with Darryl. I knew Tangie and Stephanie normally got their hair done every Saturday at a friend's salon. Usually I went to Supercuts in the mall for a trim, but you had to make an appointment at least a week in advance.

Before going to bed, I called Stephanie to ask abouth her hair appointment for Saturday. After about four rings and no answer, I hung up and called Tangie, who answered the phone like she was in the middle of some intense fucking.

"Yeah," she answered, breathing heavily.

"Damn, girl. What's going on at your place? Is Todd over there?"

"Uh-uh, just me. What's up?"

"Sorry to call so late, but are you and Stephanie getting your hair done this Saturday?"

"Yeah."

"Good—I need my hair done for my date with Darryl. Do you think you can get your girl to squeeze me in?"

"Yeah, yeah, I'm sure she can," Tangie replied in a rush.

"Great—so what time—"

"Just be at Stephanie's house around eight A.M.," she interrupted before hanging up.

What the hell was that all about? I thought. That was typical Tangie, doing God knows what with God knows who.

On Saturday I arrived at Stephanie's house right at seven-thirty. This was the normal meeting place since Stephanie lived closest to the salon.

I walked through the living room, heading toward the den. I could hear the TV as I got closer. When I turned the corner, I saw Stephanie sitting on the couch putting clothes on Brandon.

"Hey, girl," I said as I walked toward her.

She looked up. "Hey."

I sat down closest to Brandon. "Where's Tangie?"

"She just called. She should be pulling up any minute."

"Good—I'm ready to do something with this hair," I said, running through it with my fingers.

"What? Girl, please. You got that straight, white-girl hair. All you have to do is just wash and trim the split ends, Ms. Supercuts," she teased.

I giggled. "No, I don't. I need to do more than that."

"Look at my hair," Stephanie said, rubbing across her head. I need a serious perm."

"I think I need one, too," I joked.

"Whatever, Cajun girl," Stephanie replied, laughing.

Minutes later, Tangie appeared, wearing a baseball cap. "Hey, are you two ready to get this thing started?"

"Yeah," I replied. "What's with the ball cap?"

"Girl, I just woke up and got dressed. I didn't even touch my hair. Why bother when I'm about to get it hooked up, anyway? I'm going to get me some braids so I won't have to keep dealing with my hair in the morning. Just wake up, shake them out, and head to work."

We all started toward the front door.

"Hey, I'll meet you two in the car. I want to make sure Curtis has everything for Brandon." Stephanie said.

Tangie and I walked outside, passing Curtis and a group of guys in the front yard.

"You guys about to leave?" Curtis asked.

"Yeah, as soon as your girl comes out," I replied.

Curtis looked in the direction of the front door before walking toward it, going inside as Tangie and I got in my car. Minutes later, Stephanie came outside and got in the backseat with a slight frown on her face.

"Girl, you okay?" Tangie asked.

Stephanie took a deep breath and turned toward Tangie. "Girl, sometimes that damn Curtis can be a pain in my fucking ass. My horoscope said some tempers would flare today and it's starting early."

"Girl, you still reading that horoscope shit every day?" Tangie said.

"You didn't think it was shit when it helped you out with your divorce," Stephanie replied.

"I didn't need a horoscope to tell me my marriage was in chaos. That bastard showed his true colors way before you tried to get me to listen to that horoscope bullshit."

I laughed out loud.

"What's Curtis tripping about now?" I asked.

"He got all upset 'cause I asked him to go to the store and pick up some things for Brandon. All he wants to do is hang out with those thugs all day."

Tangie smirked and turned her head. I kept my eyes focused on the road.

"He can at least give up five minutes of being around them to take care of his son," Stephanie continued.

There was silence as we continued on. I looked over at Tangie who was biting down on her lip.

"Let me call him and make sure—"

"Stephanie!" Tangie shouted. "I'm not trying to hear that shit, okay? Don't let that petty shit ruin your day. Better yet, *our* day, over this bullshit. Brandon will be okay. You have your way of taking care of him and Curtis has his way. What you need to be worried about is getting that shit on your head done, more than anything else."

I laughed, caught off guard by her comment.

Stephanie dropped her head for a moment before looking up with a slight smile on her face. "You're right, girl. You're absolutely right."

"Now turn the radio up, Mya, and let's kick this day off right," Tangie continued.

When we got to the hair salon, we opened the door to see torn-up heads everywhere. It's a good thing men don't come here and try to pick up women. Seeing this would make the entire gay population in Atlanta skyrocket.

I had been to this salon a few times but had never had my hair done here. The owner's name is Peaches. She is a childhood friend of Tangie and Stephanie who started out doing their hair from her bedroom when they were in high school and developed enough clients to open her own salon. Peaches's salon was unlike any that I'd ever encountered before. We have ghetto salons in New Orleans but this salon took the cake. It was mostly filled with women there to air their dirty laundry.

Tangie had called Mary Butler, who'd agreed to fit me into her schedule. I had met her before when I was in the salon earlier that month and was confident that she would do a good job on my hair.

As we entered the salon, I saw Mary standing by her chair, organizing her work area. Mary is a big-boned sista who stands about five feet tall. She wore these worn-down slippers with a pair of white socks and dragged her feet when she walked. As Tangie and Stephanie greeted their other friends, I walked over to Mary.

"Hey, Mary. What's up, girl?"

Mary looked up and saw me through the mirror and turned around with a slight smile.

"Nothing. Trying to make some money, that's all."

"I appreciate you seeing me on such short notice."

"Girl, that ain't nothing. My next appointment is not until ten o'clock, anyway. Have a seat." She cleared off her salon chair.

I took my jacket off and placed it on the coat hanger next to Mary's workstation and took a seat.

"How you want your hair did?" she asked.

"I think a wash, condition, and maybe trim the split ends. Don't cut too much off, just the uneven ends," I replied.

"Yeah, that's all you really need 'cause your hair texture is too straight to get a perm," she replied, combing through my hair. "Let's wash and condition."

Mary escorted me to the station a few chairs down from hers where I sat back and she began washing my hair.

"You a schoolteacher with Tangie and 'em, huh?"

"Yep, dealing with bad-ass kids five days a week," I replied.

Mary laughed. "I thought about teaching school, but preferred doing hair instead," she continued, making small talk as she put the conditioner in my hair.

"Let this set for about twenty minutes and I'll be back to trim the ends before putting you under the dryer."

I nodded and looked over at Peaches, who had just finished with a customer.

"Who's next, you or Tangie?" Peaches said, looking at Stephanie.

Stephanie looked over at Tangie. "You can go first. I'm going to call Curtis to make sure he gets Brandon his things from the store."

"Oh, okay." Tangie got up and walked toward the salon chair. When she pulled off her ball cap, Peaches frowned. "Damn, girl. When was the last time I gave you a perm?"

"Girl, I don't know. I had to use hair grease and water just to keep it down all week," Tangie replied.

"Umph," Peaches sounded. "C'mon and sit down so we can get started on this head."

Stephanie dialed Curtis and apparently got his voice mail or something, because she hung up the phone in disgust without saying a word and sat back in her chair, frowning.

"You okay over there?" Tangie asked, seeing Stephanie's face.

"Hell, no. Now he's not answering the phone. Bastard."

Peaches looked up at Stephanie as she combed through Tangie's hair. "What's the matter? Your man tripping?"

"Girl, that ain't—"

"Men ain't shit sometime," a voice interrupted Stephanie.

"Amen to that," Peaches replied as she turned toward this skinny sista standing near the door.

"I got a court case pending now because of my ex," she continued.

"Are you serious? What happened?" Peaches asked.

"Girl, I had a feeling he was cheating on me but could never prove it. Then one night I followed him and caught his ass cheating with the fucking cleaning lady at his job," the girl continued.

"Whaaat?" someone shouted.

"What did you do?" Peaches asked.

"Shit, what any other nigga would do. I kicked that bitch ass. Then threw his shit out my fucking house."

Everyone laughed.

"You know how you can find out if your man cheating?" Peaches asked. Everyone waited in anticipation.

"When his ass comes home late, let him sleep the rest of the night away. But early the next morning, run his ass some hot bath water and have him sit in the tub. If his dick floats up to the top, that means his ass has been out there fucking around 'cause he ain't got no more strength down there."

The entire salon burst out laughing.

"I'm serious—a heavy dick will sink to the bottom, but an empty one will float," the sista continued.

Another girl stood up. "Girl, my man started off giving me roses, cards, and other nice gifts. But now the only thing he gives me is grief. He had the nerve one night to ask me to stop by the store and get some condoms on my way to his house. Shiiiit, I told his ass I'm already bringing the pussy, now I got to bring the damn condoms, too?"

There was continued laughter.

"Needless to say, he's my ex now," she continued.

"Your ex? I thought you two were getting married next year," Peaches said, concerned.

"We *were* until I called Psychic Cindy on his ass and she told me he was cheating."

"A psychic, girl?" Stephanie asked.

"Hell, yeah. Psychic Cindy is the shit. She told me things about myself that only me and God knows. That's why I believe she was telling the truth. Months later, just like she said, I came home one day and caught him in the act. On the same sheets I lay *my* ass on every night."

"Wow!" Stephanie replied.

"That's right. There's no price on happiness. Whatever works, girl," Peaches continued.

This went on and on throughout the course of getting our hair done. By the time Mary had finished my hair, I'd developed an appetite. When Stephanie's hair was done, we all gathered our things and said our good-byes as we walked to the door of the salon.

"Are you guys hungry?" I asked as we exited.

"Hell, yeah, I'm starving," Tangie replied.

Stephanie looked confused at the question and didn't respond.

"What about you, Stephanie? You want to go to the Cheesecake Factory?" I asked.

She paused for a moment. "I don't know. Let me call Curtis."

"What? Forget his ass. He didn't even pick up the damn phone when you called the first time."

Wrinkles formed on Stephanie's forehead. "Forget it, you're right—let's go to the Cheesecake Factory."

CHAPTER 10

Tangie

After lunch I decided to let my class have study time, primarily because my head was killing me from the new hairdo that Peaches had given me two days ago. Since I'd never had braids, I decided to try it to change my look. It was cute but the price you pay to stay beautiful can have some very painful consequences.

As I sat at my desk with eyes closed, I massaged the sore areas, trying to concentrate on something pleasant, when I was suddenly interrupted by the sound of paper crumpling in my right ear.

"Ms. Jackson, can I finish painting my pictures?" an irritating voice sounded. When I looked up, it was Tina standing next to me, holding some drawings.

"Excuse me?" I was staring at her with my eyes half-open.

"Is it okay if I finish watercoloring my drawings?"

I forced a smile. "Uh, sure, Tina. Let me get the watercolors out of the storage closet."

She smiled, following me as I got the supplies and placed them on the table in the back of the classroom used for painting.

"Ms. Jackson, can you help me paint my drawings?" she asked innocently.

I paused, trying to figure out a way to say no in my fake, high-pitched voice so I wouldn't offend her.

"I'm going to paint this one for my mother, this one for my

cousin, and this for my daddy," she continued as she displayed each picture.

When she said *daddy*, I got a hot flash and instantly my mind rewound back to how fine her dad's ass looked walking through the door the other day.

"Uh, sure, Tina. I'll help you paint." I had a huge smile on my face.

I pulled up a chair and sat down next to Tina as she took off the caps on the paint. When I grabbed a paintbrush, I reached over the open paint to soak it in the water.

"Ms. Jackson, your bracelet is getting into the paint," Tina said, concerned. I looked down and noticed that my favorite diamond bracelet was about to be covered in green paint.

"Oh, shi-shoot," I replied as I moved my arm away quickly. "I'd better take this off and put it to the side. This is my favorite bracelet and I would die if I got paint all on it."

As I took it off and placed it on the table between Tina and me, she picked it up, admiring it. "Is this real?" she asked.

"Absolutely—I wouldn't wear anything that wasn't."

"Can I try it on?" she asked.

"Sure, but just don't get any paint on it."

Tina tried on the bracelet—it hung loosely around her bony little arms. She held it up with a look of admiration in her eyes. "I really like you, Ms. Jackson," she said, staring up at me while placing the bracelet back on the table and continuing her painting.

I smiled at the compliment. "You do?"

"Yes, I want to be a teacher just like you when I grow up. I tell my parents all the time that I want to be a teacher."

"And why is that?" I asked.

"Well, I like to read, and I like to paint. Plus, teaching is fun," she continued.

When Tina and I finished her paintings, we left them out to dry. She discussed her family at great length, then talked about the other schools she attended prior to Stephenson Elementary. That gave me an idea for my class's next history assignment. Since we're learning about ancestors, I asked each student to create a collage about their family. I wanted them to gather pictures and put them on construction paper to display to the class. Maybe Tina could bring in some pictures of her dad for me to admire.

As the day went on, I watched as Tina interacted with the other students. The way she smiled or held her head a certain way, I could see her father's features—it made my mind suddenly drift away and picture him walking through the door of my classroom once more. I tried to block him out but visions of him kept reappearing out of nowhere.

Later that night Todd came over in a really good mood as he entered my apartment, holding a medium-sized brown paper bag. "Hey, baby," he said and kissed my lips.

"What are you smiling about?" I asked as I closed the door behind him. He pulled out two twelve-count boxes of magnum condoms. "From now on, condoms won't be an issue when I come over."

He took a seat in the den and continued talking as he slowly took off his shoes and socks. I walked into my bedroom and turned on some music and lit a few candles. After waiting for what seemed like ten minutes, I went back in the den where Todd was just pulling off his pants. "Todd, would you hurry the hell up?" I yelled.

He looked up as I took off my robe and let it drop to the floor. I walked back into the bedroom and lay across the edge of my bed on my stomach with my naked ass in the air.

Seconds later, Todd appeared, standing over me. "Let me jump in the shower first." He pulled off his underwear and walked in the bathroom.

Todd closed the door behind him and I heard the shower come on. After five minutes of lying there waiting on him, he finally came out with a condom on. "It's about fucking time," I said as I got under the covers.

Todd turned off the lights, joined me in bed, and quickly put his face between my legs. I bit down on my lips as the pleasure of his motion made my body weak. He climbed on top and penetrated me. I could tell he missed me by the aggressive way he moved his body. My legs were pushed back behind my ears as he dug deep inside of me. I was enjoying every stroke as I moaned in rhythm with his movements. "Ain't nobody gonna give it to you like me," he whispered as his body moved faster. Normally I would have responded but for some reason Tina's dad popped up in my mind as Todd's movements made me wetter. I tried to focus on the moment with Todd but I had a clear color picture of Tina's dad on top, fucking me. I felt myself about to climax as Todd kept his rhythm going. I was losing control, trying not to come until I saw Todd's face, but couldn't get a vivid picture of him through the candlelit darkness. Suddenly Todd gave a hard thrust that made me explode. "Ooooo-oooh, shit." I yelled as I closed my eyes at the pleasure of my climax. Tina's dad's face appeared in my mind once again with that cute-ass smile of his. I felt myself short of breath as the pleasure continued for several seconds until Todd finally climaxed and collapsed on top of me. *What the fuck was that all about?* I thought as I opened my eyes. Out of all the times Todd made me climax, this was the first time I'd had an orgasm that lasted this long. Todd continued to kiss and caress my body, but my mind was in deep thought trying to figure out why the fuck Tina's dad appeared in my head like that.

Todd got up and turned on the light. "Damn, I don't know what you did tonight, but that was some intense fucking."

I smiled in agreement. It *was* some intense fucking all right, but he shouldn't pat himself on the back for all the credit.

Todd and I held each other for a few more minutes until he climbed on top of me for round two. This time the sex took longer, but once again all I thought about was Tina's dad on top of me, which made being with Todd more pleasant. Todd was talking, but I couldn't understand a word he was saying. After a while I rolled Todd over and let my thoughts of Tina's dad go to work in my mind. I rode Todd until the beads of sweat rolled to the tip of my nose and fell on Todd's face.

Todd stared in my eyes. "You really do miss me, don't you?"

"I'm not going to lie. I do miss these moments."

"Yeah, I can tell." He caressed my back.

In the midst of our cuddling and caressing, Todd looked at the clock and noticed the time and slowly rolled over, getting out of bed. He leaned back and kissed my forehead with a look of confidence in his eyes like he was in total control of my emotions. I pulled the covers over my naked body and stared up at the ceiling.

Todd came back into the room, fully dressed. "Hey, I'm leaving. Do you want me to lock up behind me?"

I turned my head in his direction. "Yeah," I replied softly.

When Todd left I took a long, hot shower, asking myself questions, one being my fixation on Tina's dad, Walter. It was strange, because I hadn't had feelings like this since my first crush.

CHAPTER II

Stephanie

In the midst of unpacking the groceries, I received a call from Reggie that Brandon's baptism was approved by the bishop and was scheduled to take place in three weeks. In order for me to gain membership at the church I had to attend Bible study and a retreat. Reggie volunteered to be my sponsor, and we agreed to meet for about thirty minutes after Bible study as part of my preparation for membership. Things were happening fast, considering I had just turned in the applications last week. Curtis's application for membership was still on the coffee table in the den under some empty beer bottles he'd left last night after drinking with his buddies. I had given up on trying to force him to join the church and decided to try and lead by example. I figured if he saw how much I was doing at the church he would eventually come around. I think most of his influence comes from the guys he hangs around with. I swear I think the only time they see the inside of a church is during weddings and funerals.

I showered and started dinner while Brandon watched cartoons in the den. Several minutes later, Curtis came walking through the door smelling like someone had drenched him in oil. "Hey, son." He walked over and hugged Brandon before going into the kitchen to get a beer out of the refrigerator. "Hey, baby," he said. I smiled in return as I continued fixing dinner.

"Oooh, what smells so good?" Curtis asked.

"I'm frying chicken, with green beans and mashed potatoes."

"Good, 'cause I'm starving. Look, baby—made four hundred dollars today painting a few cars," he said, pulling out crumpled bills.

I shifted my eyes to the money, then back on the chicken I was seasoning. "That's good, Curtis," I replied unconcerned.

"How long before dinner?" he asked as he took off his grimy shirt and hung it on the back of the chair next to the dinner rolls I'd set out.

"Not long, and could you *please* put that dirty-ass shirt in the laundry?" I snapped.

"My bad." He grabbed his shirt and tossed it into the laundry room on his way to the bedroom.

That was a pet peeve of mine about Curtis. He would always toss his dirty clothes anywhere in the house once he got home and expected me to pick up after him. Also, he rarely cleaned the bathtub after using it and hardly ever washed the dishes.

Curtis went into the bathroom and showered before coming out with a towel wrapped around his body and grabbing another beer out of the refrigerator.

"I may be going out of town this weekend for a job. Cedric knows this guy in Columbia, South Carolina, who wants a couple of cars repaired he's trying to sell."

"Why does Cedric need you? Doesn't he have a crew at the shop that can go?"

"Yeah, but he asked me along, too. Besides, it's easy money."

"There's no such thing as easy money, Curtis. Someone is always getting screwed on the back end."

"That's not my problem. I'm just doing what I have to do to open 'Curtis Auto Repair.'"

"Don't get caught up in Cedric's bullshit. I think he's just using you because you work cheap."

"No, it's because I can do the work better than those other shops that try to rip you off."

"Says who? Cedric?"

"Says me. I did my homework. I know what these other shops charge so I just mark my price down a few dollars." Curtis took a sip from his beer.

"So you got it all figured out, huh?" I replied.

"Not all of it, just the things that pertain to me." He turned and walked into the bedroom.

After dinner, Curtis went into the den and lay across the couch watching TV. I put Brandon to bed and went into the bedroom to get my clothes together for school tomorrow. Moments later, Reggie called again.

"Hey, sister, I'm just leaving the church and was wondering if you wanted to be in the female mentor program? We meet twice a month and try to talk to kids about personal issues. It's a very successful program that has helped hundreds of kids over the years. You'll get a chance to meet a lot of other members of the church who volunteer."

"Well, let me think about that, Reggie. It sounds good, but I have a son of my own to raise, and that takes up a lot of my free time."

"Well, how about coming out when you can?" he suggested.

"Okay. That sounds better. But let me think about it before I make a decision."

"Has your boyfriend thought about the mentor program?"

"Uh, well, because he works so much he probably won't have the time to do it," I lied.

"Well, that's fine. Maybe sometime in the future we can convince him to come out. Well, sister, nice talking to you, and I'll see you Wednesday at Bible study."

"Thanks, Reggie, for everything."

Curtis entered the room as I put the phone down. With a puzzled look, he asked, "Who the hell is Reggie?"

I turned toward him. "That's the guy from the church I told you about."

"What did he want this late?" he asked.

"He just wanted to let me know that Brandon's scheduled to be baptized in three weeks."

A smile came across Curtis's face. "Oh, really? So my boy will be baptized? That's great." He walked over and kissed me.

"So tell me about this damn Reggie," Curtis asked.

"What?"

"This, uh, Reggie dude. Is he the reverend or something?"

"No, he's like a deacon, I think. All I know is that he is helping me get my life together."

"Your life together?"

"I mean spiritually, Curtis."

"Shit. I bet his ass is gay."

"What are you talking about?"

"Everybody knows that half of the so-called deacons in these big churches are fruitier than a Christmas cake."

"Curtis, I really don't know what you're talking about, and to be honest, I really don't care. If this is your excuse for not wanting to join the church with Brandon and me, that's fine, but you really need to look at yourself before you start judging other people."

"It's not about me not wanting to join. I told you I'll go when I can, but I already belong to a church. It's all a scam, anyway. The preacher stands up there with a thousand-dollar suit on, reading the Bible to the poor and confused. You said it yourself—Mya's dad is a preacher and he drives around in a Rolls-Royce. Now what kind of shit is that?"

"Mya's dad has two churches in New Orleans. If the members want to pay him that kind of money, then why shouldn't he accept it? Plus, he travels and speaks at engagements out of town. I'm sure he gets paid for that."

"All that shit is a scam. Nowadays, anyone who turns their life around is trying to preach."

"Well, then, you should make a hell of a preacher, as much shit as you're into."

Curtis gave me a strange stare before he continued on with his negative opinions about churches. I think his problem is not so much joining the church as trusting one. Now I was convinced that once he saw how involved I was getting, he would join, too.

CHAPTER 12

Mya

I was still admiring the roses Darryl gave me on our first date—they were in a vase on my mantel. Each time I passed them, it reminded me of how much of a gentleman he was. I felt like I was with the perfect man at the perfect restaurant on the perfect evening. With him fresh on my mind I picked up my cell phone and called. Before it could ring, I got his voice mail.

"Hey, Darryl—it's me, Mya. Just wanted to see what you were up to. Call me when you get this message. 'Bye."

As I sat on the couch reading through my mail, my parents called.

We haven't talked much since my dad took over as president of the Full Gospel Baptist Counsel a year ago. Before that, we talked three times a week. Now they spend most of their time traveling to different churches across the country, speaking or going to banquets and conferences. My spirits quickly rose when I heard their voices.

"Hey," I said with excitement.

"How's my girl?" my dad asked.

"I'm okay. Just working."

"When are you coming home?" my mother asked.

"Whenever you two are there. Oh, and I talked to Grandma LeVeaux the other day. She got on me for not calling."

"Well, you know your grandma. She'll speak her mind," my dad replied.

"So where are you guys now?" I asked.

"We're in Los Angeles. I have to speak at the regional full gospel convention on Friday," my dad replied.

"See? That's what I'm talking about. You guys are always traveling."

"I know, baby, but that's a part of my calling."

"I know, I know," I replied.

"So has Atlanta been good to you and are you staying out of trouble?" my mom asked.

"Of course."

"And going to church, I hope?" she added.

"Mama, of course I'm going to church," I lied, closing my eyes.

"It just worries me that you're up there all alone."

"She's fine," my dad said reassuringly. "As long as she keeps God in every decision she makes, she won't have a problem. Baby, just stay focused on God's will. If it doesn't feel right in your spirit, then chances are it's not of God."

"I know," I replied.

Those were the exact words my dad had said to me since I was a little girl. Every day before I went to school, I would hear it. Pretty soon it started going in one ear and out the other.

"Well baby, we just called to let you know we love you and to see how you were doing."

"I'm fine, just busy working."

"Okay, well, let's pray together and we'll let you go back to whatever it was you were doing."

I closed my eyes as my dad began his prayer.

"Dear Heavenly Father, we thank you for—"

As soon as my dad got into his prayer, my cell phone rang. I opened one eye and peeked at the caller ID. It was Darryl. As my dad continued, my phone rang a second time. I had my hand on the button to answer, but I was in the middle of prayer. As soon as my dad finished his prayer, my mom started praying. Seconds later the phone stopped ringing. My attention was focused on my mother's voice.

"And God, we ask that you continue to shine your goodness and mercy upon us, in Jesus' name we pray, Amen."

"Well, baby," my dad said. "We love you, and have a good night, okay?"

"Okay, I love you guys, too." We hung up.

I quickly called Darryl back, only to get his voice service again. I also checked to see if he had left me a message but he didn't.

Later that night Tangie called me on the three-way with Stephanie as I was getting into bed.

"What's up, girl?" Stephanie asked.

"Tell it. Tell it all—I want to hear about your date with Darryl," Tangie shouted in the background.

"Yeah, we want the dirt," Stephanie said.

I laughed out loud. "Girl, it was soooo romantic. His ass got me yellow roses and everything. We talked and laughed. I mean, I had a great time. He was a true gentleman in every sense of the word."

"He got you roses?" Stephanie asked, surprised.

"Yeah, and had them sitting on the table for me when I got to the restaurant. I was like, damn. Everybody around me was staring as I sat there red as a damn beet."

"That *was* romantic, girl," Stephanie replied.

"Yeah, it was all right. But don't get caught up in that shit. Brothers start off like that until they get between your legs. Then that rose becomes a thorn in your damn side," Tangie said.

"Yeah, like that thorn in my damn side named Curtis. He started out like that, and look at me now. Oh, and girls, guess what," Stephanie said.

"What?" Tangie and I responded.

"You know his ass was trippin' 'cause I was hanging out with you and Mya the other night."

"What!" I replied.

"Yeah, he started saying things like what kind of mother would hang out like I did when she could be spending time at home with her child and shit. It just made me feel bad, like I was doing something wrong."

"I know his ass ain't talking, as much as *he* hangs out. He acts like you two are married or something. You have your life and he has his," Tangie replied.

"I know, but—"

"What about all the times his ass is all up in the club? I mean, let's just keep it real. Why are you still putting up with his shit? He barely pays child support—the nerve of his ass to question why and who you hang out with."

"Yeah, I have to agree with Tangie on this one, Stephanie," I replied. "You're good, 'cause I would've dragged his ass in court a long time ago."

"Don't get me wrong. He's trying. He gives me what he can," she replied.

"Bullshit—Curtis got it made. Live-in pussy, home-cooked meals, and a free roof over his damn head. You need to shake his ass and get you a real man. He's thirty years old, working part-time, and no education. Girl, a nigga like that can't tell me shit. A thirty-year-old man needs to be in a career, anyway, and not a job."

I stayed quiet 'cause I had to agree with Tangie on that. But for some reason Stephanie just couldn't let him go and move on with her life.

"You talking about the thorn in *my* side. What about Todd?" Stephanie said. "You spend more time in bed with him than his wife does."

"Whose fault is that? He comes to me," Tangie replied.

"Yeah, yeah, yeah," Stephanie said.

"Well, it's true. I'm not like other girls, who think things are going bad at his house for him to come over. We just enjoy each other's company, that's all."

"All he's giving you are false hopes, is all I'm saying," Stephanie continued.

"Well, I—"

"Will you two let me finish my story?" I interrupted.

There was silence on the phone. "You two are never going to accept each other's situation, so leave it alone." I said.

"Girl, you just mad 'cause you ain't got no business," Tangie joked. Stephanie laughed.

"Anyway, he invited me over to dinner at his place next weekend. How should I handle that?"

"Well, that depends on you," Stephanie said.

"Yeah, what don't you want to happen?" Tangie added.

"Well, of course he ain't getting any." I poked my lips out.

"No, I'm talking about are you ready to kiss, cuddle, or something like that? Brothers expect that," Tangie said.

"I don't know. I did want to kiss him when he walked me to my car. Especially when he wrapped those arms around me before I left. Oooooh wooooo, that shit felt good."

"Tangie, save your advice—Mya's already sprung. She's going to mess around and get fucked," Stephanie joked.

We burst into laughter.

"No, the hell I'm not. What am I thinking of, anyway? I really don't know him that well to be kissing on him. I'll probably just go over there, eat, talk a little, and come home."

"And don't wear anything too sexy or revealing. Wear something that covers you up. Don't leave any room for his imagination to wander," Tangie said.

"Yeah, the more you have on, the better chance you have to change your mind if it's getting too hot for you." Stephanie said.

"Now that you mention it, let me look in my closet and see what I can wear."

I found an outfit that would be perfect. When I got off the phone with Tangie and Stephanie I put it aside to take to the cleaners after I left work tomorrow.

Darryl never did call back. I wanted so badly to call him a second time but didn't want to seem desperate, like I was chasing him or something. Instead I spent the rest of the night watching a movie before drifting off to sleep.

CHAPTER 13

Tangie

During lunch I left the teachers' lounge on my way to my classroom to get my *Ebony* magazine. I was dying to see this month's issue—it featured the twenty-five most eligible bachelors. Last year I contacted a doctor from Atlanta who was listed. We e-mailed each other for a couple of months before we went out. The first couple of dates were cool, although I found him to be a little strange. He licked his lips after almost every statement. Not in a sexy way, like L L Cool J, but like he was trying to remove something off the side of his mouth. I continued to see him because he was really cute and fine as hell. Besides, I thought licking his lips the way he did with that long tongue of his was something that could be useful in the bedroom.

It wasn't until after he lost his job that things started to change. He would get upset about the littlest things and all of a sudden start having temper tantrums. That's when I had to break off our relationship and I'm glad I did, I found out more about his true profession as a physician. He was a doctor all right, Dr. Jekyll. This man was a doctor of psychiatry at a state facility and had been diagnosed as having split personalities. He worked around mentally challenged people so much, his ass started acting just like some of them. That explains why, after an orgasm, he would make these strange noises and faces that made me feel really uncomfortable. Last I heard, he was seeking psychiatric treatment in the very hospital where he worked. The sex was good, though, and different every time. I guess it was because I didn't know who I was fucking, him or one of those crazy motherfuckers that came out of his ass.

As I continued down the hallway and past the principal's office, someone called out my name—it literally stopped me in my tracks. When I turned and faced in the direction of the voice, I was caught off guard by Tina's dad standing there with his brown suede jacket draped across his right arm. "Hi, uh, Mr. Washington? What are you doing here? Is everything okay with Tina?" I asked as I walked toward him. He stood there with a huge smile that showed off his pearly white teeth. "Yeah, Tina's fine. She has a doctor's appointment, so I'm getting her out of school early today," he replied.

"Oh, I see," I said, trying not to stare directly at him.

"How are you today?" he asked as he shifted his jacket over to his left arm to shake my hand.

As he did this, I noticed his penis as it hung down on the left side of his thigh. *Oh my god*, I thought. *That shit looks thick. I heard that guys with penises that hung on the left side were good lovers.*

I quickly looked up, right into his eyes once again. I felt a hot flash through my body that made the hair on the back of my neck stand up. "Uh, I think she's still in the cafeteria eating if you want to check down there," I replied.

"If it's okay? I know you guys have a policy about strangers lurking in the hallway. Can you take me there?" he asked politely.

I shifted my eyes down at his penis and back up at him. "Sure, I can do that," I replied.

We walked toward the cafeteria, passing a few empty classrooms on the way. Before we could make it to the entrance, Tina came walking out with a couple of her friends, surprised to see her dad. After they hugged and exchanged greetings, Tina took him by the hand and we started walking back toward the principal's office so that she could be checked out properly.

"Well, thank you, Ms. Jackson, for walking with me. I really appreciate that."

"Oh, that's no problem. It's a good thing we did because Tina looked like she was on her way out the door to the playground." I looked down at Tina. "Well, you two have a nice day." I turned away and quickly walked off.

"Ms. Jackson," he yelled as I continued on toward my classroom. I turned around and he was walking toward me. "Yes?"

"Uh, do you and your friends like jazz?" he asked.

"Yeah, my friends and I love jazz," I replied, surprised at the question.

"Well, I have a jazz band that plays around town. This Saturday we're going to be playing at the Living Room. My wife thought it'd be a good idea if I did more promoting, so maybe you and your friends can come out if you don't have plans."

The Living Room is a quaint spot in Buckhead where a lot of young professionals hang out. On certain nights, they have different types of live music.

"Oh, uh, I'll check with my friends and see if they're available," I said with a smile.

There was a moment of uncomfortable silence.

"Well, thanks. If you know anyone else, please feel free to spread the word. My band is called ACE."

"Okay—well, I'll see what I can do."

As I took a few steps forward I was dying to turn around and see that tight ass of his before he made it out the door. I counted to three and took a deep breath before turning around. But unfortunately, when I did all I saw was our principal, Mr. Ridgewell's, big ass in his tight, double-knit pants as he blocked my view of Mr. Washington. Ridgewell, as I called him, stands about six feet tall with a processed Afro and a beer belly that draped over his belt. He swears he's a playa from back in the day, and he is always trying to undress the female teachers with his eyes during conversation.

"Ms. Jackson?" he called out.

I put on my fake smile as he walked toward me. "Yes, Ridgewell, what's up?"

"You having a good day?" he shouted.

"Yes, and you?" I walked toward my classroom.

"Just fine, just fine," he said as I heard his footsteps fade in the opposite direction.

I sat at my desk, thumbing through my magazine, really not interested in any of the new bachelors that were listed. Instead I let my mind wander again to Mr. Washington. *So, he has a band. Hmmm, was that a hint that he wanted me to come to his show because he is inter-*

ested? By the way, he was checking me out the first time we met. I'd say he was just as curious as I was. What if I did go? I definitely couldn't take Stephanie or Mya 'cause I don't want to hear any shit from them. But damn, I sure would like to find out what's inside his pants.

Suddenly, my mind was made up. I was going to the Living Room this Saturday. A smile came across my face at my decision.

"What the hell are you thinking about over there?" Mya said as she and Stephanie entered my classroom.

My smile went away, as I was startled. "Oh, uh, nothing. I just read an article in *Ebony* magazine that I thought was funny."

Mya and Stephanie took a seat in the chairs next to my desk. "Girl, Ridgewell was talking to this fine-ass man a minute ago outside under the walking deck," Stephanie said.

"Yeah, he was very attractive," Mya replied. "Then again, any man standing next to Ridgewell is gorgeous with a capital G."

We laughed.

I knew just who they were talking about but sat there completely surprised as they went on and on about this man's physical features. With every description they gave, my mind drifted away with wild and crazy thoughts of Walter.

CHAPTER 14

Stephanie

I missed my seven o'clock Bible study class because I overslept after a long day at work and then came home and cooked dinner. I asked Curtis to wake me up at six o'clock so I could have time to shower and make it to class. Instead, I was awakened by loud laughter coming from our den. When I looked over at the clock it said eight-thirty P.M. Upset, I jumped out of bed and walked to the kitchen, where I could see a bunch of thugs in the den sitting on the couch drinking beer and watching TV. They turned and saw me standing with my arms folded as they looked over at Curtis. Some spoke as I focused my attention on Brandon, who was sitting on the floor next to Curtis playing with empty beer bottles. Curtis turned toward me, then quickly looked down at his watch. He stood up, facing me with a blank expression on his face. I called for Brandon and quickly turned around, heading toward the bathroom to run Brandon's bathwater. Minutes later, Curtis came walking in the bathroom and closed the door behind him.

"Baby, I'm sorry I forgot to wake you—I lost track of time."

I stood there in silence as I turned on the bathwater and began taking off Brandon's clothes.

"The guys came over unexpectedly about some more work they want me to do, and next thing I knew you were standing in the kitchen."

I looked over at him, my face wrinkled with anger.

"You want me to send them home?" he asked.

I didn't respond.

"Let me ask them to leave," he continued.

"You know what, Curtis? I don't care what you do. I really don't." I was furious.

"What's that supposed to mean?" he asked.

"We'll talk about it later." I helped Brandon into the water.

I was so upset that I started to feel dizzy. It took all the patience I had to keep from going off on Curtis in front of his friends. My horoscope this morning stated that *during rainy days we can either use an umbrella and walk to our destination or take our chances and run through it while getting drenched in its wrath.* This moment was one of those rainy days that I had to take a deep breath and walk with an umbrella.

I sat back calmly and let Brandon play with his toys in the water while I worked on a crossword puzzle.

When I finished with Brandon's bath, I put him in his bed and began reading him a bedtime story until he drifted off to sleep. I quietly got up and walked out, turning on the night-light near the foot of his bed. As I walked down the hallway, I passed Curtis, who was in the den picking up the empty beer bottles the guys had left everywhere. When he saw me enter the kitchen he walked toward me.

"Go ahead and say what it is you want to say. I know you're boiling over," he said.

"Curtis, you really don't want to hear what's on my mind right now."

"No, go ahead—say what's on your mind."

"Just what I said," I replied and began fixing a plate for dinner.

"No, I *do* want to hear it. It seems like you have a problem every time my friends come over."

Just as I was about to tell him about how inconsiderate he is, not to mention how he has my son on the floor playing with fucking beer bottles, the phone rang. Because Curtis was standing closest to it, he answered.

"It's for you. It's the faggot from church." He handed me the phone.

I walked into the den. "Hello."

"Sister, we missed you at Bible study tonight. Is everything okay?" Reggie asked, sounding concerned.

"Hi, Reggie, uh, I had such a long day that I overslept."

"Okay, I understand. That happens to me sometimes. Do you have a minute? I would like to give you a recap of what we discussed tonight."

"Sure," I replied.

"We've all decided that we're going to start studying a book called *The Purpose-Driven Life*. I have an extra copy if you can come by one day this week and get it."

"Oh yeah, I heard about that book. It's been out for a while. I know people who read it and said it changed their life. Well, can I get it from you on Sunday?"

"Sure, or if you're near the church, just come by my office. I'll be there the rest of this week until six o'clock."

"Thank you, Reggie—I really appreciate everything."

"God bless you, sister. Have a good night."

When I got off the phone, I felt a sense of calmness that took over my body when I heard the words "God bless you." I put the phone on the charger and went back to eating my dinner, ignoring Curtis, who was standing there staring at me.

"Well, before we were interrupted by your phone call, you were about to tell me about myself."

I looked up at him. "You know what, Curtis? Forget it. It's not even worth saying."

"No, it *is* worth saying if you have a problem with me. I want to know what's on your mind."

I ignored him and concentrated on eating my dinner.

"Well, let's hear it, Stephanie." he persisted.

I grabbed a forkful of food and placed it in my mouth and looked up at him as I chewed slowly.

"Fuck it, then." He took the trash bag full of bottles and placed it near the garbage can by the kitchen door and walked to the bedroom.

CHAPTER 15

Mya

As I headed for Darryl's apartment, I got lost a few times and had to rely on my instinct to finally get me there. He lives in a high-rise building that overlooks Atlanta's party spots downtown. As I drove up to the gate of his complex, he buzzed me in and met me outside in the parking area before guiding me upstairs.

"Welcome to my crib," he said and opened the door.

"Wow, this is nice," I replied, admiring the decor.

"Thank you. Make yourself at home."

I stood in the center of the den as I looked around. The brother had it looking really nice. He had vaulted ceilings in the den with track lighting and hardwood floors throughout the entire place. As my eyes wandered around, I noticed the formal dining area and the burgundy linen tablecloth with candles in the center. The view from his living room was really beautiful. It overlooked miles and miles of trees.

"You mind if I walk around?" I asked.

"No, go ahead. I'll be in the kitchen finishing up the shrimp before I put the steaks on the grill."

I walked down the hall and looked in the bedroom closest to the den. It had a wrought iron, queen-sized bed with a gray-colored dresser and nightstand set. The window had the same view as the living room area. I walked on the other side of the hall and passed what looked to be a guest bathroom. It was nice but simple, decorated in royal blue and white. When I entered the last room down the hall, I knew it had to be the master bedroom because of its size. In the center of the room was a king-sized bed made out of a cherry oak. Directly in front of it and against the wall was an armoire and dresser combination. In the corner was a sitting area with a cherry oak sofa, love seat, and coffee table set up in front of a marble fireplace. The master bathroom was just to the right of this, with a huge glass shower and a Jacuzzi. The tub had candles in the corners and a nine-inch TV mounted just above it. I walked over to his cologne tray and leaned over, admiring the different fragrances he had lined up in rows of three. I turned and walked back inside the bedroom and started for a door that was slightly open, which seemed to be his closet. As I got close to it, Darryl appeared in the room on my right.

"Oh, there you are," he said, walking over to me.

I smiled. "I love your place. Who decorated it for you?"

"I did." he replied. "I just got a few ideas out of some magazines and put them together."

"Looks really nice. You have great taste."

"Why don't you join me on the balcony? I'm getting ready to put the steaks on. Hungry?"

"Yeah, that sounds good."

I followed Darryl to his kitchen. "Wow. Your kitchen looks like something off of The Food Network."

Darryl smiled.

The kitchen cabinets were also a cherry oak with stainless steel appliances on an onyx marble countertop.

"Can I get you something to drink?" he asked.

"Yeah, I'll take bottled water."

"One bottled water coming up." He smiled again.

Darryl opened up the big stainless steel refrigerator, pulled out bottled water, and opened it.

"Here, let me get you a glass," he said.

"No, I can drink it out of the bottle."

"You sure?"

I grabbed the water and took a sip.

"Okay. I got the baked potatoes in the oven, the salad in the refrigerator, my shrimps are steaming in the corner, and my special sauce is simmering. I'd say we're ready to go."

Darryl grabbed the bowl that held the steaks, covered in a dark-colored marinade. I followed him out onto the balcony.

I sat down on one of the patio chairs as he opened the grill and placed the thick steaks in the center.

"How do you want your steak?" he asked as he turned toward me.

"Oh, medium-well is fine. I want to see just a little pink."

He nodded and moved one of the steaks closer to the edge. He began to brush the steaks with the marinade as the aroma filled the air.

"Smells good," I said, still watching him.

He smiled as he closed the lid. I took a sip of water as the nice, cool breeze off the trees below us blew my hair wildly. Darryl walked toward me and reached for my hand, gently pulling me up close to him. We stood there, almost eye to eye, for what seemed to be minutes. He reached up toward the side of my face. I slowly closed my eyes as I prepared myself for his touch. I felt his fingers comb through my hair and down the sides of my shoulders. Suddenly his touch disappeared. When I opened my eyes, he was walking away, back toward the grill.

I stood there dumbfounded and slightly mesmerized by his touch.

"You may want to sit closer to the door. You had something in your hair," he said.

Something in my hair, I thought. *What kind of shit is that?* I couldn't believe how I was taken over by the simple touch of his hand.

I sat back down, this time closer to the door. *Is he trying to tease me or what?* I thought. *Well, I'm not about to sit out here and play his game.*

"Hey, it's really smoky out here. You mind if I watch TV or something in the den?"

He turned. "Oh, no, go right ahead. The steaks will be ready in a few minutes."

"Can I do something to help?"

"Well, before you go inside, you can watch the steaks while I check on my sauce."

I nodded.

Darryl went inside while I stood over the grill, trying to dodge the smoke that was blowing in all directions. Minutes later he came back out with another bowl that had what looked to be another kind of sauce.

"Sorry it took me so long. I had to arrange the table for dinner and turn the TV on for you. Go on inside while I get the steaks."

I nodded before going inside. I passed the dining area on my way and saw the table set for two with a fresh bouquet of flowers in the center. He had linen napkins and sterling silver utensils organized in their proper places. I sat down in front of what looked to be a fifty-seven-inch TV with surround sound. I flipped through the channels as I watched Darryl's fine ass walking back and forth from the kitchen to the table every few seconds.

"Hey, I'm going to jump in the shower for a quick second and get some of this smoke off of me. The steaks are in the oven," Darryl said, walking past me.

"Sure. Take your time," I replied.

Darryl closed the door to his bedroom. Seconds later I could hear the sounds of the shower coming from behind the bedroom doors. I sat back comfortably on the couch with my head buried in the thick leather, staring at the nice African art on the wall. Below one of the paintings was a built-in shelf with lots of books. Intrigued, I got up and walked over to see what topics interested Darryl. *Hmm, Marcus Garvey, Martin Luther King Jr., Malcolm X. I'm impressed,* I whispered under my breath. There were several romance novels by various authors as well. As I reached for one, I was startled by a hard knock at the front door. I stood there, confused as to what to do. I looked across to Darryl's bedroom and could still hear the sounds of the shower. There was another knock. I slowly walked toward the door as another knock sounded, this time much harder than the last. I stopped in my tracks as I stared at the front door.

"Yo, Chris. Open up, man, it's Ray Ray," a loud voice shouted.

I turned and hurriedly made my way back to the couch and sat down. I didn't want Darryl to come rushing out of the bedroom and think I was snooping. There were two more knocks at the door before the person finally went away.

Minutes later, Darryl's bedroom door opened and he walked out, dressed in a pair of blue jeans and a casual pullover shirt.

"I'm glad to see you're still here," he joked.

I smiled.

"What are you watching on TV?" he asked, walking past me to the kitchen.

"Oh, nothing. I was just sitting here flipping through channels."

"Can I get you anything while I'm in here?" Darryl walked into the kitchen.

I got up, following behind him. "No, I'm fine."

Darryl began taking the steaks out of the oven.

"Can I *please* help with something? I feel helpless." I said.

"Uh, can you grab the bottle of wine out of the fridge and place it on the table for me?"

"Sure," I smiled.

Darryl began placing the food dishes neatly on the table in serving trays.

"Oh, while you were in the shower someone was knocking at your door."

He turned toward me. "Oh, yeah?" he replied nonchalantly. "Why didn't you answer it?"

"I'm not going to answer your door. That's impolite."

"Impolite for whom? That doesn't bother me."

"No, that's a line I won't cross," I replied.

"Well, if it was important, they'll come back," he said.

We sat down at the table. Darryl grabbed my hand and we said grace before digging in. While I cut into my steak, Darryl opened the bottle of wine and poured each of us a glass.

"Ummm, this is delicious," I said.

Darryl smiled. "Thank you."

"I'm serious. Most men brag about cooking and really can't. But, I got to give it up to you. This is really good."

Darryl continued to smile as he took a bite of his steak.

After much conversation and a lot of eating, we both took a seat on the couch. By now I was full from dinner and the wine had me feeling relaxed. Darryl sat close to me with his shoulder against mine. The TV was off and soft jazz played on the stereo.

"You know, it'll be two weeks before I see you again," he said.

"Why?" I asked.

"Work. I have to go out of town again."

"Do you ever get tired of all the traveling?"

"Yeah, especially now since I met you," he replied.

I blushed at his remark.

"Two weeks away from moments like this," he continued.

Darryl reached over and grabbed my hand. His touch was gentle as I turned and looked at him. He reached over and ran his fingers through my hair. My heart began to flutter. *I'm not going to kiss him, I'm not going to kiss him*, I repeated to myself.

Darryl's hand moved slowly behind my neck and down my back. I closed my eyes at the sensation of his caress. My heart began to pound and my breath became short. I exhaled. When I opened my eyes, Darryl was moving closer as our lips met. Darryl softly kissed my lips and pulled away. I stared at him, unsure of how to react. He shifted his body then leaned toward me again. When we kissed, I felt Darryl's tongue pierce my lips. I opened my mouth as our tongues touched. *Hmmmm*, I moaned. I pulled Darryl close to me as the kiss intensified. Darryl rubbed down the outside of my waist until he got to my outer thighs. The kiss lasted for what seemed like hours as our tongues moved in rhythm. Suddenly he reached under the back of my thigh pulling my legs up as I wrapped them around his waist. He began moving his kisses across my face toward my neck. I wrapped my arms tighter around Darryl's neck, pulling him closer. He slowly moved his hand between my legs, gently rubbing in a circular motion. *Uhhhhh*, I moaned loudly, enjoying the pleasure of his touch, I began slowly grinding against his hand. He reached for my belt and unbuckled it. Our kisses became more passionate as I began to kiss him wildly on his neck. Darryl unzipped my pants and put his hand in my jeans on the outside of my panties. By this time I was hot and wet. Darryl's fingers touched the seam to my panties and slowly began moving his finger around, pulling them aside.

"No . . . no," I whispered.

I tried to pull back but he had his hand too deep for me to move away. Please . . . no, Darryl," I repeated.

Darryl slowly moved his hand away and began rubbing my stomach. At that moment I sat up and moved out of his reach.

There was silence as I looked away.

"You okay?" Darryl asked.

"Hell, no." I replied. "This shit went too far."

"I'm sorry. I should not have—"

"No, it wasn't just you. It was me, too. I'd better go," I replied.

"No, wait. Don't go. Stay and let's just watch some TV or something."

"No, really. I'd better go." I got up and zipped my pants before reaching for my belt. Darryl sat there in silence, watching me. I grabbed my purse and headed for the door.

"Wait! At least talk to me before you leave," he said.

"And say what? I'm embarrassed enough as it is."

"Look, Mya. Things went a little too far, but not out of hand. C'mon, don't be like this. You're leaving like I'm never going to see you again."

I paused.

"Come on, can I at least get a hug?"

I smiled before hugging him.

"See, that wasn't so bad, was it?"

I nodded.

"Here, let me walk you to your car."

Darryl and I walked down to my car and hugged before I drove away. He tried to make me feel special, even though I felt like a little-ass slut.

I rode home in silence, ashamed of my behavior. When I got to my house I quickly jumped in the shower and washed myself thoroughly, trying to scrub off the guilt I was feeling.

CHAPTER 16

Tangie

It was getting late as I sat at home trying to figure out what to wear to the club tonight to see Walter's band. I tried on several different outfits and stood in front of the mirror to see if it showed enough of my figure to warrant some attention from the brothers in the club, preferably Walter Washington. About five outfits later, I decided to go with my dress jeans that showed off more of my firm hips, tight ass, and thick thighs. I did my hair before putting on my makeup, then headed out the door.

When I got to the club, it was close to eleven o'clock. I took a seat at the bar in full view of the stage and ordered a Remy XO. For the first few minutes I sipped on my drink while listening to Walter's five-member jazz band. There was a crowd of people dancing as others sat in groups talking at tables. After a few sips of Remy, the alcohol took over and I began to feel relaxed enough to start walking around the club. I scanned the room for Mrs. Washington before I got up. I already had a quick lie in place in case I saw her there. From where I was sitting, I carefully looked around a couple more times, but didn't see any sign of her anywhere.

The band played on as I walked closer to the stage. Walter was blowing the saxophone, standing in the back doing a solo, then slowly walking toward the front, his eyes tightly closed as he moved his body in rhythm with his horn. Minutes later the drummer joined in as Walter's horn slowly faded out. When he opened his eyes, he looked directly at me and a slight smile came across his face. I looked away, then back at him, and smiled. He gestured for me to come to an empty table in the corner of the club closest to the stage. I walked across the front as the men standing there eyed me. When I made it to the table I sat with my back facing the crowd, staring at the band as they played another twenty minutes before stopping for a break.

"Hey, thanks for coming." Walter took a seat across from me.

"Yeah, I like jazz, plus I needed to get out," I replied.

"Are you alone, or are your friends with you?" he asked, looking around.

"Uh, they're on their way," I lied.

I didn't want him to think I came just to see him, even though I did.

"Can I get you a drink or something?" he asked.

"Uh, no, I'm fine for now."

He gestured for the waitress and ordered himself a drink. "So what do you think of my band?"

"They're good. I like your little solo spot, too."

He smiled. "Yeah, I get up and do my thing every now and then."

"So where is your wife?"

A weird expression crossed his face. "Oh, uh, she rarely comes out anymore. She works odd shifts at Piedmont Hospital downtown."

"How long have you had your band?"

"Oh, we've been doing our thing for about eight years now. We've only been doing clubs for about three, though."

I nodded.

"You sing? We sure could use a singer," he joked.

I laughed. "No, I don't think so."

The waitress brought Walter his drink. "Put it on my tab, please," he said.

She nodded and walked away. Walter took a sip of his drink and placed the glass on the table while looking around as several people got on the dance floor.

"You care to dance? I don't have to go back on for another half hour." The house DJ was on the turntable, playing hip-hop and R&B music while the band took their break.

"Sure, why not?" I replied.

Walter and I danced about two feet apart from each other. I danced more conservatively than usual, trying to figure him out. I did turn around a couple of times and shook my ass a little to see his reaction, but I couldn't read his expression. Suddenly, the lights on stage began to flash as a signal to the band that it was time for them to continue playing. "Well, I got to get back to work. Can you hang out a little while longer?"

"Sure, I can stay about another hour."

I sat around until almost one o'clock, bored and a little bit disappointed. I thought Walter would have swept me off my feet by now or at least given me a signal that he was a little bit interested.

I got his attention and signaled to him that I was about to leave. Because he was in the middle of another solo, he nodded as I turned and exited the club.

What a waste of my fucking time, I thought as I walked to the parking lot in the back of the club. As I was about to open the door to my car, Walter came walking around the corner. "Hey, hold up a minute," he yelled.

"Aren't you supposed to be on stage?" I asked.

"It's cool—I just wanted to thank you for coming tonight."

I nodded.

"I guess your friends never showed up, huh?"

I dropped my head and looked back up at him. "Uh, no, I guess not."

There was silence as we both stood there staring at each other.

"Can I ask you something?" I said.

"Yeah, sure."

"Why did you ask me to come here tonight?"

He looked away as he wiped his hand gently across his face, then back at me. "Like I said, uh, just trying to get more people to come check out the band."

I could tell he was lying but wasn't man enough to say what was on his mind. "Okay," I replied as I turned and opened my door.

"Hold up for a second," he said as I was about to get in.

"What?" I replied.

"Why are you leaving so soon?"

"Answer my question," I said.

"I just did," he replied.

"Okay, fine."

"Wait!"

We stood there in silence for a moment.

"What do you want me to say?" he asked.

"Nothing, if that's it," I replied. I got inside my car and started the engine. "Well, have a good night."

Walter wiped his hand across his face. "Hold up for a minute."

I looked up at him. "Yes, Walter, what is it?"

"How can I say this without—"

"Just say whatever it is—it's no big deal," I interrupted.

"Well, it is for me."

"What is?" I asked.

"The fact that I'm feeling something for you that I shouldn't be feeling, because I'm married . . . not to mention you're my daughter's teacher."

"What are you feeling for me?"

"Damn, you're going to make this hard for me, aren't you?"

"Just say it."

He paused. "I guess I'm diggin' you. There, I said it. From the moment I saw you, it did something to me."

I smiled and turned away. "I knew you were feeling me when you asked me to come out here. I just wanted you to be man enough to say it. And to answer your question earlier, *no*, my friends weren't going to meet me here. I came because I'm feeling you, too."

He laughed. "So what do we do about it?" he asked, looking into my eyes.

"Well, I can come inside for a drink and we can talk about it more," I said.

"No, that wouldn't be a good idea. My wife's brother is in my band and it wouldn't look right."

"I tell you what—call me tomorrow and we'll talk about it."

"Sure thing," he said as he wrote down the number to my cell phone. I could tell he was nervous by the way he fumbled with the piece of paper, so I smiled to get him to ease up a little.

"Good night, Walter."

"Thanks for coming by," he replied.

I drove off as Walter waved in the background.

CHAPTER 17

Stephanie

Early Sunday morning, Curtis came through the door as I was getting dressed for church. As he walked past me, Brandon ran behind him playfully.

"Are you coming to church?" I asked.

"You're kidding, right? I just spent three hours on the road after working the entire weekend and you want me to sit in church? I don't think so. I'm going to bed." He headed for the bedroom.

"Okay, well, Brandon and I are about to leave as soon as I put on my shoes."

Before I walked out the door, I passed Curtis on my way to the bathroom. He was lying across the bed in his boxers, asleep and snoring loudly. All of his clothes were lying in a pile directly under his feet.

The church was packed and the sermon was really inspiring as usual. After the service, Brandon and I ran into Reggie as he stood out front talking to some of the members. When he saw Brandon and me, he ended his conversation and walked toward us with his hand extended. "Hey, sister, how are you this morning? And hello to you, young man." Brandon curled up against my leg.

"Hi, Reggie."

"You two look lovely today."

I smiled at the compliment.

"I still have the book in my office if you have a minute?" Reggie said.

"Yeah, I can start reading it tonight," I replied.

I followed Reggie to his office and he gave me the book. "I almost forgot—the baptism is set for two weeks from now. We're going to have rehearsal the day before to make sure everyone is on the same page."

I nodded.

"We'll need to have both parents as well as the godparents there to—"

Suddenly Reggie's stomach growled loudly, interrupting him.

"Oooh, I'm sorry, sister. I skipped breakfast this morning and I'm starving over here."

"I know—I was in such a hurry I missed breakfast, too."

"Would you like to grab some lunch? Gladys and Ron's Chicken and Waffle is just around the corner. It's a really nice place where a lot of church members hang out."

I didn't think twice before I answered. Besides, I *was* feeling kind of hungry, and chicken and waffles sounded really good right about now. "Uh, sure, why not?"

"Great—you can ride with me if you want and leave your car here. I have to come back to the church anyway to prepare for the evening service."

"Well, I have Brandon's car seat in my car, so I can just follow you there," I replied.

"Okay, I'm parked just around back. I'll meet you there."

When we got to the restaurant, Reggie parked next to us in his black Lexus 430. Brandon and I got out of my car and we grabbed a table once we got inside. The place was filled with church members who all recognized Reggie as they walked past where we were sitting.

During the course of our lunch, we talked about different topics like upcoming events in the church, the choir, and even a little gossip. The conversation slowed down when Reggie got on the subject of Curtis and me.

"Sister, you mind if I ask you a personal question?"

"That depends on how personal," I replied.

"How long have you been in your relationship?"

I looked up at Curtis, puzzled.

"I'm sorry, was that too personal?" Curtis looked surprised.

"No, that's fine. We've been together for a few years."

"So, are there wedding bells anytime soon?"

"Well, not yet. He's still trying to get his business together."

"Aren't you his business, sister?"

"Well, yeah. But he's been working really hard trying to get himself together, and right now I'm playing the support role."

"Do you two live together?"

"Well, yes, but . . . You know, let's talk about you now," I said, beginning to get annoyed at his questions.

"I'm sorry. I didn't mean to get too personal. I have a habit of that."

"Yeah, you *are* sort of crossing the line here," I replied.

"Well, about me. Let's see—I'm thirty-four, single, no kids, I am a real estate investor and own about twenty-four properties that I rent out. I am one of the assistants to the pastor, and I handle church affairs and I love to serve the Lord."

"I see—that's impressive. So why aren't *you* married?"

He turned away, looking out the window for a quick moment, then back at me. "Well, sister, I'm waiting on God to match spirits with the woman he's chosen for me."

"How will you know?"

"You just know. It's a feeling you get down in your soul."

"Down in your soul?" I repeated with sarcasm.

"That's right—a woman that I can share my time, my dreams, and my life with."

"I see," I replied.

"Didn't you feel that when you met your boyfriend?"

I forced a smile as I turned away, 'cause Lord knows Curtis and I don't share those things Reggie described. I was almost embarrassed to look in his direction as I noticed him staring at me from the corner of his eye. I raked across my plate with my fork, trying to find a response. "Well—"

"Sister, you don't have to answer that. I'm getting too personal again."

Good, I thought.

"Hey, look at the time. I'd better get going. I need to run a few errands before I have to get back to the church."

"Yeah, I'd better be getting back. I have to start dinner," I replied, relieved. Reggie paid the check and we exited the restaurant.

On my way home I thought about my relationship with Curtis. The only things we shared was a house and a child, and we never spent that much time together, plus his dreams were. . . . Hell, we never talked about his dreams. All he really talked about was opening an auto repair shop some day. But we never actually sat down and planned it. I felt numb all of a sudden. Reggie's questions had me second-guessing my own relationship.

When I got home, Curtis was sitting in the kitchen eating pizza from the box. Brandon ran over to him and took a bite from the slice Curtis had in his hand.

"You hungry, baby? I ordered some pizza so you wouldn't have to cook today."

"No, Brandon and I ate lunch at Gladys and Ron's Chicken and Waffle."

"That's cool. It'll be here when you get hungry later."

As I walked past Curtis sitting in the kitchen, I saw pieces of his leftovers tossed on top of uneaten pizza as he sat there eating.

"Damn, Curtis. Can't you be considerate enough to at least get you a plate?"

Without a response he tossed the leftover crust of the slice he had just finished into the box of uneaten pizza before closing it and walked to the den. Before he got up, he let out a loud, disgusting belch that made Brandon laugh. I opened the pizza box and threw the leftover crust away before going in the back to change. Curtis's inconsiderate ways began to get me so upset that I felt sweat build around my forehead. When I finished changing, I looked all over the house for the Sunday paper but couldn't find it. I wanted to see what my horoscope was for today. After checking in the kitchen, I walked in the den, where Curtis was sitting watching me. "What are you looking for?" he asked.

"The Sunday paper. I see parts of it here, but I'm looking for the section with the horoscope."

"Oh, I may have thrown it out with the trash this morning. While you two were gone, I changed the oil in my truck and used some of it to catch the dripping oil."

"Damn, Curtis. Why did you have to use that section? You know I read my horoscope every day."

"Well, how am I supposed to know that you didn't read it already?"

Upset, I walked back into my bedroom and sat down in the chair next to the bed. I noticed my copy of *The Purpose-Driven Life* on the dresser next to my purse. I grabbed it and lay across the bed and began reading.

CHAPTER 18

Mya

Monday morning my alarm went off, waking me out of a hard sleep. I slowly opened my eyes and noticed my pillows were at the bottom of the bed and my covers were in a knot around my leg. I got up and sat at the edge of the bed for a minute and thought about how I was going to start my day. As I processed each phase through my mind, I came to a sudden halt about how I was going to face Tangie and Stephanie about my date with Darryl. I still felt the afteraffects of how close I came to giving in to him.

I got up and walked to the bathroom and began brushing my teeth. Even as I looked into the mirror, I saw the eyes of a troubled woman. My problem wasn't with Darryl, but with myself. I tried so hard to keep my mental guard up that I forgot about how I would react physically. Finally, I had to tell myself how much of a gentleman he was to respect my wishes, especially at my weakest moment.

My cell phone rang as I was about to walk out the door.

"Hello," I answered.

I could barely hear a voice over the loud noises in the background.

"Hello," I repeated.

"Hey," a voice sounded.

It was Darryl. A knot formed in my stomach for some strange reason.

"Hi," I replied.

"Hey, are you still there?" he asked. "Hold on, I'm about to walk inside the airport."

I continued on to my car. The loud sounds started to fade.

"Mya?"

"Yeah, I'm here."

"Hey, I'm glad I caught you before you left for work. I know you can't take your cell phone with you inside the school but I wanted to tell you how much I enjoyed Saturday night. Also, I can't wait to see you again."

I poked out my lips as he continued. I really didn't have a response because part of me felt dirty from letting him touch me inappropriately.

"Can I see you again?" he asked.

I paused 'cause I wasn't expecting that. "Yeah," I replied softly.

"Let me get your address so that when you're on my mind I can write you." A smile came over my face as I gave it to him.

"Uh, I'll call you tonight when I get settled in, okay?"

"Okay," I replied.

"Well, have a good day."

"I will," I replied. "And Darryl—thank you for calling me."

After we hung up, the knot in my stomach turned into jitters. I realized from this phone call that I really liked Darryl. I felt like this past Saturday night was a test to see if, in fact, I was going to give in and sleep with him. Because I didn't, I felt it made us worthy of each other. *What a relief,* I thought. *I almost gave in.*

When I pulled into the parking lot of the school, I was now ready to face Tangie and Stephanie about my date. I could now claim a part of Darryl as being my man. At least, a watered-down version, if nothing else.

I walked into the teachers' lounge and saw Tangie and Stephanie next to the coffee machine.

"Good morning, ladies," I squeaked.

They both turned before walking toward me.

"Stephanie, is that a glow on Mya's face or too much makeup?" Tangie joked.

Stephanie laughed. "I can't tell. Let's see—she's not walking funny, so you know she didn't do the nasty."

"Don't make me cuss you two out," I replied.

"So do tell," Stephanie said.

"Not much to tell—just dinner, conversation, and a whole lot of kissing."

They laughed.

"How much is a whole lot?" Tangie asked. "Let me be the judge of that."

"The kind that starts while sitting up on the couch but ends when you're lying down on the floor."

We all giggled.

"That qualifies," Tangie replied. "What size was his dick?"

"What? Tangie, I don't know. Even if I did, I wouldn't tell your ass."

"It must be small, 'cause if he had a large one you would have said so or at least hinted around."

I turned to keep from laughing at her. "By the way, thanks for the tip about wearing extra clothes. I almost got weak at one point," I said.

"Could this be the one?" Tangie asked.

"I don't know. But so far, so damn good," I replied.

"Well—girl, I'm happy for you," Stephanie said with a hug.

"Yeah—me, too," Tangie said.

By this time the bell sounded and we all gathered our kids and started school. I was on a high the entire day. I even let some of my students off the hook for writing profanity on tables in the back of my classroom.

Darryl called later in the evening like he promised and by the time Thursday came, he had sent a card and a four-page letter. In the letter there was a gift card for a free spa treatment. He said that because he was going to be out of town this weekend, he wanted the spa treatment to be a way for him to stay on my mind while he was away. Our relationship was starting to heat up. We talked more about intimacy. Not fucking, but sexual romance. I started thinking more about a future with him. My guard was down and I was ready to move this relationship forward.

CHAPTER 19

Tangie

I was sitting at home looking through the newspaper when Todd called. It had been several days since we'd seen each other, and he expressed his desire to come over. Walter's lying ass was supposed to call me sometime during the week but I hadn't heard from him. I agreed to meet Todd during his lunch hour and by the time he arrived, his erection was noticeable. He went straight to my bedroom, where he undressed and got into bed. I joined him shortly and after a couple of minutes of small talk, Todd pulled me close to him, kissing my body intensely. I wasn't really into it because I was sort of pissed at Walter for not calling me. I went through the motions of kissing Todd on his neck and up the sides of his face with my eyes wide open, looking around the room nonchalantly. By now Todd was ready for sex as he reached for a condom he had placed on my nightstand. As soon as he tore the package open, my cell phone rang. I rolled over toward my nightstand. "Mr. Big," my name for Walter, displayed brightly. As Todd tried to penetrate me from the back, I turned my body at an angle which made it difficult for him to enter. By the time I was able to reach for the phone, it stopped ringing.

"What the fuck are you doing? Will you be still so we can do this?" As Todd positioned me on my back, my cell phone rang again. Once again "Mr. Big" appeared on the caller ID. I pulled away from Todd and grabbed my cell phone.

"Hey, what the hell is this?" Todd said with a frown.

"Wait—I have to take this call. It's important," I replied as I walked toward the den.

Todd rolled over on his back in disgust.

"Hello," I answered softly.

"Tangie?"

"Yeah."

"Hey, this is Walter. Did I catch you at a bad time?"

"Well, kinda sorta. I was in the middle of something," I said.

"Oh, well, I was trying to see if you were free tonight. I was going to come by."

"Tonight?" I replied, surprised.

"Yeah, I skipped band rehearsal and thought it would be as good a time as any to see you."

I began trying to figure out how to get rid of Todd's ass right away. "Uh, you'll have to give me about an hour or so to finish up what I was doing."

"That's fine. I have to make a stop first, anyway. Just give me the directions and I'll see you in about an hour."

I gave Walter the directions before walking back into the bedroom where Todd was lying down staring at me. "Will you hurry up? I only get an hour for lunch and we've already wasted thirty minutes."

By now I was completely turned off by Todd and was looking forward to seeing Walter, but his persistence made me give in and have sex. I was looking at the clock the entire time and it seemed as if the minutes were flying by really fast. Out of all the nights Todd had come over, it seemed like he picked this particular one to take his sweet time. As usual, he jumped up after sex and went into the bathroom, closing the door behind him. I got up and rushed to the kitchen and straightened up a little before going back into the bedroom. Todd was still in the bathroom as I gathered up the condom wrapper he had thrown on the floor next to the bed. The only thing I needed to do was shower after Todd left and freshen up a little bit. I went back in the kitchen and poured me a glass of wine and stood by the counter and took a couple of quick sips. I didn't hear a sound from Todd for several minutes, so I walked back in the bedroom and noticed my bathroom door was still closed. Finally, I'd had enough. I walked to the door and opened it up, only to see Todd sitting on my toilet taking a shit. The funk was so strong it choked me as I closed the door behind me. "Todd, what the fuck are you doing?" I yelled.

"What does it look like?" he replied. "I'll be out in a minute."

Damn, I thought. *If Walter comes in and smells this, I don't know what he'll think of me.*

"You're going to be late for work if you don't hurry up," I yelled.

"It's okay. I told them I was running a little behind because I had car trouble."

Great, I thought. *Now what am I going to do?*

Minutes later I heard the toilet flush and Todd came walking out and slowly put on his clothes I'd laid neatly across the bed. He left the bathroom door open as the odor began to fill my bedroom. "Todd, you got to get out of here, smelling like this . . . and why didn't you turn on the fucking vent?"

He laughed as he put on his shoes. "Aw, girl, you smelled my shit before. Stop tripping."

"Hurry up and get out," I demanded.

Todd continued laughing as he left my apartment and went to his car.

In a panic, I rushed into the bathroom and began spraying all kinds of disinfectants to cover the odor. I even opened several windows in my bedroom, hoping the cool night breeze would blow some of the odor outside while I jumped in the shower. I quickly washed off and put on some shorts and a sweatshirt before finishing the glass of wine I left on the kitchen counter. Minutes later there was a knock at my door. I closed the door to my bedroom before opening the front door. Walter was standing there with a nervous look on his face.

"Hi, come on in and sit down," I said.

He walked in and took a seat on the couch. I sat in the recliner directly across from him.

"Sorry to come by so late in the evening—this is the only time I could really get out."

"That's cool. I *did* wonder what had happened to you. I thought you were feeling a bit uncomfortable after our conversation the other night."

"Oh, not at all," he replied, rubbing his hands nervously.

"Would you like a glass of wine, a beer, or something?" I asked.

"Yeah, a beer sounds good."

I got Walter a beer and sat down in the love seat closest to him. He took a long drink and leaned forward on the couch, looking down.

"Walter, you *can* take your jacket off if you'd like," I said.

I could see this was going to be a long night. It was obvious that he wasn't feeling comfortable, so I decided to lighten the mood with a little music. Walter placed his jacket on the couch next to him. His shirt showed off his toned biceps as he leaned back and finished off his beer.

"You care for another one?" I asked.

"Sure, why not?" he replied.

I got up and went to the refrigerator. When I leaned over to reach for the beer, Walter came from behind and wrapped his arm around my waist. Startled, I quickly turned around.

"Uh, Walter—"

Walter pinned me against the refrigerator with a long kiss that made me melt into his arms. I slightly opened my legs as his hard penis rubbed against me. By this time, I was hot and wet as he pulled back, staring at me.

"Wow—I didn't expect that." I was dazed.

He smiled. "I've been wanting to do that since the day I laid eyes on you in your classroom."

"Is that right?"

"I think you knew that."

I smiled.

Walter leaned forward and gave me another big kiss, this one much longer than the first. As I started to get more turned on, his cell phone rang, stopping us. He pulled his phone from his pocket and looked at the caller ID.

"Shit, it's Tina. She's at her aunt's house. I really need to take this," he said, walking away.

I walked back in the bedroom to see if my bathroom was free of Todd's horrible odor just in case things got more heated. When I returned to the den, Walter was putting on his jacket.

"Leaving so soon?"

"Yeah, Tina isn't feeling well and is ready for me to come and pick her up." There was disappointment on his face. "Maybe we can do this some other time."

"Sure, just let me know when," I replied.

When he left, I sat on the couch and sipped the rest of my wine, reliving the episode over and over in my mind.

CHAPTER 20

Stephanie

Thursday night was the church's men's group charity basketball game. I volunteered to work the concession stand along with members of the women's group. I wasn't into basketball all that much, so I just sat in the corner talking to the ladies working alongside me. The gym was packed with church members from both our church and Victory Baptist, located on the other side of town. They had their own organization that they were trying to raise money for. Reggie was playing, and from what I hear, he's a pretty good basketball player.

We stayed sort of busy the first hour, but closer to the end of the game the crowd lightened up a little as we began putting away most of the refreshments. While carrying the leftover boxes of chips to be stored in the church cafeteria, a young man ran up to me wanting ice for an injured player. I set the box down and rushed over to the concession stand and bagged some ice and quickly ran toward the injured player, who was sitting with the team from our church. As I made my way through the crowd on the bench, I saw Reggie sitting, slumped over, holding his ankle with a look of agony on his face.

"Coming through," a voice yelled as I walked past them with the bag of ice. Reggie looked up as I placed the bag next to him. "Thanks," he grunted.

I stepped back as some guys wrapped the bag around his ankle.

As the crowd closed in around Reggie, I made my way back up to where I'd left the box I was carrying and placed it in the cafeteria storage.

As the game continued, two really tall guys helped Reggie up from the bench. When they carried him past me, he gave me a slight smile before frowning in pain. I went back to the concession stand and finished cleaning up before walking toward the church cafeteria to throw out the trash. As I left to go home, I had to pass Reggie's office to get to my car, which was parked in the front of the church, when I saw the door to his office open. As I continued on, I peeked inside. Reggie was sitting with his leg elevated on his desk.

"Sister," he shouted as I walked by.

I stopped, turned around, and went inside. "Hey, Reggie. Are you okay?" I asked, looking at his swollen ankle.

"Yeah, but I think my ankle is broken," he replied.

"Maybe you need to go to the hospital and have it checked out."

"Yeah, I think you're right, 'cause it's really beginning to swell."

"Is there anything I can do for you?" I asked.

"Yeah, can you see if Sister Pattie is still here? Her office is all the way to the end of the hall on your right."

Sister Pattie was another assistant to the pastor who helped handle the finances of the church. I've seen her around but never actually met her personally.

I walked to Sister Pattie's office. Her door was closed and locked, so I went back to the gym, where the security guard was turning off the lights. Looking out the window I could see the parking lot was vacant.

When I made it back to Reggie's office, he was sitting in agony—his ankle had swollen even more than before.

"I think she's gone for the night, Reggie."

Reggie dropped his head as he reached over and adjusted the ice pack on his ankle.

"Sister, can you give me a ride to the hospital? I don't think I can drive with my ankle like this. I'll call Sister Pattie on the way and see if she and her husband can give me a ride home."

"Sure," I replied without hesitation.

I went to my car and drove it up close to the door leading to Reggie's office. I rushed back inside and helped him up from his chair as he put his arm around me. We slowly walked down the hall, his six-foot-four frame draped over on my shoulder.

"Am I too heavy for you?" he asked.

"No, you're as light as a feather," I joked.

He chuckled as we continued to struggle to the door of the church. Seeing us, the security guard rushed over and helped me put Reggie in the car. I drove him to the closest hospital, then rushed inside and got a nurse, who came out and wheeled Reggie to the emergency waiting room. As he filled out forms, I got the rest of his things out of my car and brought them inside and placed them beside him.

Once he completed the forms, Reggie rolled himself to the window where I was sitting.

"Thanks, I really appreciate this," he said. "I owe you big-time."

"It was nothing—besides, I was going this way home, anyway," I joked.

Reggie laughed, putting his hand on mine. I looked down at his hand, then back up at him as he stared at me. There was silence for a split second until Sister Pattie and her husband came walking through the door of the emergency room lounge.

"Reggie, are you all right?" she asked, concerned.

"Yeah, but I think my ankle's broken. Look at how swollen it is."

Sister Pattie looked down at Reggie's ankle, then looked up at me. "Hi, I'm Pattie Simpson—I don't think we've met. This is my husband, Louis. And you are?"

"Hi, I'm Stephanie Hall—nice to meet you both."

"I've seen you around church but never had the pleasure of meeting you."

"I know. It's too bad we had to meet under these circumstances."

"Sister Stephanie was kind enough to bring me here. She was working the concession tonight and just happened to be there when I needed to be taken to the hospital," Reggie said.

Sister Pattie nodded as she and her husband took a seat next to Reggie. I looked at my watch and realized it was getting late. "Reggie, is there anything else you need from me? If not, I need to be getting home."

"No, sister. Thank you for all your help. I'll call you later."

Sister Pattie gave me a smile before I turned and exited the waiting room. *What was that look for?* I thought, before getting into my car and driving off.

When I got home, Curtis was asleep on the couch. I walked past him and into the kitchen, where his dirty shirt was hanging on the chair. I took it off and tossed it into the laundry room before checking on Brandon, who was in his bed asleep.

I went in the bathroom and took a quick shower. As I was drying off, I was startled by Curtis walking into the bathroom, looking at his watch.

"Where the hell have you been all night?"

"I was at church, like I told you earlier, helping out at the basketball game."

"This late?"

"Yeah—I had to help the ladies clean up," I replied.

Don't you think you could've called or something? Or at least taken care of things at home before hanging out all night? Brandon and I had to eat in the streets, spending unnecessary money."

I ignored him because I knew I was in the wrong. I couldn't tell him the truth or it would've been blown out of proportion. Instead, I just put on my pajamas before getting into bed as he continued.

"I hope you don't have to do nothing at the church again tomorrow, 'cause I have to go out of town again to do some work."

"Good night, Curtis." I closed my eyes.

Curtis got in bed next to me, still complaining about me being late. But once I got comfortable, I drifted off to sleep.

CHAPTER 21

Mya

Darryl was finally home! I was excited and anxious to see him. He called me from his car to ask me to meet him at his place, but I was too exhausted from work and really wasn't up for going out, so I decided to let my guard down and invite him over.

I had the wine chilling, the food simmering, and my body was tingling. All I thought about was the way his hands made me feel when they were all over me that first night together at his apartment. My plan wasn't to sex him up but just to enjoy his presence, physically and emotionally.

An hour and a half later my doorbell rang. I nervously ran into the bathroom for one last look at myself before going downstairs to answer the door. When I opened it, there was Darryl with a stuffed teddy bear and a big smile on his face.

"Heeeey," I said as I reached out for him.

He handed me the teddy bear as he walked inside, giving me a kiss on the lips.

"Hey, baby," he replied. "I am so glad to be home."

I smiled. "Aw, thank you for the teddy."

I grabbed his hand as we proceeded inside.

"I like your place—it's really nice," he said as we entered the den.

"Thanks," I replied. "I still have a lot to do with it, though."

"No, I like the way you have the New Orleans jazz paintings and sculptures throughout your den. That's tight."

Darryl took the teddy out of my hand and placed in on the couch. He then pulled me close to him for another kiss. Our tongues touched, and I tasted the mint flavor from the gum in his mouth.

Darryl caressed my neck on up through my hair. With my eyes closed tight, I followed the rhythm of his kiss. Caught up in the moment, I slowly put my arms around his waist up to the center of his back and pulled him closer. I could feel Darryl slowly getting an erection against my stomach. I opened my eyes and pulled away.

"Wow," I replied.

Darryl smiled as he continued to hold me.

"I'd better check on the food. I bet you're starving by now," I said nervously, walking away and into the kitchen.

"Yeah, I am. I can't wait to get a home-cooked meal for a change. Whatever it is smells really good, too," Darryl replied.

While in the kitchen I got the plates from the cabinet and placed them on the counter. My body was still shaking from his kiss. I'd waited weeks to be with him and now I was losing control of myself.

"You need some help with anything?" he shouted from the den.

"No," I replied in a panic. "Uh, I just have to put everything on plates and that's it. You just have a seat and get comfortable. You can turn on the TV if you'd like."

"Cool," he shouted back.

Minutes later I called him into the dining area. Like a gentleman he got up and washed his hands before sitting down with me at the table. He grabbed my hand and blessed the food.

"Wow, this looks good. What do you call it?" he asked.

"Oh, this is shrimp and crawfish etouffee."

"Okay, so you came with the New Orleans dish on me tonight, huh?" he replied, smiling.

I brought out a small crabmeat salad over lettuce with a spicy vinegar dressing and some French bread sticks.

"Ummm—this is delicious, Mya. I've never had this before."

I smiled. "Thank you—I'm glad you're enjoying it."

When we finished, we sat together in the den. Darryl had gotten comfortable and taken his shoes off, one leg straddling the arm of the couch. I lay stretched out, slightly between his legs and arms, as we watched *BET Comic View*. We both laughed loudly at each comedian, holding each other tighter as the night went on.

By the end of the show, we both lay there, waiting for each

other's next move. I rubbed my hand against his thighs, still staring in the direction of the TV. I could hear his heart pounding and felt the bulge in his pants press against my side. When I looked up he tilted his head forward and we began kissing. He pulled me up closer until the bulge in his pants rested between my legs. My heart began to beat faster. I let out a soft gasp. He pulled me down onto him from my waist and began to gently kiss my neck. Darryl rolled me over and got on top, then began to move his hand under my shirt up toward my breast. I shivered at his touch. Suddenly his finger came under my bra as he caressed my breast. I turned my head away, breaking our kiss as he moved down and began to kiss my stomach. Before I could open my eyes, his mouth was over my right breast as his tongue moved slowly around my nipple. I moaned as I took in the pleasure. Suddenly, my mind took over. This was the moment I had been waiting on for two weeks. Either I'm going to fuck his brains out right now or get my ass up and stop this shit. The pleasure began to take over my mind as Darryl began sucking on my left breast while his right hand worked its way past my navel. *What is it going to be, Mya?*

Before I knew it, I was lying there with no bra, no panties, and Darryl on top of me. I felt the gentle penetration and a grunting sound as my body rocked back and forth. My pocketbook, what my mother called my vagina, was throbbing with every thrust as Darryl dug deeper and deeper inside of me. I whimpered as he began moving faster and faster.

"Is it good, huh? Is it good?" Darryl repeated.

I bit down on my lip as the pleasure began to intensify. The motion continued over and over, until finally, I felt myself slowly reaching my peak.

"Oooooh," I yelled. "Ahhhhh, Darryl, just like that, just like that."

Darryl moved faster and faster as he spread my legs farther apart. Suddenly he reached the one spot that sent a bolt a pleasure from my head to my toes. I began to gasp uncontrollably as I exploded. Within seconds I heard Darryl moan loudly as he climaxed, too.

"Oooooh . . . Ooooh . . . Oooh," I continued as I came down from my sexual high.

I lay there with my eyes closed, too afraid to look at Darryl's expression. There's something about the first sexual experience with someone that makes you nervous all over again. You think to yourself, okay, now that that's over, what's next? I've given this person eighty percent of me, and now what?

Suddenly, I felt soft kisses on the side of my face. I opened my eyes slowly as Darryl smiled down on me. He took a deep breath as he continued to hold me.

"Wow, that was great. I've been thinking about this moment the entire time I've been gone. Damn, I missed you," Darryl said.

Hearing those words put a smile on my face, erasing any regrets I might have had. I reached up, pulling him down on me, and put my arms around his neck as we lay there in silence.

The next morning, after another great sexual encounter, I cooked Darryl a big breakfast—eggs, bacon, grits, and even some mixed fruit and New Orleans-style coffee. While we sat in the dining room eating, Darryl's alarm on his cell phone went off.

"Ahhh, shit," he shouted.

"What's the matter?" I replied with a confused look.

"Damn, I have to go downtown to a meeting with the other reps in my region. I set my alarm on my cell phone so that I wouldn't forget, and it just reminded me."

"Oh," I replied. "Well, can we get together later today?"

"Sure. After the meeting, I'm going straight home. Maybe you can come over or we can catch a movie or something."

"Okay, sounds like a plan."

Darryl hurriedly showered and minutes later he left. I began putting dishes from last night and this morning into the dishwasher before going upstairs and changing my sheets. I ran a tub of steamy hot bubble bath and relaxed.

After hours had passed doing laundry and running errands, I finally made it home, awaiting Darryl's call. I got a glass of wine and sat down at the dining room table with my stack of bills and began going through them, one by one, occasionally staring at the clock on the wall just above the kitchen stove. It was now four o'clock and still no call from Darryl.

I got up from the table, got my checkbook, and began writing checks and set the bills to the side to mail on my way home from work on Monday.

I glanced over at the clock again and it was now five. I got up and poured another glass of wine and sat down on the couch to watch TV. Minutes later, I called Darryl, only to get his answering service. Instead of leaving a message, I just hung up and began to get upset. Now I really began to feel like a whore.

CHAPTER 22

Tangie

On Monday, Stephanie invited Mya and me to her church's Pilates class that evening. It had been a while since I'd done any kind of workout, so I agreed to go along. Besides, Stephanie had a hand in coordinating the class and was trying to make it a weekly event—she needed as many people as she could gather to make it successful.

"Girl, I was just about to call you. You're late," Stephanie said.

"I'm here, aren't I? Besides, the thing hasn't started yet." I put my small bag down. I had gotten lost on the way and even got lost again in the parking lot.

"Well, hurry up and take your jacket off so we can take our places on the mats," Stephanie said.

"Will you calm down?" I said as I placed my jacket on the bleachers behind me. I pulled off my sweatpants and placed them alongside my jacket.

"Girl, I can't believe you came on church grounds wearing that skimpy outfit."

Stephanie looked me over.

She was complaining about the thong leotards I wore over my spandex shorts that showed off my well-shaped bottom.

"Skimpy? This is standard workout gear. When was the last time *you* worked out?"

Mya laughed as Stephanie stood there giving me an evil look. We took our places in the center of the floor.

The instructor was a petite lady who looked to be in her mid-forties and stood about five-two. She had a really squeaky, irritating voice as she yelled through a microphone that carried over the sound of the mild elevator music that played in the background.

The first couple of poses, which I thought really sucked, had my heart racing. I suddenly felt nauseous, like I was about to pass out, as was Mya, who was sweating profusely in front of me and struggling with her poses. Stephanie was into it like she was practicing for an Olympic event. The intense look on her face and her smiles between poses made it look like she'd really accomplished something. The gym was packed with women in rows of ten, covering the entire basketball court. A few were large, but most of the women were sort of thin.

Midway through the class, my hair was soaked. The perm I had gotten two days before made my hair stick to my forehead as lines of sweat ran down my face. I could hear women passing gas next to me, trying to play it off by grunting to muffle the sound as they struggled with the exercise. I frowned, trying to hold my breath at the terrible smell that followed. Finally, I'd had enough of this shit and walked over to the water fountain nearest the back of the gym. The fresh air brought a sense of relief, as did the cool water that quenched my thirst.

Both Mya and Stephanie gave me a shaming look as I wiped the sweat from my face. After a few more big gulps of water, I took a seat alongside a few women who had gone through as much of a workout as I did and decided to sit out the rest of the class.

Suddenly, the front door of the gym opened as a tall gentleman on crutches entered and stood near the entrance. He was followed by two other men wearing suits. He waved in the direction of some women closest to Stephanie. I saw a smile come over Stephanie's face as she held up her hand. The gentleman leaned over and whispered to the man closest to him and they both smiled.

Throughout the course of the workout, I watched Stephanie as she continued to roll her eyes in this guy's direction like she was hoping he was watching her. I became even more intrigued by the way he smiled when their eyes met. *Well, I'll be damned*, I thought.

Something is up with Stephanie and this guy. My first instinct was to run back out on the floor behind her and pester her about it. But my cramped leg and ass muscles wouldn't allow me to do so. It was best, anyway. I would much rather let her tell me instead of rushing into her business like that. But something was up and I was determined to find out what.

After the workout, Mya and I helped Stephanie and some other women clean up the gym. The gentlemen were still there, standing outside the door as we were about to leave.

The guy on the crutches hopped toward us. "Hey, sister, great turnout tonight."

Stephanie smiled. "Thanks, I enjoyed it. I hope everyone else did. Oh, Reggie, these are my girls, Tangie and Mya."

Reggie, huh?

"Nice to meet you," Mya and I responded simultaneously.

"I would shake your hand, but I'm so sweaty," Mya replied.

Reggie nodded as he balanced himself between his crutches.

As I stood next to Reggie, I scanned him closely. For some reason he looked familiar to me, but I couldn't think of where I knew him from. "I've seen you somewhere before," I said.

"Oh, really?" he replied as he stared back at me.

"Yeah, but I just can't think where."

"Girl, you think you know everybody," Mya replied, and we all laughed.

I cut my laughter short because I knew I knew him from somewhere. I just couldn't remember where exactly. I may not remember names for shit, but a face stands out to me.

We all walked back to our cars, then Mya and I drove off. When I pulled out of the parking lot, I noticed through my rearview mirror that Reggie and Stephanie were still talking as the two stood by Stephanie's car. *Umph, umph, umph. Something is definitely going on. Whatever it is, I'm going to find out.*

CHAPTER 23

Stephanie

I got Brandon up earlier than usual on Sunday so I could dress him in his new suit and take a few pictures before his baptism. I asked Tangie to be the godmother since I had known her most of my life. She agreed. Curtis got his cousin Gary to stand in as godfather because I didn't like the other friends he suggested. Despite his broken ankle, Reggie had to go out of town with the men's group on a weekend retreat in Baltimore, Maryland, and couldn't attend the baptism, but called the night before to make sure I had everything I needed.

Curtis, who dragged his ass in at around four o'clock in the morning, was still sleeping as I got dressed in front of the mirror.

"Curtis, get your ass up—we have to be at the church before nine o'clock." I shook his body.

He opened his bloodshot eyes, looking around in a delirious state. "Huh?"

"Get up, Curtis," I repeated.

"Uh, yeah, I'm up. What time is it?" He yawned.

"It's time for you to get up and shower. Ooooh, you reek of alcohol."

"Turn on the shower for me while I get me some coffee," he said and got out of bed.

Brandon and I waited in the den as Curtis took his time getting dressed. About thirty minutes later he came from the back, dressed in his suit and clean-shaven, looking just like the man I had fallen in love with several years ago. I had almost forgotten how handsome he really was behind all his bullshit.

While at church, all of my family—along with Curtis's family—sat in front pews. When the baptism began, godparents were acknowledged by the church as the kids were escorted to the baptismal pool. Brandon looked a bit nervous dressed in his white robe as he stood in line behind the other kids as they were each dunked in the water by the praying bishop.

Curtis stood on the altar and snapped pictures during every phase of Brandon's baptism. I was so proud that my little man was getting baptized that tears began to flow. In a way, I wished Reggie could have been there. After all, he *did* have a lot to do with this day that was so special to me.

After we left the church, we all came back over to my house where I hostessed a cookout to celebrate Brandon's special day. While I was on the patio getting ready to put some burgers on the grill, Curtis's mother came outside to smoke a cigarette. "This sure was a beautiful day for a baptism. I'm so proud of my grandson. You and Curtis are doing a wonderful job with him. I'm glad you two finally got him baptized," she said.

Curtis's mother—Mama Williams is what I called her—and I really didn't get along. She would always come over to my house and act like she ran shit. The last time she was here she had Curtis rearrange my living room and den furniture because she didn't like the way I had it so close together. She'd nitpick about how I seasoned the foods I cook and what I fed Brandon.

I forced a smile at her remark as I continued to put burgers on the grill. Little did she know that Curtis had nothing to do with Brandon being baptized, but I kept that to myself.

When she finished her cigarette, she quickly pulled out another and began smoking it, coughing after almost every puff and following it up with a sip of beer.

As the smoke began to rise from the grill, Mama Williams walked next to me. "Now when the flame starts to rise, move the burgers to the side so you don't dry out the meat. I see why the flames are so high—you put almost a whole bag of charcoal in there," she complained.

I took a deep breath and bit down on my teeth to keep from responding rudely to her as she went on. Suddenly Tangie and Mya came outside dressed in jeans and sweaters.

"Girl, what smells so good? You need help with anything?" Tangie said. "Mya and I had to get out of those dresses and into something more comfortable."

"No, I'm just doing burgers and hot dogs. As soon as this is ready, everyone can eat," I replied.

"Stephanie, while you're sitting over here talking you are going to dry out these hamburgers. I told you to move them over to the edge away from the flames. You know I can't eat nothing tough with my dentures," Mama Williams snapped. Tangie's eyebrows went up as she stared over at Mama Williams. "You can leave mine right where it is—I like it dry," she replied sarcastically.

Mya also picked up on her rudeness. "Yeah, and I *like* my hot dog a little black, being from New Orleans and all."

Mama Williams turned and stared at Tangie, then over at Mya, about to respond, but simply turned her back to them, then tossed her cigarette in the yard and went inside the house, mumbling under her breath.

"Uuuuh, I can't stand that lady sometimes," I replied.

"Just put her in her place—she'll leave you alone. Trust me, I had to do that to both of my mother-in-laws."

"Well, I don't see her that often so I just ignore her when she comes around."

"Hey, whatever works," Tangie replied. "But I would've had her out of my business a long time ago."

More members of the church came over with kids who were baptized with Brandon. Tangie and Mya helped me set the tables and serve the kids, who were playing in the den. Curtis was outside with his friends while I was inside mingling with some of the guests.

"Are all these people members of the church?" Mya asked.

"Where are all the cute guys? Like that guy who was at the gym the other night who walked into the yoga class you introduced us to?" Tangie asked.

"Oh, uh, you mean Reggie?" I replied.

"Yeah, what's up with him? Is he single?" Tangie asked.

"Yeah, that's what he said. But I don't keep up with him like that."

Tangie had a cunning stare, smiling like she was trying to look through me. "I think he likes you, girl," she continued.

"What? Oh, girl, please." I turned away.

"Well, something's up with him. But seriously, I swear I've seen him before. I just can't remember where."

"When you've dated as many guys as you, Tangie, everybody starts looking the same," Mya joked.

I laughed out loud.

"Normally, I would cuss your ass out, Mya, but this time I'm serious."

After everyone ate, we finally began cleaning up the kitchen. Curtis lay on the couch asleep, still dressed in his suit. Tangie often glanced at him, frowning like she wanted to say something, but she remained silent. After they left, I grabbed the trash bags and put them in the garbage cans outside, washed the dishes, and took a hot shower before going to bed.

CHAPTER 24

Mya

Tuesday night was the PTA meeting, which started and five o'clock. My feelings were a little hurt that Darryl and I hadn't talked in a couple of days. I wasn't going to give in and call him, either. If he wanted to talk me then he would have to make the effort to call.

I sat in my classroom as the parents of the kids came in one after the other for their conferences. As usual, the parents whose kids had good grades were the ones that showed up.

It was almost eight o'clock when the last parent left—my stomach was growling like crazy. I needed to drink some water or something to keep the noise down as it echoed in my empty classroom. As I got up to go to the water fountain, this tall, dark-skinned man came through the door and walked toward me. I sat back down as he approached my desk.

"Uh, excuse me, but are you the teacher for Kennedy Hill? I'm her father, Christopher Hill."

"Yes . . . please have a seat, Mr. Hill." I pulled out my progress reports. The gentleman sat down in the chair directly in front of my desk.

"Well, Mr. Hill, I'm Mya LeVeaux—nice to meet you. Uh, let's see. I have Kennedy's grades and performance scores right here." I passed the papers to him. He looked through the papers as I continued. "As you can see, she is doing very well in all of her subjects.

Her weakness is spelling, even though she *is* maintaining a B average. I say that because she struggles a little during verbal spelling quizzes."

He lightly scratched the side of his face. "Yeah, she gets nervous in front of a lot of people."

"But, overall she is an exceptional student. If we can break that nervousness, I think she would be the perfect candidate to represent our class in the school spelling bee."

"Really? Well, I'll work on that with her. You see, her mom and I are divorced and on the days that I have her, we spend most of our time out having dinner or around my parents' house because they don't get to see her much. When she's at home she's always in her room watching TV or something."

I nodded.

"I need to get her more involved in other activities. Do you know of any good after-school or summer programs?" he asked.

"Well, a lot of the local universities have summer programs for kids. You should check out Morehouse, Clark-Atlanta University, and even Spelman College. I think at least one of them should have what you're looking for."

I remembered I had some literature from the boys and girls club along with the YWCA that I gave to Mr. Hill to look over.

"You mind if I keep this?" he asked.

"No, not at all, I hope it can be helpful to you." I closed my desk drawer.

"You know, you're the first teacher I've had a conference with that really shows some concern."

I smiled. "Thank you, Mr. Hill."

"No, thank *you*, Mrs. LeVeaux, for everything . . . It is *Mrs*. LeVeaux, right?"

"No, it's Ms. LeVeaux, and you're quite welcome, Mr. Hill."

He got up and continued on with compliments until he walked out the door. I looked at the clock—8:20 P.M. I was happy to finally be able to leave, so I began gathering my papers and clearing off my desk. As I walked toward the door, Mr. Hill appeared out of nowhere, startling me. I jumped back, almost dropping my bags. "My God," I yelled.

"I'm sorry—I didn't mean to scare you. I just had one more

question. Uh, I know this may be inappropriate, but can we have lunch sometime?"

"Well, Mr. Hill, you're right—that would be inappropriate."

There was disappointment on his face. "Is that a no?"

"I'm afraid so," I replied.

"Is it against the rules or something like that?"

"Yeah, it's against *my* rule. I don't get personal with my students' parents."

"You can't make one exception?" He waited with anticipation.

"Mr. Hill, my answer is no. I just don't get involved like that," I replied.

He rubbed his hands together nervously. "Well, I figured it wouldn't hurt to ask."

I gave him a forced smile, "Good night, Mr. Hill." I turned and started down the hall to Tangie's classroom. By the time I got to her door, she was walking out with one of her students' dads, engaged in what looked to be a deep conversation. When I got closer to her, the gentleman quickly turned and walked off. As he passed me, he spoke softly, turning the corner at the end of the hall.

"Hey, girl, are you finished for the night?" I asked.

"Yep, that was the last parent. What about you?" she replied, talking through a devilish smile.

"Yeah, I just finished my last one about five minutes ago."

"Hold on a second so I can get my things." Tangie walked back into her classroom and grabbed some papers.

I noticed her blouse hanging from her partially unzipped skirt.

"Girl, did you know you were about to come out of your clothes?" I pointed out.

"Oh, uh, when one of my students' parents was here I had to pee like crazy but his ass kept on talking on and on. The minute he took a breath I excused myself. I guess in a rush I forgot to adjust my clothes before coming back."

Stephanie appeared, cutting off Tangie's story. "Are you guys ready?"

Tangie locked her classroom door.

"Tangie, who was that fine-ass man leaving your classroom just now? That's the same man we saw talking to Ridgewell about a week and a half ago," Stephanie said.

"Oh, girl, that was Mr. Washington, my student Tina's dad."

"Umph, he's sexy," Stephanie continued.

We all started down the hall.

"Girl, guess what? I just had a parent hit on me tonight," I said.

"What did you do?" Tangie asked, concerned.

"Basically, told his ass I don't get down like that."

"Oh yeah? Was he cute?" Tangie asked.

"Tangie. I wasn't looking at him like that."

"You know whether he was cute or not. Well, was he?" Tangie waited on my answer.

"Anyway," I replied.

"Yeah, his ass was cute," Stephanie laughed.

"That was your first time being hit on by a parent? If so, it damn sure won't be your last. I get that a lot, and not from just the men, I might add," Tangie said.

"What? You never told me about that," Stephanie replied. "When did this happen?"

"I told you about how this lady said that I had something on my pants, then rubbed her hands across my ass."

"What?" I giggled.

"Oh, yeah, I do remember. That's when you started bringing your mace to school." Stephanie laughed. "Mya, Tangie was so sick to her stomach she showered the entire night over that shit."

"You're damn right—that bitch violated me and made me feel icky," Tangie replied.

We made it outside as Tangie continued.

"What are we going to eat? I'm starving," Tangie said.

"Me, too—this mint can only do so much for my appetite," Stephanie replied.

"Let's go to Smokey Bones and get some ribs," Tangie suggested.

"What! It's after eight. I ain't trying to eat that heavy on a Tuesday night," I replied.

"Well, what do you suggest?" Tangie asked.

"Let's go to the Subway and get a salad or something light," I said.

"Great, just what I need right now. Rabbit food," Tangie replied.

"Well, what about Applebee's? It's just around the corner," Stephanie suggested.

We all agreed and got into Tangie's car, heading to Applebee's. This particular Applebee's was ghetto, and right up Tangie's alley.

"Girl, this is the spot right here," Tangie said as we pulled into the parking lot.

"It's popular," I replied, looking at all the cars that surrounded the restaurant.

"Tangie, this is too crowded—let's go someplace else." Stephanie had a look around the parking lot.

"We can get in. I know the manager. He'll hook us up," Tangie said.

Stephanie and I looked over at each other in disgust as we walked up to the front entrance.

When we opened the door to go inside, there was a line in the lobby with a crowd of people standing around in the middle of the aisle and against the wall.

"Wait right here. Let me see if Steve is at work," Tangie said.

Stephanie and I stood close together by the door of the restaurant as Tangie disappeared into the crowd.

After a couple of minutes, the line started moving forward, which gave us more room.

"I'm not feeling this shit at all," Stephanie whispered.

"Girl, me either. Ouch, what the fuck!" I yelled.

"What's the matter, girl?" Stephanie asked.

"Girl, somebody pinched me on my ass."

Stephanie laughed.

"That ain't funny," I replied, frowning. "That shit hurt."

"Here, come on this side so you can have your back against the wall," Stephanie said, still giggling.

I began looking around, trying to find the sorry bastard who pinched me. "What the hell is taking Tangie so long to find her friend?"

"You know Tangie—she's probably running her mouth," Stephanie replied.

"If she's not here by the time I count to twenty, I'm—" I said.

Tangie appeared with a short, light-skinned brother with reddish-colored hair.

"Hey, come on in. We got a table in the back." she yelled.

A few people in front of us looked over in Steve's direction. "Oh, hell naw, what kind of shit is that? Me and my girl have been wait-ing out here for almost an hour to get a table. They just walked up," a guy said, standing in line.

Suddenly more people started complaining and cussing. Stephanie and I just walked past them, keeping our eyes straight ahead, and followed Tangie to the back. I'd never seen this kind of thing be-fore. There were people sitting on tables and standing in the aisle drinking beer, some wearing white tees. There were couples kissing in the booths in the back. Some people were even playing cards at the table and on their cell phones with a pile of empty dishes in front of them. People were talking so loud you could barely hear the music playing in the background.

We made it to a booth in the back toward the bathroom and sat down.

"See, I told you my boy was going to hook us up. He said get whatever we want and he'll pick up the tab," Tangie said.

"Girl, I'm not feeling this at all. We could have gone right up the street to Subway, got a salad, and headed home," I said.

"I'm with Mya on that, Tangie. Look at this place." Stephanie pointed with her head slightly tilted.

"Girl, we're just going to eat and then we can leave. Don't pay any attention to these crazy-ass people in here," Tangie said.

"Shit, you can't help but pay attention to them. They're loud as hell," I said.

"Well, damn. What do you all want to do?" Tangie asked.

"Let's just order something to go and get the hell out of here be-fore some shit starts."

Tangie sat there with a grim look on her face. "Fine, let's just leave then. I'll tell Steve we'll catch him another time."

"We can stay. Shit, we're here now," I said.

"No, that's okay. Let's go if you two feel *that* uncomfortable. Besides, it's getting late," Tangie replied.

We sat there while Tangie got up to find Steve. They both came back to the booth and Steve walked us to the front door. We were still getting the evil eye from some of the people that were waiting to be seated as we exited the restaurant.

While outside, we passed more people sitting on the hood of their cars smoking what smelled like weed.

I dropped my head to keep from making eye contact with anyone until I got to the car. Once inside Tangie's car, we started down Memorial Drive near Stone Mountain Park.

"Let's hear it," Tangie said, staring at me.

"Huh, hear what?" I replied.

"Hear the shit you and Stephanie got to say. Every time I pick a place, it's not good enough for you two."

Stephanie cut in. "Tangie, I'm not thinking about that shit. You knew that place was fucked up when you pulled in the parking lot. No more needs to be said."

"Yeah," I interrupted, "so can we please find a Subway now? I'm starving and it's getting late."

When we came to a Subway sandwich shop, Tangie pulled in the parking lot facing the door. At that time, my cell phone rang. I looked down at the caller ID. My heart began to race with excitement. It was Darryl. I laid my head back and took a deep breath to get my composure. "Hello," I answered sharply.

"Hey, baby. What's up?" Darryl said in a soft voice.

"What's up?" I replied "You tell me. I haven't heard from you in a few days now. Where—"

"Wait, wait. Let me explain. I just got out of the hospital."

"Hospital? What were you doing in the hospital? Are you all right?"

"Yeah, I'm better now," he replied.

"What happened?" I asked, concern in my voice.

"I don't know exactly. I was downtown in a meeting and my head started hurting really bad all of a sudden. When I got up to get a drink of water, I blacked out and hit the floor. One of the guys I work with helped me up. They said my eyes were rolling back and my body was quivering, so they rushed me to the emergency room. I spent two days in the hospital having tests run on me."

"Are you okay, Darryl?" I asked.

"They found out I have high blood pressure. My pressure was so high I could have stroked out."

"Well, why didn't you call me or something? I could have come by at least."

"I didn't have time to do anything. They were in and out of my room every five minutes. I didn't even get a chance to call my parents until the day after I was admitted."

"Where are you now?" I asked.

"Oh, I'm at home now in bed."

"I'm coming over," I said.

"No, it's late and I really need to get some rest. I just wanted you to know I didn't forget about you," he said.

"Well, I'll be there tomorrow when I get off work," I replied firmly.

"Okay, that's fine. My body is just exhausted from all the examinations they did on me."

"Well, all right, Darryl. Just get some rest and I'll see you tomorrow."

"Okay, good night, baby."

When the call ended, Tangie and Stephanie were staring at me with blank faces.

"Damn," I said in a semi-low tone.

"What's up?" Tangie asked.

"That was Darryl. His ass was in the hospital for the last couple of days. He passed out while at work and someone rushed him to the hospital."

"Passed out?" Tangie replied.

"Yeah, his pressure was so high that he blacked out."

"Damn," Stephanie replied, "My Uncle Rob passed out because his pressure was too high. They found him the next day, barely alive. He's paralyzed on his whole left side."

"That's because your Uncle Rob is damn near seventy years old. How old is Darryl?" Tangie asked.

"I think he's about thirty-two," I replied.

"Thirty-two? And passing out? Hell, no, something's up with that shit. You need to check him out yourself."

Stephanie burst out in laughter. "Tangie, that's not right."

"Girl, I ain't thinking about Tangie and her crazy shit," I said.

"I'm not trying to be funny. I just don't know too many men his age going around dropping to the ground," Tangie said with laughter. "Check and see what kind of medicine he's on and look that shit up on the Internet. That alone will tell you all you need to know."

I turned and couldn't help but laugh. In her own way, Tangie knew how to make the best of a bad situation with her odd sense of humor.

"Girl, let me go inside and get something to eat." I got out of the car. We stayed in Subway until almost eleven o'clock. After that, Tangie drove us back to our cars and we all headed home.

CHAPTER 25

Stephanie

Because I was so involved in my church activities, Curtis and I had come to an agreement. Two days a week I would dedicate time to the church and he agreed to stay home with Brandon. Most weekends, when he had to go out of town with Cedric, I would stay home with Brandon.

Wednesday, after Bible study, I saw Reggie as he struggled on his crutches to get to his office. I walked up behind him as he turned on the light and took a seat in one of the chairs next to his desk.

"Hey," I said pleasantly.

Startled, he looked up. "Hey, sister, how are you? I thought you left after Bible study."

"I'm good . . . I just wanted to thank you again personally for helping me get my son baptized—you just don't know what that means to me."

"Not a problem, I just hate that I missed it," he replied.

"When I get the pictures developed I'll bring them by so you can see my little man up there on the altar."

Reggie smiled. "So, what's next on your agenda for church activities?"

"I don't know. I was supposed to be helping Sister Carol organize the luncheon for the deacon board, but I think she has enough people." I shrugged.

"Well, if you want, you can help me out," Reggie suggested.

"Sure—what do you have going on?"

"Well, uh, first I have to organize some events next month for the bishop. Oh, and I have some of the bishop's contracts that need to be placed in a safe deposit box at the Bank of America around the corner. I was supposed to get one prior to my accident and now that I'm on crutches, I'm not able to get around and take care of it."

"Sure, I can do that tomorrow," I replied.

Reggie opened his briefcase and pulled out a leather case that had a small lock on the side of it and placed it in my hand. "To start, how about putting this case inside the safe deposit box—I'll give you more next week."

"Sure, whose name should I put the account in?"

"For now you can just put it in your name in association with the church. Once I'm able to get around more, I'll get it changed over into my name," he said.

"That's not a problem."

"Whatever you do, protect this with your life. If this gets lost, the bishop will kill me," he joked.

"No problem—I'll guard it with my life." I smiled.

I put my purse across my shoulder. "Well, I really should be getting home before it gets late."

"If you got a minute, we can leave together. I just came in my office to get some papers to look over tonight."

Reggie opened a small safe behind his desk that was camouflaged by a huge flower arrangement. When the safe door opened, I glanced over and noticed stacks of money that nearly filled the safe. As he turned in my direction I quickly looked away. He closed the safe and placed a folder on the desk before grabbing his crutches.

"Well, I'm ready when you are," he said.

We both exited the church. Coincidentally, our cars were parked a couple of spaces from each other. We stopped at mine since it was closest to the church.

"Well, sister. Drive carefully on the way home."

"I will." I reached for my keys.

As I did Reggie reached over and hugged me. I was so shocked that I dropped the case I was holding.

"Oops, sorry about that—did I startle you?" He stared at me.

"No, it's just that I didn't expect that." I reached down and picked up the case that fell near my feet.

"I'm sorry, sister, it's just that I'm so used to hugging members after we leave church."

We stood there staring at each other. I must admit I felt a couple of nerves jump through my body. Not from nervousness, but from passion. I forgot what that felt like, being that I wasn't getting it at home.

"You have a good spirit, sister. I can feel it." He looked down at me.

I stood there and didn't respond. I was so confused that I couldn't think straight.

It was dark with the exception of the streetlights that surrounded the parking area. Our cars were the only two in the back lot. The sounds of the chirping crickets were beginning to fade as I stared back at Reggie, concentrating on his handsome facial features. His skin was smooth and his dimples were noticeable even when he didn't smile.

He put his hand on my shoulder. "Your boyfriend is lucky to have someone like you to come home to. I feel so comfortable around you. I can just imagine how he feels about you."

Like a magnet, I felt myself being mentally drawn to him. His words were simple but meaningful and had my undivided attention. Reggie's hand slowly began to move closer to my neck when suddenly the security guard came from behind the building in his car with the yellow light flashing.

"Uh, Reggie, I'd better be getting home. It's late."

"Y-Yeah—me, too," he said and stared down at me.

The security guard pulled into the parking space near the church and sat in his car.

Reggie turned and went to his car.

I closed my door and let out a gasp before starting my car. *Oh, my God*, I thought. *What am I thinking?*

When I got home, Curtis was sitting in the recliner with a beer between his legs watching TV. He threw up his hand as I came through the door as a sign of hello before turning his head back to what he was watching. I walked into the kitchen and got a soda from the refrigerator. "Baby, bring me another beer while you're in there," Curtis shouted.

After I gave Curtis his beer, I grabbed the newspaper that was scattered on the floor next to him and took it to the kitchen to read my horoscope. I needed to make sense out of my reaction after Reggie hugged me. When I read it the first time it didn't really make sense to me. *Stay aware and alert to the possible life lessons of this situation.* Confused, I took a sip of my soda and stared into the den at Curtis, who was picking his nose and rubbing whatever he pulled out of it between his index finger and his thumb. I was so grossed out that I yelled out at him, "Wash your filthy hands, Curtis." *Is this what I have to be aware of? Why can't Curtis be more of a gentleman like Reggie?* I thought.

Curtis got up and walked past me, passing gas as he went into the bathroom, closing the door behind him. *Ugggh*, I stared at him, annoyed. I got up and went into the den and looked at Tangie and Mya's horoscope. I didn't know Reggie's birthday to look up his horoscope so I read through all of them, pretending each was his. As my eyes shifted to the bottom of the page, my attention was caught by a huge advertisement in the corner. I was shocked to see an ad for Psychic Cindy. *This is the lady who the girl from the salon was talking about.* Out of all the times I've gone through this paper, I've never paid attention to this ad. The more I read about her, the more curious I became. At a time that I was second-guessing my relationship I wanted to see what was in store for my future. At my age I couldn't afford to waste another year with Curtis if he's not the one I'm supposed to spend the rest of my life with. Some days with Curtis feel good but most of the time I feel like this relationship is too much for me to handle. *The girl in the salon said that Psychic Cindy was good*, I thought. I grabbed a pen and my notepad from my purse and wrote down the number. *I'm going to see her. I mean, what can it hurt?*

CHAPTER 26

Tangie

The lights came on, waking me out of a deep sleep. I rolled over as the covers shifted from my shoulders, then past my legs, exposing my naked body. Walter and I finally got a chance to spend some intimate time together, and boy, was it worth the wait. He skipped band practice again to see me, which I found thoughtful. Although he didn't have Todd's penis length, he made up for it with its width. If there was anything negative about Walter as a lover, it would have to be the fact that he sweats profusely. My bed was drenched in the middle where we handled our business.

Walter stood up and put on his underwear before grabbing his pants.

"What time is it?" I stretched my eyes to look at the clock on my nightstand. "It's almost ten-thirty." I yawned.

Walter zipped up his fly.

"Are you leaving?" I wiped my eyes with both hands.

"Yeah, my wife will be home in about two hours and I have to pick Tina up from her cousin's house."

I got out of bed and went into the bathroom. When I looked in the mirror I realized that I was still wearing the long, black-haired wig, with layers of lipstick on my lips and eyeliner in the corners of my eyes, making them slanted like an Asian woman's. Walter's kinky ass loves to play dress-up. Tonight his fantasy was to fuck a Chinese hooker. We role-played like he was picking me up from a street corner as he thoroughly explained what he wanted to do to me sexually. Somehow this crazy shit turned him on, and as long as it made him hungry for me, I obliged him.

"Aren't you going to take a shower?" I asked.

"No, I don't have time. I'll do it when I get home. Sometimes my wife works over a little, so it won't be a problem."

"Okay, suit yourself."

"You know my wife will be going out of town all of next week for a seminar in Dallas. Maybe I'll be able to stay a littler longer."

"Yeah, that's fine."

"Then we can get into some more freaky stuff," he laughed.

"More freakier than this shit?"

"Oh, yeah," he replied as we laughed in unison.

Walter got dressed and left. I ran some hot bathwater and soaked for about an hour, removing the makeup from my face.

While in bed reading a magazine, my phone rang. "Hello?" I answered.

"What are you doing?"

It was Todd, and by the sound of his voice he was dealing with some serious issues.

"What's up, Todd?"

"I need a place to crash for tonight," he said.

"Why? Don't you have a home?"

"My wife and I got into an argument and she called the police and they made me leave."

"That's not my problem, Todd. I don't want your shit over here."

"I just need a place to crash for tonight. I'll be gone first thing tomorrow."

"Dammit, Todd—you know I don't get down like that."

"She doesn't know about us. I just need a place to lay my head. When you leave in the morning to go to work I'm right behind you."

I paused for a moment. "Okay, but just for tonight."

"Well, come unlock the door 'cause I'm right outside," he said.

Confused, I opened the door and Todd entered my apartment. This shit was kind of scary, because Walter had just left and I didn't feel comfortable with Todd's ass being outside my apartment like that.

"How long have you been out there?"

"I don't know. About thirty minutes or so," he replied.

"Well, you can't do that," I insisted.

"I'm sorry, but I had no other place to go."

"What about a hotel or something?"

"Girl, please. I don't have money to waste like that. Why are you so uptight, anyway? It's not like I'm a stranger."

"I'm not uptight. I just don't like people hanging outside my place like that or coming over all hours of the night without me knowing in advance."

"Girl, kill that shit and lock the door behind you." He walked inside.

Todd went into the bathroom and began taking a shower. I quickly changed the sheets, got back in bed, and turned on the TV. Minutes later my cell phone rang. "Hey, Walter," I answered.

"Hey, I just made it home and wanted to say good night and I had a really good time."

"Yeah—me, too."

I heard the water stop running and movement in the bathroom. Walter was in the middle of a conversation as I held the phone. I believe my business is just that, my business, and I didn't want either guy finding out about the other. So I rushed Walter off the phone. "Uh, Walter, I have a call on my other line—I'll see you sometime next week." I hung up.

Todd opened the door and came out naked with a smile on his face, staring at me as I put my cell phone on my nightstand.

"Uh-uh, not tonight, Todd. I'm not in the mood," I said, pulling the covers over my shoulders.

"Since when are *you* not in the mood, Tangie?" he replied, walking toward me.

"Not tonight," I repeated.

Todd stood in front of the bed, waiting on me to change my mind before finally putting on his boxers and joining me in bed. He reached over and wrapped his arms around me as we watched TV. Just when I thought I would make it through the night without him trying to make a move on me, Todd started kissing me on the back of my neck. "Todd, stop." I moved away.

Todd pulled me back as I shoved him away from me once again.

"Damn, Tangie, what's the matter?"

"I told you I'm not in the mood. Shouldn't you be trying to figure out how to get back in your house?"

"Fuck that. Our relationship was over a long time ago. We've been sleeping in separate beds for the past two months."

"Well, you need to figure out what you're going to do next."

"I already know what's next."

"Good, now go to sleep."

"I was hoping we could rekindle some old feelings and start kicking it a little stronger."

"What? Oh, no. Is that why you came over here tonight? You're trying to rekindle some old shit that existed back in high school?"

"No, I really did need a place to stay. But think about it. You and I together, like old times? That could be a hell of a relationship. We could even have a kid or two."

"Wait a damn minute, Todd. Number one, I ain't trying to have your damn kids. Two," I said as I sat up in bed, "there ain't no damn two. As a matter of fact, take your ass in the den and sleep. I don't want you up under me tonight."

Todd chuckled. "The den? What is that all about?"

"Todd, our rule was for you to come over on occasion for some physical affection. Now you're talking about a relationship and kids. I'm not trying to hear that tonight."

"You mean, all this time I came over it was just a fuck thing?"

"Hell, yeah. You didn't know?"

"I thought we were feeling each other in some way."

"Negro, please. I never gave you any indication that I was feeling you like that."

"Just think about it—we could have a good life together." He pulled me closer, confessing more of his feelings.

I shook my head in disbelief because I was thrown completely off guard by his admission of his feelings toward me, which made me really feel uncomfortable. "Todd, I'm serious—stop," I snapped.

Frustrated, Todd got up and snatched the blanket from the bed, knocking the pillow on the floor. He bent down to pick it up, then slowly rose with a blank expression on his face, holding an empty Trojan condom wrapper.

"What the fuck is this shit, Tangie?"

I looked down at the wrapper and back up at him. "What?"

"*This* is what!" He threw the condom wrapper in my face. "This ain't my shit. I use magnums. Who else you been fucking, Tangie?"

"That's none of your damn business, Todd. Besides, why are you surprised, anyway? You think I'm just sitting around here waiting on you to fuck me?"

"When we hooked up, we agreed—"

"No, *you* agreed. I told you we could get together every now and then. Plus, how the fuck can you put stipulations on me when your ass is married," I yelled.

"Stipu*lations* . . . stipu*lations?* I'm talking common sense. Do you know what kind of diseases are out there? Not only are you putting me at risk, but my family."

"Nigga, if you cared anything about your family, you wouldn't be in my bed, not to mention thrown out on the streets."

"What?" Todd replied as he walked toward me. He stood in front of me and pointed his finger in my face about an inch from my nose. I was scared at first, but the look in Todd's eyes was that of jealousy more than anything else.

"Get your fucking finger out of my face. Are you crazy, motherfucker?" I said, pushing his hand away. "This is not about your family. This is about you being jealous that someone else is sharing my bed."

"Who is he?" he yelled.

"None of your business!" I shouted back, staring directly at him.

"You ain't shit but a tramp, Tangie."

"Well, you don't have to worry about that anymore, do you, 'cause you're cut off. This little affair is over."

"Oh, hell no. It ain't hardly over. Not by a long shot. This is just the beginning."

"Whatever, Todd. Walk with that bullshit."

He kept yelling as he got dressed and finally left, slamming the door behind him. I laughed out loud. The nerve of this man thinking there was a possible future for us. How ridiculous is that?

Now that he was out of my hair, I could get on with the next phase of my life, whatever that is.

CHAPTER 27

Mya

After I left school, I called Darryl to let him know I was on my way to his place. Again, I got his voice mail. I stopped by the nearest grocery store and got a few things before calling him again. This time he answered.

"Hi, where are you?" I asked.

"Oh, I'm on my way back to my apartment. I had to get my prescription filled because I was running out of the samples the doctor gave me."

"Darryl, why don't you answer your cell phone when I call?"

"I do—I had the radio up kinda loud listening to my girl Alicia Keys and didn't hear it ring."

"Yeah, well, I need to get your home number, too, 'cause I'm tired of getting your voice mail when I want to talk to you."

"That's fine. But every time I leave home I forward my home number to my cell phone, so what's the difference?"

"The difference is that I can find your ass."

He laughed. "Girl, you're tripping."

"How are you feeling, by the way?"

"Better, now that I got some rest and the medicine has kicked in. Where are you?"

"I'm leaving the grocery store. Do you need anything while I'm in here?"

"No, I'm cool."

"Okay, I'll be there shortly," I said before hanging up.

I arrived at Darryl's apartment a few minutes later. His truck was parked in his usual spot closest to the stairway leading up to his unit. When I walked inside, he had the TV on and the curtains to the patio open with a view that overlooked the trees from his deck. He walked up behind me and grabbed me around my waist, pulling me close.

"Ummm, it feels good to have you in my arms again," he said.

I smiled and rested the back of my head on his chest. "I'm still mad that you didn't call me when you were in the hospital," I said softly.

"Baby, I'm sorry. Things happened so fast, I didn't think." He rubbed his hand across my stomach. I closed my eyes, mesmerized by his touch.

Darryl's cell phone rang, breaking the mood. I turned toward him as he reached for it.

"Don't answer your phone," I said, holding on to him.

"Wait, let me see who it is. Oh, I need to take this. It's one of my boys."

I dropped my arms from around Darryl's waist, walked over to the couch, and sat down in front of the TV, slumped over on one side. I grabbed the remote control and began flipping through channels as Darryl paced the floor behind me, laughing wildly with the phone pressed tightly against his ear.

I sat back on the couch and turned toward him. He stared at me as he continued his conversation. To get his attention I began unbuttoning my shirt from the top, one button at a time. His laughter slowly dissipated. When I got to the last button I took my shirt off and tossed it to the side. I stood up and began taking off my pants and let them hit the floor. I was standing there in a black lace bra and thong, staring directly at him. I could see the bulge in his pants began to get bigger. I took off my shoes before walking slowly and sexily down the hall to Darryl's room.

When I walked into his bedroom, I took off my bra and thong and threw them in the hall. I could hear Darryl stutter in the background as he tried to get off the phone.

Completely naked, I got into bed and pulled the covers over me. Darryl appeared in the doorway with one shoe on and his shirt off.

"Hey, man, let me call you right back," Darryl said. "Uh, yeah, that's cool but give me a few minutes or so before you come by . . . Yeah, yeah, later."

Darryl got completely undressed and got into bed. We began kissing as our naked bodies touched.

Darryl was kissing me hurriedly all over my neck and on my breasts.

"Hey, slow down. We've got all night."

"No, baby. Actually, we don't. My boy is on his way here to discuss some business. I've been putting him off for about a week now, so let's do this." Darryl caressed my body.

"Let's stop then, 'cause I don't want a quickie." I grabbed his hand.

"Come on, Mya. Haven't you ever had a quickie before? They can be just as romantic," Darryl said.

"What can be romantic about you ramming your dick inside of me?"

"I can show you better than I can tell you." Darryl kissed me around my neck. I felt his tongue move its way up in my ear as I shivered.

Darryl rolled over and opened the nightstand drawer to his right. He fumbled around with some papers before quickly running to the bathroom. I heard cabinet doors opening and closing, drawers being opened and shut. Darryl came out of the bathroom and stood in front of the bed.

"What's the matter?" I asked.

"I can't find the condoms." He looked confused. "Oh, yeah." He kneeled down and looked under the bed. "Here they are."

As soon as Darryl stood up, there was a knock at the door.

"Shit, that's Greg. Quick, go in the den and get your clothes while I get dressed in here."

I gave him a puzzled look. "Why don't you just bring them in here? I have to go to the bathroom, anyway."

"Uh, yeah." Darryl ran out of the bedroom.

Seconds later he appeared, holding my clothes in one hand and my shoes in the other. "Here—put these on and make up the bed before you come out."

"What? Make up the bed?"

Another knock sounded, this time much louder than the first. "Shit, let me get the door," Darryl shouted.

By this time Darryl had his clothes on. He dashed out of the bedroom.

I got up, still naked, and closed the bedroom door behind him before walking into the bathroom and getting dressed. I took my sweet time as I fluffed my hair with my fingers. I walked out of the bathroom and over to the bed and began straightening the ruffled covers. I heard sounds of laughter outside the door as I placed the pillows neatly in their place. *Let me go on home.* I tossed the last pillow on the bed.

I walked into the den where Darryl and this guy with braids sat at the dining table with papers scattered everywhere. When I appeared, Darryl quickly got up.

"Hey, there you are. I'd like for you to meet my good friend, Greg Parker."

Greg stood up, staring at me like I was a piece of meat. "Hey, nice to meet you," he said and shook my hand.

I smiled and returned his handshake. "Well, Darryl, I think I'm going to head on home. I'll call you tomorrow, okay?"

"Are, you sure, 'cause you're welcome to stay," he said. "I'll just be a couple of hours at the most. You sure you don't want to watch TV or something?"

"No, you have business to take care of, so I'll just go."

"You sure?" Darryl repeated.

"I'm positive. Go on and take care of your business."

"Okay, well, let me walk you to your car," he replied.

I grabbed my purse and Darryl and I headed out the door to my car. I unlocked the doors with my remote as we approached and Darryl opened the driver's-side door. "Be careful on the way home and call me when you get there," he said before slamming the door shut.

CHAPTER 28

Stephanie

I left my classroom right after the final bell rang. I zipped past Mya on her way to the teachers' lounge as I walked out the door toward my car. I was in a rush to make my four-thirty appointment with Psychic Cindy. After much thought, I finally got up the nerve to call and set up an appointment the day before. Deciding to talk to a psychic was totally different from reading my daily horoscope. Especially when you have someone gifted enough to tell you your future, so I was anxious.

I arrived at the address that I got out of the paper. Her office was actually a trailer behind a house on the side of the road off the main highway. I pulled up, composed myself, and walked to the door. Before I could knock, a petite white lady with long red hair and freckles met me at the door. "You must be my four-thirty appointment. Stephanie Hall, right?" she said softly.

"Uh, yes, ma'am," I replied nervously.

She stared at me with a frown, looking me up and down for what seemed like several minutes. "Come with me, please." She turned and walked away.

We went into an empty room on the right that was filled with several candles. She grabbed a lighter from her pocket and lit them one by one before sitting down at a desk facing me. "Have a seat, please," she said and pointed to a chair.

I sat down facing her as she continued to stare at me. "I was—"

"Shhh," she interrupted as she continued to stare.

For several minutes, she kept the same frown on her face as the two of us sat in silence. I looked around the room, not knowing what to do next. Suddenly, she reached down and pulled out another candle and placed it on the desk near me and closed her eyes. After saying a few words, she lit it and put it behind her next to the other candles. I thought it was odd because all the other burning candles were white but this particular candle was black. It had a really strong odor that quickly filled the room. I didn't know what to think at this point, but it made me kind of nervous. The room had no windows and no furniture other than what we were sitting in along with the desk that separated us.

She smiled as she pulled out a deck of playing cards and began shuffling them before laying three of them faceup on the desk. "I see your finances are in order. As a matter of fact, it looks as though they are going to get better. That's if you keep your focus."

I nodded.

She shuffled the cards again and placed three more on the desk. "I see happiness with your career. Do you work around a large number of people?"

"Uh, yes. I'm a schoolteacher," I replied.

She turned over three more cards. "You seem to have positive energy. I see that your students seem to like being around you."

I smiled.

After placing three more cards on the desk, she grunted out loud. "Wow . . . it seems like things are about to get pretty interesting at that job of yours. As a matter of fact, things are about to get pretty interesting in your personal life as well."

I looked puzzled, wanting to ask for the specifics as she continued on.

"You're surrounded by a lot of lies and deceit. It's a wonder you can think straight," she said, staring at the cards.

"Huh?" I replied, confused.

"And who are these men in your life?"

"Men? What men?"

"I see three men in your life, pulling you in three different directions. All want a piece of you."

"What?"

Psychic Cindy opened a drawer on the side of her desk, pulling out a piece of white cloth and a bottle that contained a red liquid. She opened the bottle and poured a drop of the liquid on the cloth and began rubbing it in her hands. A few seconds later, she opened her hand and placed the cloth on the desk directly in front of me. I looked at the cloth, as it was now the color of the liquid.

"Umm-huh, yeah, I see three men in your life. There's no doubt about that. One you love with your heart and he really needs you. One you love with your body and he wants you. And one you love with your spirit and you're really compatible with him. You're going to have to make a life-changing decision about which way you are going to go. The wrong choice could be a drastic change in your life."

"Can you describe the person I am going to choose?"

She closed her eyes tightly and took several deep breaths before opening them and looking directly at the cards in front of her. "I can't say which one because the spirit is not showing me a face. But I can see that two out of the three men will have an important impact on your life."

"How so? I don't understand."

"Do you feel empty or unfulfilled at times, almost like you're waiting on someone to move you in the right direction as opposed to you always having to move others? I see you finding that person if you open yourself up a little more. You seem uptight or edgy, like you are about to lose your mind. Just relax and follow your heart. That person will come to you."

I listened as Psychic Cindy went on and on about these three men she claimed she saw. I expected more information, according to what the girl in the salon had told me. I was just as confused when I left as I was before I got there. It seemed as though my horoscope gave me more information than she did. Plus, it only cost me fifty cents for the paper as opposed to the eighty dollars I gave Psychic Cindy.

CHAPTER 29

Tangie

Exhausted, I drove through the heavy Atlanta traffic. Today I was the recess monitor and my feet were killing me from all the walking around the playground during lunch. I had just remembered that I needed to stop by the market and pick up something for dinner. While inside the market, I received a call from Todd but didn't answer. It was one of the many calls he had flooded my cell phone with since I put him out of my apartment the other night.

When I made it home, I unpacked the groceries before taking a hot shower and lying in bed watching TV. Several minutes later, there was another call on my cell phone. I looked at the caller ID and noticed Todd's number again. I ignored that call, but then there was a knock at my door. I looked outside my window and saw Todd's truck parked next to my car. Seconds later there was another knock. I got extremely angry and wanted to rush out and cuss his ass out for disrespecting me like this, but decided to ignore him. The knocks continued for several minutes, followed by another call on my cell phone. I peeked out the window and saw Todd sitting in his truck with his cell phone against his ear. Suddenly my cell phone rang again. At this point, I was fed up and grabbed my phone from the nightstand.

"What the fuck do you want?" I yelled.

"Hey, hey, what's the matter?" a voice replied.

It was Walter. I paused for a moment to gather myself. "Oh,

sorry—it's just that someone has been calling my house, annoying me."

"Are you okay?" he asked.

"Yeah, I guess. How are you?"

"Good, but I'd be even better if I could see you."

"Well, I don't think tonight would be a good night for you to come over."

"Why? I think it's the perfect night. My wife is out of town until Friday and my daughter is spending the rest of the week with her cousin."

I peeked out the window once more and Todd was still in his truck on his cell phone. I really wanted to see Walter but couldn't think of any other way to get together.

"Tangie, I don't think we'll get another chance like this to be alone. Tomorrow I have a gig and Friday my wife will be home."

"I know, but it's just that—"

"Look, how about coming to my house?" he interrupted.

"What? Are you out of your mind?"

"C'mon, you're risking your career for me. I just want you to know that no matter how much we kick it, I'm risking just as much. Besides, no one will see you. You can park your car in my garage."

Normally, I would decline the invitation outright, but Walter did have a point. His wife was out of town and we both really wanted to see each other.

"Okay, Walter. But it'll have to be later tonight," I said.

"Sure, just call me when you're ready to leave and I'll give you the directions," he said excitedly. "And bring that blonde wig with you. I think I want something different tonight."

"Sure." I smiled before hanging up.

It was still kind of early, so I lay back in bed, looking out my window from time to time until Todd was finally gone.

I quickly packed my short dress, the blonde wig that I bought the week I got my short black wig, and my high-heel shoes before rushing out the door. I called Walter on his cell phone and got directions. I sped through the light traffic, looking through my rearview mirror the whole way to see if Todd was following me. Luckily, I didn't see any signs of his car.

When I turned into Walter's subdivision, it was late in the

evening and the sun was going down. Before I arrived at his house, I called so he could open the garage door and guide me inside.

I got out of the car with my bags in hand. "Hey."

Walter was standing at the door inside the garage wearing a robe. "Did you have any trouble finding my house?"

"No, I found it okay," I replied as I walked inside. "Are you sure it's cool to be here, 'cause I don't really feel comfortable."

"Well, have some wine. Maybe that'll ease your nerves a little. Besides, my wife is out of town—I just got off the phone with her."

I sipped some wine and followed Walter to his family room, where we sat down next to each other on the couch. He turned on some music with his remote control and we talked. I was still a bit nervous being in a strange house, and I found myself looking over my shoulder every couple of minutes.

"Are you sure you're okay?" he asked.

"Hell, no. I'd feel much better if you showed me around," I replied. "I'd at least like to know where the doors and windows are in case I have to run out or something," I joked.

He grabbed my hand and escorted me around every room in his house. It was a beautiful two-story home with five bedrooms. When we got to Tina's room, I walked inside and looked around for a minute, admiring her neatness and the way her room was furnished. Walter then guided me to what looked to be his bedroom, where I stopped in my tracks.

"What's the matter?" he asked.

"I know you're not about to take me into your bedroom."

"Yeah, what's wrong with that? I'm just showing you around," he replied.

"I'll pass. That's one room I'd rather not see."

He took me to the rest of the rooms in the house until we found ourselves back on the couch, where I began to loosen up a little. I went into the bathroom down the hall and got dressed for our role-playing. Once the kissing started, we ended up in one of the guest bedrooms. As the hours passed, I noticed it was getting late. My clothes were scattered from the bedroom to where we started in the den. The alcohol had me feeling paranoid—I began to feel more nervous about being in Walter's house, thinking his wife would walk in at any moment. I sat up in bed and let my eyes roam the room.

"Walter, it's getting late. I'd better go." I got out of bed, gathering my clothes.

Walter got out of bed and put on his robe. All of the lights in the house were off as I struggled in the dark to find my thong panties. When I finally got dressed, I walked to my car and waited for Walter to open the garage.

"Damn, you're just going to run out like that? Don't I get a hug or something?" he asked.

"Yeah," I replied as I leaned over. "Now, open the garage so I can go," I said. Walter stepped back inside the house and used the remote to open the garage door. I quickly backed out of the garage and left his neighborhood. I didn't feel comfortable until I drove onto the main highway, heading home.

When I turned into my apartment complex I decided to park in the unit behind mine and slowly walked to my door. As I put the key in the lock, there was a piece of paper taped below the doornob. It read, *Just a little something to let you know that you can't ignore me.* I crumpled the paper up and opened the door to my apartment. I walked inside and reached for the lamp switch and bumped my knee on something hard and solid. "Ouch—what the fu—" I mumbled as I turned on the light switch on the wall to my far right. *Oh, shit,* I thought as I stood by the front door, staring into my den. All of my furniture was rearranged. My stereo was neatly organized in a corner against the wall. My couch and love seat were completely changed around, facing each other, with the coffee table centered between the two and magazines neatly stacked on them. My end tables were placed on both sides on the couch, a lamp in the center of each. The paintings on the wall were taken from their original positions and placed on the walls opposite each other. My magazine rack was right below my leg—I'd kicked it when I walked in.

I rushed into the kitchen and grabbed a knife before slowly walking to my bedroom, turning on the lights. My heart was racing really fast as I tiptoed to my closet door. I took a deep breath before quickly opening it, making a stabbing motion on the inside. I walked to the bathroom and checked the showers, repeating the stabbing motion before looking under the bed. I went back into the kitchen, grabbed my house phone, and called Stephanie. When no one answered, I called Mya, still hysterical. Mya asked a million questions but I was too frantic to explain. I put Mya on hold and called my friend Burton Williams. Burton owns a detail shop in Buckhead—he's a straight-up gangsta and just the person I needed to handle this kind of shit. After hearing my story, he was ready to take action on Todd's ass right away, but I had him stand down for now. I was merely calling him to give him a heads-up just in case I needed him.

Before leaving, I called Mya from my cell phone, then packed some clothes and rushed over to her place.

CHAPTER 30

Mya

Tangie came to my place with her bags in tow. She had a frustrated look on her face as she talked on her cell phone and entered the doorway, heading straight to the kitchen. She poured herself a glass of wine and closed the phone. "That Todd is about to get his ass kicked," she said.

"What are you talking about?" I asked. "What's going on?"

"Girl, Todd is on some other shit. While I was gone, he broke into my place and rearranged my damn furniture."

"What?"

"You heard me right. He rearranged my furniture."

"I don't get it, Tangie. Why would he do that?"

"Last week his wife called the police on his ass and then kicked him out of the house. He called me and wanted to spend the night and I agreed. But later on he started acting weird, talking about he didn't love his wife anymore and wanted us to be in a committed relationship. When I said no, he started going off until I kicked him out. Since then, he's been calling me and hanging outside my apartment all times of night. That's when I came home and saw that this fool had rearranged my shit."

I wanted to laugh but I held it in because of the look of disgust on Tangie's face. I have to admit, that is the craziest shit I'd ever heard of, and I really had no words of comfort for her. Instead I let her finish off the half-bottle of wine before she finally calmed down and dozed off on the couch.

The next day after school, Stephanie, Tangie, and I drove over to Tangie's apartment to gather some of her things to take back to my place for the night because she didn't feel safe staying home. When we opened the door to her apartment, we did so with caution and then slowly walked inside. We stayed close together and checked every room in her apartment before settling back into the den.

"See what this fool did?" Tangie said, pointing wildly.

"Well, the brother did a damn good job, if you ask me. It actually looks better," Stephanie joked.

Tangie rolled her eyes at Stephanie as I chuckled. "That shit ain't funny. That's okay. When Burton catches up with him he's going to rearrange his ass."

Minutes later, Tangie was finally at ease. She looked around her apartment and actually laughed at her ordeal.

Stephanie and I took a seat on the couch as Tangie checked her answering machine. She was so out of date that she still had the answering machine that looked like a portable tape recorder next to her phone. The volume was turned up so loud that Stephanie and I could hear her messages from the den.

The first four messages were hang-ups; the next message was from her friend Burton, checking on her, and the last message was from her cousin Crystal Branch, inviting all of us to her party.

Tangie's cousin Crystal was a real estate agent with lots of high-class friends. Her parties were really boring. According to Tangie, Crystal grew up poor and now that she had a little money, she tried to flaunt her wealth by having these little parties to impress her friends. Most of them only talked about how many cars they had and how many trips they'd taken over the last year and, who they knew. I just flat-out wasn't interested in going. Crystal only wanted us there so that we could wait on them hand and foot.

When Stephanie and I heard the message, we both looked at each other and nodded our heads in disbelief.

Tangie came walking from the bedroom holding some clothes. "Hey, Crystal has invited you two to her party next weekend."

"Next weekend? Oh, I can't make it. Vicki Winans is performing at the church that night," Stephanie said.

Tangie looked over at me. "I'll see what Darryl and I have planned and let you know."

"You gotta see what Darryl has planned? Girl, you better stop tripping. Set your own damn schedule and stop working around his."

"It is not like that. He might just have something special planned."

"You can bring him if you'd like. Crystal won't mind," Tangie said as she walked back to her bedroom.

I looked over at Stephanie. "What are you going to do?" I whispered.

"Just what I said I was going to do. Go and see Vicki Winans."

"You know Tangie is going to keep bugging us until we give in," I said.

"So I—"

Tangie walked back in the den and into the kitchen, talking about Crystal's party and asking us over and over about going. She wouldn't take no for an answer until I finally gave in. Soon after, Stephanie— after a long plea from me—also gave in. Then she left while I waited for Tangie to gather up the rest of her things.

On the way home I called Darryl, only to get his voice mail again. I left a message and put the phone back in my purse. I could feel Tangie looking at me as I kept my head turned away to keep her from saying anything about my relationship with Darryl. When we made it home, I cooked dinner and Tangie and I sat in the den talking. In the midst of our conversation, I picked up my cell phone and called Darryl once again, and just like the call before, his voice mail picked up. Disappointed, I tossed the phone on the coffee table.

"What's that all about?" Tangie asked.

"Nothing," I replied.

"That's the second time in my presence that you called someone and you had a frustrated look on your face. What's up? Was that Darryl?"

I turned slightly and nodded.

"Girl, don't put yourself out there like that. Let him look for you sometime. If a man thinks you're desperate, he won't respect you."

"I'm fine. Besides, he's not like Todd," I joked.

"Todd's just an exception to the rule. But like all rules, if you break them, there are consequences."

Later in the night as I lay in bed looking up at the ceiling, I thought about Tangie's words about chasing after Darryl. I kept telling myself that I was worried about him. After all, he was just diagnosed with high blood pressure. God only knows what else is wrong with him. I was tempted to call once again but noticed how late it was before drifting off to sleep.

CHAPTER 31

Stephanie

I opened the account for the church after school and gave Reggie the papers that night after Bible study. He put them in the safe in his office, then gave me a small envelope to be put in the safe deposit box along with the other papers the following day. I took a seat in his office and began talking about Bible study. Our conversation was interrupted by an incoming call on Reggie's cell phone. I sat there for about five minutes, staring around the room, until I noticed a crossword puzzle on Reggie's desk. I reached for it and started to work on it. Minutes later, Reggie hung up and laughed out loud.

"What are you so excited about?" I asked.

"I just closed another deal worth a lot of money," he replied.

"Oh, well, congratulations," I said as I smiled in return.

"Thanks . . . I feel like celebrating. Have you had dinner? It's still early. Why don't we grab a bite at the restaurant around the corner."

I thought about it for a quick second before realizing I really needed to be heading home. "Maybe next time—I have to get home before my son goes to bed."

Reggie had a disappointed look that he tried to hide. "I keep forgetting you're in a relationship."

"Well, there's nothing wrong with having dinner with a friend. It's just that I can't do it tonight."

"I understand," he replied.

I put the crossword puzzle and pencil back on Reggie's desk.

"Oh, so you couldn't answer any of the questions either?" he joked.

"I did. As a matter of fact, I answered three of them," I said, smiling just a little.

"Let's see." He leaned over and looked at the puzzle. "Hmmm, okay, I see where you filled in a few. Well what about this one?" he pointed to clue 23 Down.

I got up and pushed my chair closer to him to get a better view. He handed me a pencil as we went through the leftover clues. By the time we finished, another hour had passed.

"Oh, look at the time!" I said as I looked at my watch. "It's almost nine o'clock. I need to be getting home."

I grabbed my purse, rushed out the door, and jumped in my car to head home.

When I walked inside the house, all the lights were off and the TV was on in the bedroom. I put my purse on the kitchen table and went into Brandon's room, where he was sound asleep. I felt bad that I had missed giving him his bath and putting him to bed. I walked over to him and gently gave him a kiss on the cheek before going to my bedroom. As I entered, Curtis got out of bed. "Do you know what time it is? What the hell is wrong with you, coming in this late?"

"I was tied up at the church and lost track of time."

"Ain't nobody preaching no sermons this time of night."

"I was helping Sister Pattie with some event planning for next week," I lied. "We got to talking and we both lost track of time."

"Well, if these so-called church events are going to have you coming home this late, then I think it's time for you to give them up."

"What? Boy, you must be crazy. I enjoy what I'm doing and it's only a couple of nights a week, anyway."

"What about Brandon? He was staring out the window all night waiting on you to come home until he fell asleep on the floor."

When I heard that, I felt a sinking feeling in my stomach. I was having so much fun that I did lose track of time. But I should be more responsible than to forget about my child. As I was caught up in my thoughts, Curtis continued to rant and rave. I walked into the bathroom and turned on the shower, closing the door behind me. I stayed in the shower for over twenty minutes before getting into bed to Curtis's snoring. I tried to sleep but I couldn't help but think about Reggie. I was beginning to feel more comfortable around him each time we talked. He was warm, friendly, and very easy to talk to—unlike Curtis, who seemed angry at the world and blamed everyone for his mistakes instead of trying to do something about it. I got out of bed and went to the refrigerator, where I made a sandwich. I opened the paper Curtis left on the table and started working the crossword puzzle in the back. I smiled to myself as I filled in most of it and thought about Reggie when I couldn't figure out the others. I started to have strange feelings suddenly that really made me feel guilty. But I didn't really feel bad about it. Besides, Reggie was just a friend filling a void in my life that Curtis doesn't even try to fill.

It was almost midnight before I decided to throw away my sandwich and make my way back to bed. As I got comfortable, Curtis reached over and held me close like he always did throughout the night. But it wasn't his affection that made me feel so comfortable. It was the fact that I had finally found a special place in my heart for Reggie, and it made me feel more complete. Now I knew what it felt like to have a true male friend that I can talk to with no strings attached.

CHAPTER 32

Tangie

I finally felt comfortable enough to come home. Plus, I was getting tired of Mya's behavior with Darryl, like he owned her ass. I had my own mess to straighten out.

I got my cell phone from my purse and saw that there were seven missed calls and five messages from Todd. Because I had my people backing me up, I was ready to deal with him once and for all. While I was at home sitting on the couch, Todd called my cell phone once again. I could tell he was shocked that I had answered by the way he paused after I said hello. Before he could get a word out of his mouth, I went off. "You must be out of your fucking mind to think that you could scare me. And yeah, I got your message—breaking into my apartment and shit. Just wait 'til you get *my* message. One that I don't think you'll like very well. Are you insane?"

"All you had to do was talk to me, Tangie," he replied.

"We said all that was needed to be said the other night. Get it through your head that this friendship is over."

Todd paused once again before the phone went dead. I jumped up and ran to my bedroom, turned off the lights, and peeked out the window to get a view of the back parking lot to see if Todd was out there. When I didn't see him from that angle, I dashed into the den and looked through the peephole. Again, I didn't see Todd. I got really nervous and called Burton.

"What are you doing?" I asked, out of breath.

"I'm just finishing up some things here at work. Are you cool?"

"Yeah—Todd just called, bugging me again."

"Look, how about letting me put a stop to this nonsense? Tell me where he lives or works, and I'll go by and talk to him."

Just as I was about to give Burton Todd's information, I thought for a minute. "Well, Burton, I don't want you to get in trouble on my behalf," I said.

"Don't worry about it. That's the least of my worries," he replied.

"No, wait. Maybe I just need to get me some pepper spray in case something goes down."

"What?" he responded.

"Some pepper spray to stun him and then I can beat the shit out of him."

Burton laughed. "Girl, you tripping—pepper spray won't do nothing but make him more upset."

"Well, what do you suggest?"

"Well, I have a stun gun at the office if you really want to put him down," Burton suggested.

"Yeah," I replied, excited. "First I can stun his ass. Then, while he's down, pepper spray him, then beat the shit out of him until I can call the police or something."

"Or until you call me," Burton replied.

There was silence after his response.

"Can I come by and get it, maybe this weekend or something?" I asked.

"Well, I'm going out of town this weekend, but I can make sure my receptionist leaves it out for you. Better yet, I can drop it off at your place tomorrow."

"No, that's too far for you to come. The pepper spray will do until I'm able to pick it up," I replied.

"It's no trouble, but whatever you want to do," he said.

"That's fine. I'll be cool until then."

Later that night, Stephanie and Mya called on three-way to check on me. I talked to them while I took a bath, ate my dinner, and lay in bed. We planned another girls' night out since it had been a while. Plus, I needed a perm badly. We realized that we were all consumed with men and needed to hang out and clear our heads. In the midst of the conversation, Walter called on my cell, so I got off the phone. He was on his way home from playing at a function with his band. It had been a while since we'd talked. He explained how his wife came back from out of town and wanted to be more supportive of what he was doing with the band. As he tried to go on, I cut him off, explaining my rule to him. I don't discuss personal issues between husband and wife. I just needed to know when and where we were meeting next. Walter thought it was cute, but I was serious. I'm only interested in us, not them.

Because his band had another gig this coming weekend, we agreed to meet. The plan was to come back to my place, but with all of the drama I was going through with Todd, I wasn't comfortable with it. I suggested a hotel near the venue they played in, but Walter was adamant about not wanting to be seen in public like that. So my place was the agreed-upon setting, unless his wife was going to be at his gig. In the middle of our conversation, Walter cut me off. "Hey, let me call you back tomorrow sometime," he said in a rush.

"Okay, but is everything all right?" I asked.

"Uh, yeah, but my wife is coming out of the restaurant with our food, so I have to go."

"You mean she's—"

I was cut off by the phone going dead. I couldn't believe he'd called me while his wife was around. Walter was either insane or stupid. Well, he was too fine to be insane, so I believe his ass was just plain stupid. I needed to let him know not to put me in a situation like that again. Besides, I'm just a fling. I ain't no hoe, so do not treat me like one. Call me when you got time to talk, not when you want a quick conversation about your next booty-call.

I got up to check my locks and windows once again before getting into bed. Just as I did, Walter called once again. "Hey, sorry to hang up so fast but my wife is with me. She had to rush back inside to get some condiments."

"Look, Walter. Don't play me like a hoe. Call me when you're alone next time. I don't like my conversations rushed," I said firmly.

"I'm sorry. I didn't mean to offend you—I was just missing you, that's all," he replied.

"That's fine, but just remember what I said. Now, enjoy your time with the wife and call me when you're able to talk. It's still here waiting for you."

CHAPTER 33

Mya

Saturday evening, Stephanie, Tangie, and I were over at Tangie's apartment getting ready to go to Crystal's party. Stephanie picked me up on her way from the Mall of Georgia and I rode with her. I didn't want to drive because I had already made plans with Darryl to ride home with him after the party.

After Tangie finished getting dressed, Stephanie and I followed her to Crystal's neighborhood clubhouse. Crystal lives in a really nice area in Alpharetta. Her subdivision faces the famous Country Club of the South. This is where celebrities like Usher, Michael Vick, and Whitney Houston live, to name a few.

When we pulled into the parking lot, there were only four cars. Crystal was standing outside, pointing people in different directions as they carried what looked to be food trays into the clubhouse.

We parked, got out, and walked toward Crystal.

"Hey," Tangie shouted.

Crystal turned and came over to us.

"Hey, I'm glad you all could make it. How's everyone doing?" she asked. Stephanie and I looked at each other before turning toward Crystal.

"It's only seven o'clock. The guests won't start arriving for another two hours or so. I'm glad you could come early," she said.

I looked back over at Stephanie, who was staring at Tangie with a frown.

"Do you need any help with anything?" Tangie asked.

"Girl, yeah. I still have to decorate the bar and dining area. I've been running around all morning trying to get things together. I tried this new catering company, thinking they would do all this, but the only thing they do is cook and set up the food."

"Don't worry about that—we'll help you out," Tangie said cheerily.

Crystal smiled as we all proceeded inside the clubhouse.

"You brought your sneakers?" Stephanie whispered, leaning toward me.

"Shit, for what? I'm just helping her put napkins on the table and that's it," I whispered back.

Crystal and Tangie walked in the back as Stephanie and I stood near the doorway inside.

"Tangie had me thinking we were running late, the way she was rushing," Stephanie said.

"Well, I'm not helping her clean this shit up. I plan on being with Darryl all night," I replied.

"When you two leave, I'm right behind you," Stephanie continued.

Tangie and Crystal came from the back part of the clubhouse, rolling a cart filled with decorative napkins and trinkets.

"Here, can you two put these on the tables along the walls in every room?" Crystal said, looking at Stephanie and me.

"Sure," I replied dryly.

Stephanie just nodded.

"Make sure when you place them on the table that you stack them neatly so that the design will show each time a napkin is taken. Uh, Stephanie, you can start placing the napkins near the bar area the same way."

I grabbed a stack of napkins and proceeded to the main dining area. The room was huge, with a chandelier in the center of the ceiling. The lights were mesmerizing. In the back was a bay window that went from the floor all the way up to the ceiling. The view from there overlooked a lighted pool and patio.

Tables were set up in every corner of the room. I walked back and forth from the cart to the main dining area, setting up napkins. Every couple of minutes, Crystal would come in and look over what I had done, often adjusting the way I had placed the napkins. When I finished, she walked me to another room in the back corner of the clubhouse.

"Can you place glasses in rows of five on the tables next to the punch bowls? Thank you," Crystal said as she exited.

I took a deep breath and slowly let it out. Stephanie appeared seconds later as I began placing the glasses on the table.

"Girl, if Crystal asks me to do one more thing, she might get cussed out," Stephanie said.

"You must've read my mind," I replied. "After I finish with these glasses, that's it. The only other glass I'm lifting will have some wine in it," I said.

Stephanie laughed.

Minutes later, Tangie walked into the room as Stephanie and I continued placing glasses on the tables.

"There you two are. Isn't this place nice?" Tangie asked.

"We wouldn't know—all we've been doing since we got here is work," Stephanie replied.

"Yeah, and where have you been, Tangie?" I asked.

"I was helping Crystal and the bartender put the liquor and wine behind the bar, and making sure she had enough ice for drinks."

Crystal appeared again with a glass of wine in her hand. "Well, that should do it. I think we're all set. The guests should arrive within the hour. The band is setting up and the food is all set out. Oh, I may need you to help me make sure the guests are comfortable."

I gave Crystal a stone-cold look. "Crystal—"

Tangie cut in. "Hold up, Crystal. My girls came here to have a good time, not wait on your guests. Come on, enough is enough. They helped you set up—"

"Well, Tangie, I just want to make sure things go right tonight."

"Then you should have hired people for that. I can't let you take advantage of my friends."

Crystal looked over at Stephanie and me. "Is that what you think? If so, I'm sorry. I didn't mean to give you that impression. With all the rushing back and forth, I didn't realize I was acting that way."

"Crystaaaaal," a voice yelled.

"Excuse me for a second—that's one of the guys in the band," Crystal said.

When she left, Tangie turned toward Stephanie and me. "Let's get a drink and get our party on. I know you two are pissed. I can see it in your eyes."

Stephanie and I laughed.

"Well, I'm not going to lie. I was about to lose it for a minute," I said.

"I know—I saw you and Stephanie trying to hold back your anger. Crystal was wrong and I had to let her know that. Sometimes she can get carried away."

We all took a seat at the bar and got glasses of wine. By the time the guests arrived, I was feeling really mellow. Time passed by quickly, and when I looked down at my watch, it read ten o'clock. *Where is Darryl?* I thought as I looked around.

"What's wrong?" Tangie asked.

"Nothing," I replied nonchalantly.

"Let's walk around and check out the guys," Tangie suggested.

"You go ahead. I'm fine," I replied.

Tangie and Stephanie got up and walked around. I sat at the bar and sipped my wine.

Guys came over trying to engage in conversation but I wasn't interested. I looked at my watch again. This time it read ten fifty-five.

I got up from the bar and walked in the back of the clubhouse to the restrooms. As I opened the door, my phone rang.

I pulled it out of my purse and looked at the caller ID. It was Darryl. "Where are you? I can't believe you stood me up again. I—"

"Hey, calm down, baby. I'm getting off Georgia 400 and will be there shortly. I just wanted to apologize for running late, that's all."

A sigh of relief came over me. "You are? If you had stood me up, I promise, Darryl, I would have been through with your ass," I said.

"C'mon, Mya. Don't be that way. I had no control over the other times," he replied.

"Well, do you know how to get here?" I asked.

"Yeah. Oh, I brought one of my boys along, too. I hope it's okay," he said.

"What? Darryl, I thought we were going to spend tonight together. I rode here with Stephanie, thinking I was going home with you."

"I can still take you home. That's not a problem," Darryl replied.
I was hot. "Okay, fine. I'll see you shortly."
I walked back to the bar and got a fresh glass of wine.

Darryl appeared in the doorway, along with another guy. I got up and walked toward them. When Darryl saw me, he walked over and gave me a big hug and kiss.

"Hey, are you still mad at me?" he asked, holding me.

"I should be, but I'm not. Glad you could make it, though."

"Oh—this is my boy, Jeff Cook." Darryl pointed to Jeff.

I reached out and shook his hand. "Nice to meet you, Jeff."

"So you're the Mya I've been hearing so much about, huh?"

I smiled and looked back over at Darryl. "Do you two want a drink?" I asked.

"Yeah, sure," Darryl replied.

Jeff nodded.

We walked over to the bar, where Darryl and Jeff both got a Heineken from the bartender.

Stephanie came by minutes later and stood next to me as I sat next to Darryl.

"Hey, you're still sitting here. You're not going to get up and dance?" Stephanie asked.

"No, I'm fine now that Darryl's here," I replied.

Stephanie looked behind me and leaned over to my ear. "Is that Darryl?"

I smiled slightly. "Yeah, that's him."

"Damn, he looks better than before. I hear you, girl." She tapped my shoulder.

I turned and got Darryl's attention. "Hey, you remember my girl, Stephanie? She was with me the night I met you."

Darryl looked up. "Yeah, I remember," he replied, getting up. "Hey, Stephanie. Nice to see you again," he said, shaking her hand.

Darryl gestured for Jeff to come over. "Stephanie, this is my boy, Jeff Cook. Jeff, this is Mya's friend, Stephanie."

Jeff shook Stephanie's hand and they began talking. Darryl and I walked away from the bar and over to the main dining area. The band was really good. They played everything from Frankie Beverly and Maze to Anita Baker.

Darryl and I danced through several songs before taking a break and going back to the bar for a refill on drinks. Stephanie and Jeff had taken a seat at the bar facing each other, still conversing. Tangie was there also, talking to some guy drinking a glass of wine.

I tapped Tangie on the shoulder. "Hey, sorry to interrupt you, but I wanted to introduce you to Darryl," I said.

Tangie turned around to face Darryl. "Oh, so you're the Darryl I've been hearing so much about."

Darryl smiled. "What's up? Nice to meet you."

Tangie looked over at me and smiled. I turned, getting the bartender's attention, and got a napkin to wipe my face.

I grabbed Darryl's hand and guided him to the room with the food. "Are you hungry?" I asked.

"Yeah, a little . . . Damn, this is a nice spread." Darryl looked over at the food.

"I'll fix us a plate together. Tell me what you want," I said, grabbing a plate.

"It doesn't matter. Whatever you put on there is cool. Make sure you put a couple of chicken wings on there, though."

I neatly placed food on the plate and we took a seat in the corner of the room at a table. It was much quieter than the rest of the clubhouse. Minutes later, other couples gathered around the food table and sat in chairs near Darryl and me.

Later, Jeff and Stephanie came walking through the door. They both fixed themselves plates and joined Darryl and me.

"Are you having a good time, Jeff?" I asked.

"Yeah, this is a nice little get-together. The food is good. Did you make any of this, Stephanie?" Jeff asked.

Stephanie looked over at Jeff, smiling. "You know this food was catered," she replied.

"No, I didn't know. Can you cook, by the way?" Jeff asked.

"Yeah, why?" Stephanie replied. "Can you?"

"Yeah, I can burn." Jeff laughed. "So *you* can cook, huh?" he repeated.

"Yes, I can cook. I can eat, too—watch me," Stephanie joked.

Darryl burst out laughing, as we all did. Jeff nodded in embarrassment as he kept on eating.

Darryl and I got up and walked outside near the pool. The dark skies were lit up by the tiny stars spaced across it. The half-moon generated a light beam that reflected off the water in the pool. Darryl held my hand as we stood there enjoying the picture-perfect moment. A slight breeze in the midnight air made me shiver as I moved closer to Darryl.

"You okay?" Darryl asked as he held me close.

"Yeah, I am now." I replied.

Darryl took off his jacket and placed it around me. We walked over to some chairs closest to the door of the clubhouse and sat down.

"You looked beautiful tonight, Mya," Darryl said.

"Thank you. You look rather handsome yourself." I blushed.

We sat there in silence for a moment, gazing into the night skies. Suddenly, Darryl's cell phone rang. I looked over at him as he reached for it.

Darryl didn't even look at the number. He just turned his cell phone off and put it in the pocket of the jacket I was wearing. He slid his chair closer to me and put his arm around me. I tilted my head on his arm and continued looking up at the stars. We stayed outside, cuddling and talking, for an hour.

"It's getting a little chilly out here. Let's go back inside," I suggested.

The guests started leaving the party at around two o'clock in the morning. I was sitting at the bar alone with Darryl while he finished his beer. Jeff and Stephanie stood behind us against the wall, still engaged in conversation.

As Crystal walked the last guest out, Tangie began cleaning the tables in the dining room. I turned toward Stephanie. "Hey!" I shouted over the music.

Stephanie looked over at me. I pointed in the direction of the dining room. Stephanie looked over at Tangie and a smile came over her face. She excused herself from Jeff and walked over to me.

"Hey, I'm about to leave. I'm not staying here all night cleaning up," Stephanie said.

"I'm right behind you," I replied.

I leaned over to Darryl. "Hey, are you about ready to go?"

"Sure, whenever you are," Darryl replied, getting up from the chair. "Let me get one more beer for the road."

The lights came on in the clubhouse and the music was turned off. Jeff walked over to us. "What's up? Is everybody leaving?"

"Yeah, the party's over," Stephanie replied.

"But we're all still going to hang out, right?" Jeff asked.

"Not me—I have to go home to my son," Stephanie replied.

"Aw, c'mon—doesn't he have a babysitter?" Jeff asked.

"Yeah, his father," Stephanie replied with her eyebrows up.

"Oooooh, I get it. That's cool. I didn't know it was like that," Jeff said with a shameful smile on his face.

Jeff walked over to Darryl and began talking. I leaned over toward Stephanie. "Damn, girl. That was cold."

"No, it wasn't. Earlier, he asked me for my number and I politely said no, and then he asked if we could get together sometime and I politely said no. I don't know why he should be surprised at that. I told him I had a son."

"Then I guess asking you to hang out with us is out of the question, huh?" I asked.

"Hell, no . . . Besides, I don't like his spirit," Stephanie replied.

"Spirit. What are you talking about?" I asked.

"I just don't get a good vibe from him. His ass is too strange for my taste, always wanting to know things."

"That's just your crazy ass, girl. I don't see anything wrong with just hanging out for a while."

"You can do what you want, but I'm going home."

"Hey, Tangie. We're about to leave."

"Oh, okay. Crystal and I are almost finished here, so I won't be too far behind you,"

"Crystal, thank you for inviting me to your party, and for letting my friends come, too," I said.

"Yeah, thanks," Stephanie added.

"No problem. Thanks for all the help and I apologize if you felt like I was using—"

"No, don't worry about that," Stephanie interrupted.

Crystal nodded.

Stephanie and I turned and walked toward the front door, where Darryl and Jeff were waiting.

Jeff walked Stephanie to her car as Darryl and I waited inside his truck.

Moments later, Jeff trotted back to Darryl's truck with an odd grin on his face as he got inside.

"Is everything cool?" Darryl asked, driving off.

"Hell, no," Jeff replied. "Mya, your girl is tough to break. I just asked her out to lunch and she gave me a million and one excuses why she didn't want to go."

"Well, Jeff, right now she's going through some things."

"Oh, with her baby daddy," Jeff joked.

No one laughed at his silly humor as he continued. "Why aren't they married if they are supposedly together?" Jeff asked.

I sat there in silence.

"See, that's what's wrong with these sistas today. When good men try to approach them, they treat *them* like shit. I don't feel sorry for women when they get dogged out by the thug brothers they love so much."

Jeff was beginning to annoy me really bad. I tried tuning him out by just looking out of the window, but he kept on.

"Mya, does she live with her baby daddy or something? What's up?" Jeff asked.

"What did she tell you?" I replied sharply.

"Something about how she and her man are working through some shit. You know, the usual bullshit when you try to blow a brother off."

"Well, Jeff, you know more than I do," I replied.

Darryl cut in. "Damn, Jeff. Just give that shit a rest, man, and take what she said for what it's worth. You act like this every time you get a few drinks in you."

"Man, I'm just trying to figure out what's up with her, that's all," Jeff replied.

"C'mon and just give it a rest. I'm not trying to hear your gripes all the way home."

"Yeah, yeah, all right. I'm through with it, then," Jeff replied. "It's her loss, anyway."

Jeff sat back in his seat and remained quiet the rest of the ride home. I was glad, because I don't think I could have taken many more of his remarks.

When we got to Darryl's apartment, Jeff was asleep in the backseat. Darryl opened the back door of his truck and helped Jeff to his feet.

"Jeff? Are you okay to drive home, man?" Darryl asked.

"Huh, uh, yeah," Jeff replied, laughing out loud.

"Darryl, help him upstairs and put him on the couch or something. If he drives home, there's no telling what will happen," I said.

Darryl nodded as he held Jeff up.

Once we all got inside, Darryl laid Jeff on the couch before walking to the bedroom. I was already undressed and in bed with nothing on but my panties and bra when he walked in.

"Is Jeff okay?" I asked.

"Yeah, he just needs to sleep off some of the alcohol."

Darryl got undressed and climbed into bed. He reached over and pulled me closer as he caressed my stomach on up to my breast. I politely moved Darryl's hand away.

"What's wrong?" Darryl whispered.

"I can't do anything with Jeff in the next room," I replied.

Darryl reached over and caressed my breast again as he kissed the back of my neck.

"Darryl, no."

"C'mon, Mya. I'll be quiet."

"No, I wouldn't feel comfortable."

"Jeff is drunk on his ass. He's not about to get up."

"No, Darryl. Can't you just hold me instead?"

Darryl took a deep breath out of frustration as he wrapped his arm around my waist.

Within minutes, he was asleep and breathing heavily on my neck.

I stayed up all night, tossing and turning, thinking about Jeff in the next room. Darryl began to snore loudly as the smell of alcohol filled the room.

I closed my eyes, trying to concentrate on sleep, but a burning sensation in my stomach made it impossible.

Finally, I got up and went into the bathroom in search of medicine of some kind that could help me settle my stomach. I looked around for several minutes but couldn't find anything but toothpaste, mouthwash, and bathroom cleansers. *Maybe some water will help my stomach*, I thought.

I turned on the faucet and drank several handfuls of water before sitting down on the edge of the bathtub.

From where I was sitting, I could see what looked to be medicine bottles in a shaving bag on top of Darryl's sink. I got up and looked at each bottle. *Hmmm, what's this?* I thought as I looked through each one. *Darryl Cooper, 2211 Tonlours Dr., Marietta, GA. Take one Tarka pill with a full glass of water . . . I can't take this. I can't take this one, either,* I thought.

I walked back inside the bathroom, taking deep breaths, and sat on the edge of the bathtub again.

With my head down, I stared at the floor until I felt myself getting dizzy and breaking a sweat. Suddenly, I felt a lump form in my stomach that began moving up toward my chest to my throat. *Oh, God*, I thought. I rushed over to the toilet and dropped to my knees, letting out a loud roar as I threw up my insides.

My heart started racing and I began to have hot flashes on my neck and face. After flushing the toilet, I got up and walked over to the sink, where I splashed water on my face and rinsed my mouth out. *Damn, I never should have drunk that wine and eaten that greasy food*, I thought.

I sat back down on the edge of the bathtub again with my head down. I felt a little better, but I needed to lie down again.

I got up and slowly walked back into the bedroom to a snoring Darryl. I got under the covers, lying on my back, and softly rubbed my stomach in a circular motion until I drifted off to sleep.

I was awakened early in the morning by the smell of bacon that made my stomach quiver. I rolled over to Darryl, but he was gone. Minutes later, he came inside the bedroom with a tray in hand.

"Good morning, sleepyhead," Darryl said, walking toward me "I made you some breakfast."

I sat up as he put the tray in the center of the bed. "Thanks, but I don't think I have much of an appetite. The wine or something I ate last night made me really sick."

"All you need is something in your stomach. That'll make you feel better."

I looked at the tray filled with small plates of eggs, bacon, grits, toast, and two glasses of orange juice. I reached over and grabbed a piece of toast and ate it. My stomach began to quiver and a lump began to form. I grabbed the glass of orange juice and took a couple of small sips. I felt the lump begin to follow the same path as before, up to my throat. I quickly jumped out of the bed and ran to the bathroom again, throwing up.

When I looked up, Darryl was standing at the door with an odd look on his face.

"Damn, Mya. Are you okay?" he asked.

I ignored him as I released another roar with my face in the toilet.

"I'll be back. Let me get you a Sprite to settle your stomach," Darryl said before exiting.

I got up and rinsed my mouth out once again before walking back into the bedroom and getting into bed. Darryl appeared with a can of Sprite.

"Here, drink this. It should settle your stomach." He handed me the Sprite.

I sat up and took a sip. I could feel the cool liquid flow down my throat into my empty stomach. Within minutes I felt a little better than before from the cold, bubbling sensation.

"Darryl, I just need to go home and get into my own bed," I said.

"Oh, okay. But why don't you wait a while until your stomach is settled," he suggested.

"It feels much better now. I just want to be home in case it starts again."

Darryl paused before finally nodding in agreement.

I got dressed and headed out the door. Jeff was up, watching TV and eating what looked to be grits and eggs. I got into Darryl's truck and we started on our way to my town house.

Minutes into the ride, Darryl's cell phone rang again. Without looking at the number, he silenced the call. He looked over at me as I slowly closed my eyes. *He must've read my mind*, I thought.

CHAPTER 34

Stephanie

Curtis came walking through the door just as I was serving dinner. I was surprised to see him home so early. He entered the kitchen and placed his lunch box on the counter.

"Hey, baby," he said, then walked down the hall toward the bedroom.

I nodded as I placed Brandon's plate on the table next to him. I opened the cabinet and grabbed another plate for Curtis's dinner. When I finished fixing our plates, I placed both on the table and waited for a moment for Curtis to come out of the back room before I sat down to eat. I was glad to see that he was home, because it had been a while since we had eaten dinner as a family. I got a bottle of beer out of the refrigerator and placed it next to Curtis's plate.

After several minutes had passed I got up and walked toward the bedroom. Before I got to the door, Curtis was walking out dressed in jeans and a sweatshirt.

"Where are you going?" I asked.

"I have to make a run with Cedric. He's taking some cars to South Carolina tonight. We'll be back early in the morning."

I stood there stunned for a minute before responding. "I thought you came home early to spend time with us."

"No, I'm getting five hundred dollars for this. Besides, I need the money."

My disappointment turned to anger as tears formed in my eyes.

Curtis walked past Brandon and kissed him on the forehead before grabbing his beer off the table and walking out the door.

I slammed my body in the chair next to Brandon and ate a spoonful of green beans from my plate with my other hand, covering my eyes so that Brandon couldn't see the tears as they flowed down my cheeks. At this moment I realized that I had finally reached my limit in this relationship. No longer could I stand by and live my life seeing Curtis two or three days out of the week. I was trying to do the right thing by getting back into church, being more of a mother to my child, and even trying to be a supportive girlfriend to Curtis. But he is just not trying to understand my efforts. *I can't take it*, I thought.

I watched as Brandon finished his dinner, then gave him his bath before I put him to bed. Later on that night, I got a glass of wine and took a hot bath before getting into my own bed. I called Mya, hoping she could give me some comforting advice, but all she seemed to talk about were her own problems with Darryl, and I wasn't in the mood to hear about that. I thought about calling Tangie, but I couldn't stomach her drama, either.

I put the phone in my lap as I sipped my wine and put it back on my nightstand table while watching TV. Suddenly I thought about Reggie. I never thought I'd feel so lonely that I'd want to call someone outside of my girls, but he crossed my mind. Throughout the short time I'd known him, his words seemed genuine, which is what I needed right now. *Fuck, it*, I thought as I dialed his number from my cell phone.

When he answered, I instantly felt guilty.

"Hello?"

"Uh, hi, Reggie," I replied.

"Sister?"

"Yeah, did I catch you at a bad time?"

"No, I'm just sitting here working on a crossword puzzle."

"Are you serious?" I replied as a smile came over my face.

"Yeah, I got it out of today's paper," he said. "Do you have it handy?"

"Uh, yeah, hold on one minute." I ran to the kitchen and grabbed the paper off the counter and dashed back into the bedroom.

I went through the paper until I found the puzzle Reggie was working on. He gave me the answers to the clues he had completed before we continued working on it.

I was having the best time. We often had friendly little arguments over an answer until we both agreed on one. I got up a couple of times to go to the bathroom and refilled my glass with wine as we completed the puzzle. Afterwards, we pretended to argue about who knew the most. The conversation took a turn when Reggie asked me about Curtis and why he wasn't home.

"You sure it's cool for you to be talking to me this late? I know if you were *my* woman, I wouldn't stand for it," he said.

"Well, Curtis had to work and he won't be home until later tonight."

"I understand—he's got to do what he got to do, huh?"

"Yeah . . . I guess I just wish we had a normal life. We hardly see each other sometimes, and I can't even remember the last time we had dinner out together."

"Well, have you said something to him about it?"

"When I try, it usually leads to an argument or he just ignores me altogether."

"Well, maybe it's your cooking?" Reggie joked.

Caught off guard by his comment, I laughed. "I was taught by the best."

"Yeah, and who might that be?"

"My grandmother and my mother."

"Well, I guess that does qualify. It's hard to meet a woman who is domestic. Either she can cook and can't do anything else or she can do any and everything but cook."

"Is that right? What was your worst relationship?" I asked.

"Let me see—oh, I dated this girl in college who was very possessive. She always thought I was cheating on her. She would have people follow me around or have girls call my apartment to see if I was cheating."

"Were you?" I asked, curious.

"Well, not at first. I did when I couldn't take it no more. That's when the problems started."

"What happened?"

"I came home from working all day at a painting company and when I walked in my apartment, it was completely trashed. She bent every piece of silverware I had into the shape of a horseshoe."

"Oh, my God," I replied, but I couldn't help laughing a little.

"Then she saturated my mattress with the fish grease that was on the stove from the night before."

"Are you serious?" I laughed harder.

Reggie began laughing, too. "When I went into the bathroom to get a towel, I looked over in the bathtub and saw my DVD, stereo, and TV submerged in water."

"Oh, no," I replied in total disbelief. "What did you do next?"

"I picked up my phone to call her but she'd cut my phone cord at the tip where it connects to the wall. So it was time to pay her a little visit. As I opened my closet door to change shirts, I noticed a pair of scissors lying on the floor next to a pile of clothes. When I turned on the lights, I looked up at my clothes and they were cut completely in half."

"What?"

"Yeah, one half was still on hangers and the other half on the floor. I was so furious that I drove to her apartment and started banging on the door, only to find that her dad was waiting on me with a gun."

"Wow. Then what happened?"

"Her dad and I got into an argument and her mother called the police. They threatened to take me to jail."

"Why? You didn't do anything," I said.

"I know, but my ex made up this story about me wanting to jump on her because she was pregnant."

"Well, was she?"

"She said she was and that I made her have a miscarriage, which we found out to be a lie. The next week I left school and never saw her again."

"Now *that* was pretty scary," I said.

"Yeah, and ever since that episode I've been very particular about the women I date."

"And rightfully so," I added.

"Now it's your turn," he said.

I looked over at the clock. "Oooh, well, look at the time—it's one-thirty A.M. I have to get up in a few more hours to teach."

Reggie laughed. "Okay—evading the question, huh? That's all right. I'll get it out of you next time."

We laughed, then seconds later there was silence.

"Reggie, thanks for your friendship tonight. You don't know how much I appreciate it."

"Anytime, sister, you know that."

"Good night," I said as I hung up the phone.

CHAPTER 35

Mya

Wednesday morning I woke up feeling sluggish. My body was aching all over and my eyes were bloodshot. I did the best I could with my hair and headed out the door for work.

When I arrived, I walked into the teachers' lounge and grabbed some bottled water before going to my classroom.

I sat at my desk and organized my papers for class. Tangie and Stephanie appeared shortly afterward and sat down beside me.

"Damn, Mya. You look like shit," Tangie said abruptly.

"Girl, I feel like shit. The food I ate at Crystal's party this weekend has me feeling and looking like this."

"Are you sure? I ate the same thing you did and I feel and look like a damn princess," Tangie joked.

Stephanie laughed. "I feel fine. I'm glad I didn't eat what you had."

"Maybe the food along with the wine I had didn't agree with me," I said.

"Here, I have some Visine you can use to clear your eyes," Tangie said, looking in her purse. It looks like you've been getting high all morning," she continued.

"Thanks a lot," I replied.

"Yeah, girl. And did you even *try* to comb your damn hair?" Stephanie joked.

"Girl, get yourself together before class starts," Tangie urged.

I got up and went to the bathroom and did what I could to make myself presentable before the bell rang.

The day seemed like it was just dragging. By the time my last class period ended, I was rushing out of my classroom into my car, heading home. When I got there, I jumped right into bed.

I slept so hard that I didn't even hear the phone ring. When I woke up, there was a message from Stephanie checking on me, and one from Darryl asking me to call him as soon as I could.

I got out of bed feeling much better as I walked downstairs to get some water. My appetite still hadn't come back and I was a little hesitant to put something solid in my stomach just yet.

I relaxed on the couch and called Darryl.

"Hello," he answered.

"Hey, what's up?" I asked in a soft tone.

"How do you feel?" Darryl asked.

"I feel a little better. I'm going to try and eat some soup later."

"Good, that may be what you need," he agreed.

"How was your day?" I asked.

"Well, not so good, I have to fly out tomorrow for a conference in Little Rock, Arkansas."

"What? Oh, no. For how long?"

"I'll be gone for a week and then I have to turn around and go to another conference in Cleveland for this new heartburn medicine coming out."

I got quiet with disappointment.

"Are you still there?" Darryl asked.

"Yeah, I'm here. Can you come by before you leave?"

"I don't know. I have people with me now. I'm already running behind and my plane leaves at five-forty A.M."

"Okay," I said sadly. "I guess I'll see you when you get back."

"Mya, don't be like that. I promise I'll call you every day, okay?"

"Yeah, I understand."

"Okay, I'm going back to the office and pick up a few more things, then run some more errands and I'll call you later tonight."

"That's fine," I replied.

I hung up and lay back on the couch. I was really disappointed that Darryl didn't even try to make an effort to come by.

I got up and went to the kitchen to heat up some chicken noodle soup. I went back into the den and ate as much as I could before I lay back on the couch again.

I was still feeling down and needed someone to talk to. I picked up the phone and called my Grandma LeVeaux. She always knew how to cheer me up.

"He-hello," she answered softly.

"Hey, Grandma. How are you doing?"

"I'm fine. Mya, is that you?"

"Yeah, it's me, Grandma."

"Lord, girl. How you doing?"

"Not so good. I'm trying to get over a stomach virus or something. I've been sick since Saturday."

"Oh, I see. Do you have the runs?"

"Aw, Grandma, no." I laughed. "I did throw up a couple of times, though."

"You did? Well, get you some flour, mix it with some hot water, and drink it before you go to bed tonight. That should settle your stomach."

"I had some soup earlier."

"No, baby. You'll be up shittin' all night eating that. You need something heavy like the flour."

I laughed out loud. "Grandma, you crack me up with your remedies. You know, I wish you had a remedy for men."

"Men? What for?" Grandma replied.

"I'm just tired of always feeling like I make more of an effort to make things work."

"That's because you fall in love too easily. Let them fall in love with you first and then you can learn to love them later. That's the problem with these fast-ass girls today. They think dropping their drawers is love. A man wants much more than that. Why, when I courted your grandfather, he couldn't even hold my hand, let alone kiss me."

I smiled. "Yeah, times certainly have changed since then, Grandma." I replied. "How was your day, by the way?"

"Good. The Lord let me live to see another one," she replied.

"What did you cook?"

"I made some red beans and rice, fried chicken, and some cabbage greens."

"Really, red beans with the spicy sausage?"

"Well, you know Grandma can't eat it spicy anymore but I did put some sweet sausage in it."

"Ooooh, Grandma. That was one of my favorite dishes."

She laughed. "Some of your cousins came by and ate with me."

"Oh, yeah? Who?"

"Lonnie, David, Jimmy, and his wife."

"Wow, you had a lot of company."

"Yeah. I see everybody but you."

"I know, Grandma. I'll be home for Christmas, I promise."

"I'm going to hold you to it, baby."

"Okay, Grandma. Well, I just wanted to say hi and tell you I love you."

"I love you too, baby," Grandma replied before hanging up.

I got into bed and tried to sleep but still felt a little queasy. Grandma was right. The chicken noodle soup only gave me the runs. I was in and out of the bathroom until midnight. Finally, I'd had enough. I got some warm water and mixed it with some flour before getting back into bed. Darryl finally called as I lay there rubbing my stomach.

"Hey, sorry to call you so late, but I'm just getting in," he said.

"Huh, yeah. That's fine," I replied softly.

"Are you still sick?" Darryl asked, concerned.

"Yeah, if I don't feel better by tomorrow I'm going to make an appointment to see my doctor," I replied.

"Yeah, you should."

"Where are you now?" I asked.

"I'm on my way home to get a few hours' sleep before I have to catch my plane."

"Okay—I'm going to try to get some sleep, too. I feel exhausted."

"Do that and I'll call you tomorrow and check on you when I get settled."

"Yeah, just leave me the name of your hotel in case I miss your call."

"Uh, well, just call me on my cell phone in case I'm out," he suggested.

"All right," I replied.

"Okay—good night, baby. I hope you feel better."

When we hung up I turned my head and before I knew it I was sound asleep When the alarm clock went off the next morning, I just rolled over and hit the snooze button. I was too tired to do anything else. My body was aching and I didn't have the energy to go to work.

I got the phone and called the service at the school and notified them of my absence so they could get a substitute teacher in before school started. *What I need is a full day of rest*, I thought as I closed my eyes.

That evening, my phone rang several times, but I was still too sick to answer it. I wasn't in the mood to talk to anyone, anyway.

About an hour later there was a knock at my door. I ignored it and rolled over on my side, staring at the wall.

The knocks got louder and louder until I couldn't stand it anymore. I got up and walked downstairs to my front door and peeked out the peephole.

"I see you, bitch, so you may as well open the door," a familiar voice shouted. It was Tangie standing there with a smirk on her face. "Mya, open this door," she said firmly.

Fuck, I thought to myself. I wasn't in the mood for company right now, but she knows I'm here. *I'll pretend that I was asleep and maybe she'll leave.*

I slowly opened the door, looking pitiful. Tangie was standing there next to Brandon with a grocery bag in her hand and Stephanie was walking toward the front door from her car.

"Girl, we were worried about you. We called you several times and got worried when you didn't answer," Tangie said as she walked inside.

"No, no, I'm fine. I was just asleep, that's all."

"Oooh, Mya girl. You don't look so good. Did you go to the doctor?" Stephanie asked, walking in behind Tangie.

"No, I'll have to schedule an appointment tomorrow maybe," I replied.

"Well, in the meantime, we brought you some soup and crackers to settle your stomach, some orange juice, and some wine for me and Stephanie to drink while we prepare it for you," Tangie joked.

I forced a smile.

"Well, you can have some wine, too, if you like," Tangie said.

"Yeah, maybe the alcohol will help you sweat. I hear that's a good thing when you're sick," Stephanie said.

"Guys, thanks, but really, I just want to be alone and go back to bed."

Tangie looked over at Stephanie.

"I do appreciate everything, though. But I just want to sleep," I continued.

"Girl, you've been sleeping all day and it hasn't done you any good. Trust me—eat the soup and crackers and then we'll leave," Stephanie insisted.

"Guys, I'm fine," I replied.

"Mya, don't make me turn into a grandmother on your ass about this," Tangie said.

I knew it wasn't going to do me any good trying to make up excuses for them to leave because their minds were already set on making me eat that damn soup. Besides, they are my girls and were just looking out for me. Instead I just sat in the den with Brandon while the two of them were in the kitchen preparing the food.

I turned on the TV to watch the news. Minutes later, Tangie and Stephanie came into the den and sat next to me on the couch.

"Here you go, girl. This will make you feel a lot better," Stephanie said, placing the tray of soup and crackers in front of me.

I smiled. "Thanks—what kind is it, anyway?" I asked.

"It's the real deal," Tangie said. "It's that beef vegetable soup from Progresso. You know, the kind that stays in your stomach and makes a turd."

I laughed as I blew on a spoonful of soup close to my mouth. Stephanie almost spilled her wine laughing.

We all watched TV as I continued eating my soup and crackers. I was glad they were there because it made time pass and I didn't miss Darryl as much.

My appetite was back because I managed to eat two bowls of soup and a handful of crackers. We sat in the den gossiping while Stephanie and Tangie finished off two glasses of wine apiece. Before we knew it, the time was close to ten o'clock. Tangie dozed off on the recliner as Stephanie and I continued talking till almost ten-fifteen.

"Tangie—wake up so we can go," Stephanie shouted.

Tangie's eyes opened slowly. "Huh, uh, yeah. I'm ready when you are," she said.

"Well, let's go, 'cause it's a little after ten P.M.," Stephanie replied. Tangie's cell phone rang as she stood up. A smile came over her face as she looked at the number. She seemed completely energized. "Hey," Tangie answered. "Huh? Oh. I'm over at Mya's house. She was sick, so we came by to look after her."

"Who is that you're telling my business to?" I asked sarcastically.

"Get some business first," Tangie whispered, covering the mouthpiece.

Stephanie shook her head. "Girl, let's go."

Tangie nodded as we all walked toward the door. Tangie hugged me as she continued holding the phone to her ear and walked out.

"Will you be at work tomorrow?" Stephanie asked.

"Yeah, I think I'm able to make it," I replied. "Thanks for everything."

"Girl, you know we've got your back."

I smiled.

I watched them as they backed out of my driveway before closing the front door. I walked into the den and put the dishes away before going upstairs to my bed.

I woke up feeling one hundred percent on the next day and ready for some bad-ass kids to teach. Each time there is a substitute teacher, my class gives them hell. I walked into my classroom to a big message on the board that read: "Get Well Soon." It threw me for a loop and made a big smile come over my face.

Mr. Ridgewell appeared in my classroom as I gathered my papers together.

"Hey, how are you feeling today?" he asked, walking toward me.

"Oh, I'm better. I think I just had a stomach virus or something."

"Well, good. Stephanie told me you were ill. I'm glad you feel well enough to come back to work. That sub they sent was terrible. I had to come in here two or three times to make sure the kids weren't driving her crazy."

"Oh, really?" I replied, surprised. "Well, I'll get on them about that today because they know better."

"Oh, no, no, no. That's all right—I took care of it," he replied.

"Yeah, but you shouldn't have to do that. I've told them that when I'm gone, how they act reflects on me."

"Well, I came in to make sure they didn't get out of hand," he continued. Tangie walked into my classroom. Mr. Ridgewell turned and stared at her as she got closer.

"Where is Stephanie?" he asked, smiling.

"I guess she's in her classroom," Tangie replied with sarcasm.

"Oh, okay. I have to ask her something," he replied as he walked out of my classroom. "You two have a good morning."

Tangie shook her head. "That man loves him some Stephanie."

"That's Mr. Wanna-be playa-playa," I replied, laughing.

"What was he talking about?" Tangie asked.

"Oh, he told me how my kids ran the sub crazy yesterday and how he had to come and put them in check."

"What? Girl, Mr. Ridgewell is lying his ass off. He kept coming in here flirting with your sub all day yesterday. When she and I talked in the break room she told me some of the things he was saying," Tangie said.

"Like what?" I asked, curious.

"Like 'Oooh, let me help you with this, let me help you with that. We could sure use someone like you over here at our school. You're so good with the kids. Here's my card. Call me if I can help you with anything.'"

I laughed.

"Girl, I wouldn't listen to that mess he's talking," Tangie continued.

"Oh, *I* see," I replied.

Stephanie came walking into the classroom, a disgusted look on her face.

"Why are you frowning?" I asked.

"Mr. Ridgewell came to my classroom trying to flirt again."

Tangie and I laughed.

"Yeah, he just asked about you," I replied.

"That man is so disgusting. Did you see the clothes he was wearing?" Stephanie asked.

"Girl, I wasn't looking that hard," Tangie replied.

"You can't help but notice those tight purple pants and that white shirt. Anyway, he kept trying to stand close to me so I could see his thang. Uhh, that's disgusting."

Tangie and I laughed harder.

The bell sounded for class as we walked outside to meet the kids for school.

Later that night I was really hungry. It would have been nice if Darryl was in town to grab dinner together at a nice restaurant. Instead I went home and cooked some baked chicken, yellow rice, and a green salad. I sat at my dining room table with the lights down and my candles lit and had a nice dinner, sipping on the wine Stephanie and Tangie left the night before. In the middle of my intimate evening, Darryl called me on my cell phone. I turned up the lights in the dining room as I answered.

"Hey, baby. How do you feel?"

"Fine," I snapped.

"Are you still sick?"

"Nope," I replied sharply.

"What are you doing?" he asked.

"Nothing—just having dinner alone, that's all."

"What's wrong with you?" he asked.

I was silent.

"Mya, what's going on?" Darryl repeated.

"Well, Darryl, where should I begin? Let's see. I'm sick as a dog and you can't even come by for a minute to check on me before you go out of town. I didn't hear from you yesterday, and now you call me tonight like everything is fine."

"Wait, what are you trying to say?"

"I'm not trying to say nothing. It is what it is," I replied.

"Damn, Mya. Did you ask me about my day? Did you bother to call me? C'mon, it works both ways. I'm under a lot of pressure at work. I can't do everything."

"Can't you make more of an effort, at least?" I asked.

"Damn, where is all of this coming from? I called to let you know I miss you and you come at me like I just don't give a fuck about you."

I was quiet.

"Look, I apologize if I'm not more attentive but you have to meet me halfway," Darryl continued.

"Yeah," I replied.

"I know I'm not perfect—"

"I'm not asking you to be perfect, Darryl. I just want you to be more considerate that's all. I needed you and you weren't there for me is all I'm saying."

Darryl paused. "Why does it always have to be me that's fucking up? I don't complain about your shit."

"What shit?" I replied, defensive.

"When you don't call, I don't take it personally," he said.

"I do call—you just never pick up the phone."

"You know what, Mya? You're making this argument too personal."

"Too personal? You're supposed to be my man and I can't get you to pick up the phone when I call. I've noticed how you ignore your calls sometime."

"Your man? Hold on, Mya. I thought we were taking it one step at a time."

"What do you mean?"

"Now you're labeling our friendship?"

"Friendship? What friendship? We got beyond friends when we were intimate," I replied.

"Hold up a minute—it's obvious we have a lot to talk about. Our understanding of this is completely mixed up," Darryl said firmly.

I stood there holding the phone, completely stunned. "What? How can you say that? What about all the time we spent together and the nights we—"

"We were enjoying our passion at the moment," Darryl interrupted.

Tears began to well in my eyes. "Are you out of your fucking mind? I don't 'enjoy passion' with a friend like that. I thought we had something special."

"Wait a second, Mya, slow down here. The times *were* special. We just never discussed anything further. Let's wait 'til I get back into town and talk about this."

"There's nothing to say. You have just made it clear to me that we have nothing. So fuck it," I replied angrily.

Darryl was silent. I began to breathe heavily as I wiped my eyes.

"Let's stop right now. I don't want to argue over the phone like this. I'm stressed and you're upset. Why don't we get some sleep and I'll call you tomorrow," Darryl suggested.

I was silent.

"Mya? . . . Mya?" Darryl repeated.

" 'Bye, Darryl." I hung up.

I stood there, holding the phone in disbelief. Seconds later, the phone rang again. I looked at the caller ID and it was Darryl calling back. I put the phone back in its charger and ignored the constant ringing.

Then I sat back in my chair as tears began to flow. I quickly wiped them away before they rolled down my cheek. *You know what, Darryl? You're not worth one drop of my fucking tears*, I thought.

CHAPTER 36

Stephanie

I was walking out of the Bank of America after putting the envelope Reggie had given me in the safe deposit box when he called
me on my cell phone. This was the first time either of us called the
other since we'd talked the other night.

"Hello," I answered.

"Hey, sister, how are you? Are you coming to the church tonight?"

"No, I have to go grocery shopping after I pick my son up."

"Oh, I wanted to see if you could put another package in the safe
deposit box for the bishop."

"Well, I can stop by the church on my way home and get it if you
need me to."

"No, I'll just put it in my office safe until I see you next week."

"Are you sure? 'Cause it's not a problem."

"No, it's not *that* important. It can wait . . . You doing okay?" he
asked.

"Yeah, I'm good. What about you?"

"I'm good, too. I'll be even better when I get this cast taken off
my leg."

"When is it supposed to come off?"

"I have a visit with the doctor on Friday. Hopefully he'll take it
off then, 'cause I can't wait to get back on the basketball court."

"Yeah, you'll just have to be more careful next time," I said.

"I'm going to take it slow. I just miss playing with the guys."

Reggie and I stayed on the phone from the time I left the bank until I picked up Brandon. From there I went grocery shopping and then home. As usual, Curtis wasn't home, so I started dinner, fed Brandon, gave him his bath, and we both sat in the den and watched TV as he dozed off. About an hour later Curtis walked through the door, making so much noise that it scared Brandon out of his sleep. I got up and put him to bed before going into my room to finish watching the end of a show on HBO. Curtis jumped in the shower. As soon as he came out of the bathroom, he went into the kitchen and heated up the dinner I had left for him on the stove. When he finished eating he joined me in bed.

"I am so tired," he yawned.

I ignored him and continued watching TV.

"What are you watching?" he asked.

I turned toward him. "*The Wire*," I replied.

He continued to make small talk, much of which I basically ignored. It was like we were strangers sharing the same bed. I had to think long and hard just to make conversation. I felt like he was doing the same, because he was talking about cars and what he worked on at the shop, which didn't interest me in the least. Finally, minutes before the show ended, Curtis was snoring.

When I got dressed for work the next morning, I turned and stared at Curtis as he lay in the bed asleep. I stood there and watched him for what seemed like hours, wondering what we had and what direction this relationship was heading in. I knew I loved him, but was my love based on the time we'd spent together or was it because of our child? I needed to know if I was *in* love with him. We don't spend time together, we don't go out, we barely make love, and when we do, there's no passion. We don't have a decent bank account and he doesn't have a decent job. Am I crazy to think this relationship could work out? I turned and stared in the mirror as I put on my lipstick. *Look at me*, I thought. I look pitiful. Look at my hair and how I wear it. Maybe I need to cut it or change the style. My face looks like it's breaking out. *I just look plain ugly*, I thought. I walked into the kitchen, got a cup of coffee, and walked out the front door to get the paper off the front porch. I opened it up to read my horoscope. *No more negative talk . . . Great things will happen if you start thinking positively. Sometimes you may have to push a littler harder,* it read. *This is so true*, I thought. *Right now my mind is so twisted*. I sipped my coffee and started thinking about my day. Minutes later, Curtis appeared in the kitchen and poured himself a cup of coffee before sitting down next to me at the kitchen table. I closed the paper, not wanting Curtis to see me reading my horoscope.

"I want to apologize to you," he said.

Confused, I looked over at him. "Huh?"

"I said I want to apologize to you."

"For what?"

"Well, I know our relationship hasn't been a bed of roses for you, but I promise it's going to get better."

"What makes you think something's wrong?"

"C'mon, Stephanie, I can see it in your eyes, by the way you act. Even in bed when we're asleep. You don't even let me hold you like I used to."

"It's *has* been strange lately, Curtis."

"I know, but it's going to get better. As soon as I get a few more jobs and can open my own shop, I can hire some people to work for me and then I can work the nine to five, and come home to you and Brandon so we can have dinner together and do things a family should do. Just bear with me a little while longer," he pleaded.

I took a sip of coffee. "Curtis, I know you're doing your best, and yes, sometimes I think you take us for granted. But why can't you just get a job at a local body shop and save money that way?"

"I would, but I won't be able to make the money I'm making now. Plus, they may not hire me because of my criminal record," he said.

Great things will happen if you start thinking positively, great things will happen if you start thinking positively, I kept saying over and over, reciting my horoscope while he was talking.

"I want a better life just like you do. I told Cedric that I would make a couple of more trips with him to South Carolina and that's it, and that I needed to spend more time with my family. I should have enough money soon to start buying my own tools and other supplies."

I reached over and grabbed his hand. "Okay, Curtis."

I know that wasn't much of a response, and I wanted so badly to give him my little speech about how selfish he's been. I let it go, though, because I know it took a lot for him to open up to me like he did.

He smiled and leaned over and kissed my cheek before getting up and getting back into bed. I finished my coffee and went into Brandon's room to kiss him before I left for work.

CHAPTER 37

Tangie

I stopped by Peaches's salon to pick up some pepper spray she'd gotten from her sister, who is a security guard at the Fulton County courthouse. After I told her about my ordeal with Todd, she went on about the level of potency in each kind of pepper spray and assured me that her sister had just the one I needed. I expected to see Walter tonight so I managed to get a perm, too. The stress I'd been through these last few days had my hormones racing and I was really horny. Just as I was leaving the salon, Walter called me.

"Hey, what's up?" I said as I walked to my car.

"Nothing much—about to head to the club to set up for my gig tonight. What are you up to?"

Just as I was about to answer him, Peaches ran out of her salon with my favorite bracelet in her hand.

"Hold on for a second, Walter."

"Girl, you dropped this in my chair," Peaches said as she handed the bracelet to me. "This is the third time you've done this. Next time, I'm going to keep it," she joked.

I gave Peaches an evil look as I got in the car and resumed my conversation with Walter. "Okay, I'm back. Uh, I'm just on my way home. Are we on for tonight?"

"I don't know yet. My wife's sister is in town so I think they're going to want to come to the show tonight."

"Really?" I replied.

"Yeah, my sister-in-law's husband is a Navy recruiter and is stationed in Memphis, so she flew in last night to see my wife."

"That's cool—I had a backup plan just in case," I lied.

"Well, I just wanted to hear your voice in case I don't see you tonight," he said.

"Okay—well, that was nice of you."

"Yeah, I think so, too. Well, let me go—I'll try to call you later if I can."

"Okay. 'Bye, Walter."

I hung up, very disappointed. I was looking forward to seeing him, but I guess that's the price you pay when you're just a fling.

When I got to my apartment complex, I slowly pulled into the parking lot and parked closest to the view of my bedroom window. I looked around before taking out my pepper spray, with my index finger on the trigger. I was ready for Todd's ass if he was hiding somewhere near my apartment. I put my purse around my arm and briskly walked toward the door. As I reached for the knob, I heard a sudden noise in the bushes behind me. Surprised, I jumped back and screamed while pressing down on the pepper spray.

"Ugggh," I yelled.

Suddenly I went blind for a quick second, and I rubbed my eyes to regain my vision. I dropped to my knees, trying to catch my breath. When I opened them I saw a cat jump out of the bushes. Suddenly my eyes started burning and I felt my throat begin to swell. I took deep breaths, trying to stay conscious as I staggered toward the door. When I managed to make it inside, I fell to the floor, rubbing my eyes repeatedly. I rolled over and crawled to the kitchen and pulled myself up enough to find the sink and dash water on my face. The cool water was only a minor relief as I reached for a paper towel to put over my face. I staggered back toward the door and locked it before slamming my body on the couch with the paper towel on my face. My eyes, throat, and face were burning as my heart raced out of control. It felt like I was going to die.

After about thirty minutes, I removed the paper towel from my face. The burning sensation seemed to have slightly gone away. I slowly got up from the couch and got bottled water from the refrigerator before going into the bathroom. I looked into the mirror and was in total shock. My face looked like someone had literally kicked the shit out of me. My eyes were bloodshot red and swollen around the edges. I took a sip of water but it was still difficult to swallow. *This is some potent shit*, I thought.

I jumped in the shower and let the cool water run down my face, hoping it could help reduce some of the swelling but that didn't do much good. Afterwards I spent the remainder of the evening on the couch with an ice pack over my face. Later in the night I got a call from Walter, who was at intermission at the club.

"Guess what?" he asked, surprised.

"What?" I replied softly.

"My wife is going to Memphis next weekend with her sister. She is leaving on Friday and flying back on Sunday, which gives us a chance to spend more time together. I have a gig that weekend, so how about meeting me at the club to start the weekend off right?"

My throat was slightly sore. "That sounds like a plan," I whispered.

"I don't understand. You don't sound excited."

"I am, Walter. It's just that, physically, I'm not feeling well."

"Ahhh, I wish I was there to make you feel better," he continued.

"I know—maybe you can do that for me next weekend. Trust me, you wouldn't want to see me right about now. My eyes are all swollen and I feel terrible."

"Okay, well, make sure you keep me locked in for next weekend. . . . Well, we're about to go back on. I'll call you tomorrow if I get a chance," he said, before hanging up.

I hung up, feeling a little bit better. I guess it was because I was finally going to get me some. I'm just glad it wasn't tonight.

After I finished watching *The Tonight Show*, I turned off the lights and headed for bed. Suddenly my phone rang. *Maybe that's Walter checking on me again*, I thought. Without looking at the caller ID, I answered.

"Hey, are you on your way home?" I said.

There was silence.

"Hello?" I said as I climbed into bed.

"Am I on my way home? You must have me confused with your other lover," the voice replied.

Oh shit, I thought. *It's Todd.* "Aren't you tired of playing games?"

"It seems like you're the one into games, fucking me while you're laying up with someone else."

"I don't play games, Todd, and I certainly don't play anyone else's, so for the last time, leave me the hell alone."

"Why don't you come outside and tell me that. I want to look in your eyes when you say it this time."

"Outside?" I replied as I got up and looked out my window.

Todd looked up in my direction as he sat on the hood of my car with a sarcastic look on his face. My heart began racing as I got up and ran to the den where I got my pepper spray. "Why are you outside my apartment, Todd?"

"Come outside and find out," he replied.

I hung up, only to get several other calls back-to-back until I answered. "Look, dammit, don't make me call—"

"Call who? The police? Go ahead."

"No, call some real brothers to come over and kick your ass."

"Are you fucking them, too?"

"Fuck you. Now I can see why your wife kicked your dumb ass out," I shouted.

He laughed out loud.

"And now you're going to bring that shit over here," I continued.

Suddenly Todd's laughter turned into a long, steady cry. I watched as he lay back on the hood of my car, throwing his arms wildly in the air. Suddenly he jumped back into his car and sped off. That really made me nervous because I'd never seen him react this way. I got really paranoid, so I placed two of my pillows in my bed to make it look like I was in there asleep. Meanwhile I slept on the floor between the couch and the coffee table in my sweatpants and sneakers in case he tried to break into my house again. He'd expect me to be in the bedroom, and then I could run outside to my car and get away.

CHAPTER 38

Mya

Each day that went by was more difficult. I continued to ignore Darryl's calls, but deep inside I was fighting the temptation to answer.

It was Saturday, and I needed to get out. I didn't want to stay home, knowing Darryl was in town and wondering what he was doing.

I suggested a girls' night out with Tangie and Stephanie at the Cheesecake Factory at Perimeter Mall.

After I went shopping for a couple of hours, we all met at Stephanie's house. We got a late start because she was waiting for Curtis to pick her clothes up from the cleaners. As usual, he arrived later that she expected and had his same crew of guys with him as he walked through the door.

"What's up, Tangie . . . Mya?" Curtis said as he walked in.

"Hey, Curtis," Tangie replied.

"Hey," I replied.

Curtis walked with his friends to the back of the house. Stephanie came out with a smile on her face. "You all ready to get your drinks on?"

"We *been* ready," Tangie replied as we exited the house.

On the way to the Cheesecake Factory, Tangie and Stephanie did all of the talking. I just sat back, staring out the window, thinking about what Darryl was doing at the moment.

"Hey, you know today is officially supposed to be our hair day," Tangie said.

"Oh, really?" Stephanie replied. "I forgot all about that. I need to do something with this hair of mine. Tangie, your hair looks fine."

"I know—I got it done earlier in the week," she said.

At this point, their voices faded out as I kept my eyes straight ahead.

"Mya? Mya? Girl, where is your mind?" Stephanie asked.

"Girl, your mind is running ninety miles north with no direction. Are you okay?" Tangie asked.

"Girl, yes. I'm fine."

Tangie kept on talking. Several minutes later, we made it to the Cheesecake Factory. There were crowds of people walking in and out of the mall and into the restaurants and sports bars surrounding it.

We parked in the middle of the parking lot, not too far from the door, and made our way inside.

"Damn, look at all these people in here. I hope we can get a seat," Stephanie said.

The hostess came over.

"Welcome to the Cheesecake Factory. Table for three?" she asked.

We nodded in unison.

"Smoking or nonsmoking?" the hostess asked.

"Well, it really doesn't matter, as long as we get a seat within the next five minutes," Tangie said.

"Well, there's at least a fifteen-minute wait for either smoking or nonsmoking," the hostess continued.

"That's fine. I can deal with that," Stephanie replied.

"Okay, what's the name?" the hostess asked.

"Oh, put it under Jackson," Tangie replied.

"Jackson . . . Okay, it'll be about fifteen minutes or so," the hostess said as she scribbled in her pad.

We all stood next to the glass counter and waited, watching others get seated. The glass counter is where all the different kinds of cheesecake were displayed. As Tangie and Stephanie stood by it admiring the flavors, I was admiring couples as they entered and exited the restaurant. Seeing this put Darryl back in my mind and the urge to call him began to build. I watched as couples sat close together, trying each other's dinner, laughing and enjoying one another's company. I remember times with Darryl like that over at his apartment.

"Jackson, table for three!" a voice yelled, breaking my concentration. I snapped back to reality. "Jackson, table for three!" the voice repeated, a little louder.

"Hey, guys. Our table is ready," I said.

We were seated in the middle of the restaurant, where we had a great view of the front entrance.

"Your waitress will be here shortly to take your orders." The hostess placed a menu in front of each of us.

We grabbed our menus and began looking them over. Seconds later, our waitress came over, full of energy with a big smile on her freckled face.

"Good evening, ladies. How are we doing? My name is Stacey and I'll be your server tonight. Can I start you off with something to drink while you look at your menus?"

"Yes," I replied. "Can I get a margarita and a glass of water?"

"Oooh, that sounds good," Stephanie replied, looking up, "I'd like the same thing."

"Frozen, or over ice?" the server asked.

"Over ice," Stephanie and I replied.

"And you, ma'am?" the waitress asked, looking at Tangie.

"Uh, do you guys have any drink specials?" Tangie asked.

"Yes, we have beer on tap for two dollars and also three-dollar martinis."

"Oh, good. Let me get an apple martini," Tangie replied.

"Okay, that'll be two margaritas over ice with water on the side and an apple martini."

We all nodded.

"Okay, I'll go and place your orders while you decide on your food."

We sat there in silence, reading our menus.

"Oooh, girl. Look at what just walked in," Tangie said. Then she pointed.

There were two females wearing tight jeans and boots with a lot of makeup looking like straight-up hooches. Men who were sitting with their wives glanced discreetly over at them as they passed by. Noticing the attention, the girls winked at some of the men they caught looking in their direction as they went to their seats. I kept staring at the girls, who obviously loved the attention, and saw one exchange smiles with a man whose wife had just walked away from their table. Apparently, Tangie saw the same exchange of pleasantries.

"See, that's the kind of shit that makes you think twice about marriage," Tangie said.

"Why?" I asked.

"Shit, you don't want that kind of girl around your man," Tangie replied.

"If you keep your man satisfied, he won't creep," I said.

"What! Girl, it doesn't matter how happy your home is, a man will be a man. If a nice piece of ass walked his way, I don't care if your household is like the Cleavers, she's good as fucked. At least one time," Tangie said.

Stephanie laughed. "So you don't think that men can be faithful?"

"Hel-l-l, no," Tangie replied. "There's no way. With women like those two girls walking around, it's impossible."

"Now, I totally disagree," I replied. "There *are* some good brothers out there."

"Where? They damn sure don't live in Atlanta," Tangie replied.

The server brought our drinks. "Have you decided on what you want to eat?" the waitress asked as she placed our drinks on the table.

"I think I'll just get some hot wings. I'm not very hungry," I said as I put my menu on the table.

The waitress looked over at Stephanie. "I'll get the sampler appetizer," Stephanie said.

"Okay," the waitress said before looking at Tangie. "I'd like the club sandwich and fries," Tangie ordered.

The waitress repeated our order before walking off.

"So, back on these hoes," Tangie continued.

"Girl, your opinion of men is so negative. You don't believe any man can be faithful?" Stephanie said.

"That's right. Enjoy the moments while you're with your men. Once they're out with their friends, they're cheating—trust me."

I picked up my drink and took a big gulp. Tangie's remarks put my mind back on Darryl.

"So you don't think a man can settle down and have a family?" Stephanie asked.

"Yeah, I think they can get married and have families, but settle down? Hell, no. When he's not with you, chances are he's cheating or has cheated at some point and time in his marriage."

Stephanie nodded. "Girl, you kill me with your bullshit."

"I second that." Stephanie and I tapped glasses.

"Okay. But remember, I've screwed married men who, up until Todd, never thought twice about leaving their wives for me. They cheat for the thrill. A wife's at home, thinking she has her Prince Charming, the man of her dreams, but if she only knew."

"So you're no better then those girls that just walked in, who, by the way, you know nothing about," I said.

"Yeah, I guess you're right. But there's one difference—I'm not trying to break up anyone's home. I don't play that. Once you get his attention, there are other ways of getting a brother's information before the night is over."

"And that makes it right, huh?" Stephanie said.

"No, not at all. But that's just me," Tangie replied.

"Think about what you just said, Tangie. That doesn't make any sense to anyone but you," I said.

"I wasn't with Todd for anything but that D. I didn't want his money, I didn't try to take him from his home, and you damn sure didn't see me sweating his ass," Tangie replied.

"Anyway," I said, "you'll never convince me that what you're doing is cool."

Tangie laughed.

We sat there sipping our drinks until the waitress brought out our food. My margarita was really good. After I finished my first one, I ordered another. In fact, we all ordered another drink while we continued to eat.

We continued to laugh and enjoy our night out together. Tangie shared her little ordeal with the pepper spray that had Stephanie and me rolling out of our seats. I must admit, I was having the time of my life.

As a couple of hours passed, I drank three margaritas and ate most of my wings.

Stephanie seemed worse than me after drinking four and a half margaritas. Tangie only had two apple martinis because she was the designated driver.

"Hey, are you guys ready to go?" Tangie asked.

"Yeah, I'm tired and it's getting kinda late," Stephanie said.

We left the restaurant, heading back to Stephanie's house. I was feeling really mellow by the time we pulled into her driveway.

"Okay, everybody inside," Stephanie said loudly.

"It's getting late—I need to go home," I said.

"Girl, you know you're not able to drive after all those drinks," Stephanie said.

"Yeah," Tangie agreed.

"Really, guys, I'm okay," I insisted.

"Okay, but I'm going to call you and talk you home the entire way." Stephanie said.

"Yeah, yeah, yeah," I replied as I walked toward my car.

I got in and drove off. Truthfully, I was a little tipsy but I wanted to get home and sleep in my own bed.

As soon as I got on the road, my cell phone rang.

"Yeah, Stephanie. I'm fine," I said as I answered.

"So, I'm still going to talk your ass all the way home. I don't see why you didn't just stay the night," Stephanie said.

"Where's Tangie?" I asked.

"Oh, she left right after you did." Stephanie said.

We kept our small talk going until I pulled into my driveway. "Okay, you happy now? I'm home," I said as the garage door opened.

"Okay, good night," Stephanie said before hanging up.

I parked in the garage and got out of my car, walking toward the mailbox in the front of the yard to get my mail.

Out of nowhere, a truck pulled into my driveway. Startled, I jumped back, looking at the truck nervously.

"Mya!" a voice sounded.

I took a deep breath in relief. It was Darryl. He got out of the truck and walked over to me.

"What are you doing here, Darryl? You scared the living shit out of me, pulling up like that."

"I'm sorry, but I had to see you. I've been waiting here all night, wondering where you were."

"Why?" I asked.

"I wanted to talk to you. I think we got off on the wrong foot and if we're going to act like this, we at least need to talk about it face-to-face," Darryl said.

I just stood there, looking up at him. My buzz still had me light-headed as I tried to stand still and stay calm.

"Well, can we go inside?" Darryl asked.

I took a deep breath. "Yeah, I guess."

We went inside and sat in the den. I was on one end of the couch, Darryl on the other.

"You look beautiful," Darryl said.

"You know, Darryl, don't," I replied, turning away.

I don't know if it was the alcohol, but he was looking really good. It was hard for me to maintain control of my feelings.

Darryl moved closer to me and grabbed my hand. My heart began to race out of control.

"Look, Mya. I know we've been through a lot. Uh, I think you're a really nice and beautiful woman, but—"

Before I knew it, I pulled Darryl close to me and began kissing him. When our tongues touched, I felt a tingle down my spine.

"Hey, Mya," he whispered.

I continued to kiss him on his neck as I took his jacket off.

Suddenly, Darryl turned me over and was on top of me. He began taking off my shirt and bra. I felt his mouth cover my breast, and his tongue began to move in a circular motion around my nipple. I moaned softly as Darryl continued to work his way down my stomach.

"Let's go upstairs," he whispered.

We got up and walked upstairs, throwing clothes on the floor as we made it to my bedroom. Darryl held me up as I staggered to the bed, then stood over me as he opened a condom. I closed my eyes as I felt Darryl penetrate me. When I opened them to look into his eyes, the room began spinning as pleasure filled my body. We both began to moan softly as we made love. Darryl opened my legs wide as he pushed himself deep inside of me.

I moaned louder at the feeling of his power. I began to feel my climax getting closer and closer. "Don't stop, don't stop," I repeated.

He began to move faster and harder.

"Uh, yeah. Oooh, ooooh," I shouted as I reached my peak.

Soon after, Darryl let out a loud moan.

I pulled him close to me. "I love you, Darryl," I said.

"What?" Darryl replied.

"I said, I love you so much," I repeated.

The last thing I remember was closing my eyes, falling fast asleep.

The next morning I woke up with a smile on my face. I rolled over with my arms stretched out, reaching for Darryl.

I moved my arms around and felt the pillows next to me. When I opened my eyes, Darryl was gone. I sat up in bed and let out a big yawn.

"Darryl!" I shouted as I got out of bed. "Darryl!" I repeated.

I walked downstairs to the kitchen and Darryl was nowhere in sight. I picked up my clothes from the night before, then walked over to the window and looked outside in the driveway. Darryl's truck was gone.

What the hell is this? I thought.

I walked over to the phone and called Darryl's cell phone but got no answer. I went back upstairs and put my clothes on the chair in the corner of my bedroom. I walked back over to the bed and lay across it, staring at the floor. The condom package was crumpled up next to the used condom at the front of the nightstand. Frustrated, I just held my pillow as I closed my eyes in thought.

CHAPTER 39

Stephanie

Even after our little chat the other day about trying to see more of each other, things between Curtis and me didn't seem like they were getting any better. After I left school, I was on my way to the church for the Wednesday night Bible study. I was excited, because tonight we were going to have a guest speaker talk about building your finances and getting out of debt, followed by refreshments in the church cafeteria. I had promised Sister Pattie I would arrive early to help prepare the decorations. As I walked into the cafeteria, Curtis called to tell me that Cedric needed to go to South Carolina and wanted to pay him double the usual money if he could go along with him on such short notice, and he had immediately agreed. I tried to get him to pick Brandon up from day care and bring him to the church, but he went on to explain that he had left hours ago without telling me and that they were minutes outside of South Carolina. He and I had a few words as I tried as much as I could to keep from using foul language on church grounds. I finally hung up on him. Instead of picking Brandon up, he took it upon himself to call me hours after he had already made the decision to go. I was so upset that I had to sit down and take a few deep breaths to calm my nerves. My child was at the school with no one to pick him up, and now I had to drive in traffic all the way across town to get him. As I walked over to Sister Pattie to explain why I had to leave, Mya called me. She sensed the anger in my voice as soon as I answered. When I explained my situation, she insisted on picking Brandon up and keeping him at her place for as long as I needed her to. Relieved, I went to the bathroom and put some cold water on my face to cool off for a minute before going back to help the other ladies with the decorations.

The church was packed. The guest speaker related debt to several scriptures and showed us how the Bible teaches us how to overcome it. The service lasted about an hour, then everyone assembled in the cafeteria. I looked all around for Reggie, but he was nowhere to be found. When I opened my purse to get my cell phone to check on Brandon, I noticed I had a message from him. I went outside to the parking lot and dialed Reggie's number.

"Hey, sister, how was the service?" he asked cheerfully.

"It was great, but you missed it. Is everything okay?"

"Yeah, I got the cast taken off, but my ankle is still sore. It was too painful to be on it for long, so I decided to stay home tonight."

"Well, I hope you feel better," I said.

"What I called you for is to see if you could stop by and pick up the bishop's papers to be put in the safe deposit box tomorrow. I told him I had already done it but I lied. Is there any way you could stop by my place tonight and pick it up? I would really owe you big-time."

"Uh, well, I'm at the church right now and have to help Sister Pattie clean up. Is it really important?"

"Well, it is, but if you can't come tonight, I understand," he replied, disappointed. I thought for a minute, realizing that Mya had Brandon, and Curtis wasn't going to be home until sometime in the morning. So I could stop by on my way to pick up Brandon.

"Sure, let me help Sister Pattie and I will leave soon after."

"Thank you, sister."

Reggie gave me the directions to his house. I left and minutes later arrived at his subdivision. When I drove through the neighborhood I admired what looked to be million-dollar homes. After turning a few corners, I pulled up to this huge house on a hill that seemed to sit higher than any house in the neighborhood. The gate was open on the side that led me to the back of the house. When I got out of the car, Reggie was on his crutches, walking toward the car from the back door.

"Hey, sister," he said.

"Hey, you have a beautiful house," I replied.

Reggie looked at my car and turned his head toward his driveway that was on the other side of the gate.

"Did I come in the right way?" I asked, confused.

"Well, this part is my private driveway to my garage. I forgot to close the gate behind me. Normally, guests come in and park in the front driveway," he explained.

"Oh, well, let me back out and park there."

"No, don't worry about it. You can pull up some more so that it'll be easier to turn around." He closed the gate, using a remote.

"Well, I am not going to stay," I said.

"Come in for a minute."

"Uh, I really need to be going. I have to pick up my son from my friend's house."

"Okay, I have the papers here on the kitchen counter," he replied, hopping away.

I followed him as we made our way up the back stairs and into this huge kitchen. I couldn't believe how beautiful his house was.

Reggie had two stacks of envelopes on the counter next to a glass of wine. He grabbed the stack and handed them to me as he sipped his wine.

"Wow, Reggie, your house is like nothing I've ever seen."

"Thanks—let me show you around."

I really wanted to see more, so I ran to the car and placed the envelopes inside before going back into the house. He walked back into the kitchen and refilled his glass. "Would you like some wine?" he asked. "They only sold three thousand of these in the world, and it's really fresh."

I looked at the way he sipped the wine, and the fact that it was rare piqued my curiosity. "Sure, I'll try a small glass."

Reggie and I walked through his house like we were touring a museum. He explained every piece of art, from who painted it to why he bought it and why he put it in that particular room. The bedrooms each had their own bathrooms and were bigger than my den. The basement had a huge theater, a workout room, and an indoor swimming pool.

By the time we made it back to the kitchen, Reggie took a seat on the couch and elevated his ankle grimacing in pain.

"Are you okay?" I asked.

"Yeah, it's just that my ankle is starting to hurt again." He sipped the last drop of wine. "Can you do me a favor? Can you bring me the wine from the kitchen?"

When I got the wine bottle, I noticed a huge pot of Alaskan king crab on the stove—it looked very tasty. Also on the stove was a simmering pot of jambalaya filled with sausage, shrimp, and chicken.

I walked back in the den and poured Reggie another glass of wine before putting the bottle next to his glass.

"How do you like the wine?" he asked.

"It's really crisp. I've never had this merlot before."

"Have some more?" he suggested.

"No, I have to drive home . . . I see you're a good cook, too."

"Yeah, I had just finished cooking before you came. You care to try some? I promise it won't kill you," he joked.

As much as my heart wanted to say no, my stomach took over. "Well, I'd love to try just a little. All they had at the church was cookies, cake, and punch."

Reggie directed me to where he kept his plates and utensils. I set the plates on the coffee table, where we sucked crab legs and ate jambalaya. He even convinced me to have another glass of wine. Before I knew it, we were doing the dishes and laughing like we had known each other for years. Reggie was so dramatic verbally that it almost put you in a trance. I'd never seen this side of him—sensitive, yet unique. The wine was starting to take effect as I stared at him more and more intently.

As I handed him the last plate to dry off, it slipped from my hand and fell to the floor, breaking into pieces.

"Oh, shii—Reggie, I am so sorry. Here, let me clean this up," I said as I bent down to pick up the glass pieces.

"No, sister, don't worry about that. I'll just get the vacuum cleaner and get it up."

"No, I can get it. I just need a broom for the little pieces," I said as I continued.

Before I knew it, a sharp piece of glass cut through my index finger—I let out a loud scream. The blood began to trickle between my fingers as I jumped up and put my finger in the sink and began running cold water on it. Reggie came back into the kitchen and grabbed a towel to wrap around my finger.

"Hold this while I get the first-aid kit from upstairs," he said.

He struggled to move with his crutches as the blood started to seep through the towel.

"Where is it? I can just run upstairs and get it. I know your ankle is hurting."

Reggie gave me the directions to the bathroom in his bedroom, where I found the first-aid kit in the medicine cabinet. As I stood there running cold water on my finger, once again Reggie appeared behind me. "Here, let me look at it," he said as he held my hand.

Reggie gently squeezed my index finger in the middle to control the bleeding and then applied some ointment to relieve the pain and treat the cut. Finally he wrapped my finger in gauze before tapping it at the end. I stood there, amazed at how gentle he was.

"Now, this should make it all feel better," he joked, kissing the tip of my finger. Before I knew it, I pulled him closer and we embraced in a long kiss. Our tongues touched as we kissed wildly and off beat until we got used to one another's rhythm. I was nervous and turned on at the same time, because it was the first time in years that I had kissed anyone other than Curtis. Reggie squeezed my body, pulling me closer to him. Before I knew it, we started backing up until we ended up in Reggie's bed, still keeping our kiss going. He reached for the buttons on my shirt and I moved my arms to give him easy access. I was in a trance and it felt good. I kicked my shoes off and spread my legs apart as he climbed on top. Reggie pulled up my skirt and I felt his hands slowly moving up my thighs. I let out a short whimper as he moved between my legs. He caught my panties at the top and gently began to pull them down. I felt his rock-hard penis against my leg as he moved his kisses down to my stomach.

Just as my panties made it to my ankle, there was a loud ringing of what sounded like chimes. I tensed up, caught off guard by the sound. We tried to ignore it but the ringing continued. "Wait one second. I don't know who could be ringing my doorbell like that this late at night," Reggie said as he grabbed his crutches and hopped away.

I lay in bed with a smile on my face, waiting for Reggie to come back and take me. It was as if this moment has been building ever since we met. I pulled my skirt off and tossed it neatly on the floor next to my shoes, then got under the covers with nothing on but my bra and shirt.

Suddenly, I heard yelling downstairs, and I sat up in bed. Minutes later, the yelling started to fade away. I got up, put on my panties and skirt, and tiptoed into the hallway. The yelling seemed muffled as I walked to the edge of the steps. I continued on until I got to the door to Reggie's basement. I could hear Reggie and another male arguing back and forth. The door was ajar, so I opened it slightly to listen more clearly.

Reggie started cussing and made threats like nothing I'd ever heard. Then I heard a third voice in the background that sent a chill down my spine. I would know this voice anywhere, and to confirm it, I walked down the steps and peeked around the corner for a closer look.

"Oh shit," I said under my breath. Curtis was standing there next to another guy with Reggie's finger in his face. My knees got weak as I tried to walk quietly back upstairs to the main floor. Once I did, I darted upstairs and grabbed the rest of my things and rushed out the door. I fumbled with my keys, trying to find the right one to open my car door, but dropped them in the grass. I got down on my knees, rubbing my hands through the blades until I found them. When I got the car started, I backed up, only to stop in my tracks because the gate was closed. I got out of the car and rushed back toward the house, praying that they were still in the basement. When I made it to the back door, I stopped and peeked through the window and saw the gate remote next to Reggie's keys on the kitchen counter. I opened the back door, grabbed the remote, and ran back to my car, opening the gate as I backed up, then tossing the remote in the yard. I sped down the street until I got on the main highway heading toward Mya's house. When I got close, I was a nervous wreck. I called her to let her know I was around the corner and to have Brandon waiting at the front door. I pulled up in the driveway, composed myself, and got out of the car, walking quickly toward the front door. Before I could knock, Mya opened it, holding a sleeping Brandon in her arms. "Thank you, girl. Sorry it's so late, but I got hung up at the church," I lied.

"You could've let him stay the night instead of having to drive way over here," Mya said.

"It's no problem. I really appreciate it. I owe you big-time," I said, then turned to leave.

I got in my car and turned my cell phone off. I didn't want to talk to Reggie under these circumstances, or in case he told Curtis I was at his house. I needed to calm down first and gather myself. When I felt more at ease, I drove away.

When I made it home, I didn't see Curtis's truck in the driveway, so I rushed inside, put Brandon in the bed, and got in the shower. By the time Curtis came walking through the door, I was lying down, wide awake. My heart was racing and I was terrified. I don't know what they were arguing about but it had to be something really bad. *I wonder if Reggie told him about me. If so, I'll deny every damn word*, I thought.

Curtis came toward the bedroom and stood in the doorway. I reached over and turned on the lamp. He had a look on his face unlike any I've ever seen. "Stephanie, we need to talk," he said in a somber voice.

Tears began to well up in my eyes. I was surprised at how calm he was. I started thinking of a lie as I got out of bed and headed toward the kitchen. Curtis was sitting at the dinner table with his head down. When he looked up at me, he had tears in his eyes. *Oh, shit*, I thought. I said a small prayer from the time I pulled the chair out until I sat down in it. Then I took a deep breath and looked Curtis in the eyes.

"I can't believe this shit is happening to me. Stephanie, tonight I've lost everything. I mean everything, over some bullshit," he continued.

I clenched my teeth and began rubbing my hands together nervously.

"Cedric set me up," he said.

Shocked, my heart dropped and a lump formed in my throat as I tried to swallow it. "Say what?"

"Cedric set me up. He had me thinking that the trips to South Carolina were all for his auto repair business, when in fact they were a cover-up to run drugs for his cousin."

"What?"

"Tonight on our way home from South Carolina, Cedric was speeding. When the cops got behind us, instead of him stopping, he sped up and there we were, in the middle of the highway, on a high-speed chase. This motherfucker has been trafficking drugs with me in the car the entire time and he knows I have a prior drug conviction. When we finally lost the cops, he turned onto a dirt road where we both jumped out and ran like hell. Afterwards he called his uncle, who later came to pick us up.

"When we drove back to the spot where we ditched the car, the perimeter was blocked and about ten police officers were all over the place. Some of the officers detoured traffic and others searched the vehicle. I later found out that the drugs belonged to Cedric's cousin, who threatened our lives if we don't come up with his money for the drugs."

I sat there, stiff as a board, in total shock. I tried as hard as I could to understand Curtis's pain but my mind was fixed on my own problems. It wasn't until after I took several deep breaths that I was able to pull myself together. I felt too guilty to be mad.

"How much?" I asked.

"Huh?" Curtis looked up at me, confused at my calmness.

"How much money are we talking about?"

"The entire stash was two hundred and fifty thousand dollars. I'm responsible for half and Cedric is responsible for the other half."

I got up and walked toward the stove, shaking my head in disbelief. Not just for his ordeal but for mine as well. "How much do you have saved?" I asked, turning toward him.

"I have about thirty thousand in cash . . . I can pawn my tools— they should be worth another twenty-five thousand."

"Curtis, that's not even half."

"I know . . . How much do you have?"

"I don't know, maybe ten thousand or so. But that's all the money I have in the world, Curtis. Do you have any other options?"

"The only other option is to give G-man fifty thousand in cash and continue to do runs for him until it's paid back. But if I do that, I risk going to jail for life."

"Who is G-man?"

"That's the guy's name. I met him for the first time tonight at his house."

"I don't know what to tell you, Curtis. This is all such a shock to me that I can't even think straight."

"Damn, all I wanted to do was provide for my family." Curtis slammed his hand on the table.

I looked at the hurt in his eyes, but felt completely helpless and unable to think about how I could comfort him because of the guilt that was eating me up inside. But I had to play the role of a loving girlfriend and figure out later how I was going to handle my situation with Reggie.

CHAPTER 40

Tangie

I met Walter at Level Three, a club in downtown Atlanta. I was casually late as I walked inside and stood near the bar and ordered a drink. Level Three is a club that has three floors with three different parties going on. I spotted Walter right away as he wooed the crowd with his saxophone solo. I took a sip from my drink as I walked toward the band. Walter spotted me and a huge smile came over his face. I acknowledged him, smiling in return before taking another sip from my drink.

Several guys came up to me wanting to dance but I politely refused. Instead, I stood in the same spot until the band took a break, at which time Walter and I went upstairs to the second level so we could get away from his brother-in-law and other members of his band. We sat at a table, where we chatted for a while. He was just as eager as I was to get our night started.

"I'll give you the signal when we're about to play our last song for the night. That way, you can leave and I'll meet you at your place," he said.

"Let's just get a room downtown. I'm still having issues at my place that wouldn't make the night as comfortable as I'd like," I replied.

"I can't do the hotel. I'm just not comfortable with that."

"Well, it seems like we have a problem."

"Well, not really. My wife is in Memphis until Sunday. We can go to my place," he suggested.

"I don't know about that, either."

Walter took my hand and rubbed it across his leg. I felt his penis grow in a matter of seconds.

"Damn," I said, under my breath.

"How about it? I'll even call my sister-in-law's house just to make sure she arrived," he replied.

I thought long and hard. Then I discreetly reached under the table once again and felt his huge bulge. "Hmmm—okay, but we can't keep doing that. You're lucky I'm horny as hell."

Walter laughed as he finished off his drink. "Let me get back downstairs. I'll give you the sign, then you can meet me at my house in about an hour. You still remember how to get there, right?"

I nodded as I finished off my drink and watched Walter walk away.

Later that night, after I got the signal for the last song, I left the club, heading to the liquor store to get a bottle of wine. While there, I took my time looking through the different types of Rieslings. When I found one I wanted to try, I checked out and headed to Walter's house.

I called as I turned into his subdivision, and once again, he suggested that I park in the garage. Walter was like a madman as we made love on the floor of his den. My clothes were scattered everywhere. My earrings even fell out as Walter tried one of his kinky positions. We didn't even get to the bottle of wine until I was about to leave. We drank it, mainly because we were both thirsty. But as usual, I left his place more than satisfied.

Once I got to my apartment, I rode around the complex until I saw one of my neighbors pull up. I got out, ran to my door, and entered my place. I went through my same routine and checked every inch of my apartment until I was convinced Todd wasn't there. I went into the bathroom and took a hot bath before getting in bed. Before I got comfortable, I peeked outside my window to see if I saw Todd lurking around my car.

For most of the night, I jumped at almost every sound I heard. I did manage to get a few hours of sleep and didn't get out of bed until almost ten o'clock. After a quick breakfast, I got dressed and drove to Burton's Detail Shop in Buckhead to pick up the stun gun. When I pulled up to the front entrance, Burton was outside talking to a few of his clients.

"Hey, baby," he greeted me.

I smiled. "What's up? Did I catch you at a bad time?"

"No, come on inside. I have your package for you," he said, trying to be discreet. I followed Burton to his office and took a seat as he opened his drawer and pulled out a small package and handed it to me.

"Be careful with this stun gun. It's the kind the police use and is guaranteed to put you on your ass for a while."

"That's exactly what I want." I took the package.

"Make sure you read the directions carefully before you try to use it," he said. I opened the package to get a better look at the stun gun.

"Hey, let me detail your car while you're here," he offered.

"Sure, is it free?" I joked.

"Baby, you can have anything I got," he replied, laughing.

I gave him my keys as he left his office. I opened the box, pulled out the instruction manual, and began reading.

Several minutes into reading the manual, I got up to get a drink of water. I walked down the hallway to the water fountain near the waiting room, leaned over, and took a few sips. As I turned to swallow my last drop, I spied a well-dressed gentleman sitting with his legs crossed, reading the newspaper. He looked very familiar. I stared at him for what seemed like minutes, trying to figure out where I'd seen him before. When he looked up, I quickly turned my head and walked back down the hallway to Burton's office. As I got back to reading my manual, it hit me where I've seen this man before. "That's Stephanie's friend from her church," I murmured under my breath. I got up and peeked down the hallway to see if I could see him from Burton's office, but I couldn't. When I walked back into the waiting room, he was gone. I looked outside and there he was, standing next to Burton and engaged in conversation. Seconds later, the guy got into a black Lexus and drove off. Burton came inside with my keys in his hand.

"Well, Tangie, you're all set." He handed me my keys.

"Burton, who was that guy you were talking to?"

"Why? I'm not good enough for you anymore?" he joked.

"No, I'm serious. Who is he?"

"Oh, that's G-man—he's one of my loyal customers."

"G-man," I replied, confused.

"Yeah, he comes here every Saturday to get his car detailed. Why?"

"My girl knows him, and when she introduced him to me I thought he looked familiar. What's up with him?"

Burton paused and looked around before motioning me into his office, closing the door behind him. "Tangie, you're my girl and you know I look out for you, right?"

"Yeah?"

"Well, you may want to tell your girl not to get involved with someone like G-man."

"Why, what's wrong with him? Is he gay?"

"No, he's one of the biggest drug dealers in the South. He's so large in the game that if he wanted to, he could have your ass killed right now."

My eyes widened in surprise. "Are you serious?"

"Hell, yeah, I'm serous. Half of my customers are dealing drugs. Why do you think I'm doing so well?"

"Damn, I need to tell Stephanie. I think she is feeling him."

"Don't mention my name and get me involved in any kind of shit. I'm just telling you that 'cause you're my girl."

"No, it's cool. I won't mention you."

Burton began giving me details of G-man's operations and some of the things he'd done to people. Shocked, I sat there until I couldn't stand to hear any more.

When I left the detail shop, I couldn't get out of the parking lot fast enough so I could call Stephanie. Before she could say hello, I started talking.

"Girl, I got some shit to tell you. I'm just leaving Burton's and I saw your boy from church in here. You know, the one you introduced me and Mya to."

"Who, Reggie?"

"Well, around the streets he goes by G-man, and girl, I heard he is one of the biggest dealers in the South. I know he's your boy and all, so whatever feelings you have for this brother, you'd better shut them down now."

"Girl, please. Is that what you called me for? Besides, I only see

Reggie at church. Whatever he does outside of that is his business. Don't call me with no shit like that."

I was shocked at how offended Stephanie had gotten and changed the subject right away. It was obvious that I'd struck a nerve, and knowing Stephanie for as long as I have, I knew something was definitely wrong. But I could tell this wasn't the time to find out by the way she reacted to the information I gave her.

CHAPTER 41

Mya

It had been two days since I'd last seen or heard from Darryl. In thinking more about that night, I was convinced that Darryl had been about to open up to me about his feelings but I spoiled it by turning the night into a sexcapade.

After work, I went home and called Darryl but got no answer. This time I left him a long voice message asking him to call me.

I don't know what I possibly could have done to deserve being ignored like this, but it was obvious that Darryl had issues with "us."

Later that night I called Darryl again, only to get his voice mail. I knew he was out of town, but he could've at least picked up the phone to talk to me. I was even more confused now. I tried to sort things out in my mind, but I needed some help. I felt really alone and needed some answers because my mind was too twisted to think rationally. How could a man treat you so nicely one minute, and all of a sudden turn coldhearted, like everything we had meant nothing.

I needed to vent, so I called Stephanie. Maybe she could be the voice of reason behind my problems.

"Hey, girl. You got a minute?" I asked, sounding desperate.

"Yeah, what's up?" Stephanie replied.

I took a deep breath. "Well, I don't really know where to start."

"Huh? Uh, hold on a minute. Let me go in this other room where I can hear you. Brandon has the TV up too loud in here," Stephanie said.

The noise from the TV began to fade as I held the phone in silence.

"Okay—now, what's going on?"

"Well, it's a long story. Can you call Tangie on the three-way?"

"Yeah, hold on."

Seconds later, we all were on the phone.

"What's up, Mya?" Tangie asked.

"It's Darryl," I replied.

"What about Darryl?" Tangie asked.

"Well, lately Darryl and I have been really having some problems about our relationship, or, as he puts it, our *friendship*," I said.

"I don't understand," Stephanie said.

"Wait, Stephanie, let her continue. I think I know where this is going," Tangie said.

"Well, all this time I thought we were a couple, but Darryl thinks this is just a casual friendship. We got into a big argument a week ago about this and I basically hung up on him."

"Why does he think you two are just friends?" Tangie asked.

"I don't know. After all, we've been intimate and shared special moments together. We did shit that you just don't do as friends."

"Umh, well, when was the last time you talked to him?" Stephanie asked.

"Last Friday, the night I got home from your house. Darryl pulled up in my driveway and begged me to talk to him. We went inside and before you know it we were in bed having sex."

"What? Damn, Mya. You gave up the goodies even after he made that remark about being friends?" Stephanie replied shocked.

"Yeah, I was a little tipsy and he was looking so good that I couldn't help myself. The next morning when I woke up he was gone. No good-bye, no nothing. His ass just disappeared like a thief in the night."

"Well, it's your fault," Tangie said.

"What? What do you mean, it's my fault," I replied, surprised.

"Just like I said. It's your fault. I told you from day one that you give in to this man entirely too much. Now you're feeling all out of whack because you're not a challenge to him anymore. A lesson learned, so move on," Tangie said.

"What? That's not it at all," I replied defensively.

"Wait, Mya. Tangie is just bitter. Misery loves company. She didn't mean it—"

"I'm not bitter," Tangie interrupted. "If I didn't care for Mya, I wouldn't bother to even comment on this shit. I just think she should let it go and move on."

"I don't, and I think you should let him cool off and hear his side of the story, Mya. But next time, keep your damn clothes on," Stephanie joked.

"What do you really know about this man, Mya?" Tangie asked.

"He's nice, he's successful, he's a loving person—"

"Yeah, yeah, yeah. He has a hook in his dick, he has a mole on his balls, give me a break. I mean what do you *really* know about this man? All men are nice when you first meet them."

"I don't know what you're asking, Tangie," I replied.

"I'm asking, what did you bother to learn about this man before you decided to sleep with him?"

"Uh, well—"

"Don't sit around feeling down and out. Go over to his place and confront him about this shit. Let him know how you're feeling. Take control and tell him about himself. If he's not willing to listen, then you would've gotten everything out of your system and just move on," Tangie said.

"Yeah, now I *do* agree with Tangie on that," Stephanie replied, "Go over and talk to him about it. You're not getting anywhere waiting on him to make the first move. So what, you made a mistake. We all make mistakes. But you still have time to make it right."

"Well, he's out of town now. But, I'll do it when he returns on Friday. Thank you guys for being there for me and listening to my problems."

"That's what friends are for," Stephanie replied.

"Yeah, you know we got your back, girl," Tangie said.

There was silence.

Maybe it *was* time for me to take control of my life. How dare Darryl try to control me? If Mohammed won't come to the mountain, then the mountain will just have to come to Mohammed.

* * *

Friday took its time getting here. I had gone over in my head everything that I was going to say to Darryl. I did, however, try to call him again on his cell phone but I got his voice mail.

I waited until around seven o'clock before getting in my car and heading over to his apartment. I figured he'd be home, relaxing from his trip. The butterflies in my stomach were really making me shaky. Tangie and Stephanie called my cell phone on my way to give me some last-minute encouragement.

When I pulled up to Darryl's complex, I drove around looking for his truck but it wasn't there. I decided to park in the back parking lot in a space closest to the stairway leading up to his apartment door. I could see his bedroom window and the side of his patio from where I was parked.

An hour had passed and still there was no Darryl. I sat in my car with my seat reclined with the radio volume low. The night sky was black as the street lights' bright rays covered the parking lot. Several cars and trucks came in but none were Darryl's. I began to grow frustrated as I sat there waiting.

Suddenly, my attention was focused on Darryl's bedroom as his light came on. I sat up in my seat and turned the radio off. My heart began to race. *His ass has been home all this time*, I thought. I got out of the car and walked up the stairs to Darryl's front door. I took a deep breath and knocked.

I waited but no one came to the door. Immediately I knocked again, this time a littler harder. But again, no one came to the door. I walked back downstairs and looked up at his bedroom window. The light was now turned off. I began to grow furious. I ran back upstairs and began knocking on the door even harder than the last time.

"Darryl, I know your ass is in there. Why don't you be a man and open this door?" I shouted.

I began to knock on the door again, hurting my fist as I hit it with all my might.

"Darryl! Darryl, open this door and talk to me!" I shouted.

Suddenly, the door swung open. "What in the hell is wrong with you, lady?" said a deep voice.

Frightened, I jumped back. The person at the door wasn't

Darryl, but a tall, dark-skinned man with a scary-looking frown on his face.

"I-I'm sorry, but I'm looking for Darryl Cooper. He lives here," I said. A woman standing in the background wearing a robe was staring at me angrily.

"No, you got the wrong place. Darryl doesn't live here. I do," the man replied sharply.

"That's impossible. I've been here several times with Darryl. This is his place."

"Lady, I've been living here for over two years and Darryl doesn't live here."

I took a deep breath in anger. "I don't understand what's going on, but Darryl and I spent time in this apartment," I said.

"That may be true, but he doesn't live here. He stays in my apartment when I'm out of town, and I'm tired of him bringing his shit to my place."

"What? You mean—"

"Yes, I mean Darryl doesn't live here."

I paused and looked away.

"Well, do you know where I can find him?"

"Look, lady, don't waste your time. I'm not going to tell you where he lives nor am I going to get involved with his personal life. The best thing for you to do is just go."

The man slammed the door.

I was devastated. My heart sank to my stomach as I began to hyperventilate. I took deep breaths, struggling to walk down the stairs to get to my car. When I got inside, I called Darryl's cell phone frantically. When I got Darryl's voice mail, I lost it. "You sorry-ass, lying, motherfucker! I just left the apartment and some man told me all about your ass. How could you be so dirty, you bastard! I hope you had your fun, you motherfucker," I shouted, then hung up.

I called Stephanie, out of control.

"Hello," Stephanie, answered.

"Ahhhh, that low-down, dirty motherfucker!" I shouted.

"Hello? Mya, what's wrong?" Stephanie asked, concerned.

"Lies—that motherfucker was lying to me the whole time," I continued.

"Mya, calm down. What's the matter?" she said.

"Darryl—he's being lying to me about everything!" I replied.

"Mya, Mya, hold on a minute!" Stephanie shouted.

I struggled to breathe. "I'm at the apartment where Darryl used to bring me. He told me that this was his place. When I knocked on the door, this man answered it and said Darryl doesn't live there— he just house-sits for him when he's out of town."

"And you believe him?" Stephanie said.

"Right now, I don't know what the fuck to believe. It's obvious Darryl doesn't care. He's not answering his phone or anything."

"Mya, where are you now?" Stephanie asked.

"I'm sitting in the parking lot at the apartment."

"Look, get out of there now and come to my place," Stephanie suggested.

"I need to calm down first—my entire body is trembling."

"Mya, get the hell out of there and come over here right now."

"Okay, okay," I replied. "No, I think I'm just gonna go home. I need to be alone."

"Go home and calm down. Tangie and I will be over at your place in an hour."

"You know what? I don't want to be alone. I'm on my way over," I replied.

"I'm here for you, Mya," Stephanie said before hanging up.

I composed myself and drove to Stephanie's house in complete silence. I just thought about every moment Darryl and I had spent with each other and how convincing he was each time. *I must be the biggest fool ever,* I thought.

When I arrived at Stephanie's house, Tangie was pulling up behind me. As I parked and got out of the car, Tangie was already at my door wearing a big tee-shirt, sweatpants, and house slippers. "What the hell is going on that I'm giving up some dick for?" Tangie said.

I closed my car door quietly and looked over at Tangie. "You were right," I said quietly.

"Huh? Right about what?" Tangie asked.

"About Darryl. He ain't shit, just like you said."

Stephanie opened the front door and Tangie and I walked in. "What's going on, Mya? Did you step to his ass like I said?" Tangie asked.

We headed toward Stephanie's den. Brandon was sleeping on the couch under a blanket as I began to explain.

"I went to his apartment and knocked on the door, but this man answered and said Darryl's ass doesn't even live there," I said.

Stephanie picked up Brandon and carried him to his room as Tangie and I sat down on the couch.

"What do you mean, he doesn't live there?" Tangie asked.

I paused.

"Mya, what do you mean?" Tangie repeated.

"She doesn't know for sure," Stephanie interrupted as she walked back into the den.

"I was there, Stephanie, and from the way the man looked at me I'm almost certain that Darryl doesn't live there," I said.

"Girl, you don't guess," Tangie said. "Didn't you investigate his ass at all while you were there? When you go over to a man's house, the first thing you do is look around. You check his mail when he walks into another room or look at pictures on the wall to see if his ass looks like those people. If I'm really curious, I'll ask his ass for a glass of water or some chips to see if he knows where things are. If he has to fumble around, chances are that's not his place. That's when I grab my shit and get the hell out of there."

"Come on, Tangie, she already feels bad as it is," Stephanie said.

"I'm not trying to make her feel bad. I'm just preparing her for next time," Tangie said.

"No, I'm cool. It is what it is," I replied. "I just wish I had one last chance to see him in person so I could cuss his ass out."

"Girl, forget that. He's not worth it. Just move on and find you another man," Tangie urged.

I looked down toward the floor. "Yeah, I guess you're right."

"Stephanie, do you have some wine or something. I'm parched," Tangie urged.

"Yeah, I could use a glass to calm me down," I seconded.

"Well, you need to talk about it and get the shit out of your mind," Tangie said. "That's always the best therapy."

Stephanie got some wine and put it on the coffee table along with three wineglasses and poured each of us a glass. I grabbed the one closest to me and held it to my lips for a moment before taking a sip. Stephanie and Tangie were going back and forth in conversation as I sat there reliving my night in my head.

It was getting late and we were pretty exhausted from talking all night. I just leaned my head back and closed my eyes. Tangie was in the chair across from me, curled up in a ball, and Stephanie was opposite me on the couch asleep with her hand still wrapped around the wineglass. I just put my feet up on the couch and dozed off again.

The next morning I was awakened by a banging noise outside. I sat up, stretching my arms as I looked around the room. Tangie was still asleep in the chair across from me, but Stephanie was gone. I got up and walked toward the window where the sounds were coming from and pulled back the blinds. There, standing next to a car, was Curtis, hammering on something under the hood.

I turned and walked toward the bathroom down the hall past Stephanie's bedroom. When I walked by her door, I saw her lying in the bed with covers around her legs and bottom. I looked in the direction of Brandon's bedroom, which was down the hall, and saw that his door was closed. I continued on to the bathroom.

When I came out and walked past Stephanie's door, she was sitting up in bed wearing a tee-shirt and shorts. She got up and I followed her to the den.

"Tangie's ass is *still* asleep?" Stephanie asked.

Tangie turned her head, facing Stephanie and me. "What time is it?"

Stephanie looked over at the clock on the wall. "It's seven-forty-five in the morning."

"What? Seven-forty-five in the morning? That early?" And who in the hell is making all that damn noise outside?" She wiped her eyes.

I grabbed my purse. "Well, I'm about to go. I want to get home and take a nice bath."

"You all right?" Stephanie asked.

"Yeah, I feel a little bit better now. Thanks," I replied.

"You don't want breakfast before you go?" Stephanie asked.

"No, I'll eat something later when I get home."

"I do," Tangie said as she got up from the chair. "I want some grits, sausage, and two eggs fried hard with cheese on them."

"Well, you better call it in and pick it up at the Waffle House around the corner, 'cause all I have is cereal," Stephanie laughed.

"Cereal? I *know* it's time for me to go, then. I'm not a cereal person. I got to have something that'll stick to my ribs."

Stephanie giggled.

"Mya, hold up—I'm right behind you," Tangie said as we both exited.

We walked to our cars and waved to Curtis standing at the end of the driveway before driving off.

I didn't go straight home. Instead I drove around the city for a while to clear my head. I passed the Martin Luther King Center, the Underground of Atlanta, and finally the Georgia Dome, then got on Interstate-85 North heading home.

When I pulled in the garage I looked at the clock in my car and noticed the time read one o'clock P.M. *Wow—I've been gone for hours*, I thought.

I walked inside, heading upstairs to my bedroom, and began getting undressed for a nice, hot bath. I ran some water while I brushed and flossed my teeth.

When my bathwater reached midway in the tub I dipped my toe in to check the temperature.

I sprinkled in some skin gel and let it melt as I got a hairpin and put my hair up before getting into the water. I slowly let my body sink in until the water covered every part of me, then closed my eyes, enjoying its soothing sensation.

I tried to keep focused on my bath but thoughts of Darryl kept running through my mind, depressing me. I opened my eyes, staring up at the ceiling. Suddenly the moment didn't feel relaxing—I began to feel uncomfortable and closed-in. The bath began to feel irritating and I became fidgety. I sat up and grabbed my towel off the rack next to the bathtub before standing and drying myself off. I went inside my bedroom over to my dresser and grabbed my undergarments, shorts, and a shirt.

As I bent over to put my towel in the laundry basket, I began to feel light-headed and short of breath. I quickly walked over to my bed and lay across it. My stomach began to growl a little as I turned on my left side. I needed to eat something, but I didn't have much of an appetite.

I rolled over again, trying to get comfortable on my right side. I reached over and grabbed the phone on my nightstand. *I need to talk to my mother,* I thought. *I need some of her encouraging inspiration to energize me.*

"God bless you," my mother answered pleasantly.

"Hey, Mom," I said.

"Hello, baby. How are you?"

"I'm okay. Just not feeling well," I said.

"Not feeling well? What's wrong?" she asked.

"I don't know. I'm just tired, I guess."

"Oh well, baby, are you getting enough sleep? You know how you are when you stay up late—cranky and irritable," my mother continued.

"No, Mama, it's not that. I just—"

"I wish you were here with me. Remember the fun we used to have together? I'm about to meet the ladies at the church for a lunch before going to visit some members who are ill. You remember Sister Johnson? You know, the one whose husband left her for their daughter's best friend's mother? Well, she had a nervous breakdown. It seems that her ex-husband and his new girlfriend are getting married, and the wedding is at our church. That's right—the new wife-to-be is going to become a member. When Sister Johnson saw this in the church bulletin, she went home and passed out. Lawd have mercy, the devil sure is busy."

I held the phone as my mother went on and on about other people's business. For a church-going woman, she sure could gossip.

"Well, Mya, get you some rest. I'm about to walk out the door."

"Mama, go on before you're late," I said dryly.

"Well, I'll tell your dad you called. He's at the church with the men's group. They're doing a mentor program for the kids today."

"Okay, Mama. Just tell him I said hi," I replied.

"Okay, baby, and remember, keep God in your heart so He can direct you down *His* path so you don't venture down the path of the devil. *Amen.*"

"Yes, ma'am."

"Okay, baby. Let me go and I'll talk to you later." She hung up.

I held the phone to my ear before calling my Grandma LeVeaux. The phone rang three times before she answered.

"Hello?"

"Grandma?" I replied cheerfully.

"Hello—Mya, is that you?"

"Yeah. What are you doing, Grandma?"

"I'm just sitting here talking to some friends of mine from down the street."

"Oh, I'm sorry, I can talk to you later if you're busy."

"Is everything all right?" she asked.

"Uh, yeah. I just wanted to say hi, that's all. Go ahead and entertain your friends. I'll call you sometime later in the week."

"Okay, baby." Grandma hung up.

I sat up in bed and took a deep breath. I was really feeling lonely with no one to talk to. It seemed like all the people around me were living their lives the way they wanted except for me.

I got out of bed and walked downstairs to the kitchen. I was still feeling light-headed but not as bad as before. I drank a glass of orange juice and ate half of a bagel before sitting on the couch in the den.

I fumbled through a number of magazines on the table for a while, then I turned on the TV but nothing could hold my attention. It seemed like the day was just dragging by.

I couldn't sit in here the rest of the day, feeling like I'm about to lose my mind, so I got dressed. I needed to get out and do something to get my mind running again. I drove to school and went to my classroom to straighten up for Monday. While I was there, I rearranged the bookshelves, moved some chairs to different areas of the room, and even managed to clean up a little. I washed my chalkboard and got rid of some old papers that were just lying around. I scrubbed each student's desk that was stained with paint. By the time I was finished, the night began to fall.

CHAPTER 42

Stephanie

Curtis had just arrived from South Carolina after making another drug run for Reggie. Every time he left the house I was terrified that he wasn't going to come back home. I would pace the floor, a nervous wreck until he called or walked through the door. In addition, I was really feeling guilty about going over to Reggie's house and letting myself get caught up in my own misery and self-pity. I should've been woman enough to control my emotions and not fall into such a lustful state.

Together, Curtis and I had managed to pay about forty thousand dollars on the one hundred twenty-five thousand he had to give Reggie for the lost drugs. The money was given to Cedric, who paid Reggie. According to Curtis, Cedric was the only one who was to contact Reggie—or G-man, as *he* knew him—for anything.

Throughout the week, Reggie had been calling, leaving messages, trying to find out why I left his house the other night all of a sudden and asking me to call him. I was hesitant because at this point, with all of the drama going on, I really didn't have anything to say to him.

Curtis and I were sitting in the den feeling depressed, flat broke, with no other options available for us to get more money. I don't think I've ever seen Curtis this down since we've been together, and never have I felt so helpless. The TV was on, but I don't think either of us was watching it. Curtis would often look in my direction like he wanted to say something, but would hesitate. Suddenly he grabbed my hand.

"Uh, Stephanie, I don't think I can do this anymore," Curtis said softly.

"Well, you don't have a choice, Curtis. Maybe after a few more runs it'll be over and then we can get our lives back."

"I don't think it's that easy. Look at us—the only other things of value that we have are our cars and this house."

I sat there speechless as anger started to come over me and I realized the financial state we were in. Reggie is destroying my life and he doesn't even know it. It was obvious that if Curtis didn't make his drug runs, Reggie would probably have Curtis hurt—or worse, even killed.

Curtis got up, grabbed his keys from the table, and walked outside. Seconds later I heard his truck start and he drove off.

I got up, walked into Brandon's room, and sat on the edge of his bed and watched how peacefully he slept. I burst out in tears. I had no clue what I was going to do. With me having the only income, we were in a lot of trouble.

Moments later I heard Curtis come through the door. He walked into Brandon's room, where he saw me sitting with the tears flowing down my face. Without saying a word, he dropped his head before walking off. I got up and went back in the den, where he was sitting in the dark, drinking a beer.

"I'm sorry, Stephanie. I'm sorry that you had to fall in love with a man like me. All I ever wanted was to make you happy and give you a good life."

"No, Curtis, we're going to get through this. We just have to pray," I said.

"Pray? I'm beyond prayer. We have nothing at all because of me. I can't even provide for my family like a real man should," he said.

"No, a real man would do something about this situation. A real man wouldn't give up. That's what you have to do."

"But this fool wants me to make drug runs for him twice a week and risk going to prison for the rest of my life."

"Well, you're already in prison if you give up. So just do what you have to do to get us out of this."

"I just need to know that you're going to be with me no matter what happens," he said.

"Curtis, like you said, we're a family and families stick together."

"So whatever happens, you're with me?"

"Every step of the way." I grabbed his hand.

I was trying to encourage him so he could get stronger. But deep down inside, I was losing control. I walked to my bedroom, grabbing my bills on my way, and started looking over them. Between my savings and checking account, I only had about five hundred dollars, and that was because I just recently got paid. Pretty soon the bills were going to start piling up and I might have to pull Brandon out of day care. I wrote a few checks and placed them in envelopes to send off the next morning. Afterwards, I lay in bed with my eyes closed, trying to figure out a way to pay the debt that Curtis owed Reggie. If I talked to Reggie, I risked the chance of him telling Curtis about our night together, and if I don't talk to Reggie, I risk losing Curtis to prison or even worse. Either way, it was a fucked-up situation. For now, I had to stop helping out at the church and try to get a job on the side tutoring or something to bring in some extra money. Maybe it's for the best because I didn't need to be around Reggie, knowing what I know about his secret life. I was amazed at how he could cover up his drug-dealer status by being a prominent figure in the church. His business as a real-estate investor was a pretty good front.

Since I was scheduled to help Sister Pattie with a clothes drive on Saturday, I knew I could tell her to take me off the list for future events. My thoughts were cut short as Curtis entered the bedroom and joined me in bed. He reached over and pulled me close to him and held me tight. I rolled over and gave him a light kiss on the lips before closing my eyes as we both drifted off to sleep.

CHAPTER 43

Mya

Days had passed and I was really going through withdrawal from not seeing Darryl, but I didn't let it show. I focused my thoughts on my career and my students. I spent a lot of time at the bookstore, sitting in the café and reading.

By the time I got home each night and took my shower, I had just enough energy to get to bed. My appetite faded as the days went by. I had already lost about ten pounds, and each time my head hit the pillow, I passed out like a light. My hair was a mess, too, and I just pulled it back and tied it up with a rubber band before going to work.

By the end of the week, it hadn't gotten much better. Saturday was the day for our hair appointment. I was really looking forward to this because I was ready to change my look. I wanted my hair cut really short into the Halle Berry-style of old. I felt a change in my hairstyle might bring a change in attitude.

Early Saturday morning I got up and met Tangie at her apartment. Stephanie was supposed to join us, but she had to do some work at the church.

As usual, Tangie wasn't ready. I waited for her to get dressed.

"Girl, you're going to make me miss my appointment," I shouted from the next room.

"We're okay. I just got off the phone with Peaches and she's just opening the shop," Tangie replied.

"What about Mary?"

"No. She's not there yet, either. From what Peaches said, she's the only one there," Tangie replied.

We drove off as I combed my fingers through my hair, feeling its length for what would be the last time.

"Tangie, how do you think I would look with my hair short?"

Tangie looked over at me. "How short?"

"I don't know. I was thinking something like the Halle Berry of old," I replied.

"You know, I think that would really be a good look for you. What made you want to cut your hair? Or should I say, who?" she joked.

"What do you mean, who? I just think I'm ready for a change, that's all."

"I'm just teasing, Mya. I think that would look really nice on you, and I think Darryl would love it, too," she laughed.

I forced a smile. I didn't think it was funny, because she was right in a way. I wanted a new look so in case I ran into Darryl somewhere he could see what he is missing.

"Good morning all," Tangie shouted as we entered the salon.

Everyone looked up and smiled and replied verbally or with a gesture. I walked over to Mary as she stood beside her salon chair.

"Hey, girl," I said, smiling.

"How have you been, Mya?" Mary asked.

"Oh—so-so, I guess."

"Really, is that good or bad?"

"You don't want to hear my drama."

Mary laughed. "So, do you want the usual? A wash and a trim?"

"No, I think I'll try something different. I want it cut kind of short. Something like Halle Berry in *Boomerang*."

"Oh, okay. You want to jazz it up a little, huh?"

"Yeah." I looked at myself in the mirror.

Mary combed through my hair, spraying it with water until it was straight. While this was going on I shifted my eyes over to Peaches, who was putting what looked to be a conditioner in Tangie's hair.

Minutes later, several more women came walking through the door and took seats.

Peaches had all of the TVs around the salon on BET, which was playing music videos. The volume was turned up loud enough to hear the music but low enough to still hear the people in the salon as they carried on various conversations.

Mary turned my chair around facing the mirror. I looked at my reflection and saw how long my hair was—past my shoulders.

Mary grabbed some scissors and began to cut. I closed my eyes as thoughts ran through my mind as to whether or not I was making the right decision. I got nervous and my hands began to sweat. The sound of the scissors echoed through my ears and around my head as she continued to cut away.

As Mary made her way around my head, she turned my chair back around facing the TV.

"Damn—Mary is cutting all that woman's hair off," someone whispered.

I cut my eyes in the direction of the voice. There were several women looking at me with their mouths open. I looked back over at the TV, where I focused my attention. Several minutes later, Mary touched my shoulder. "Okay, Halle, I need you to sit over here so I can wash out the loose hair," she joked.

I got up looking straight ahead to keep from looking into the mirror. I didn't want to see my hair until it was completely finished.

I sat down near the back of the salon as Mary reclined the shampoo chair far enough for my head to reach the sink. She began to lather and rinse my hair several times before adding conditioner. Mary then began to massage my scalp with her fingers, occasionally combing through it.

"Okay, let the conditioner sit for a while, then I'll wash it, roll it, and let you get under the dryer."

"Okay," I replied.

I grabbed a magazine from the rack next to me and began looking through it.

"Hey-y-y," a voice screeched, catching my attention.

When I looked up toward the door, there were two women walking in wearing scarves on their heads. It was the same two girls Tangie knew who were talking negatively about men. I think one's name is Shannon.

"Am I late? Where's Flo?" Shannon asked, looking over at Peaches. Flo is short for Florence. She works at the salon also, and has a chair in between Mary and Peaches.

"Oh, girl. Flo won't be here today. Didn't she call you?" Peaches replied.

"Hell, no, she didn't call me. Where is she? She is supposed to give me a perm and a trim. I have a date tonight. What am I supposed to do now?" Shannon yelled.

"Well, she was supposed—" Peaches continued before being interrupted.

"See, black folks, I tell you the truth. I specifically told her that I needed to come in early because I had plans tonight," Shannon shouted angrily.

"Well, let me see if she made it home yet," Peaches replied.

"Home? You mean she's somewhere out of town?" Shannon asked sharply.

"Well, uh, you see. Look, Shannon, I don't want to talk about Flo's business like that," Peaches said.

"What happened, Peaches? I should at least know *something* after dragging my ass out of bed this early in the morning!"

Everyone in the salon got quiet. Someone even had the nerve to get up and turn the volume down on the TV.

I slowly moved the towel from around my ears to listen as Peaches walked over closer to everyone.

"Well, you see, and don't say anything to Flo about this, but last night Flo's husband came home drunk as hell at like three o'clock in the morning, stumbling everywhere, waking her up. He walked in the damn closet, thinking it was the bathroom, and pissed all over the clothes and everything. Hearing this, Flo jumped up and they started arguing and cussing each other out. Flo said he turned to leave and she grabbed the back of his shirt to stop him and the shirt tore from behind halfway down his back. She said he had lipstick on the inside of his collar, and scratches on his back like he was in a fight with a damn bear."

Every mouth dropped as Peaches continued.

"Flo said they went to fighting. She said she hit his ass with everything that wasn't tied down. Then suddenly her husband James turned around and knocked Flo's ass across the room. Their son saw this shit and ran over to help Flo get up, but James's crazy-ass pushed him out the way and went to punching her over and over."

Their son grabbed the phone and called 9-1-1, and a few minutes later the police came and took both their asses to jail. Flo said her lip and eye are so swollen on the right side that she can barely see or talk."

"Ooooh-weeeee," someone shouted. "Now that's an old-fashioned ass-whipping."

"Oh hell, no," another girl shouted. "I know she's filing for divorce after that."

"It only takes a man one time to put his hands on me," Mary cut in.

"That's right. James better be glad she called 9-1-1, 'cause if that was me they would've been calling a medical examiner for his ass," Tangie added.

I sat there in disbelief. That was the craziest thing that I'd ever heard of. A man beating a woman like that is terrible.

"Well, damn. I didn't know all that shit had happened," Shannon said. "And I do feel sorry for her, but what about my damn hair? Can you do it, Peaches? How many customers do you have this morning?"

"I'm pretty booked. I'm getting ready to wash Tangie's hair and then I have about eight more heads to do."

"Shit!" Shannon hissed.

There was silence as Shannon stood there in thought.

"You can go next," someone said. "I'm just getting a wash and condition, anyway."

Shannon's face lit up with relief. "Girl, thanks—I owe you big-time. I'm supposed to be going out with one of the Atlanta Falcons football players tonight, and I need to look my best if I'm going to hook him."

Conversation persisted about Flo's situation—everyone was laughing among themselves, talking about the things they would do in her situation. To me, it was frightening to have a man beat on you like that.

When my hair was dry enough, Mary took the small rollers out and began to style it. The women in the salon stared as she combed through it. From the smiles I received by the onlookers, I was anxious to see the results.

"Oooh, Mya. I think you're going to like it," Mary said.

Minutes later, Mary turned my chair around and I faced the mirror. When I looked up, I couldn't believe my eyes. My hair turned out exactly the way I had imagined it. *I truly had the Halle Berry look!* A smile spread across my face. I stood up to get a closer look.

"Wow, Mary. You did a really good job with my hair," I said.

Mary smiled. "Thank you, Mya. I'm glad you like it. You made a good choice."

Tangie walked over to me. "Mya, you look great."

"Yeah, I like your hair," this girl sitting in the salon chair said.

"Thanks," I said and blushed.

When Tangie's hair was dry, we left the salon and headed to downtown Atlanta to grab some lunch.

"Girl, can you believe that story about Flo?" I said.

"Yes, girl. Flo and James fight almost every weekend. That's why Shannon was like '*so*? What about my hair?' James has been messing around on Flo ever since they started dating," Tangie replied.

"That's some strange love," I replied.

Tangie nodded in agreement.

"What do you want to eat today?" Tangie asked.

"I don't know, but I'm kind of tired of Buckhead. Let's go someplace like Lithonia or Marietta," I suggested. These were outskirts of Atlanta that had pretty decent eateries.

"Oh, you know what? I heard they've built some new restaurants in Marietta." Tangie said.

"Oh? Well, let's check those out. We may find a place we like."

We got on 75-North heading toward Marietta. When we came to Barrett Parkway, we exited and drove down the street, checking out the restaurants on both sides of the parkway.

"What's it going to be?" Tangie asked, looking at the different restaurants.

"What about Bugaboo's, farther up on the right?" I suggested.

"Bugaboo's? What kind of place is that?" Tangie asked.

"I don't know," I replied. "I've never been, just wanted to try something new."

"That's fine with me. I'm just hungry," Tangie replied.

I got in the far right lane, turned at the light off Barrett Parkway into the parking lot of Bugaboos', and went inside.

The inside didn't look like your typical restaurant. The theme was something like a safari, with pictures of camping equipment hanging on the wall.

"What do you think?" Tangie asked.

"Yeah, it's doable," I said.

We sat in the front near the entrance. As people walked by, I noticed a lot of women staring at me as their eyes shifted upward toward my hair. Even guys sitting alone stared over at me. The new look was definitely giving me confidence.

After lunch, I was stuffed. The restaurant had one of the best salads I've had in a while. I even managed to force down their delicious hot fudge brownie and ice cream. As we exited the restaurant, I noticed a shopping plaza not too far away.

"Hey, look over there," I said, pointing. "Let's see what kind of stores they have in Marietta."

"I bet they don't have any good stores," Tangie replied.

"It looks fairly new—they might have some good sales going on," I said.

I let Tangie drive because I was stuffed. She got back on the main street to get to the shopping plaza. When we pulled into a parking lot, we were disappointed to see everything but clothing stores. There was a Blockbuster video, a music store, and other little small businesses that sold things that didn't interest us.

"Girl, let's get out of Marietta. I knew there was a reason I didn't come here regularly," Tangie said.

"Yeah, you're right," I replied as I sat back in my seat.

We turned around in the parking lot to get back on the side street that would lead us to the highway. We sat there in a line of traffic waiting on the light to turn green. It seemed like the light would turn red after every third car, which began to irritate Tangie.

"What the hell is up with these traffic lights? It's going to take forever to get back on the highway," Tangie said with anger.

Minutes later, we began to move. Suddenly Tangie slammed on the breaks. "Will you go!" she shouted.

I looked up, startled at the sudden jerk. Tangie stopped about an inch away from the back of the car in front of us. Other cars in all directions started blowing their horns.

I get nervous when Tangie starts driving with an attitude. I began fidgeting in my seat, looking around in all directions.

Cars on the main highway started moving as some got into the turning lanes and yielded at the oncoming traffic heading in our direction. We began to move once again, closely behind the cars in front of us. I kept my attention on the cars on the main highway as we turned to help keep Tangie from being blindsided.

Suddenly my attention was focused on a truck in the turning lane directly across from us. "Holy shit! . . . Holy shit!" I shouted.

Tangie looked over as she swerved into another lane. "Mya, what's wrong?" she asked in a panic.

"Look, over there! It's Darryl," I said, pointing.

Tangie looked toward the left at the black truck. Darryl was sitting at the light, rocking his head to music without a care in the world.

"That *is* Darryl," Tangie shouted.

She turned on her right signal light.

"Why are you turning?" I shouted.

"Oh, we're going to stop his ass so you can confront him about his lies," Tangie said as she turned into a restaurant parking lot.

I got really nervous. This was happening all of a sudden, and I didn't really know what I was going to say if I confronted him.

My heart began racing out of control. "Girl, forget his ass. I'm over that."

"Bullshit," Tangie said. "There's only one way to get over this, and that's to deal with it. And that's just what we're going to do."

I took a deep breath and composed myself. "Okay, you're right," I replied with doubt in my voice.

I looked back and Darryl was still in the lane waiting to turn. Tangie was maneuvering her way through the parking lot, apparently to cut him off. When we rode behind the back of a small building, I lost sight of Darryl's truck. After we passed the building I looked over in Darryl's direction again and his truck was gone.

"He disappeared," I said, looking at the cars turning.

We both looked around as Tangie got closer to a side street.

"There he goes," she said, pointing. "Look—he's going down that street!"

Tangie put on the left turning signal and darted out into the street about two cars behind Darryl's truck.

"I'm on his ass now. Mya, you better get your words together, 'cause you are about to see him up close and personal," Tangie said.

I was trying to think of something to say, but my mind was blank.

Suddenly the car in front of us put on their left turning signal and had to yield to the cars in the opposite lane before turning.

"Fuck, fuck, fuck," Tangie yelled. "Keep your eye on his ass, Mya."

Darryl's truck disappeared as it continued down the street. The car in front of us finally turned as Tangie sped up.

"Do you see him, Mya?" Tangie asked.

"No, I lost him," I said, looking around.

Tangie slowed down and cruised past several neighborhoods. I looked up at the street names as we passed each one.

Suddenly, the street name "Tonlours Drive" appeared on one of the street signs. For some reason, that name rang a bell in my mind.

"Turn here, Tangie," I shouted.

Tangie sharply turned down Tonlours Drive. "Do you see him?" she asked.

"No, but the name of this street seems familiar to me."

Tangie slowly drove down the street while we both looked at each house carefully as we passed them by.

Suddenly we came to a house that had a bunch of cars in the driveway and along the front of it.

"Look! There's Darryl's truck," I said and pointed.

Tangie continued on past the house and turned around in someone's driveway. We drove back up to the house where Darryl's truck was and she parked across the street.

"Well, Mya. Here's your chance to get him straight," Tangie said.

"I don't know, Tangie. We don't know who lives here."

"Girl, fuck that. This man lied to you and treated you like shit. You shouldn't care whose house this is. This is a chance for you to get some closure."

I bit down on my teeth. "You're right. I'm just going to walk in and confront him about all his lies."

"Do you need me to go with you? 'Cause I got my mace and stun gun if his ass gets physical," Tangie replied.

"Uh, yeah, that would be a good idea, 'cause I don't know how he's going to react," I replied.

Without hesitation, Tangie got out of the car. I slowly opened my door and we began walking across the street into the driveway.

"Don't worry about anything, Mya. I got my finger on this mace," Tangie said.

We walked up to the door, where I paused for a moment and took a deep breath. Seconds later, I reached over and rang the door-bell. My heart raced uncontrollably as we waited.

Seconds later, I heard someone on the other end fumbling with the locks. When the door opened, we saw a brown-skinned, petite woman who looked to be in her thirties with black, shoulder-length hair wearing a party hat, smiling.

"Hello, can I help you?" she asked politely.

I cleared my throat. "Yes. Sorry to bother you, but I'm looking for a guy who drives that black truck. His name is Darryl Cooper. Do you know him?"

"Yes, I do," she replied as the smile disappeared from her face. "Is there anything I can do for you?"

"Well, no, thank you. I just want to talk to Darryl if I could, please."

"May I ask what this is pertaining to?" the woman asked.

"Well, I'd much rather discuss it with Darryl, if you don't mind," I repeated.

The woman paused and looked down at the floor. She looked up again at us with a mean look in her eyes.

Suddenly there was a voice behind the door. "Baby, hurry up. Everyone is ready for DJ to blow out the candles."

When the door opened completely, Darryl was standing behind it wearing a party hat and holding a young boy who looked to be two or three years old. When he saw me, he froze. You could have knocked him over with a feather.

"Darryl, do you know these ladies?" the woman asked.

"Uh, no. Well, uh, not really," he stumbled.

"What?" Tangie replied.

"Well, do you or don't you, Darryl?" the woman asked again.

Darryl got quiet as he put the baby down. "Go inside with Grand-ma, okay DJ?"

"No, DJ, stay *right* here with Mommy," the woman replied as she picked up the little boy.

"No, let him go inside," Darryl insisted.

"Darryl, are you going to answer me or not?" the woman replied sharply.

"No, but I will," I replied. "Miss, I don't know who you are—"

"I'm his wife," she interrupted sharply.

"Wife?" I looked confused. "Darryl, you never told me you were married."

"Baby, this is a misunderstanding. I met this woman when I was out with the fellas and—"

"You're a damn liar, Darryl," Tangie interrupted.

"No, baby, listen to me. We just—" Darryl struggled to continue.

"Look, I'm sorry to bring this to your home, but I swear to you, I didn't know he was married. Darryl and I met at a club and we dated for a while," I said.

The woman broke down in tears, shouting loudly. Hearing the commotion, people came from the back with confused looks on their faces.

"Dating? Darryl, is this true? How could you bring this kind of shit to your son's birthday party? What kind of man are you? You promised me you were being faithful. How could you do this in front of all my family and friends?" the woman screamed. Suddenly the baby started crying and an older lady walked over and took him from Darryl's wife.

"Would you all get the fuck off of my property?" Darryl shouted, looking at us as he reached over to console his wife.

"Get your hands off me," the woman said and pushed him away.

"Baby, I'm sorry, this is all a misunderstand—"

"There's no misunderstanding. I'm tired of your lies, Darryl. It's over. You hear me? It's over. I've had enough of your shit. I should've known you wasn't going to change after the first time you cheated on me," his wife shouted.

First time he cheated, I thought.

Suddenly, a lady put her arms around Darryl's wife and walked her inside the house as she continued her hysterics.

Darryl turned and walked in my direction. "I'm going to fucking kill you for this shit, Mya. You tramp! You were nothing to me but a piece of ass. How you just going to come to my house and fuck up my life like this?" Darryl reached out at me.

Several men jumped in front of him and held him back.

Tangie pulled out her can of mace and held it by her side as Darryl wrestled to get away from the men holding him.

"Ma'am, would you all please leave—I don't know how long we can hold him," one of the men said.

I stood there staring at Darryl, whose eyes were fiery red with anger. "Look, lady, would you please leave? You've done enough to hurt this family," the man repeated.

"Girl, let's get the hell out of here before somebody comes running out here shooting," Tangie said and pulled my arm.

We turned and quickly walked across the grass and back to the car before pulling off.

I turned around one last time in Darryl's direction as the men wrestled him to the ground in his front yard. Seconds later, Tangie sped off.

"Girl, can you believe what just happened?" I said.

"Ooooh-weeee, that was wild! I was standing there shaking like a leaf. But I kept my eyes on both Darryl and his wife, though. I just knew they were going to start swinging at one of us," Tangie laughed.

"Damn, I can't believe what we've done," I continued.

"What *we've* done?" Tangie replied, turning toward me. "It was Darryl's curious dick that got him in this predicament."

"Girl, he said he was going to kill me. Did you hear that? I was about to turn and start running for my life until the men grabbed him."

"I know, 'cause I pulled out my mace and held it by my side just in case he got away."

"I know one thing—I'm not going home tonight," I said.

"You'd be a fool if you did," Tangie replied.

"Do you mind if I stay with you the rest of the weekend?" I asked.

"Not at all. We'd better head to your house right now and get you some clothes. Ain't no telling if Darryl got loose and is on his way there before us," Tangie suggested. "God, wait 'til I tell Stephanie. She's never going to believe this shit."

CHAPTER 44

Tangie

It wasn't until midnight that I finally got to bed. Mya stayed at my place and we called Stephanie to tell her about our run-in with Darryl's wife at their child's birthday party. We laughed until Curtis came home and she had to get off the phone. I sensed that something was wrong with Stephanie, but I didn't want to bring it up over the phone. When I made some joking comments about Curtis, she seemed very defensive—something she hadn't done in a while.

I was glad that Mya was staying the night because with her in the next room I could finally get a good night's sleep without thinking about Todd trying to break in. Still, I had my mace under my pillow and my stun gun on the nightstand close to me.

Monday morning Mya and I rode to school together. I would've overslept if she hadn't decided to stay an extra day. I jumped in the shower and got dressed, then grabbed my watch and put it on as I rushed to the kitchen to fix a cup of coffee.

"Girl, will you hurry up?' Mya snapped.

"I'm almost ready—as soon as I get my bracelet and my keys I'm out the door." I grabbed my keys off the counter and rushed back into the bedroom to get my favorite charm bracelet, but it wasn't on my dresser. I looked in my jewelry box and even on the floor next to my bed but still I didn't find it. Suddenly I began to panic. This was the bracelet my grandmother had given me before she passed.

"Mya," I called out. "Do you see my charm bracelet in there somewhere?"

Minutes later she responded. "No, I've looked everywhere in here. Where did you put it?"

"Hell, if I knew that, I wouldn't be asking you," I snapped in return.

I looked at the clock and realized that we needed to be leaving in the next ten minutes. I walked back into the kitchen and grabbed my cup of coffee. "I'm ready," I said, annoyed.

"Did you find your bracelet?" Mya asked.

I gave her an evil look.

"I guess not," she said under her breath as she turned toward the door.

"I don't know—maybe I lost it trying to rush out of Darryl's yard the other day," I replied as I locked the door behind me.

While driving to school I kept trying to trace my steps but still couldn't pinpoint any possibilities of where I could've lost it other than over at Darryl's house. *Maybe it'll come to me later,* I thought.

During recess, I walked outside to my car to get some papers for my class when I noticed Stephanie sitting on the steps of the gymnasium alone, staring at the ground. Puzzled, I walked over toward her as she sat there in deep thought.

"Hey, girl, what are you doing sitting out here by yourself? Are you okay?"

She forced a smile. "Yeah, I'm fine. Just thinking, that's all."

"Whatever it is it must be really deep. Let me guess. Curtis, right?"

She took a deep breath and looked away. "Well, yeah, kind of, but more complicated than that."

"Do you want to talk about it? Because if you do, you know that I'm here for you, right?"

"Yeah, girl, I know. But it's nothing that I can't handle."

Suddenly Mya appeared. "Hey, I was wondering where you two were. What are you talking about?"

"Nothing. We basically just wanted to get out of the building for a while and think," Stephanie replied.

After school, as I was leaving my classroom, I saw Walter's wife coming through the door. She had her coat over her arm, and the outfit she was wearing made her look like she'd added another ten pounds to her chubby frame. We crossed paths and spoke as we passed each other by. She looked me up and down like she was admiring the way I was dressed or something, but we didn't stop to talk.

I walked into the teachers' lounge, where I turned and watched as she disappeared down the hall toward my classroom door. I walked over to my mailbox and grabbed my mail, then turned around facing the doorway where I saw Walter's wife and Tina coming from around the corner. They continued out into the parking lot, and I watched them as they got in the car and drove off.

When I got home I searched my entire apartment and my car for my bracelet. I was so upset that I couldn't find it that I was almost in tears. I tried retracing my steps for the third time, only to end with the same result: I must have lost it in Darryl's front yard, rushing to get out of there before his ass went postal. I called Mya and had her look in her car one last time just in case I missed some spots, but there was still no sign of my bracelet. I wasn't going to give up. I was determined to keep looking until I found it.

Later that night I got a call from Walter, who was leaving rehearsal. I was just getting out of the shower, trying to dry off. "I can't wait to see you again," he said.

"Yeah, speaking of which, I saw your wife at school today picking up Tina."

"Oh, really? She didn't mention to me that she was going to pick Tina up. She was supposed to be working until six o'clock. Oh well, maybe she got off early." As he continued to talk, I was blocking him out 'cause my mind was still on my bracelet. Suddenly I said, "Oh, shit, Walter, when you get home make sure you look around your house to see if I left my bracelet over there."

"What?" he replied. "Your bracelet?"

"Yeah, I can't find it but I'm sure I had it on this past weekend—or at least I think I did. Anyway, just look in your house just to make sure."

"It could only be in one of two places—either the den or the guest bedroom. I'll make sure I check it when I get home and call you right back." He added nervously, "Do you really think you left it at my house?"

"I don't know. Just check to make sure."

After we hung up I finished drying off and put on my pajamas before calling Mya to check on her. We only talked for about ten minutes because she wasn't feeling well.

Minutes later, Walter called again. "Hey, I don't think you left it here. I searched everywhere and I couldn't find it. Maybe it's somewhere else," he whispered.

I felt relieved because the last thing I needed was more drama in my life if his wife stumbled on it.

CHAPTER 45

Mya

After Darryl didn't contact me by phone over the weekend, I didn't feel like he was going to hurt me. After all, he had his wife to deal with. *Wife*, I thought. *I can't believe he was married all this time.*

That explains all the times Darryl claimed to be out of town. He was probably saying that because he was at home with his family. Even the times he didn't answer his phone, he was probably with another woman, or his wife was calling.

What an idiot I was, I thought. I need to just focus on me from now on and put all this mess with Darryl behind me.

The next day after school Mr. Ridgewell brought in a cake for one of the teachers' birthday. All the teachers met in the teachers' lounge and surprised Mrs. Hawthorne as she walked in from her classroom. Tangie cut the slices from the angel food, white-icing cake and placed them on paper plates while Mr. Ridgewell passed them out to us as we stood in line.

I didn't have much of an appetite, so I got a piece and wrapped it in a napkin to take home for later.

When I got home I sat in the den and graded papers before going into the kitchen to get something to eat. I got some bread, turkey, smoked ham, lettuce, and tomatoes and made me a sandwich. I put it on a plate and added some chips before going back in the den to finish my work.

After eating only three bites of my sandwich and a few chips, my appetite went away. I tried to force down another bite, and because I couldn't, I just threw the rest in the garbage and headed upstairs to my room. I sat down on the edge of the bed and turned on the TV and watched a couple of sitcoms before getting up to take a shower.

As I walked toward the bathroom, my stomach began to quiver. The food I had just eaten felt like it was bubbling around and pushing its way toward my throat. I turned on the shower and went downstairs to get a glass of water. When I returned to my room I felt short of breath with hot flashes around my neck after walking up the stairs. I got my face towel and ran some cold water on it and placed the towel on the back of my neck as I leaned over the sink.

After a moment of gathering myself together, I turned the shower off and lay across the bed looking up at the ceiling. Sweat beads began to form around my face and my heart began to flutter. I could hear the TV on in the background as I took three deep breaths to calm me down. Moments later I began to feel relaxed. I closed my eyes as my heart rate slowed down. Several minutes later, I began to drift away. The last thing I remember hearing was a commercial about tampons.

Suddenly, in the midst of dozing off, it hit me. "Oh, shit!" I shouted as I jumped out of bed. "Tampons! Fuck—my period! My period hasn't been on in over two months. Oh God!"

I paced the floor frantically. My body felt numb as tears began to fill my eyes.

"It can't be possible. It just *can't* be," I repeated.

I took a deep breath to calm myself and sat down on the edge of the bed, thinking back to my moments with Darryl. *We used condoms each time*, I thought. Then the details of our first encounter came to mind. "Oh shit! Oh no. The first time we were intimate, we didn't use protection. What the fuck was I thinking?"

I got up and paced the floor again, rubbing my temple. "God, I can't be pregnant. I just can't be."

I turned the TV off and got back into bed under the covers and began to shiver with nervousness. *But what if I am?* I thought. *I can't have no fucking baby now. How can I function in school around my students? Better yet, how can I face my parents with this shit? My father is the president of the Full Gospel. I can't ruin everything he's worked so hard to achieve.*

An hour had passed, and I was still in bed under the covers running scenarios through my mind about being pregnant. I cried so much that the tears drenched my pillow and my nose was so stuffy, I could barely breathe through it.

But what if I'm not? I thought as I came to my senses. *This may very well be the flu or a simple stomach virus. There's only one way to find out—a pregnancy test.*

I got out of bed and walked into the bathroom to wash my face. My face was puffy, and my eyes were bloodshot. I blew my congested nose and put on a baseball cap.

I walked back into the room and put on the sweatpants that were on the floor in my closet, then rushed out the door to my car.

I drove past the supermarkets I frequent—I didn't want to go there and be seen by people I see on a regular basis.

I kept on driving until I found a little mom-and-pop store several miles away. When I got out of the car, I put my sunglasses on and went inside. The store was small, with about three people inside shopping. It only had about two aisles, which would make my search a little easier.

As I walked down the first aisle, I passed the gum, potato chips, canned peanuts, and other snacks until I made it to the end near where the beer was stacked in the coolers.

I slowly turned down the second aisle, where I passed the detergent, paper plates and napkins. When I walked closer to the end of the second aisle, I saw the pregnancy tests in the corner next to the headache medicine. I reached down and looked through each one until I grabbed the most familiar box, the Easy Pregnancy Test, or EPT.

I blew off the dusty box as I looked throughout the store to see who was around before walking up to the register. The man behind the counter looked to be of Latin desent, which made me feel comfortable. *Good—someone I may never see again in my life*, I thought.

When I paid, I grabbed the bag and quickly exited the store and got into my car. My nervousness began to build, the closer I got to home.

When I parked in my garage, I sat in my car for a minute and said a quick prayer before walking upstairs.

I went into my bathroom and opened the box, placing its contents on the sink. I took out the instructions and began to read over them carefully. When I finished, I sat back on the toilet seat, looking up at the ceiling, and took a deep breath before grabbing the test instrument.

After going through the process, I placed the instrument on the sink to wait for fifteen minutes as instructed. My watch read six-ten P.M.

I got up and walked downstairs and lay on the floor quietly with my eyes closed. I started shaking nervously, thinking about the outcome. Minutes later, I glanced at my watch again. It now read six twenty-two P.M. I got up and walked upstairs toward the bathroom. I rubbed my sweaty hands together as I walked inside. *Well, this is it. Whatever the outcome, I guess I'll have to live with it.*

I leaned over and grabbed the instrument. *The instructions said that a plus sign means pregnant, and the minus sign means you're not.*

I brought the instrument close to my face and looked down at the result. "Ahhh," I screamed.

The instrument clearly showed a plus sign. I threw it to the floor and ran back to the bedroom, crying hysterically. I couldn't believe it. I'm fucking pregnant. *What am I going to do?* I thought. I began to cry loudly. Minutes later, I felt the sandwich I had eaten earlier start to come up. I rushed in the bathroom and buried my head in the toilet until I threw up. My stomach began to cramp badly as I felt my insides start to tighten. Afterwards I rinsed my mouth out with water and staggered to my bed and curled up with my pillow. My entire body began to ache as I lay there until I dozed off.

I couldn't sleep, often getting up in the middle of the night, running back and forth to the bathroom. My alarm went off, but I wasn't up to going to work and called in sick. I called Stephanie and told her I wouldn't be in because I wasn't feeling well, so she didn't think Darryl had something to do with my absence. Mentally and physically, I wasn't at all up to being in class all day and especially around kids.

I stayed in bed trying to gather my thoughts together as to what my next move would be. The day seemed long. Every minute that went by felt like years. I rubbed my stomach, thinking about the life that was being created inside of me. I always pictured my life with a husband before any kids would come. I tried to treat people like I wanted to be treated, thinking life would deal me the perfect poker hand. Instead, I was sitting here carrying a child by a man who was married and who didn't give a damn about me.

I couldn't tell anyone about this, not even my Grandma LeVeaux. For some reason, I think this would make her disappointed in me. I started feeling really dirty inside, not knowing what my next move would be.

Later that evening, while in bed sitting in the dark, my doorbell rang. *Who could that be?* I thought as I got up. I put on some shorts and ran downstairs and looked out the window. It was Tangie and Stephanie. Out of all the times they'd come over, this was the worst timing.

As I got closer to the door, the bell rang again. I took a deep breath and let them inside.

"Hey, girl. You played hooky today, huh?" Tangie said as she and Stephanie walked in.

I dropped my head as they both passed me. "I just wasn't up to it today."

"You know we had to come by and check on you. Plus, I'm in a good mood—I found my bracelet yesterday. Come to find out, it was on my desk at school under some papers. Do you have anything good to eat? I'm starving," Tangie rambled.

I composed myself and followed them into the den. "Yeah, there should be something in there."

Stephanie walked out of the kitchen with a glass of wine and sat down at the dining room table.

Minutes later, Tangie joined Stephanie, eating a sandwich and holding a glass of wine. "So Mya, what's up with skipping work today?"

Both Tangie and Stephanie looked up at me. I stood there frozen momentarily.

"Uh, just—"

"Is it that time of the month, girl, 'cause my cramps were kicking my ass a few weeks ago. I thought I was going to die," Tangie continued

I turned and walked away toward the stairway before turning

around and taking a seat on the sofa. I became fidgety, feeling really uncomfortable.

Tangie, noticing my nervousness, frowned. "Girl, what's the matter? You on crack?" she joked.

Tears flowed down my cheeks.

"Mya, what's wrong?" Stephanie asked, concerned.

"Did Darryl come by here or something and threaten you? 'Cause if he did, I'll call Burton and 'em to deal with his ass," Tangie said.

"Mya, what's wrong with you?" Stephanie sat beside me on the sofa.

I quickly turned my head. "Uh, nothing. Nothing's wrong, I'm fine," I responded. "I guess I'm just in an emotional mood today."

"No, you're not. What's wrong? Why are you crying?" Stephanie asked.

Tangie walked toward me. "I know you aren't crying over that sorry-ass Darryl."

"Tangie, stop that shit, okay?" Stephanie snapped. "Mya, are you all right?

I broke down, crying uncontrollably.

"It's okay, Mya. You can talk to us. What's the matter?" Stephanie grabbed my hand.

I took a deep, quivering breath as I turned toward her. "I-I'm pregnant," I cried.

"Oh my God," Tangie said softly.

"Pregnant?" Stephanie replied. "What? How do you know that?"

I wiped my eyes. "I just took a home pregnancy test and it came back positive."

"Uh, is it Darryl's?" Tangie asked.

I gave Tangie an evil look. "Of course it's Darryl's. I haven't been with anyone else."

"Sorry, damn. I'm just asking," Tangie replied.

"Where is the pregnancy test now?" Stephanie asked.

"It's upstairs in my bathroom somewhere."

"Tangie, run upstairs and get the pregnancy test, please," Stephanie asked.

Tangie put her wine on the coffee table and walked upstairs. Stephanie put her arm around me, trying to keep me calm, gently rubbing my shoulders.

Minutes later, Tangie came downstairs with the testing instrument in her hand. "Yep, she's pregnant all right. This shit is showing a dark-red plus sign."

Stephanie got up and looked at the instrument, then looked over at me. "Well, hey, Mya, don't fret. We're here for you, whatever you decide."

"What do you mean, whatever she decides?" Tangie replied. "There's only one decision to make."

"And what's that?" Stephanie asked.

"A fucking abortion," Tangie said.

"What?" Stephanie looked surprised.

"That's right." Tangie said. "She don't know this man well enough to be having his baby."

"Tangie, it's not even about him right now. It's whatever is best for Mya and the child," Stephanie replied.

"Look, Mya, all I'm saying is think about your future. Hell, I had an abortion one time and I'm doing pretty damn well because of it," Tangie said.

"Well, I thank God for bringing Brandon into my life. Because without him, I don't know where I'd be," Stephanie replied.

I stood up, wiping my eyes. "Look, I haven't thought about anything yet. This is all still a shock to me. I need confirmation from the doctor to be totally convinced that I *am* pregnant."

"If confirmation is what you need, then you have it right here. EPTs don't lie. Trust me—I know," Tangie continued.

"Well, after I see the doctor and find out for sure, then I'll decide what I need to do."

"Man, I can't believe you're making keeping this child an option. You just found out Darryl ain't shit. Plus, he's married with a kid, I might add, and you're letting your love for this man make you act like, like uh—"

"Like what?" I snapped.

"Like *this*—you know, fucked-up-in-the-head," Tangie replied. "I know a clinic downtown that can have you in and out in a couple of hours."

Stephanie put her arms around me. "Mya, go to the doctor and do what you need to do. Know that we're here for you no matter what decision you make."

Tangie paused, picked up her wine, and took a sip. "Stephanie's right. I just don't want to see you mess up your life for this dog of a man, that's all. But I'm here for you too, girl."

I nodded as I sat down on the couch. I felt a little relief after talking to my closest friends about being pregnant.

After going back and forth about my pregnancy for several minutes, everyone sat in different corners of my den in complete silence. It was like no one knew what to say next. I definitely was at a loss for words.

"Hey, I'm going upstairs to my room. I just need to be alone right now," I said. No one else said anything. They just nodded as I got up and headed toward the stairway.

Once inside my room, I closed the door, got back into bed, and put the pillows over my head. Later on in the night, Stephanie came upstairs to let me know they were leaving and would lock the door behind them.

The next morning I woke up feeling well enough to teach. Once I got inside my classroom, my mind stayed on my work. The day went on as usual and I was able to get a lot done. During lunch I called the doctor, trying to get the earliest appointment possible. There was an opening for Saturday morning at nine o'clock. I made the appointment.

That night, Tangie and Stephanie went out and had dinner and drinks. They wanted me to come along, but I wasn't up for it. I came home, showered, and got into bed. I was nervous about my upcoming appointment, hoping there was a chance the EPT was wrong. My body was aching as I tried to convince myself that the heartburn and nausea I felt was the result of something I had eaten earlier. But the fact of the matter was that deep down inside, I knew I was pregnant.

The next morning I got up at around six o'clock. I lay in bed for a couple of hours thinking about how I would react to whatever good or bad news I received. I said a small prayer before putting on a pair of jeans and a Louisiana State University sweatshirt. The drive to the doctor's office seemed long, although it was only five miles away from my house.

I parked, went inside, and walked up to the window to sign in.

"Can I help you?" the nurse asked.

I shifted my eyes over to a gray-haired nurse who looked to be in her late fifties. "Yes, nine o'clock appointment for Mya LeVeaux," I said.

"Okay, I just need your insurance card and a picture ID, please."

I gave the nurse my information and took a seat in the lobby. Minutes later, a few more women came in and walked up to the window. As one signed in, the others waited patiently in line.

"Ms. LeVeaux, here's your information back," the nurse said. "The doctor will be with you shortly," she continued.

"Thank you," I replied as I turned and walked back to my seat.

The women at the window all sat down near me and grabbed some magazines to read. My palms began to sweat as I rubbed my hands together. Several minutes passed by as I got increasingly restless.

"Ms. LeVeaux, the doctor will see you now," the nurse announced.

I got up from my chair, weak in the knees as I struggled to walk toward the second nurse standing at the door.

I forced a smile as I walked through the door. She had a light-brown skin tone and looked to be in her mid-to-early twenties. I followed her down the hall as we passed several examination rooms until we made it to the end. When we got to the last room, she opened the door and gestured for me to go inside.

"Have a seat, please, while I ask you a few questions," the nurse said.

I sat in a chair against the wall as I stared up at her. The nurse leaned over on the counter and opened a folder with my name on the outside tab.

"Okay, Ms. LeVeaux, what brings you in to see us today?" the nurse asked politely.

I took a deep breath. "Well, I've been feeling really nauseous and light-headed lately. Just last night I felt a burning sensation like heartburn around my chest."

The nurse began writing in the folder as I continued. "I ate something the other day that really didn't agree with me and I threw up."

"How long has this been going on?" the nurse asked.

"Oh, I'd say the first time was about three weeks ago."

The nurse nodded and continued writing.

"Okay, let me check your pressure," she said.

I rolled up my sleeves. Once the nurse finished, she wrote the results into my folder. "Okay, let me give this information to the doctor and she will be right with you."

"Thank you," I replied.

The nurse walked out and closed the door behind her. I leaned over with my elbows on my knees and stared at the floor. I could hear different voices outside the room as people walked by. I'd never felt so alone before in my life. I thought about my Grandma LeVeaux, and how much I needed her right now. *Maybe I should just leave and come back some other time*, I thought. *I can tell them it was just a simple case of the flu or something and that I feel better.*

I stood up and paced the floor, contemplating what to do. Suddenly, the door opened and the doctor appeared.

"Good morning, Mya," the doctor greeted me.

Dr. Hall stood about five-seven with a medium build. Her skin color was a dark red complexion similar to that of a Native American and her long black hair was in a ponytail down her back. She was one of the few African-American doctors in Atlanta who had mostly white patients.

"Good morning, Dr. Hall," I replied.

"Go ahead and take a seat on the examination table and tell me what's going on. I'm looking at your symptoms and I must say they suggest a number of possibilities," she continued.

"Well, to be honest, Dr. Hall, after the symptoms started reoccurring I realized that I had missed my period and decided to take a home pregnancy test. When I did, I received a positive result, in which case I felt I needed to come and see you for confirmation."

"That was going to be my first question. When was the last time you had your cycle?" Dr. Hall asked.

"Uh, I would say about two months ago," I replied, unsure.

"Well, that's not uncommon, in some women. So, let's do this—I'm going to have the nurse get a urine sample and we'll go from there."

I nodded as Dr. Hall walked out of the examination room. A couple of minutes later, the nurse reappeared. "Okay, Ms. LeVeaux, if you would follow me. We're going to get a urine sample from you."

I got up and followed the nurse to the bathroom on the other side of the doctor's office. "Okay, Ms. LeVeaux, take this cup inside.

Once you finish, put it on the rack next to the mirror and I'll take you back to the examination room."

I nodded as I entered the bathroom.

The wait for the results seemed like days. I put my head in my hand and began praying again to myself, this time pleading with God not to let the test results show that I'm pregnant.

Twenty minutes had passed. Then another ten. Finally I got up from the chair and stood against the wall. A few minutes later, Dr. Hall appeared in the examination room. Her expression was blank and hard for me to figure out. She gestured for me to sit down as she pulled up a chair close to me. "Mya," Dr. Hall smiled.

Seeing the smile, I felt a burst of relief.

"Let me be the first to congratulate you on your new bundle of joy. You are definitely pregnant," Dr. Hall said as she hugged me.

"Oh God," I said under my breath.

"As a matter of fact, you are approximately two months," Dr. Hall continued.

Two months, I thought.

As I sat back in the chair, it took everything I had to keep my cool. I was stone-faced as Dr. Hall continued talking about her kids and how she felt during her first pregnancy. I could tell she would've talked all day if she hadn't gotten paged during the course of her long story.

I left the doctor's office in complete shock. It wasn't until I was at home, sitting on my couch, that I came to the realization that I was definitely pregnant. Now what do I do?

CHAPTER 46

Curtis

I received a call from Cedric the night before that we had to take two cars to South Carolina to pick up some drugs. I would be in one car and a new guy who owes G-man some money was to drive the other. I was nervous because all of the other times we made the trips, Cedric and I did them together. I was curious why someone new was now involved. When I asked Curtis about it he just ignored my question and talked about the business at hand.

I tossed and turned in bed, thinking about the worst that could happen and how my freedom and my family were on the line. Cedric said that G-man had a major supplier from Miami who was going to meet us in Atlanta once we made it back from South Carolina. From there, I was supposed to move the drugs from my car to theirs, then return to the shop for further instructions. I got out of bed in the middle of the night and sat in the den, dripping with sweat. I was having a bad feeling about this trip and needed an excuse to get out of it. I walked into the kitchen and got a beer out of the refrigerator and stood in the middle of the floor, where I took three big swallows. I walked into Brandon's bedroom where he was sleeping and looked down at him, thinking about what it would be like not seeing my son again. My mind was made up. I wasn't going on this run tomorrow. I leaned over and kissed him on the forehead and walked back to my bedroom where I got back in bed. I reached over and pulled Stephanie close to me as I drifted off to sleep.

When Stephanie left for work, I rode to the shop looking for Cedric but he hadn't come in. I tried calling him on his cell phone but I got no answer. I needed to tell him that I wasn't going to make the trip tonight. I waited for almost two hours before deciding to leave. As I was walking to my truck, Cedric called me on my cell phone.

"Hey, man, I've been trying to catch you all day. Where have you been?" I asked.

"I had some work to do on the other side of town. What's up? You ready for tonight?"

"That's what I called you for. I can't do it tonight—I got some other things that came up."

"What? Man, G-man ain't tryin' to hear no excuses. He's about to clear your debt after a few more runs, so you can't back out now."

"I understand, man. But, I just can't do it tonight," I insisted.

"He's got a major deal going down, man. A lot of people got some serious money riding on this. You don't want to get him pissed off over some bullshit excuses."

"I know, man. But I—"

"But nothing, Curtis—have your ass there at six o'clock. You don't understand how G-man operates. I've seen him have brothers shot for double-crossing him. I'm telling you as a friend—make sure you show up."

I got upset. "Don't call me your friend, motherfucker. It's because of you I'm in this shit. Hear this—once I'm finished making these runs, I'm finished with your ass, too."

"Hey, whatever, man. Just don't be late." Cedric hung up.

I waited at home until Stephanie came walking through the door with Brandon. I had to see them before I left for the night. I followed her into the bedroom where she changed into something comfortable.

"Are you hungry?" she asked.

"No, baby, I'm fine. I won't be here, anyway. I have to make another run."

"What? Tonight?" she replied, concerned.

"Yeah, I'm about to leave in a minute. I just wanted to see you and Brandon before I left."

"What's the matter? Why do you look so nervous?"

"No, I'm fine. I'm just sick of doing this shit."

"Well, what time will you be back?" she asked.

"Hopefully, sometime in the morning, but I'll call you when I can."

I kissed Stephanie and went into the den and kissed Brandon as he sat on the floor playing with his toys. Stephanie walked me to the door as I got into my truck and pulled out of the driveway.

When I got to the shop, Cedric was standing next to two cars, talking to a man wearing a New York Mets baseball cap. I parked and walked over to them.

"Hey, Curtis, this is Lonnie Mitchell. He's going with you tonight."

Lonnie looked over at me with his hand extended. "What's up, dog?"

"Yeah, what's up?" I replied dryly.

Cedric tossed me a set of keys and directed me to a black Mustang before giving us instructions as to who we were to meet once we got to the car repair shop in South Carolina. As he did this, I noticed Lonnie taking sips from a bottle of liquor that he had in his jacket pocket.

"Yo, man—you may not want to be drinking while we handling business," I said.

"Don't worry about me, man. You just hold your weight. I got this over here," he replied arrogantly.

I looked over at Cedric, who laughed at Lonnie's comment. "Call me once you guys make it to South Carolina," he said.

I started the car and pulled off as Lonnie followed behind me in a 3 series BMW. When we got on the highway, Lonnie, who was to follow, took off ahead of me, driving extremely fast. I watched in frustration as he faded from my sight. I maintained the speed limit and cruised all the way to the South Carolina state line, at which time I saw Lonnie parked on the side of the road with his emergency flashers on. When I pulled over, I noticed Lonnie coming out of the bushes zipping up his pants.

"Hey, man. What the hell is wrong with you? Slow this car down. If you want to take a piss, pull over in the rest stop a few miles up the road and use the bathroom."

Lonnie laughed. "Man, chill out. We're okay. Besides, we're almost there."

Once we got to the shop, we exchanged money for the drugs and I put two keys in my car and the other two keys in Lonnie's car. As I tried to conceal the drugs in the trunk, I noticed Lonnie pull out a bottle and take another sip. Without saying anything, I just got back into my car and we drove off.

When we got back on the highway, I noticed a lot of police officers were patrolling interstates. I slowed down, paying close attention to the speed limit as I continued on. Lonnie sped up, passing a few cars in front of him, and got behind a pickup truck. I got over in the left lane to try and catch up with him. Before I could get close enough, he jumped in the fast lane, sped up, and passed the pickup truck in front of him. Suddenly a South Carolina highway patrolman came out of nowhere and turned on his lights. "Shit," I yelled as I watched nervously.

Lonnie sped up as he appeared to try and outrun the patrolman. He moved in and out of lanes, speeding really fast. I sped up just enough to see what was going on, but was soon forced to slow down when I saw another patrolman coming up from behind. I got into the right lane and let him pass as he sped down the street. I was really nervous as I pulled off on the next exit into a convenience store and got out of the car. I watched as two other police officers got on to the highway with their sirens on. "Damn, Lonnie," I said under my breath. "I hope they're not after you."

I walked to the back of my car. *I need to get rid of these drugs*, I thought. I waited a few minutes, trying to think of a place to ditch them. I looked around and saw a wooded area behind the convenience store, so I got out and ran over to it. I saw a pothole over a ditch near the corner closest to the highway. I ran in the convenience store and bought a box of trash bags and put the drugs in one and tied it to a hook under the manhole cover before getting back into the car and hitting the highway heading toward Atlanta. I was really nervous, but didn't see any patrolmen around as I continued on. A few miles down the road, I saw a road sign ahead that read GEORGIA STATE LINE 40 miles. I didn't see any sign of Lonnie on or off the highway. *Maybe I can turn off at the next exit so I can go back and pick up the drugs*, I thought as I began to calm down. I picked up the cell phone to call Stephanie. When I dialed the first digit of the telephone number, out of nowhere two patrolmen pulled up behind me with their lights flashing. With my heart racing out of control, I gently tapped on the brakes as the car began to slow down. When they got closer, one of the cars pulled up directly behind me and the other pulled in front and boxed me in. My hands began to tremble, so I tightly gripped the steering wheel to keep from swerving. I slowly pulled over as the officers rushed toward the car with their guns drawn. "Let me see your hands, now!" they shouted.

I held both my hands in the air as they opened the door and pulled me out, slamming me against the car. "What did I do, officer?" I asked desperately.

"Shut the fuck up and spread your legs," one officer shouted.

I spread my legs as one searched me and the other held me at gunpoint. Next, they handcuffed me and threw me in the backseat of the patrol car. "Are you going to tell me what you stopped me for?" I asked.

Suddenly another patrol car pulled up and parked next to the Mustang with Lonnie in the backseat. The officer got out of the car and pulled Lonnie out and walked him toward me. "Is that him?" the officer asked.

"Lonnie looked at me with an evil smirk. "Yeah, that's him. We were here to buy drugs. He has two keys in the back of his trunk under the spare-tire panel."

"Is that true?" the officer asked me.

"Hell, no—I don't know what he's talking about."

"Do you admit to knowing him?" the officer asked me.

"Not really—we just work for the same body shop," I replied.

"Then you don't mind if we search your car?" the officer asked.

"Sure, but it's not my car. It belongs to my boss."

The officer put Lonnie back in the patrol car as the other officer began to search the Mustang. One officer looked under the seats while the other looked in the trunk, taking everything out and putting it on the side of the road.

"I got something," one of the officers said.

He walked back toward me, holding part of a joint. It was so small that it could hardly qualify as marijuana. He rubbed it across my nose to confirm the smell.

"Take 'em in," the officer said.

The officer got into the patrol car and took me to the local police station. They placed me in one holding cell and Lonnie was put into another in a separate building. Later I was fingerprinted and a mug shot was taken before they put me in an empty room with a table and two chairs. I sat there for about an hour before two men dressed in suits came in. They introduced themselves as DEA agents and told me how Lonnie had identified me as part of a drug trafficking ring from Atlanta to South Carolina. He gave them details of how I paid him to transport drugs for the buyers where he would cut and distribute it to other dealers to be sold on the streets. I sat there, shaking my head in disbelief at the accusations, until they showed me a copy of my prior drug conviction.

"Look, I need to call my lawyer before I say anything. I told you guys that I didn't have any drugs and you continue to accuse me of this bogus trafficking charge."

"You want to call your lawyer? Go right ahead," one agent replied.

They took me to another room with a phone, and closed the door behind them, giving me privacy. I grabbed the phone and called Stephanie collect. When she accepted the charges, I could hear the panic in her voice.

"Baby, before you say anything crazy, I'm innocent and they have nothing on me. They're holding me over some hearsay shit, and I need you to find me a reputable lawyer here in the city of Aiken."

"What are you talking about, Curtis? What happened?" she asked frantically.

"Stephanie, calm down," I said.

"Curtis, you know we can't afford a lawyer. We barely have enough money to pay our bills. What happened? Are you okay?"

Damn, I thought. She was right. We just gave G-man every dime we had. There is no way I could afford to pay bail, not to mention a lawyer. "Call my mother and see if she can get the money to get me a lawyer."

Stephanie started crying. "Curtis, what happened?"

"I'm in jail here in Aiken, South Carolina. But I'm totally innocent."

"Aiken? Oh, my God. I'm on my way," she replied.

"No—wait, Stephanie, I need for you to help get me out of here. Try to find me a lawyer any way you can."

She calmed down enough to start thinking rationally. "I'll call around and see who I can find that can recommend a good lawyer for you there. Afterwards, I'm coming up to see you."

Seconds later, the DEA agents came into the room. "Time's up."

"Stephanie, see what you can do and I'll try to call you back later."

The agents quickly escorted me back to the cell where they left me for the rest of the night.

CHAPTER 47

Stephanie

I got up and called in sick and took Brandon to preschool before getting on the highway heading toward Aiken, South Carolina. Once I made it to the city limits, I pulled over and got directions to the county jail where Curtis was being held. I missed his arraignment earlier that morning where he was formally charged, and had to wait for hours before I was able to see him. I waited in a large room, sitting at a table where two guards stood at each exit, staring at me with a mean expression.

Minutes later, the door opened and Curtis came in with handcuffs, wearing a blue jumpsuit with the initials SCDC (South Carolina Department of Corrections) on the front right-hand pocket, being escorted by a guard. Seeing this, tears started rolling down my cheeks and I dropped my head. The guard guided Curtis to the table, where he sat down facing me.

"You have ten minutes," the guard said firmly before walking off to stand next to the other guards by the door.

"God, Curtis, what happened?" I asked, wiping my eyes.

Curtis looked over his shoulder, then back at me. "I don't know. Cedric got this new guy to drive for him who was drinking and shit during the run. After we made the pickup, he was speeding down the highway and got caught by a highway patrolman. I turned off on an exit and took everything out of my car and tossed it, then got back on the highway heading home. A few miles down the road, out of nowhere two patrolmen pulled me over and searched my car."

"But you didn't *have* anything if you got rid of it," I said excitedly.

"They claim they found a joint in the car."

"A joint? They're holding you for a joint? So, how much was your bail?"

"Bail was denied," he replied.

"Denied? For a fucking joint?" I yelled.

"No, this is about more than a joint. They found two keys in the other car that the new guy Lonnie was driving. He told them about me. He had to—that's why they pulled me over. Now Lonnie is telling all that he knows and I'm dead in the middle of this shit. The DEA agents are involved."

"Oh my God . . . Have you talked to anyone else?"

"I called Cedric last night to tell him where I was, but that's all. He was at the arraignment this morning and left soon after my hearing. By the look in his eyes, I could tell there was something going on. Did you get me a lawyer yet?"

"No, I haven't had a chance to talk to anyone," I replied.

"Then don't. Not yet, anyway. I'd rather take my chances in here than out on the streets where G-man can get to me. He probably thinks that I'm talking, too."

"Did they schedule a trial date for you?"

"Yeah, January 8," he said.

"That's three months from now, Curtis. You mean you'd rather stay in jail that long?"

"Hell, yeah. It beats getting killed somewhere out there in the streets."

Seconds later, the guard came back to the table where we were talking. "Time's up," he said.

I leaned over and gave Curtis a kiss before he got up from the chair.

"Go pick my truck up from Cedric's shop when you get a chance. Don't talk to anyone, okay?" he said as they escorted him away.

I sat there until they walked him through the door. I pulled out a tissue and wiped my eyes before going back to my car. I sat inside for a minute, trying to take in everything that was happening with Curtis.

Later, I pulled off, heading to Atlanta. Before going home, I decided to ride by the shop where Curtis's truck was parked. Maybe I could get Tangie to drive it home with the spare key on my key chain. I got off the exit and drove a couple of blocks down to the shop. Before I could get to it, I saw the streets blocked off and police cars everywhere. I turned onto a side street in view of the shop and parked as I watched officers search the building and cars on the premises, including Curtis's truck. "Oh my God," I said softly. Suddenly I saw Cedric and two other guys being escorted from the shop in handcuffs. I sped off before they could see me and headed to the school to pick Brandon up before going home.

While sitting in the dark, trying to get my thoughts together, Sister Pattie called me twice in ten minutes on my cell phone. A couple of minutes later, she called me once again. I looked at the phone and answered it on the second ring.

"Hey, sister, how are you?" she asked, sounding out of breath.

"Fine, Sister Pattie. How are you?"

"Look, the police just came by and arrested Reggie at the church. I'm trying to call all the members I can so that we can meet later and say a prayer for him."

"What happened?" I asked, trying to sound concerned.

"I don't know. They wouldn't tell us anything. They just stormed inside and arrested him. I can't believe they would do that to such a good man. Can you come down to the church in support for him?"

"Uh, yeah—I'll try to come later," I lied.

I got up and paced the floor. *The shit has really hit the fan now*, I thought. Within minutes, I got a call from Tangie.

"Girl, are you watching the news? They just arrested the guy at your church."

"I know."

"Hurry up—turn to channel 5 news," she said.

I turned on the TV and caught the end of the story about Reggie. They had him in handcuffs as they put him in the patrol car. DEA agents were all over the church as they searched Reggie's office. Another shot showed the agents at his home as officers walked in and out of his front door. The DEA spokesman wouldn't go into details about the arrest but I already knew what was going on.

I went into the kitchen and got a glass of wine and took one big gulp followed by one small sip as I walked toward the bedroom, where I stared at an empty bed. I took another sip as I stood in the doorway, realizing that Curtis wasn't coming home. Before I knew it, I lost it. I dropped the wineglass and screamed out loud, then dropped to the floor in tears.

Brandon ran down the hallway crying out to me as I tried to muffle the sound of my screaming. I grabbed Brandon and held him gently as he gradually calmed down. I had nowhere to turn and no one to talk to. *My girls*, I thought. *I need to call my girls*. Once Brandon was quiet, I let him get into my bed with me before picking up the phone and calling Tangie.

"Hello?" she answered.

I cleared my throat. "Hold on," I said as I called Mya and added her on the line.

Without hesitation, I began to tell them every detail of what was going on with Curtis and me. I told them how I met Reggie and how close I came to cheating on Curtis, on up to how Curtis was now in jail and that it had something to do with Reggie getting arrested today. Once I finished, there was complete silence on the phone. I sat there waiting to receive any criticism Tangie had, but instead she sounded concerned.

"Damn, girl, what are you going to do?" Tangie said.

I don't know. I really don't know yet, Tangie."

"How is Curtis holding up?" Mya asked.

"As good as can be expected, under the circumstances. I'm going back to Aiken on Friday. I'm supposed to go to a singles ministry tomorrow and help Sister Pattie set up for an event, but I don't think I'm up for it."

"Then don't go, girl," Tangie said. "You have enough going on in your life."

"Yeah, but maybe it'll do me some good to get out," I said.

"Yeah, it does beat climbing the walls at home," Mya added.

"I can't believe Reggie was a damn drug-dealing deacon. He is going to burn in hell for that shit for sure," Tangie said. "Stephanie, you'd better be careful, because I heard some terrible things about him from Burton."

"Yeah, but what can he do if he's locked up?" Mya replied.

"Girl, don't you watch *The Sopranos*? They can get your ass any place or any time. Stephanie, you and Brandon may want to stay with me or Mya."

"No, I'm fine," I replied.

They tried their best to comfort me, but nothing helped. The conversation soon became redundant, so I got off the phone and tried to think of my next move.

CHAPTER 48

Tangie

Walter called after I got off the phone with Stephanie and Mya. I could hardly concentrate on what he was saying because I was thinking about what Stephanie was going through. Walter rambled on and on and didn't get my attention until he talked about getting together.

"Well, you know the holidays are coming up. What are your plans?" he asked.

"Nothing special. Normally I spend it with my family here in Atlanta. We sometimes have a few relatives visiting from out of town. What about you?"

"I think this Thanksgiving and Christmas, my wife's sister and her husband are coming to visit. You know what that means?"

"No, what?" I asked, confused at the question.

"That means that we can only see each other maybe a couple of more times before the holidays."

"When is your next gig?"

"I have one Friday at this hole-in-the-wall on Ponce."

"Is your wife going?"

"I don't know. I'll have to check her schedule, but if not, we can set something up. I want you to wear the blond wig I like with tons of makeup and lipstick. I saw some flavored gel I'm going to buy that I want to lick off of your body."

"Oooh, that sounds good. Maybe we can meet over here. I think things have cooled off a little."

"That sounds great. Oh, uh, hold on one second." Walter paused. Seconds later he came back to the phone. "Hey, that's my wife pulling up. Let me call you back tomorrow."

"Good night," I said and hung up.

I got up and made some hot tea and sat in bed, pulling the covers over my legs as I read *Essence* magazine. In the middle of an article, I found myself getting sleepy. I rolled over, took one last sip of my tea, and turned off the lights before closing my eyes.

I drifted into a pleasant dream that almost seemed real. Walter and I were making love on the beach—I could feel the cool night breeze running up my spine. I could see Walter's chiseled body on top of me as my hands moved slowly up and down his back. It felt so real that I could almost smell his very distinct cologne as he kissed my neck while holding me tight. Then I dreamed we were naked at a villa in the Virgin Islands. Suddenly a noise sounded that erased the setting in my mind. When I finally drifted off again, I kept having one dream after the other, each different from the one about Walter.

My last dream was interrupted by the alarm clock going off. I opened my eyes and let out a loud yawn. When I rolled over to turn it off, I screamed at the top of my lungs. Directly next to my bed, my breakfast chair was positioned at an angle facing me. I immediately reached under my pillow for the mace. I was so hysterical that I accidentally knocked it out of my bed. My heart raced out of control and I struggled to catch my breath. I looked around for my stun gun and saw it on my dresser by the closet. I sat in shock momentarily before I jumped up and ran toward my dresser to grab my stun gun.

I ran around the bedroom frantically turning on all the lights. Noticing the bedroom door half open, I ran toward it, slamming it shut and locking it. I walked by the window, where I saw Todd getting into his car and speeding off. *You motherfucker,* I said under my breath as I ran in the den. I checked the front door—it was still locked. I walked over to the windows and checked each one to make sure they were secure. When I turned toward the sliding glass door, I noticed it was slightly open. I closed it and pushed down on the lock. When I did this, the lock wouldn't catch. I opened the door and looked down at the lock and noticed that someone had cut a hole in the latch. *So this is how he's been getting into my place*, I thought. I walked back into my bedroom—I could smell Todd's cologne. *He was here watching me sleep the entire night. He could have cut my throat or something*, I thought. I quickly called Burton, who showed up at my apartment about an hour later. As I told him the details of what happened, I could see he was boiling with anger.

"Enough is enough, Tangie. Tell me where he lives right now so I can put an end to this shit. He could've killed you last night."

"Maybe I should call the police or something," I replied.

"And tell them what? They don't have any evidence that he did anything. It's your word against *his*. It's not like he's never been here before."

Burton was right. I couldn't prove anything. The only way to stop Todd from harassing me was to fight fire with fire, so I got a pen and paper and wrote down every address and phone number I had for Todd and gave it to Burton.

"When I get through with his ass, he's going to wish you had stunned him with that gun," Burton said as he exited my apartment.

I hurried out the door to school. By the time I got there, the kids were lining up, about to go inside. I could see Mr. Ridgewell looking out his window as I parked and trotted over to my class.

I got a call from Walter on my way home, confirming Friday. I had to cancel because I hadn't heard from Burton about confronting Todd and didn't want to take any chances on him waiting outside my apartment when Walter showed up. Walter was disappointed because his wife was working a double shift at Piedmont Hospital, which meant he could stay out later than usual.

When Friday came I found myself on the couch eating half-burnt popcorn, watching a rerun of *The Bernie Mac Show* in my sweats. I wanted to go out, but I didn't have any place to go. Mya was still sick because of her pregnancy and Stephanie's house was filled with so much depression it made me sad just thinking about it. As time passed, I got up and turned off the lights. As I walked into the bedroom, my cell phone rang. It was Walter.

"Hey, what's up?" I said.

"Guess where I am?" he asked, excited.

"Where?" I replied.

"I'm in a hotel with candles around the room and wine on ice waiting on you."

"A hotel room? I thought you didn't do hotels?" I replied, surprised.

"I don't, but I have to see you tonight. The gig ended early and I have a couple of extra hours to kill. Can you make it here in thirty minutes?"

"Uh, yeah. Where are you?"

"I'm at the Sheraton in Buckhead, room 212."

"You charged a hotel room?"

"No, a friend of mine from out of town who played with us tonight has had the room since yesterday. Because we ended early, he went back home."

A smile came over my face. "I'll be there in thirty minutes."

"Hey, why don't you come dressed in your tight red dress, high-heeled pumps, and your sexy black lace stockings with the dark red lipstick I like . . . Oh, and don't forget your blond wig."

"Are you serious?"

"Hell, yeah, I'm serious," he replied.

"You are so damn kinky. 'Bye," I said as I hung up.

I quickly jumped in the shower and pulled out the outfit Walter requested. I would've changed into it when I arrived at the hotel but we only had a short time to handle our business, so I put on everything except the wig. I thought I'd wait until I got to the door of the room.

Within thirty-five minutes, I was pulling up to the Sheraton. I got out of the car and covered up with my short leather jacket as I struggled to walk in the pumps. When I got off on the second floor, I went to room 212 and put on the long blond wig before knocking on the door. Walter answered, wearing a pair of black pants and a wifebeater. He smiled and gently pulled me in by my arm and pinned me against the wall. The only lighting was from the candles he had positioned throughout the room. He had a glass of wine in his hand that he put up to my mouth. "Drink it," he whispered.

I took a sip from the glass as he pulled me closer and kissed me. "I want to drink the wine from your mouth," he said as he kissed me.

He began gripping my ass with his right hand as he sucked my bottom lip. I pulled back as I stared at the red lipstick that covered his mouth. "You ready for me?" I whispered.

Walter began taking short breaths and his eyes were half shut. "Oooooh, yeah," he replied.

"Then take me."

Walter guided me to the bed, where I lay down looking up at him as he stood over me and got completely naked with a hard-on. I tried to entice him by slowly taking off my clothes. He touched himself as I pulled off my dress and tossed it on the floor. As I began to pull my panties down, he slowly walked toward me.

All of a sudden the hotel room door opened. I jumped back against the wall as Walter turned toward the door. Instantly, the lights came on and a woman appeared, slamming the door behind her. She looked at Walter, then back at me before reaching in her purse, pulling out a gun. She was light-skinned with short black hair. "What the fuck is going on here, Walter?" she slurred, waving the gun at him. "I thought you said you had to meet your wife for dinner tonight . . . And who is this bitch?"

Walter's hard-on went limp as he reached for his pants.

"Don't move, dammit! Stay just like you are," she shouted.

"Wait, Caroline. What are you doing here?" Walter asked nervously.

"What am *I* doing here? I'm the one who got the room. Or have you forgotten you fucked me in it this afternoon?"

My mouth dropped wide open as I sat in the corner of the bed, balled in a knot.

"Why don't you put the gun down so we can talk?" Walter said calmly.

"Shut the fuck up, I'm doing the damn talking. Who is the hooker you got in my room?"

"Put the gun down, Caroline," Walter pleaded.

"I thought you said you loved me. How can you do me like this?" she shouted.

Suddenly she began to break down in tears as she waved the gun wildly. I flinched and pulled the covers up to my face. "I thought we were going to be together. You said that you and your wife were getting divorced."

Walter looked at me, then back over at Caroline. "It's complicated. I can explain it if you just put the fucking gun down," Walter said.

"No, no. I'm not listening to your bullshit anymore. If you can't end it, then I'll do it. Call your wife right now. Pick up the phone and call her," she demanded.

Walter reached for his cell phone on the dresser behind him, then quickly ran toward Caroline. When he got close I heard a gun shot. Suddenly Walter dropped to the floor, holding his right side. I screamed out loud as Caroline pointed the gun at me.

"Oh my God, help me!" she screamed. "Get up and help me!" she repeated as she put the gun in her purse.

I quickly got up from the bed and looked down at Walter, who was moaning loudly.

"Call 9-1-1!" she shouted.

Caroline dropped to the floor and began to scream out of control. I reached for the hotel phone and called 9-1-1. I talked to the operator, who asked me all sorts of questions as I heard the siren from the ambulance in the background. I began to put on my dress, then rushed over and cracked the door open. Within minutes, the paramedics came in and started examining Walter's wound before picking him up butt-naked and placing him on the gurney. One of the paramedics grabbed his pants and took his wallet as I covered his privates with a towel. Caroline, who was still screaming frantically, followed the paramedic as they loaded Walter into the ambulance. I was right behind her. The police tried to question Caroline, but she climbed in the ambulance with Walter as the ambulance pulled off. I rushed to my car and followed close behind. Piedmont Hospital was only a few miles down the road, so the ambulance quickly pulled up to the emergency room. I parked and ran through the door, where I saw the paramedics pushing Walter toward the back. They stopped Caroline and escorted her to the waiting room. Shortly afterwards, the police arrived. When she saw them, she began to lose control.

"It was an accident, it was an accident," she shouted repeatedly.

One officer questioned me outside. I gave him the full story as he wrote in a small pad. Minutes later, another officer came out and stood next to the officer questioning me.

"The young lady inside admitted to the shooting," he said. "She said she walked in and caught her boyfriend with some hooker and lost control. They wrestled for a second and the gun went off. We found the gun in her purse and we're about to take her to county."

Hooker? I thought, offended by their comment.

The officer turned toward me. "Okay, you can go. If we need more information, we'll contact you."

I nodded and walked back inside. I saw one of the paramedics come from the back, holding a folder. "Excuse me, sir."

The paramedic turned around and faced me. "Yeah?"

"Is the gentleman you brought in going to be okay?"

"Yeah, he was lucky—the bullet just went in and out of his side. But he'll be fine."

I exhaled in relief.

"Right now, he's inside with his wife," the paramedic continued.

Wife, I thought. *Oh, shit, is this the hospital his wife works at? Let me get out of here.*

I turned and rushed toward the door. I passed the officers taking Caroline away in handcuffs and made it to my car. I looked back and saw Walter's wife in her uniform run up to Caroline, screaming at her at the top of her lungs. I started my car and quickly drove away, heading home. By the time I got inside, I realized I had left my blond wig in the waiting room. "What a night," I said under my breath. I jumped in the shower and began scrubbing the makeup from my face.

CHAPTER 49

Stephanie

I got up early Saturday morning to see Curtis at the Aiken County jail. When I walked into the visiting room, Curtis was already sitting behind the desk.

"Hey," I said as I reached over and gave him a kiss. "How are you holding up?"

"I'm good," he replied. "The DEA guys told me they arrested Cedric and G-man yesterday. Apparently, they're putting all this drug shit on me. I'm supposed to be extradited to Atlanta sometime next week to be formally charged for distribution."

I got nervous because it was just a matter of time before he realized G-man and Reggie were the same person. Also, it was just a matter of time before Reggie realized that Curtis was my man. I sat there trying to think of what to do so this matter didn't spin out of control. The *best thing for me to do is to tell Curtis*, I thought.

"You remember the guy from my church named Reggie?"

"Yeah, the fag that called you almost three times a week," he replied.

"Well, he and G-man are the same person."

"What? What are you talking about?" He looked puzzled.

"Sister Pattie called me and said that Reggie had just been arrested at church and wanted all the members to come out and show their support. When I turned on the news, I saw them escorting Reggie out and they said his alias was G-man."

Curtis frowned. "The same guy you've been spending all that time with?"

"No, my time was spent at the church," I responded.

"Then what was he calling for?" he asked.

"For me to come to the church, to help out," I replied. "There was nothing else going on."

"You mean to tell me that you spent all that time at church, coming in all hours of the night, and nothing was going on between you and this uh, Reggie? I find that hard to believe."

"Why? You know me, don't you?"

"I don't know anything anymore. I'm in jail on a bogus charge and now you break this news to me. I-I-give up." Curtis threw his hands up.

"No, Curtis, wait—" I replied.

Before we could finish our conversation, the guard came over and took Curtis away. I sat there for a couple of minutes, trying to figure out what to do next. Once Reggie finds out that Curtis is my man, he's going to tell him about my visit to his house and blow it out of proportion.

I left the jail totally confused and headed back to Atlanta. After the two-hour drive, I rode around the city, thinking of ways to help Curtis, but nothing came to mind. When I looked up, I saw the Fulton County jail, where Reggie was being held. *Fuck it*, I thought.

I turned off the exit and pulled into the parking lot of the Fulton County jail and got out. I walked inside and asked the guard for information on Reggie, and the guard guided me over to where the inmates were being held. After about an hour, I was finally allowed to see Reggie. I walked into a room with several other people and sat at a table that was partitioned in the middle as Reggie was escorted in my direction by the guards. Seeing me, a smile came over his face. "Sister, how are you? I want you to know that these charges against me are totally bogus. I think they have me confused with someone else," he said.

"Stop it, Reggie. I already know what's going on."

"What are you talking about, sister?"

"I know who you are, Reggie Gaines, or G-man. My boyfriend, Curtis, is in jail in Aiken right now because of you. We paid you almost every dime we had for your lost drugs and you still tortured us with your bullshit."

His eyebrows went up. "Sister, what are you saying?—"

"Reggie, stop it—I know who you are," I interrupted.

He looked to the sides and behind him before leaning over closer to the partition, his face menacing. "Then if you know who I am, you know I'm not one to be fucked with, don't you? Your little boyfriend decided to run his fucking mouth and now he's going to do the time. Do you honestly think I don't cover my bases?"

My eyes shifted with nervousness. I had never seen this side of Reggie and I was frightened.

"Oh, and I'll remember to tell him how sweet his little lady tastes when I see him. I hear I'll be seeing him real soon," he said with an evil smirk.

I couldn't say a word. My heart sank to the pit of my stomach as I sat there, staring at him as he grinned at me. "Take me back. I'm done here," he shouted arrogantly.

The guards came and escorted Reggie out the door. I left the Fulton County jail and sat in my car in tears. When I finally regained my composure, I drove to Mya's and picked up Brandon before heading home.

I hadn't had much of an appetite lately but I was feeling a bit hungry so I boiled some hot dogs for Brandon and me. I opened a bag of chips and poured him a cup of Kool-Aid as we sat at the table and had dinner. When the phone rang, I took a bite of my hot dog as I answered the phone.

"Hello?"

"Collect call from the Aiken County jail. Will you accept the charges?" the operator asked.

"Uh, yes, I'll accept," I replied.

"Hey, baby, I want to apologize for earlier today. It's just that I'm about to go crazy in here," Curtis said.

"Don't worry about that. It's okay," I replied.

"How is my little man?"

"He's right here eating dinner. Hold on," I said as I put the phone to Brandon's ear. Curtis talked to Brandon for about five minutes before I got back on the phone.

"Damn, I can't wait to see him. You know they're going to bring me to Atlanta on Saturday. They're taking me to the Fulton County jail," he said. "I don't know what's going to happen from there. I guess I'll have to call my mother and see about getting a lawyer to fight this."

"Yeah," I replied softly. "Just hang in there, Curtis. In the meantime, I'll try to think of something."

After I got off the phone, I gave Brandon a bath before putting him to bed. I opened the paper and read over my horoscope, which only depressed me more. As I got ready for my bath, Sister Pattie called.

"You know the women's group is meeting Friday in the church hall. I have you down to bring beverages and cups," she said.

"Well, uh, Sister Pattie, I don't know if I'll be able to make it. I have some personal issues that I need to take care of on Friday," I lied.

"Oh, no. We were depending on you to bring the beverages," she continued.

"Well, I can stop by and drop them off after I leave work, but I don't know if I'll be able to stay."

"If you can do that, we would really appreciate it," she replied.

Sister Pattie gave me the specific refreshments she needed and I wrote it on my notepad. After I finished my bath, I sat in bed in the dark thinking about Curtis and how he must be feeling at this moment. I rolled over and rubbed my hand across his space in bed, then reached for his pillow and held it tightly in my arms.

CHAPTER 50

Mya

While at home over the weekend I decided, after thinking long and hard, that the best thing for me to do was to have an abortion. After getting confirmation from the doctor about being pregnant, reality set in: I couldn't bring a child into the world this way. A single parent with no support is no way to live.

I sat in bed looking through the phone book at some women's clinics as far away from Atlanta as possible, narrowing my decision to two in Macon, Georgia, a small city about an hour and a half away.

I wrote the numbers down and placed them in my purse to call first thing Monday morning.

With my mind made up, I was able to get back to my normal life. My appetite was back and I was able to hold down hearty meals with no problem.

I called Tangie and Stephanie that evening to share my decision with them. Tangie took the news well, but Stephanie didn't really give off any signs of support. I didn't take it personally, because this was something I felt that *I* had to do.

On Monday I awakened to a cold morning. I got dressed, went downstairs, and made some hot chocolate. I poured some into my coffee mug and headed to my car. As I left my house, a little rain began to fall. The traffic on my way to school was bumper-to-bumper, not unusual for that kind of weather. I did manage, however, to take the back roads and make it to school on time.

During my first break of the day, I went to my car and called the women's clinic. I tried to get the earliest appointment possible, but the only available opening was a week from today. I hung up and called the second possible choice and got a date later than the first one. Immediately, I went into panic mode. I rushed back inside from the cold weather and into the teachers' lounge. I sat down, thinking about another option out of town, but nothing came to mind. Everything was either too far or too near. Then I thought, *My only other option is here in Atlanta.* I was already three months, and the longer I waited, the harder it would be to get it done. I grabbed the phone book in the teachers' lounge and thumbed through it until I got to the section on women's clinics. There were about a dozen located throughout the city, which made it possible for me to get an appointment this week. I tore a section of advertisements out of the phone book and rushed back to my car. I sat there for another thirty minutes until I got an appointment for Thursday of this week at the Women's Clinic of Atlanta, located in Decatur.

Later that night I called Tangie and Stephanie and asked if one of them could take me to the clinic Thursday. Tangie was more than willing to take me. Stephanie offered, but only as a last resort because her time was limited with Curtis being in jail and all. I needed someone to drive me home after the procedure because of the anesthesia.

Tuesday went by fast. I stayed late after school to put up the Thanksgiving decorations the students had created. I talked to my mother on my cell phone as I worked. She was planning a big Christmas dinner for our family and wanted a few tips from me on desserts. I was excited about going home for Christmas because cousins I haven't seen in years were supposed to be home. It would be a welcome ending to a really tough year.

I left work at around seven-thirty and missed most of the rush-hour traffic. Because it was late in the evening, I stopped by a Popeye's fried chicken and got a two-piece spicy dinner special before going home. I sat in the den, where I ate and watched TV before showering and turning in for the night.

Later that night, I awoke with the worst case of heartburn. I felt a burning sensation from my throat down to the pit of my stomach. I got up and took a couple of spoonfuls of Pepto-Bismol. About an hour later it seemed like the burning sensation had gotten worse. I went downstairs and took some Alka-Seltzer and lay on the couch for the rest of the night with a cool towel on my stomach.

The following morning I woke up cranky due to lack of sleep and got dressed for work. *Just one more day of morning sickness*, I thought as I brushed my hair in the mirror.

When I got to school, I felt really bad. My stomach was turning like crazy, making me dizzy. I walked to the teachers' lounge and got a cup of hot tea before going to my classroom. I closed my door and put my head on my desk, taking deep breaths, hoping to relieve some of my pain.

Halfway through my cup of tea, Tangie came walking through the door.

"What's up, girl? You okay?"

I took another sip of my tea. "Hell, no," I said, wiping my eyes. "My stomach has been hurting me all night."

"Well, after tomorrow you won't have to worry about that anymore. What time do we need to be there?" Tangie asked.

"At least by eight o'clock," I replied. "How long does this usually take?"

"Not long at all. You'll be in and out before you know it," Tangie reassured me.

"Oh, man, I can't wait," I replied, rubbing my stomach.

Stephanie came walking through the door, carrying a box of Krispy Kreme doughnuts.

"Hey, you two want some doughnuts? I had a taste for something sweet this morning."

"Ooooh, yeah. I love Krispy Kreme doughnuts. Are they hot?" Tangie asked.

"Yeah, and they're good, too."

Tangie opened the box Stephanie was holding and picked up a doughnut.

"Mya?" Stephanie put the box in front of me.

"Mmm, uh, none for me, thank you." I frowned.

"What's the matter?" Stephanie asked.

"Girl, she has morning sickness," Tangie said, chewing. "But I'll take another one."

Stephanie gave the box to Tangie and walked toward me. "You probably need a Sprite or something to settle your stomach."

"I'm feeling a little bit better now since I've had some hot tea."

Stephanie nodded. "Okay, well, let me know if you need anything else today."

The bell sounded for school to begin. I slowly got up and walked outside to meet my students.

Once I started teaching, it pretty much took my mind off the pain I was having. When school was over, I left right away to get home. Once inside, I took my clothes off and tossed them on the floor before getting into bed. Shortly after my head hit the pillow, I was asleep.

Three hours later, I awoke having to go to the bathroom. It was now getting closer to seven P.M. The nurse said that I couldn't eat anything after ten P.M. I wasn't really hungry, but I needed to put something in my stomach so I wouldn't get hungry later tonight.

I went downstairs and poured a bowl of cereal and sat down on the couch. The cold milk really felt good going down and gave me some temporary relief from my heartburn.

As the night wore on, I began to get nervous about the procedure. I didn't know what to expect and was getting worried that something might go wrong. I couldn't sleep, so I began praying and telling myself that everything would be okay. I did this over and over for a time until I ran out of things to pray about. I turned my TV on Trinity Broadcast Network (TBN). T. D. Jakes was preaching. I listened to his encouraging words of faith in God that let me know everything was going to be okay. I left the TV on and got under my covers and fell asleep.

The next morning Tangie called, waking me up from a deep sleep. Nervousness came over me as I sat up in bed.

"Hey, are you up yet, 'cause I'm on my way."

I looked over at the clock. "It's only six o'clock."

"I know, but you want to get there as early as possible. They don't care about an appointment. They start taking the first person sitting in the waiting room."

I cleared my throat. "Okay, I'll be ready when you get here."

"Oh, and you might want to wear something heavy because it's freezing outside."

I got up and looked out the window. The morning looked dreary and dry. There was a shiny glaze over the grass that looked to be ice. I went in the bathroom and brushed my teeth before grabbing some sweatpants from my closet. I put on a baseball cap, grabbed my coat, and walked downstairs to wait for Tangie.

I looked at the clock—it read six-forty-five. I paced back and forth in the den, looking out the window for Tangie's car. My hands began to shake. I rubbed them together as I walked.

Minutes later, Tangie pulled into my driveway. I opened the front door and met her outside. The cold winter wind sent chills down my spine that made me quiver as I made my way to Tangie's car.

"How do you feel?" Tangie asked.

"I'm okay. I'm trying not to think about anything right now. I just want to get this over with." I closed the car door.

"I understand—it'll be over before you know it," Tangie explained.

While in the car, I turned up the radio and concentrated on the music. It felt really pleasant inside Tangie's car as the heat penetrated my clothes.

The drive seemed really long. The main expressway was packed with people headed to work. Tangie maneuvered her way down some back streets, only to end up in more traffic. I looked at the clock in Tangie's car.

"Don't worry, we're almost there," she said.

I nodded as I turned my head toward the window.

A few miles later we turned down a two-lane street, passing several small buildings about three stories high. When we got to the first traffic light, Tangie put on her right turn signal. As we turned the corner there were crowds of people standing outside with signs.

"Aw, shit," Tangie shouted. "I had a feeling their asses would be out here."

Puzzled, I looked over at Tangie. "Who?"

"Nothing—don't worry about it. It's just picketers outside the clinic," Tangie replied.

"Huh? You mean abortion activists?"

"Yeah, but just ignore them as we go inside."

"Shit, I don't need this right now," I said.

"Don't worry about them, Mya. Just walk right past them and keep looking ahead."

We pulled into the women's center lot and parked in the back. Tears began to form in my eyes.

"Okay, let's go, Mya," Tangie said.

My heart began to race as I got out of the car. I walked with my eyes straight ahead.

The people with the picket signs looked in our direction and walked toward us, shouting. Tangie grabbed my hand and began walking faster, pulling me with her. As I walked on I saw a little boy wearing a shirt that read. I'M HERE BECAUSE MY MOTHER DIDN'T MURDER ME.

The tears that were building in my eyes began to fall.

Tangie looked over at me. "Girl, don't pay any attention to that shit."

I looked around and saw other signs that were just as bad. I dropped my head as we made it to the front door of the clinic. Tangie closed the door behind me as the people stood outside yelling obscenities.

"Girl, I don't know if I can do this," I said emotionally.

"What? Look, we're here. The hard part is over," Tangie replied.

I stood there, frozen.

"Let's go over to the window and sign in," Tangie said.

The nurse came to the window as I wrote my name on the log. "When you finish signing in, fill out this form, turn it in to me at the window, and have a seat in the lobby area until your name is called," the lady at the window instructed.

"Thank you," Tangie replied as she grabbed the forms.

We sat in a chair as I started filling out the paperwork. For the first few minutes, Tangie thumbed through several magazines. I read over the forms carefully, looking at the frightening questions that I had to answer about my sexuality, and who to call in case of an emergency, etc . . .

When I finished answering the pertinent questions, I got up to give the forms to the woman at the window.

"Hey, wait. Let me check the information you wrote," Tangie said.

"What?"

"Let me see something," Tangied insisted.

I stood there watching as Tangie went through each page.

"No, wait. Have a seat, Mya. First of all, don't put your real address on here. Girl, they'll send you all kinds of magazines and abortion shit in the mail. When you leave here today, you don't want a trail of this following you."

Tangie got up and walked to the window. Minutes later, she came back with some new forms. "I'll fill these out for you."

I watched as Tangie lied about everything except my name. She was going to lie about that, but I had already given them my real name when I signed the log.

When she finished, I turned the paperwork in at the window and walked toward the back. There were about fifteen women sitting in chairs with swollen eyes and sad looks on their faces. I tried not to stare and just looked down at the floor as I made it to an empty chair.

I waited as they called one person after the next into the back of the room. By this time an hour had passed and there were only about six people left, including Tangie. I sat up as my nervous legs began to shake uncontrollably. All I could think about was the little boy outside the clinic wearing the tee-shirt.

"Mya LeVeaux," the nurse shouted.

I looked around and then over at Tangie. She had a strange look in her eyes that worried me. I took a deep breath and walked over to the nurse standing at the door.

"Just follow me, please," the nurse said.

We walked down a long hallway with doors on both sides. I could hear a strange sound, like a drill, coming from the inside of some as I passed by. When the nurse stopped, she gestured me into an office.

"Just have a seat—someone will be with you shortly." The nurse closed the door. I looked around the room at the different degrees and certificates on the wall. There were papers scattered across the desk and Post-its placed on folders stacked near the edge closest to me.

Minutes later, another nurse entered the room with a folder in her hand. She looked to be in her mid-forties. Her blond hair was pinned up on her head above her ears as she sat behind the desk. She showed no emotion as she adjusted the papers on her desk and placed them to one side.

"Good morning, Mya—or should I say, Ms. LeVeaux?" the nurse asked.

"Uh, either is fine," I replied.

"Ms. LeVeaux, I'm Cathy Jones, one of the nurses here on staff. Before the surgery, I need to ask you some general questions."

I nodded.

"Are you allergic to any medications that you know of?" she asked.

"Uh, no," I replied.

"Do you suffer from high blood pressure, anxiety attacks, or any heart-related illnesses?"

"No."

"Are you on prescription drugs of any kind?"

"No."

"What about over-the-counter drugs?"

"No, only when I have my period—I take Advil. But other than that, nothing."

The nurse paused for a moment and began writing in my folder.

"Do you understand the procedure we are about to administer?"

"No, I've never done this before," I replied, puzzled.

"Okay, what's going to happen is you're going to be put under an anesthetic, at which time you will be asleep. Then the surgery will be performed. The process should last approximately thirty minutes, at which time you will be placed in the recovery room until you are coherent enough to leave the facility. You are to refrain from taking baths, using tampons, and sexual intercourse for a period of four weeks. Do you have any questions?"

"No," I replied softly.

"Is someone here with you who will be able to make sure you get home safely?"

I nodded.

The nurse got up from her desk and walked over to the door. "Okay, Ms. LeVeaux. If you would follow me, please."

I slowly pushed back my chair, got up, and followed the nurse out of her office to a bathroom at the end of the hall. Once inside, she opened a linen cabinet and pulled out a folded gown, some rubber slippers, and an empty brown paper bag. "Okay, take off all your clothes and put them in this bag. Put this gown on and have a seat in the waiting area outside this door until someone calls your name," the nurse said, pointing ahead.

I slowly undressed and put on the gown. I folded my clothes and placed each piece in the bag before slowly walking outside the door.

As I walked through the doorway, there was another waiting area with about five women sitting there, wearing the same gown and slippers. Some of the women looked nervous, while others looked like they didn't have a care in the world.

I took a seat in a chair nearest the door and placed my bag in my lap. I looked down at the floor, trying to keep from making eye contact with anyone.

Minutes later, a nurse came from a door to the left of the waiting area and called a woman to the back. As she got up and started toward the nurse, she broke down hysterically. I stared at her as she passed me, gripping my bag as tight as I could. My heart raced with fear as she walked through the door.

"It's too late to cry now. She should've thought about the consequences before she spread her legs," one girl said.

Shocked, I turned and looked at her. This girl was a light brown sista with her hair in a twist.

"I know—that's right," another girl responded. "It's too late to cry now."

I turned back around, looking straight ahead.

A tear fell from my eye.

"You okay over there?" a girl asked.

I shifted my eyes back over in the direction of the girl with the twist.

"You okay? You look scared, too," she continued.

"I'm fine," I replied.

"Well, it's going to be all right. You won't feel a thing after they put you to sleep."

I nodded.

"What's your story, by the way?" she asked.

I turned my head and looked at her. I couldn't believe she had the nerve to ask me why the hell I was in an abortion clinic. But then again, I didn't want to rub anyone the wrong way. "Uh, I just got caught up in a bad situation, that's all," I replied.

"Hell, didn't we all," another girl replied. "I had one in high school and swore I would never do this again. But now I have two kids and the man I'm pregnant by just got locked up, so I have no other choice."

"Me, either," the girl with the twist hairdo cut in. "This is my second one, too. The sorry-ass man I'm pregnant by has three kids already that he's not taking care of. I have a son that I'm barely making it with, so I know damn well I'm not taking a chance with his deadbeat ass."

The other women sat there in complete silence as the two women continued to talk. One, a younger-looking, dark-brown sista with long black hair, sat near the corner in a daze.

A few minutes later the nurse came back out and called three more women to the back. Two of the three were the sista with the twist and the other girl she was very vocal with, leaving me and the younger-looking sista in the waiting room.

Well, it won't be long now, I thought. My stomach began to quiver uncontrollably. I got up and walked over to the water cooler on the other side of the room and drank two cups of water before sitting back down.

The young girl began to sniffle aloud, catching my attention. I looked over at her as she wiped her eyes with the sleeve of her gown.

"Would you like some water?" I asked politely.

"No, ma'am, thank you," she replied.

Suddenly she broke down crying. I didn't know how to react or what to do. I just stared at her as she continued.

"I'm not a bad girl," she whispered. "It's not my fault. Why is this happening to me?"

Finally, I got up and sat next to her. "It's okay—I know it's tough. I'm feeling the same pain as you."

"You don't understand," she replied. "I want to keep my baby. I could never do anything like this to my child. This is the same as killing it myself."

"I don't understand. Then why are—"

"When I told the guy I was dating I was pregnant, his ex-girlfriend and some of her friends jumped me and started kicking me in my stomach. The doctor said that the damage caused bleeding that could affect my baby if I go through the full term, so I have no other choice."

"Oh, my God," I replied.

I couldn't believe what I just heard. This little girl is willing to do everything to keep her child and is bawling because she has to give it up. Instantly I felt sick, like I was about to throw up. I jumped up and quickly walked to the bathroom. While inside, I let it go right in the toilet for what seemed like five long minutes. I walked over to the sink and rinsed my mouth out before going back out to the waiting room. When I walked out, the young girl was gone. In her chair I could see the teardrops she had left behind. As soon as I sat down in my chair, the nurse came to the door.

"Ms. LeVeaux, come right this way, please."

I stood up, grabbed my bag, and followed the nurse. As we walked down the hall, we passed what looked to be the recovery room. Through a glass window I could see the girl with the twist lying on a cot with her eyes closed with an expression that looked like pain.

My hands started shaking as the nurse guided me to an examination room. When I walked through the door, there was a doctor and another nurse waiting inside.

"Hi, I'll take your bag," the nurse said. "Just lie down on the examination table." As I lay down on the table, I saw a strange-looking machine with three tubes hanging from it. Nervously, I lay back and stared at the ceiling. All sorts of things started running through my mind. *Why am I doing this? It's a blessing to bring a child into this world. What reason could justify killing my baby?*

Suddenly a voice sounded in my right ear. "I'm going to put this over your nose and mouth. I want you to count backwards, starting at ten."

I shifted my eyes in the direction of the doctor standing next to me. He put a mask over my face that had a funny smell coming from it. *Oh my God. Oh my God.* I repeated. Seconds later, I felt my eyes getting heavy. *I can't do this*, I thought. With the little strength I had left, I reached up and pulled the mask from my face.

"Ms. LeVeaux, what are you doing?" the doctor yelled.

The nurse tried to grab my arm but I pulled away. "I-I c-can't do this, I-I want to k-keep my baby," I replied as I slowly passed out.

I woke up lying in bed fully dressed with a nurse standing around me. "How do you feel?" she asked.

"My baby, my baby?" I whispered.

"Don't worry, everything went fine. As soon as you feel up to it, you can go home."

"No, my baby. Please tell me you didn't harm my baby," I cried out loudly.

The doctor appeared next to the nurse. "Ms. LeVeaux. How are you feeling?"

I covered my mouth to muffle the sound of my crying. I felt someone grab my hand.

"Your baby is fine—we didn't do the procedure. My concern was that you inhaled enough gas to put you under, and we had to keep you here until you were coherent enough to be released."

I turned, staring at the doctor as he stood there with a grin on his face.

"Will the gas I inhaled harm my baby? I asked.

"No, everything is fine," the doctor replied.

"T-thank you, thank you so much, Doctor," I whispered.

"Is there someone here to take you home?" the nurse asked.

I nodded.

"Okay, as soon as you feel strong enough to sit up, let me know and I'll call your friend back here to get you."

I nodded again.

I put my hand on my stomach and began rubbing it. Before I knew it, I was out once again.

When I awakened the second time I still felt a little drowsy but was able to sit up. The nurse came over and helped me.

"Are you okay to stand up now?" she asked.

"Yes, I feel a little bit better."

"Who is the person that's going to take you home?"

"Her name is Tangie Jackson."

The nurse left as I sat up on the cot. Minutes later, she appeared with Tangie behind her.

"Ms. LeVeaux, I have Tangie here with me. Can you stand up?"

I nodded as I got out of bed.

"Put your arm around me," Tangie said.

"No, I'm fine. I think I can make it to the car," I replied.

Tangie and I walked out of the recovery room and through double doors that took us to the lobby.

"You wait here and I'll go outside and get the car," Tangie said.

She rushed out the door and minutes later reappeared, gesturing for me outside. I walked toward her and followed her to her car. The protesters were still outside, yelling obscenities, but I could barely understand what was being said.

I got into Tangie's car and we drove off. I sat in the passenger seat with my head tilted back on the headrest, eyes closed. Tangie was quiet the entire ride back to my house. Once I got inside, she helped me upstairs to my bed, where I fell asleep.

Later that evening when I woke up, I walked downstairs where Tangie and Stephanie were sitting on the couch watching TV as Brandon sat on the floor playing with his toys. Stephanie got up and walked over to me and gave me a hug.

"How do you feel?" she asked, concerned.

"I'm fine, but I—"

"Don't you feel better that it's over now?" Tangie asked. "Now you can go on with your life."

"That's kind of insensitive, don't you think, Tangie?" Stephanie said.

"Well, I'm just saying," Tangie continued.

"Guys?" I interrupted. "I'm fine, because I decided to keep the baby."

"What?" they both replied in unison.

"But, you were knocked out when I got you out of the recovery room. I think your ass is in denial or still drugged out."

"Yeah, I got the hell up out of there as soon as the doctor put that gas on my face. They thought I was crazy and were trying to hold me down. But I had decided right there that I wanted to keep my child."

Stephanie looked over at me with a smile. "Girl, I prayed for you all morning. I asked God to help you make a conscious decision, and you did."

"I don't know what it was, but I just couldn't go through with it," I replied.

"Are you sure this is what you want to do?" Tangie asked. "Have you thought about raising this child and how it's going to alter your lifestyle?"

"Yeah, I'm one hundred percent sure. And no, I haven't thought about that but I'll deal with it when the time comes."

"Well then, dammit, I guess I'm going to be an aunt. Between you two hoes my hair will be white as snow by the time I turn thirty-five," Tangie joked.

We all laughed.

"Hey, what's for dinner? I'm starving over here," I said.

CHAPTER 51

Stephanie

I was leaving the supermarket after getting some beverages for the women's group meeting. Because I wasn't going to be staying, I parked in front of the church so I could take the drinks to Sister Pattie and leave. When I passed Reggie's office door, I felt a knot in my stomach as I continued on toward Sister Pattie's office. She was sitting behind her desk talking to a woman who sat in a chair directly across from her.

She looked in my direction. "Hey, sister," she said and stood up.

I smiled back. "Hey—sorry to interrupt your conversation. I just wanted to drop this off for the meeting."

"Here, I can take them," she said as she put the bags next to her desk.

"Oh, where are my manners? Stephanie, this is my youngest sister, Angela."

"Really? Hi, nice to meet you," I said with a smile.

"Nice to meet you, too," she replied.

"Well, I'll let you two get back to what you were doing. I'm parked in front of the church, anyway, and probably need to move my car." I turned to walk away.

"Wait—I'll walk you out," she said, following behind me.

We passed Reggie's office as we turned the corner of the hallway. "I still can't believe the police think Reggie is a criminal," she said.

I pressed my lips together.

"I've been down there twice to see him just to let him know that he's in our prayers. I've been taking his work over since he's been away, you know?" she continued.

I nodded. "You and your sister look so much alike, especially the nose and eyes," I said, trying to change the subject.

"Yeah, that's what everyone says. Bless her heart. She's going through some marital difficulties at the moment, so I invited her to meet with the bishop twice a week for counseling," Sister Pattie explained.

"Oh, I'm sorry to hear about that."

We made our way out the front door to my car.

"Girl, between us, he's trifling. I told her not to marry him from the start."

I opened my car door. "Well, I hope you all have a good time tomorrow. And by the way, Sister Pattie, I might not be able to help out as much anymore until I get some things straightened out personally."

"I understand. Do what you can when you can," she replied.

I closed my door and drove off. As my car moved a few feet away I thought about the safety deposit box I opened for Reggie with the bishop's papers. I stopped, backed up, and rolled my window down.

"Sister Pattie," I yelled.

She stopped in her tracks and turned, walking in my direction. "Yes?"

"Uh, since you've taken over Reggie's work, I need to give you the papers in the bishop's safe deposit box."

Sister Pattie stood there, a strange look on her face. "What papers?" she asked. "Why would Reggie have the bishop's papers? He's just in charge of the youth group. All the bishop's affairs come through me."

"Oh," I replied, confused.

"Well, whatever it is you have, you can bring it to me anyway. I'll just put it with the rest of Reggie's things," she continued.

Suddenly my curiosity took over. *If Sister Pattie takes care of the bishop's affairs, then what are those envelopes that Reggie had me put in the safe deposit boxes?* I looked at my watch: a quarter to four. The bank closes at four, which meant I had about fifteen minutes. I hurried to the bank parking lot.

I walked over to the teller and got the key to the safe deposit box, then went into the private room in the back of the bank. I sat down and opened it, pulling out all of the envelopes and putting them on the table.

As I began to open one of the envelopes, there was a knock and the door slowly opened. "Ma'am, the bank will be closing in five minutes," the security guard said.

"Thank you," I replied.

I grabbed the envelopes, stuffing the small ones in my purse and carrying the large ones in my hand as I put the safe deposit box back in its place and returned the key to the teller before exiting the bank. I sat in my car and opened one of the larger envelopes. What I saw completely blew me away. There were about five 8 X 10 pictures of the deacons in the church having sex with multiple women and snorting a white substance that looked to be cocaine. "Oh, my God. What is this?"

The employees of the bank were walking to their cars, so I quickly put the pictures back in the envelope and headed to the preschool to pick up Brandon before going home. Once inside, I put Brandon in the tub for his bath and went in my bedroom, where I opened the envelopes, putting them in separate piles. Each envelope contained what looked to be different financial transactions. There were deposit slips for large sums in overseas accounts with Reggie's name on them. There were papers that had the names listed as Colombian Cartel Miami, Colombian Cartel New York, as well as payoffs to local and state politicians by name and the amount paid to what account.

In the last envelope was a list of warehouses labeled "production," which listed in keys how many drugs were manufactured in addition to a list of names and locations where they were to be transported. Highlighted in red were the drug runs that Curtis had been doing. I sat back in my bed in disbelief.

Finally I had some hope of clearing Curtis's name and getting him released. What I lacked was a plan.

I got up and cooked dinner for Brandon and let him play for a while before putting him to bed. I had too much nervous energy to eat, so I poured a glass of wine to calm myself down. *The first thing I need to do is make copies*, I thought. *I'll get up in the morning and go to Kinko's before going to the Fulton County jail, where Curtis will be arriving tomorrow.*

Mya had agreed to keep Brandon. I told her I was going to see Curtis, when, in fact, I was going to see Reggie. I got up early and made copies before going to the Fulton County jail. I had rehearsed over and over in my head what I wanted to say to Reggie. While waiting for about an hour in the visiting area, Reggie finally came into the room. He had the same evil smirk on his face that he had the time before. I was nervous as he took a seat at the table, staring at me as I rubbed my hands together. He sat there in silence until the guards walked away.

"What do you want? Didn't I tell you we have nothing to talk about?" he said firmly. "Unless you came to tell me you still want to give me that sweet ass of yours when I get out," he laughed. "Oh wait, let me guess—you're trying to make one last plea before your boyfriend arrives . . . Well, forget it. His ass is done. By the time I finish talking, I'll be walking out to my normal life first thing Monday morning."

I sat there, getting hotter by the minute at his cockiness, but remained calm as I began to speak. "Well, you won't be the only one talking," I said as I placed a list with the names of the politicians in front of him.

Reggie's evil grin slowly faded as he stared at the names, then back at me. "What's this?" he chuckled. "Is this supposed to mean something to me?"

"Well, I thought it would, but if not, maybe the DEA may have some use for these names as well as the other information I have from the safe deposit box."

His mouth slightly opened as he stared at me. "I don't know what you're talking about. All I gave you were the bishop's contracts and other important papers that belong to him. Anything else I can say that you put in there. After all, it *is* your name on the account. And along with that and the evidence they have on your boy, that will just make their case stronger," Reggie continued.

I sat up in the chair closer to Reggie. "Look, let's cut the bullshit. Sister Pattie already told me that you don't have a damn thing to do with the bishop's affairs. You're in charge of the youth group, and as religious as she is, I'm sure she'll be willing to testify to that in a court of law. I have information that will link your ass to things that could put you away for the rest of your life. But you know what? I'm not interested in that. I just want my man out, free and clear.

Now, if you want to sit here and play games, then I can just walk away right now and the next time you'll see my sweet ass, as you put it, will be in the courtroom watching them sentence you to life."

I stood up as he stared at the paper. "Oh, yeah, you can keep this copy. I have plenty more where that came from." I turned to walk off.

I continued on until I was about to open the door.

"No, wait!" he yelled.

I came to a halt and released the door before turning around to face him. I wasn't sure he would go for my bluff, but he did. I turned and walked back to my chair.

"Please, sit back down and let's talk," he said.

I stood there for moment and rolled my eyes at him before sitting down.

Reggie bit down on his bottom lip. "How do I know you're not working with the DEA? You could be wired or something," he whispered.

"If I was working with the DEA, I wouldn't be sitting here talking to you. Besides, I would've taken everything I had to them from the start."

"You could still do that, anyway. What is it that you want?" He leaned back in his chair.

"I want everything you took from me."

He tilted his head, confused at my question. "What do you mean?"

"You took my money, my man, and my trust, then used them for your own pleasure. I want it all back."

Reggie sat up. "Want *what* back?"

"First of all, I want Curtis cleared of all charges. I don't care how you do it or who you blame it on, but I don't want him serving one day in prison for this shit you've concocted. Secondly, I don't want any mention of me being at your house. That was a big mistake on my part that I truly regret. And since nothing happened, it should be forgotten. The last thing I want is two hundred and fifty thousand dollars in cash given to Curtis for all of the legitimate work he's done for you and Cedric."

"Two hundred and fifty thousand? How do I do that in here?" he asked.

"I don't know how, but you make it happen and make it happen fast."

Reggie dropped his head for a moment, then looked up at me. "How do I know that after I give you what you want, you won't turn against me?"

I leaned in closer. "That's my point—you *don't* know. But if I don't get what I want, you'll definitely find out." I got up from my chair. "Make it happen, Reggie. I mean it—make it happen." I turned and walked out the door.

When I made it to my car, I was shaking. I couldn't believe I'd had enough courage to confront Reggie.

CHAPTER 52

Curtis

I was being transported back to the Fulton County jail by a couple of Atlanta police officers. We arrived at around two o'clock as the officer pulled around the back of the jail. Seeing it brought back memories of my first arrest on drug charges a few years ago. I had knots in my stomach thinking about G-man and Cedric being in the same jail and how they were going to react when they saw me. Lonnie was going to be transported tomorrow—I heard through one of the agents that he was cooperating with the DEA and was put in some kind of protective custody.

I went through processing before I was placed in a cell with two other guys awaiting arraignment. They had anger in their eyes, staring me up and down. When the cell door closed, I walked to the corner where a bench was bolted to the floor and took a seat. The toilet was near me and smelled of piss with stains on the outside rim. There was graffiti on the wall where two beds with old mattresses were stacked on top of each other. I was tired from my ride, but didn't want to take a chance on fighting for one of the available beds, so I just leaned my back against the wall and stared at the ceiling. One of the guys walked toward me and pulled his pants down and sat on the toilet to take a shit. The smell of his feces filled the tiny cell. I kept my eyes on the ceiling, trying to ignore the horrible odor and his presence near me.

When he flushed, the toilet ran over and the water began to

overflow around me. I lifted both my legs and placed them on the bench to keep the water from getting on my Timberlands as I watched the water settle in a corner. He didn't make any attempt to stop the overflow but instead walked away, jumped in the lower bunk, and turned to the side, facing the wall. I was really missing home. I wished I could be in bed with Stephanie or on the floor playing with my son Brandon. *I wonder what they're doing now. I bet Stephanie is probably at home cooking dinner while Brandon's at the table writing in one of his books.* A smile came over my face but slowly faded away as reality set in and I looked around the jail cell.

I was bored and lonely with only four walls to keep me company, sitting with two men I didn't trust, afraid to close my eyes. For once in my life, I felt like I was about to lose control. Three years ago, I didn't care about jail because I had no dreams or ambitions. But now I have a beautiful girl and a wonderful son. I began to feel nervous as I stood up and walked to the front of the jail cell, looking around at other people as they sat in their cells across from me.

A few hours later, a couple of corrections officers came and got the two inmates and myself and walked us in a line with other inmates to the jail cafeteria. We sat at a long table as men with carts came around and placed trays in front of us with plastic utensils on the side. I looked around as other inmates were being escorted in. Within minutes the cafeteria was packed to capacity as conversations echoed around the room. The two guys in the cell with me began eating as I stared at my food. I grabbed my utensils and began eating the cold vegetables and what looked to be meat loaf with gravy that was tossed on my plate.

About thirty minutes into my meal, an alarm sounded and the corrections officers came over to where we were eating and signaled for us to stand before escorting us back to our cells. The two guys in my cell climbed in the beds and fell asleep. I laid down on the bench, staring at the ceiling, occasionally dozing off minutes at a time and waking up at the lightest sounds.

A few hours later, the lights around us went off except for the one in the hall. In one-hour intervals I could hear the sound of footsteps as corrections officers passed our cell. I shifted my body to get comfortable as I felt exhaustion begin to take me over. The next thing I remember was being startled awake by a cold feeling on my left hand. I opened my eyes, and quickly raising my hand, which was in the water that leaked from the toilet next to me. I grabbed some tissue from the back of the toilet seat and began drying my fingers, tossing the paper on the floor next to me. From that point, I just couldn't sleep. I stayed up staring in the dark until the sunlight filled the hallway of the cell block. About an hour later, the other two guys got up, yawning loudly. A corrections officer appeared and brought each of us a paper bag that contained a toothbrush and toothpaste.

After giving us time to brush our teeth, we were escorted to the cafeteria for breakfast and then back to our cells. Before I could get comfortable, a different corrections officer walked up to our cell door and stood facing us.

"Which one of you is Curtis Williams?" he asked.

"I'm Curtis Williams." I stood up.

"You need to come with me," he ordered.

The corrections officer had me put my hands outside the cell bars, where he handcuffed me before escorting me to another building and into a small room with a mirror in the back of it. I took a seat facing the door as two DEA agents walked into the room with their IDs outside of their suit pockets. Both were white. One was slim with dark hair and the other was sort of a husky guy with red hair and freckles. The husky agent sat down at the table across from me and opened a folder.

"Okay, Curtis. You've been extradited back to Atlanta to be charged with drug trafficking with the intent to distribute. I understand that you're not represented by an attorney at this time, so the courts will appoint one for your arraignment on Monday. Your court-appointed attorney will be here sometime today to speak with you regarding your case. Is there anything that you don't understand about the charges being filed against you?"

"Look, man, I told you I had nothing to do with trafficking drugs," I snapped.

"Then tell us about your relationship with a Lonnie Figures, Reggie Gaines, a/k/a G-man, and Cedric Nichols," the dark-haired agent asked.

"Like I told the other agent, I been knowing Cedric for a few years. We're old friends from the neighborhood. I just met G-man a few weeks ago. I just met Lonnie the night we went to South Carolina to work on some cars."

The husky agent looked at me in disgust. "Look, Curtis, I'm tired of your bullshit. If you're not going to cooperate, then we can't help you. We already know all of you were in this trafficking shit together. We found drugs in Lonnie's car while you two were on the same highway heading back to Atlanta. Do you expect us to believe that was just a coincidence?"

"I don't know anything about that. I told that to the agents in South Carolina and now I'm telling you. I don't know anything. They found that shit in Lonnie's car, not mine. I only went to South Carolina to work on some cars."

Suddenly, the door opened and another agent popped his head in, a black guy with a bald head and a beard. When the two agents turned in his direction, he gestured for one of them to come outside. The dark-haired agent turned and walked out as the husky agent and I continued to go around in circles. Minutes later, the dark-haired agent came through the door with the bald brother and leaned over to the husky agent, whispering something in his ear. I watched the two go back and forth for a couple of minutes before they stopped and looked at me. My eyes shifted from one agent to the other before the brother walked closer to me.

"Well, it looks like this is your lucky day, Curtis."

I looked up at him, puzzled. "What are you talking about?"

"It seems as though Reggie has turned state's evidence against Cedric and Lonnie. Your story about not having any knowledge of the drugs was confirmed—you were set up by Lonnie for Cedric. Reggie admitted having some connection to Cedric's drug dealings and made a shitload of money to invest in real estate, then got out. The drugs found in Cedric's auto body shop backs up this story, and the fact that we found drugs in Lonnie's car and not yours proves Lonnie was involved. I'm still not convinced you're as innocent as you try to appear, but I have to go by the facts."

"What does all this mean?" I asked desperately.

"It means you're free to go and all charges against you have been dropped by the DEA and local law enforcement."

My heart leaped as a smile came over my face. The agents continued to stare at me with a cold look.

I don't know how and why Reggie would rat out his own cousin, but I didn't care. The fact that I was a free man was my only concern.

"Well, when can I get out of here?"

"We're working on it now. Just give us a couple of hours and you can go," the brother said.

"Can I use the phone to call my girl?"

"You don't have to. The front desk has been calling every half-hour. Apparently she's been sitting in the visiting room all morning, waiting to see you. I'll walk down and let her know the news. Until then, just sit tight and we'll hurry up and get you out of here. Oh, and Curtis—don't let me catch you in my jail again. Next time, you won't be so lucky."

The agents turned and left. I sat in the room as tears rolled down my face. I was numb with excitement and couldn't wait to see Stephanie and Brandon.

CHAPTER 53

Stephanie

I was in the waiting room sipping on a cup of coffee as I paced the floor. I had been waiting for hours to see Curtis and was wondering what was going on. I called Mya last night and explained to her that Curtis was still being processed. She agreed to keep Brandon overnight.

Each time I went to the desk wanting to see Curtis, the corrections officer kept giving me the same answer—he was still being processed. I grew furious at the fact that no one would give me any straight answers. I went outside to get some fresh air to try and calm my nerves. I walked the grounds for a few minutes before coming back inside. As I walked through the door, the corrections officer at the front desk signaled for me to come toward her. I walked to her, still pissed about my long wait.

"Ma'am, there's an agent that wants to talk to you about the guy, Curtis, you've been asking about. He's in the visiting room down the hall and to your right."

I followed her directions to a room where a bald, black guy was sitting in a chair drinking a Coke. "Have a seat," he said as I walked inside. "I'm Greg Smith with the DEA. I understand you've been waiting here all night to see your boyfriend, Curtis Williams."

"Yes, I'm Stephanie. What's going on? Is he all right?"

"Yes, he's fine. I just want to let you know that he'll be released in a couple of hours. Please understand that we had to hold Curtis based on the evidence against him. The DEA would like to apologize for any inconvenience to you or your family."

I exhaled in relief. It seems as though Reggie took my threats seriously. I dropped my head and cried. I couldn't believe this ordeal was finally over and that Curtis was actually coming home. I pulled a napkin from my purse and wiped my eyes.

"Can I get you something to drink while you wait?" he asked.

"No, thank you. I'm fine," I sniffed.

Greg got up and walked out. I composed myself before getting up and going to the bathroom, where I ran some cold water on my face, then walked back to the waiting room and took a seat.

About an hour later, Curtis came walking through the door escorted by a corrections officer. I jumped up from my chair and ran into his arms. We held each other as we stood in the middle of the hallway for what seemed like hours before separating for a short kiss.

"I can't believe this is over," he said as we headed for the door.

"Yeah, I know. I hope I'm not dreaming," I replied.

"Let's hurry up and get the hell out of here."

I looked over at Curtis and grabbed his hand as we walked to my car before pulling out of the parking lot. As we drove down the street, Curtis looked over his shoulders in the direction of Fulton County jail, nodding his head. "I don't ever want to see this place again. Ever."

I smiled. "Where to, baby?"

"I want to see my son. Where is he?" Curtis asked.

"Oh, he's at Mya's."

"Let's pick him up and go out and get something to eat. I'm craving a thick and juicy hamburger from Fuddruckers."

I smiled.

We continued down the highway while Curtis stared out the window as we passed the cars and trucks alongside the road. Suddenly he frowned and looked over at me. "You know, I still can't understand why G-man turned on Cedric, his own cousin. It just doesn't make sense."

I looked over at a puzzled Curtis. "Yes, it does make sense."

"What do you mean?"

"Let's just say I made him an offer he couldn't refuse."

"What?"

"I played him just like he tried to play us."

I explained to Curtis in detail about how Reggie used me to put all of his drug transactions in a safe deposit box under the bishop's name and how just in the nick of time I was able to get the information and threaten to go to the police if he didn't do what he could to get Curtis out of jail. By the time we made it to Mya's house, Curtis was sitting there, stunned, his mouth partially open from surprise.

"Are you okay?" I asked.

"Yeah, I'm cool. I just can't believe how stupid I acted over the last few months, not supporting you in what you wanted because of my selfishness. Then you go and stick your neck out for me. I love you, Stephanie."

I smiled in response because I knew now, more than all the other times Curtis told me he loved me, that this one was sincere. "I love you, too," I replied.

The next morning, while Curtis was in the shower, the phone rang. It was Reggie calling me collect from the Fulton County jail. I was nervous after I accepted the charges, not knowing what to expect.

"Sister?" he whispered.

I cleared my throat. "Reggie, what are you doing calling me?"

"You know why I'm calling. To make sure we're still in agreement."

"Yeah, but there's one thing you left out of our agreement and that's the—"

"Wait, shhhhh. Not over the phone. I want you to come by later today so we can talk."

"No, I'm not going back down there, Reggie. You're going to have to figure out another way."

There was silence.

"There is no other way, unless you want to wait till I get out?"

"No, I don't know when that will be. Don't you have something lying around?"

"No, I don't have anything. Wait—yes, I do. Look on the back of one of the papers you have from the envelope and you'll see some instructions. Follow them and afterwards we should be cool."

"Okay, I'll do that," I replied.

"And, sister, don't cross me. Whatever you do, don't cross me," he said before hanging up.

I put the phone on the charger and took a deep breath before running into the room and opening the envelopes one by one. When I got to the third one, I discovered some writing on the back corner of one of the papers. It was titled OFFICE SAFE and had numbers with directions next to each one. I assumed this was the combination to Reggie's safe in his office. I grabbed my notebook from my purse and began writing each number down.

Later that afternoon I drove down to the church and rushed inside through the front door. When I entered, I saw a group of people finishing up what looked to be a meeting of some sort. I walked on toward the back of the church and down the hall leading to Reggie's office. As I got close enough to reach for the door, a young lady appeared out of nowhere, almost running into me. "Oh, excuse me," I said as I moved to the side, avoiding her.

"I'm sorry. I'm not looking where I'm going," the woman replied. "Wait. Stephanie, right?"

"Yes," I replied, looking surprised.

"Hi—I'm Angela, Pattie's sister. I met you the other day."

"Oh, yeah, I remember. How are you?"

"I'm fine. I'm going through a divorce and came down here today for counseling from the bishop."

"I'm sorry to hear that."

"Yeah—anyway, have a good day," she said as she walked off.

I waited until she was out of my sight before I turned toward Reggie's door. But a group of women started coming down the hall, stopping to have conversation. Suddenly Sister Pattie appeared.

"Hey, sister, what are you doing here?" she asked.

"Oh, uh, I was just in the area and saw some cars outside and decided to stop by."

"Well, come on to my office—we're just finishing up choir rehearsal."

I followed Sister Pattie to her office and took a seat. Minutes later, Angela appeared and we talked for what seemed like hours.

Angela seemed really nice and was around the age of twenty-nine, close to my age. She really didn't have much of a life outside of spending time with her child. I began to feel really sorry for her.

Before she left, we exchanged numbers because I thought it would be good for her to hang out with Mya, Tangie, and me on one of our girls' nights out.

I looked at my watch and decided it was time to go. If I couldn't check the safe today, I would just have to come back some other time. I left Sister Pattie's office and walked up to Reggie's office and looked around before turning the doorknob. The door squeaked as I slowly pushed it open and closed it behind me. There was a lamp on Reggie's desk that shed enough light for me to find my way to the safe. I pulled out my notebook with the numbers and put it under the lamp so I could see clearly. I pulled back the painting and began turning the dial and opened the safe. I reached in and pulled out stacks of paper from the front, making my way to the back until I felt what seemed to be neatly stacked bundles. When I pulled the bundles out closer to the light, it was stacks of money. I opened my purse and put the money inside, then reached inside and pulled out several more bundles, also putting them in my purse, until the safe was empty. I gathered the stacks of paper from the desk and put them back in the safe before closing it and walking toward the door. Still nervous, I slowly opened it and rushed out of the church to my car and drove home.

When I arrived, Curtis was sitting on the couch. "Hey, baby. Where have you been all this time?" he asked.

I sat down on the couch beside him and emptied my purse. His eyes opened wide as the bundles of money fell on the table. He picked up the stacks of money and thumbed through them. "Where did you get this money? It's got to be at least two hundred thousand dollars here."

"This is the rest of the deal I made with Reggie. I told him that in addition to your freedom, he had to give us back our money plus some extra to compensate us for putting us through this horrible ordeal."

"What?"

"Yeah, he had some money in an office safe at the church. Now you can open the body shop you've always wanted. Plus, have some money left over to buy some brand-new equipment for your shop."

"We can't justify having all this money, Stephanie," Curtis said, getting up from the couch.

"We can just keep the cash in the house or in a safe deposit box, then lease a building based on my income. The cash can be used when necessary," I suggested. Curtis paced the room in deep thought, often staring at the bundles on the table next to me as I sat back on the couch looking at him.

"What's the matter, Curtis?"

"I don't know if it's a good idea to take this money. I just got out of jail and I ain't trying to go back."

"Curtis, this money belongs to us. This is our opportunity to get our lives back on track and do the things we've always wanted to do."

Brandon came running from his bedroom and into my arms. Seeing this, Curtis smiled as I kissed Brandon on the forehead.

"Okay, Stephanie. You're right. This is a chance for me to be legit and run my own business. Let's do it," he said as he walked over and hugged both me and Brandon.

CHAPTER 54

Tangie

Monday was difficult for me because of my traumatic weekend experience with Walter. I was still having nightmares, seeing that crazy bitch walk through that door waving a gun at us. It served Walter's ass right for trying to play me for a fool. *I wonder how he's doing, by the way*, I thought.

The bell sounded as I met my class out front and guided them to the classroom. While inside, I took roll, only to discover that Tina was not in class. At first I felt relieved, but later began to feel sorry, knowing that her dad could've indeed died that night. During lunch, as I sat in the teachers' lounge talking to Stephanie and Mya, Mr. Ridgewell came in with a look of concern on his face.

"Ms. Jackson, can I see you for a moment?" he asked politely.

I nodded and followed Ridgewell toward his office. Halfway there, I saw Tina's mom through the window, sitting in Ridgewell's secretary's office looking over some papers. Upon passing the window, I quickly turned my head in the opposite direction to keep from having eye contact with her as I walked into Ridgewell's office.

"Have a seat," he said.

I sat down, puzzled. "What's up, Ridgewell? What's so important that you pulled me away from my lunch?"

"Well, I want to let you know that I was just notified that one of your students' parents was involved in an accident this past weekend and is in critical condition."

"Oh, my God. What? Is Tina's dad okay?"

"What?" Ridgewell said, confused.

"You're talking about Tina's dad, Walter—uh, I mean Mr. Washington, right? Suddenly Mr. Ridgewell's secretary entered the room with papers in her hand. "Mr. Ridgewell—oh, I'm sorry for interrupting. I didn't know you had someone in here."

"Is there something you need?" Mr. Ridgewell asked.

"Well, I just need you to sign these papers for me," she replied.

Mr. Ridgewell looked up at his secretary, grabbing the papers. "No problem . . . Now, Ms. Jackson, you were saying something about Tina's dad, Mr. Washington. What about him? I'm referring to Patrick Harris's parent. You know, the little redheaded, freckle-face kid."

Tina's mom appeared behind Mr. Ridgewell's secretary. "How did you know about my husband?" she asked firmly.

I glanced at Ridgewell and his secretary before looking at Mrs. Washington. All of them wore looks of confusion.

I sat there, silent for a moment, as she came closer to me. "How did you know about my husband?" she repeated even more firmly.

"Mrs. Washington, what's going on?" Ridgewell asked.

"I want to know how Ms. Jackson knew my husband was involved in an accident," she replied in a threatening tone.

"Ms. Jackson?" Ridgwell asked. "What is this about?"

I looked up at Mrs. Washington. "Uh, I—"

I grabbed both sides of the chair with my hands and quickly pushed myself to my feet in case she tried to attack me. Upon doing so, my bracelet fell from my left arm to the floor. Before I could reach down to pick it up, Mrs. Washington grabbed my bracelet and held it in the air.

"What's this?" she said, dangling it in front of my face. "It was you all along, wasn't it? This is the bracelet my daughter found under my den couch."

"What? That's ridiculous," I replied as I reached for it.

Mrs. Washington pulled the bracelet out of my reach. "My daughter showed me this bracelet and told me that her teacher Ms. Jackson had one just like it. Thinking my daughter had taken something that didn't belong to her, I made her return it a few weeks ago. It all makes sense now. You've been fucking my husband in my house. You were with him this past weekend at the hospital—

the woman the police said ran out of there in a hurry. That's how you know about my husband because I haven't told anyone else about his accident!" she shouted.

"Now hold on a minute, Mrs. Washington. This is a school. You must keep your voice down," Mr. Ridgewell said as he walked around his desk.

Before I could open my mouth to respond, Mrs. Washington threw a punch that hit me directly in my right eye. It made me stagger.

"Bitch, you must be out of your mind, thinking you could get away with some shit like that."

Before I could regain my balance, she ran toward me, grabbing my hair and causing us to spill onto the floor outside Ridgewell's office. She dug her nails into the side of my neck as we both rolled around, yelling and screaming. Ridgewell and his secretary tried to separate us as I started swinging wildly at Mrs. Washington. Suddenly the door to the teachers' lounge opened and several teachers, including Stephanie and Mya, ran out.

"Somebody help me separate them, please!" I could hear Ridgewell shout.

Mrs. Washington and I fell to the floor once again, this time with me on top of her. When I tried to throw another punch, I felt someone pull me off her body.

"Tangie, what the hell is going on here?" Stephanie shouted as she pushed me back into Ridgewell's office.

"Bitch, you better be glad they pulled me off of your ass, you hear me?" I shouted.

"You just leave my husband alone!" she yelled in return.

Mya came inside and closed the door behind her as Stephanie backed me up until I dropped down into a chair.

"Tangie, what the hell is going on here?" Stephanie muttered angrily. "Why are you fighting someone at your job like some damn child?"

"That bitch put her hands on me, and where I come from, that shit will get your ass kicked."

"Well, what's going on?" Stephanie asked sharply.

The door flew open as Ridgewell walked in, slamming it behind him. "Ms. Jackson, is what she's saying true? Have you been sleeping with this woman's husband?"

I looked at everyone staring at me, waiting for an answer. I touched my face with my fingertips where the pain was throbbing and looked directly at Ridgewell.

"You know I didn't do anything like that," I lied calmly. "Just because this crazy woman comes in here and accuses me of something, you take her side."

"I'm not taking anyone's side. I just need to know the truth so I'll know how to handle this mess," he snapped. "Now, did you or didn't you?" he asked, looking directly into my eyes.

I looked back for a couple of seconds without blinking. "No," I replied softly.

Ridgewell took two steps back and wiped across his chin with his right hand before taking a deep breath, still making eye contact. "Okay, well, that's all I need to know."

"What are you going to do now, Ridgewell?" Mya asked.

"I have no choice but to call the police. One of my teachers was just assaulted."

Stephanie gave me an evil look as she followed Ridgewell out the door. Mya reached over and gave me a tissue from Ridgewell's desk.

"Here, you have a scratch that's starting to bleed," she said.

Stephanie appeared minutes later with a wet towel, throwing it in my lap. "How could you do that to that woman, Tangie?"

"What?" I replied, wiping the towel on my face.

"You know what the hell you did. You fucked that lady's husband."

Mya got up and closed the door.

"I could see the lie in your eyes. Todd is one thing, but your student's parent. How low are you willing to go?"

"Look, don't judge me, all right. I made a mistake."

"You're always using that excuse."

"Stephanie, I don't need this shit from you right now. I said I made a mistake, so just drop it, okay?"

"Ridgewell is going to call the police and have this woman arrested over some shit you started. Why is it that you only care about yourself?"

Mya walked between Stephanie and me.

"Look, this is not the place to be discussing this. What if someone was to walk in? The bell is about to ring any minute and the kids will be returning to class soon. They don't need to see you two in here going at it like this."

Stephanie turned and walked out of the office with Mya close behind her. Seconds later, the lunch bell sounded. As I was about to get out of my chair, Ridgewell walked back in.

"Sit back down, Ms. Jackson," he said as he took a seat behind his desk. "Stephanie pleaded with me not to call the police and have Mrs. Washington arrested, but I *do* have to file a report to the school board to protect myself. Mrs. Washington has been escorted from the school premises. Now, are you sure you don't have anything to tell me?"

I moved the towel from my face. "No, you saw what happened. She came in here and attacked me."

"Do you want to file charges of any kind or have any comment to make on my report?"

"No, it's over now, so let's just drop it. Thanksgiving is in a couple of weeks. I would like to take leave until then. I don't want to be around my kids with my face looking like this."

"Sure, take some sick time and I'll get a sub in here to cover until you return. Besides, I wouldn't feel comfortable with you being in the same class with Tina until this thing blows over," he continued. "As a matter of fact, go on home now."

Later that evening, Stephanie and Mya came to my apartment, where Stephanie started lecturing me again. She continued on until I finally came clean to them about how Walter and I met, then what happened up until the night I almost got killed by his other mistress. It wasn't until then that Stephanie finally calmed down enough to feel a little sympathy for me seeing that I got played on top of almost getting my ass kicked. Stephanie left, and Mya, who didn't have much to say, was right behind her as I sat in the apartment, speechless, thinking about my day.

CHAPTER 55

Stephanie

On my way home from Tangie's house, I asked Angela to stop by my place to pick up some canned goods I wanted to donate to the church for their annual Feed the Homeless Food Drive for Thanksgiving. I would have taken it myself, but Curtis called and said Brandon had come down with a slight fever and I didn't want to have him out in the cool air.

When I got home, Curtis was on his way out the door to meet a real estate agent to look at a vacant building, a possible location for his new body shop.

In the midst of giving Brandon another spoonful of chicken noodle soup, Mya called.

"Girl, what are we going to do about Tangie? I can't believe she fought that woman at the school today."

"Yeah, I know. That's why I was hard on her, 'cause she knows better than to do something that stupid like sleeping with her student's parent, risking her career. She better be glad Ridgewell didn't call the police."

"I know, 'cause it could have gotten ugly. The school board could've gotten involved and everything. Who knows? That lady may still report it."

"I don't think so, 'cause Ridgewell and his secretary saw her throw the first punch. She would risk going to jail as well," I said.

"Yeah, I never thought about that," Mya replied.

Brandon coughed loudly. "Here—just take one more spoonful of the soup and you're finished, baby," I said.

Brandon coughed once again. "Is he okay?" Mya asked.

"He's not feeling well. I'm about to put him to bed as soon as my friend Angela gets here to pick up the canned goods I'm donating to the church for Thanksgiving."

"Speaking of which, are you and Curtis going to have a big dinner this year?"

"I don't know. We really haven't discussed it. What about you? Aren't you going home?"

"I *was*, but changed my mind. I'm just not ready to break the news about my pregnancy to my parents yet. I know they're going to go off when they find out."

"Mya, you're a grown-ass woman. Why does it matter what they think? Besides, your father's a bishop. He'll understand."

"No, he won't. Nor will my mother. You have to understand— my father is on the national council of bishops for the Full Gospel. They make the laws for most of the churches across the country. His daughter being pregnant, especially without being married, could ruin everything he worked so hard to accomplish. My mother will never forgive me."

"Damn, it's *that's* deep?" I asked.

"Girl, you just don't understand how deep. Besides, I'm still having some morning sickness. I can't be around them like that."

"Well, since you'll be here, let's plan something together."

"I got an idea. Why don't we all come over to my house for Thanksgiving? I can make the turkey and dressing. You can do the greens and macaroni and cheese, and Tangie can make the pies."

"You mean, Tangie can buy the pies. You know Tangie can't do nothing in the kitchen but make a sandwich. She'll probably go to Kroger's or something," I joked.

Mya laughed. "Come to think of it, I don't think I've ever seen Tangie cook."

"Thank you. But, that sounds like a plan. Let's do it," I agreed. "I'll call Tangie later and let her know. She may come if she's not still mad at the way I talked to her today."

"She'll be fine," Mya reassured me.

Suddenly there was a knock at my door. "Mya, I think that's my friend Angela. I'll call you later." I hung up the phone.

I opened the door and let Angela in. "Hey, oooh girl, I like your house," she said, looking around until her gaze fell on Brandon, still sitting in the kitchen. "And is that your son over there?"

"Yeah, that's him." I smiled. "He's not feeling well, though."

Angela walked over and stood in front of Brandon before kneeling down and pinching his cheek. "I have a son, too. Maybe I can bring him over so the two of them can play someday," Angela said.

"I'm sure he'd like that," I replied.

Angela played around with Brandon while I made sure I had all the canned goods bagged up.

Curtis came through the door from his meeting earlier than I expected and greeted Angela before giving me a kiss. He turned and walked toward Brandon, who was getting out of his chair to run toward Curtis. "How's my little man doing?" Curtis said, picking Brandon up.

"He's still not feeling well. I'm about to give him a bath and put him to bed shortly," I said.

"No, baby, I'll do it. You entertain your company." Curtis walked in the back toward the bathroom.

I turned into the direction of Angela, who had a smile on her face. "That's wonderful. It reminds me of how my husband and I used to be before he, well, started tripping."

She looked down at the floor, then back up at me, trying to keep the tears from building.

"Are you okay?" I asked.

"Yeah, thanks—I just miss those times," she replied as she rubbed her eyes.

I wanted to know the details behind her pain, but didn't want to pry. Angela reminded me a lot of Mya because she is so emotional. I wanted her to meet Tangie and Mya and maybe hang out with us on one of our girls' outings one weekend. Then it dawned on me that Thanksgiving was just around the corner. This would be a good time for her to meet everyone together.

"Angela, what are you doing for Thanksgiving?"

"Well, my sister invited me over to her house for dinner, but I don't know if I'm going. I'm not ready for all the questions about my marriage from my other family members. Plus, my son will be with his father at his parents' house. I may just sit at home and have some quiet time alone," she replied in a disappointed voice.

"No, why don't you have dinner with me and my friends. We're going to meet at one of my girls' house and have dinner together. I really want you to meet them. I think you'll like them a lot."

"Oh, I don't know. I don't want to intrude," she replied.

"You're not intruding. It'll just be my family and closest friends. C'mon, I would feel bad if you were just sitting at home alone."

"Well, okay. What can I bring?" she asked with a grin.

"You don't have to bring anything. We've got that covered," I replied.

"No, I have to bring something. I know—do you guys drink wine?"

"Yeah, all except for Mya. She's pregnant."

"Well, I'll bring wine for us and some soda for Mya," Angela said.

"Yeah, that'll be great," I replied excitedly.

Curtis walked into the kitchen and grabbed a beer from the refrigerator. Angela looked over at him, then back at me. "Well, I'd better be going and let you two get back to your son."

Angela, still wearing her smile, stood up and leaned over, giving me a big hug before grabbing the canned goods I placed by the front door.

"Call me tonight if you feel like talking," I said.

Angela got into her car and pulled off, fading away down the street.

I turned around to Curtis, standing there with his beer in hand. We both walked toward Brandon's room as Curtis began telling me about his day.

CHAPTER 56

Mya

Thanksgiving was only two days away and I was just picking up the turkey from the supermarket. After trying three different stores, I finally found a turkey I thought would feed my guests. Then I decided to get the rest of the ingredients I needed from the same store.

When I made it home, my phone rang as I walked inside, placing the grocery bags on the floor in a rush. By the time I got to the receiver, whoever it was had apparently hung up. Immediately, I went back to the foyer, picked up the groceries from the floor, and placed them on the kitchen counter.

Later, after changing into something more comfortable, I went back downstairs and began seasoning my turkey to be cooked tomorrow evening. After cleaning up the kitchen and washing the dishes, I headed upstairs to take a hot bath. Suddenly, my doorbell rang as I made it to the top of the stairway. Annoyed, I turned around and walked down to the door, then leaned forward, looking through the peephole to see who could be coming to my home this late in the evening. As my eyes adjusted to the image through the tiny hole, I jumped back, pinning myself against the wall next to the door while putting my hand over my chest in total shock. *Oh, my God*, I thought as I tried to compose myself. I took a deep breath and slowly opened the door.

"Surprise!" everyone shouted as they rushed inside.

It was my father the bishop, my mother Cathy, Grandma LeVeaux, my favorite cousin Rodney, and his brother Flip. Each, with the exception of Grandma LeVeaux, had their suitcases in hand.

Flip, who is tall and light brown with short, curly hair, is the one cousin my dad respected. Rodney, a tall, muscular, light-skinned brother with green eyes who was just released from prison a few months ago, is the eldest of the two. Flip is a graduate of Oral Roberts University and is studying to be a minister under my father's tutelage. Rodney, on the other hand, is the one person my father despises in the entire family. I think that's why he and my father and Uncle Edward don't get along. In fact, they hardly speak. My Uncle Edward is not a member of my father's church, nor do you ever see them together at any family functions. My mother says it's because my Uncle Edward resents my father's success, being that my father is the youngest of the two. Frankly, I'm surprised to see my father and Rodney in each other's company without being at each other's throat.

"Oh, my God," I said out loud, still in total shock. "What are you guys doing here?"

My mother rushed over and hugged me as her honey-brown hair moved with the motion of her head. "Well, when you told me you couldn't make it home for Thanksgiving, I called everyone and we all decided to surprise you and come to Atlanta to spend it here with you," she said and smiled. "We tried calling earlier but no one answered . . . Oooh, Mya, I see you cut your hair. I like it." My mother ran her fingers through it.

I smiled.

My dad, a tall, light-skinned man with a husky build, leaned over and kissed my forehead. Flip kissed my cheek. Grandma LeVeaux stood in the background, grinning from ear to ear as Rodney stood beside her holding his bags.

"Grandmaaaa," I said, reaching out and grabbing her frail little body and kissing her rosy cheek. "Look at you, Grandma. You look great! I'm so happy to see you."

Grandma LeVeaux smiled as she returned my hug.

"So, you forgot about old Rodney, huh?" Rodney put down his bags, reaching out to me.

"Of course not." I kissed Rodney's cheek and hugged him.

"How on earth did you get my father to let you tag along?" I whispered, still in his embrace.

"I didn't. Grandma did. He raised all kinds of hell when he found out I was going," Rodney whispered in return. "He's been on my ass the entire ride here."

I giggled before turning around to face everyone. "This is really a surprise," I said, forcing a smile.

After putting their suitcases away, we all settled in the den, where we began talking about old times. I sat next to my grandma with a pillow over my stomach, self-conscious about the little weight that I had gained that apparently had gone unnoticed. Don't get me wrong, I was happy to see my family. It's just that the timing was completely off. Rodney sat next to me and across from my father, who stared at him menacingly from time to time.

My parents grabbed my photo album and passed pictures around, reminiscing about them. My mother talked in detail about the pictures we took as children, while my father focused on the pictures of my teenage and college years with the family because Rodney wasn't in them. That was during the times Rodney was in and out of jail before finally going to prison. As each picture was passed, Rodney asked why he wasn't in them, at which time my father would remind him that he was locked up, which led to small arguments throughout the night between the two, causing my Grandma LeVeaux to intervene.

In the midst of conversation, everyone seemed tired from their long trip. My mother, who normally drank wine only before going to bed, asked for a glass of merlot. I directed her to the kitchen, where she poured a glass for my father and herself.

"Baby, you have an entire turkey in the refrigerator, seasoned and everything. Are you planning a big dinner or something?" my mother asked.

"Oh, yeah. Because I decided to stay home, my friends and I thought it'd be a good idea to have dinner over here."

"Well, good—I've never met your friends. Do you guys have everything you need? Surely, this is not enough to feed all of us. Tomorrow we'll go to the store and get more food."

"Well, we've each agreed to bring something. Maybe we can just get another turkey."

"Oooh, that's wonderful," she replied excitedly.

* * *

The next day I got up early because the morning sickness had me nauseous. My mother, who slept in the bed with me, was snoring loudly as I tiptoed into my bathroom, gently closing the door behind me before kneeling over the toilet. I turned on the vent to muffle the sound, often lifting my head to catch my breath. I got up and splashed cold water on my face. Then I brushed my teeth and climbed back in bed and slept until I heard my mother making noises as she went through her suitcase trying to find something to wear. I sat up staring at her sitting on the floor.

"Good morning, Mama," I said and wiped my hand across my face, yawning.

"Hey, baby, are you about to get up? I want to go to Macy's and buy this dress I saw."

"Yeah, give me a minute." I slowly got out of bed.

"You want some breakfast?"

"No, I'm fine." I walked to the bathroom.

When I made it downstairs, everyone was sitting in the den watching TV, with the exception of my father. He was still in the guest bedroom having his prayer time. He usually prayed for about an hour each day after he got up before starting his day. He'd been doing that ever since I was a little girl.

Thanksgiving Day, Mother helped me set the table for dinner. Tangie and Stephanie were both running behind schedule. Tangie had lost track of time while visiting her parents and Stephanie was still waiting for her friend Angela to arrive at her house so that they could all ride together.

At three-thirty, Tangie walked through the door with a cake and a couple of pies she'd bought at the supermarket. She was greeted by my parents and Grandma LeVeaux as she walked to the den where Flip and Rodney were watching TV. Later she came into the kitchen with me and placed her bags on the counter.

"Damn, who are those fine-ass brothers in the next room?" she asked, looking over her shoulder.

"Girl, don't even think about it. Those are my cousins, Flip and Rodney."

"Which one has the green eyes?"

"That's Rodney, and no, I'm not hooking you up."

"I'm just asking, that's all. You just scared I might wind up in your family," she joked.

We both laughed.

Minutes later, Stephanie, Curtis, and Brandon arrived. After being introduced to my family, Stephanie came into the kitchen to heat up the food she'd cooked as Curtis and Brandon joined my family in the den.

"Where is your friend?" I asked.

"Oh, she's running behind. Apparently there was an accident on Interstate-285. I gave her the directions, so she should be here any minute. You'll like her, girl. She's really cool."

I nodded as we rushed to get the food ready to be served.

Because Brandon is not a turkey eater and was feeling a little under the weather Stephanie fed him a happy meal from McDonald's and put him to bed upstairs in my room.

Once the food was all heated up and placed in serving bowls, we all began taking our places. The men sat on one side, with the exception of my father, who sat at the head of the table. The ladies sat on the opposite side, except for my Grandma LeVeaux, who sat at the other end of the table, facing the doorway.

As we placed the food on the table, the doorbell rang. "I'll get it. That's probably Angela," Stephanie said, walking toward the door.

Minutes later, Stephanie appeared with this really cute, petite woman with a caramel skin tone and black hair in braids that hung down slightly past her shoulders.

"Everybody, this is my friend Angela from my church," Stephanie said.

"Hi, Angela, I'm Mya—welcome to my home," I said, then introduced her to everyone at the table. When I got to Tangie, she had a puzzled look on her face and gave Angela a dry hello. My guess is that she was intimidated by the way my cousin Rodney was staring Angela up and down from the moment she walked into the room. "You can have a seat next to me," I said, and directed her to a chair in the middle of the table.

Angela had a bag that Stephanie took and placed on a table behind us where the refreshments were kept. I scanned the table to make sure I had all the food set out, only to realize that I forgot to get the dinner rolls. I rushed back to the kitchen and pulled the rolls out of the oven and placed them in a bowl. Before I could turn around, I bumped into Tangie, who cornered me by the doorway.

"I almost forgot the rolls," I said as I tried to get past Tangie.

"Girl, forget the damn rolls. I think I know that girl," Tangie said, her face wrinkled in thought.

"Who? Stephanie's friend, Angela?" I replied. "Girl, you don't know her. You're just mad 'cause Rodney was checking her out and not paying you any attention," I said as I walked by Tangie.

She pulled me back into the kitchen. "Girl, I'm for real. I think I know her."

"Whatever, Tangie," I replied.

"We're starving out here. Will you please hurry up so we can eat?" my dad shouted from the next room.

I passed Tangie as she followed me back into the dining room. I took a seat, placing the rolls on the table in front of me before my dad said grace.

After his five-minute-long prayer, he finally cut the turkey before everybody dug in and began to eat. There was silence at first, until everyone took several bites. Some chatter began soon after among people who sat closest to one another, but nothing widespread until my father began going around the table one by one, asking everyone to tell a little about themselves. As each person shared something personal, I noticed my father's facial expression changing from pleasant to what looked to be concern. First, it was Stephanie and Curtis, who weren't married and were living together with a child. Second, it was Tangie, who had been divorced twice, both marriages resulting in issues related to her own selfishness. As my father got around to me, my grandma gestured for me to get her another glass of water from the kitchen.

When I returned to the table, I noticed Angela was walking around, pouring wine. I reached over to place Grandma LeVeaux's water in front of her as Angela reached for my glass. Noticing this, I quickly turned around, placing my hand over the top of it. "None for me, thank you." I said politely.

"Oh, I'm sorry—I forgot you're pregnant. When is the baby due, by the way?"

Suddenly there was instant silence as everyone stared directly at me. I turned and looked right into my father's eyes as he sat there stone-faced.

"What did you say, young lady?" my father said as he stood up, staring at Angela. Stephanie dropped her head as Tangie's mouth flew open in disbelief.

Angela looked around the room confused at the silence. "Uh, I asked if—"

"I heard you, young lady. Mya, what is she talking about?" my father interrupted in a loud tone.

My eyes shifted in every direction and my body was frozen stiff.

"Answer your father, Mya Cynthia LeVeaux," my mother demanded.

"Um, uh, I was going to tell you—"

"Tell us what?" my dad said angrily.

I sat there speechless as my father continued to chastise me as if I were some high-school kid coming in after curfew. All my friends were staring—I knew they were embarrassed for me.

"That you've been out here throwing your life away. For who? Some thug that doesn't have the decency to marry you first before he knocks you up, or better yet, even show his face at your dinner table on Thanksgiving like a real man. Who the hell is he, anyway?"

My body felt numb as I tried to find the right words. All I could think of saying was, *I'm a grown-ass woman and this is my life, not yours*, but as I opened my mouth, my Grandma LeVeaux stood up.

"Enough, Franklyn. We'll talk about it later. Don't embarrass her in front of her friends."

I looked over at my grandma with tears in my eyes. Out of all the times she's been there for me, this was the one time I needed her the most. But then I realized that for once in my life, I had to stand up for myself.

My dad cut in. "No, Mama, I want to know who the man is that's responsible for getting my daughter pregnant and I want to know *now*. All this time you're out running in the house of the devil, when you should've been running in the house of the Lord," he continued.

"Amen, Bishop," my mother shouted.

I stood up slowly and looked directly at my father as tears began to flow like a river. "I knew you would react like this. That's why I didn't tell you yet."

"Forget all that. Who is he, Mya? Call him up and tell him to come over here right now." His voice got louder with each word. "Get him on the phone. Who is he?"

"Yes, Mya. Who is this person?" my mother cut in.

"Look, this is not the time or the place," my grandma replied loudly.

"With all due respect, Mama LeVeaux, this is *my* child. I think you need to stay out of this for now." my mother interrupted.

"Wait a gotdamn minute! Who do you think you're talking to?" my grandmother said and pointed at my mother.

Suddenly voices were going back and forth until I just couldn't take it anymore.

"All right!" I shouted above the voices. "Darryl, his name is Darryl—Darryl Cooper," I sniffled.

Angela, who was sitting beside me, shouted, "Oh God, Darryl Cooper? That's my husband."

Tangie cut in. "I knew it. I told you I knew her from somewhere. She looks slightly different with her hair braided but that's the girl that answered the door the day we followed Darryl's ass home. I knew you looked familiar."

"What?" Stephanie replied loudly, looking at Angela. You mean your husband is Darryl Cooper? The one you're divorcing?"

Angela gave Stephanie a half nod before dropping her head.

I turned and looked at Angela, who was wiping tears from her eyes. Then it hit me that this *was* the girl that answered the door that day we followed Darryl home. I, too, was thrown off by Angela not wearing her glasses and with her hair in braids.

My dad cut in. "You mean you've been sleeping with this woman's husband? My God, sinners ya'll, sinners who are going straight to hell with gasoline drawers on. I can't believe I'm at the dinner table breaking bread with these fornicators, jezebels, and thieves. Lord, forgive me!" he shouted as he slammed his fork on his plate.

Angela looked over at Stephanie. "I have to go." As she grabbed her purse and jumped out of her chair, Stephanie got up and reached for her, but Angela ran out the door.

Seeing this, my dad looked around the table as he continued talking loudly. "I refuse to stay here one minute longer. Baby, get your bags. We're leaving," he said to my mother.

"Flip, run upstairs and get your things. I'd rather sleep in my car than in the comfort of the devil. Mya, from this day forward, you and your, your *bastard child* are not welcome in my house."

I wailed loudly at his remarks. Tangie rushed over and put her arms around me, rubbing my shoulder. Everyone else at the table was stunned as my dad turned to walk away.

"Wait one damn minute, Franklyn!" my Grandma LeVeaux shouted. "I'm not going to let you embarrass my baby like this in front of her friends—or any other time. I thought me and your father raised you right, but I can see that *you* need a quick wake-up call."

"Mama?" my father said and walked toward my Grandma LeVeaux. "This is not about me. This is about your granddaughter and the shame she's brought on herself and this family."

"How dare you, Franklyn, have the nerve to judge her and use God's name in the process. I can't take it any longer," my grandma continued.

"Mama!" my dad shouted.

"What is going on here?" my mother asked.

My grandma walked by my dad and stood alone near the doorway.

"Mya, Rodney, Flip, there's something you must know that has been a secret in this family for years. And each time I looked at you all, it broke my heart to know this lie."

"What are you talking about?" my mother asked nervously.

I turned toward my Grandma LeVeaux as her eyes shifted around the table.

"Rodney, you and Mya are not cousins. You're brother and sister."

"What? Brother and sister?" Rodney interrupted, almost with a chuckle. "Come on, Grandma. What are you talking about?"

"Mama, wait! Don't do this!" my dad tried to cut in, but my grandma kept on talking. "It's true, son. Mya, the real reason your Uncle Edward and your father don't speak is because your father slept with his wife, your Aunt Margaret, and they conceived a child, your brother Rodney."

My mother interrupted. "Oh no, the hell he did! That can't be possible. I've been married to Franklyn for over thirty years and the only child he has is Mya."

"For your information, you didn't know Franklyn then," my grandma replied.

"Mya, when your father was in college finishing up his last semester at the seminary, your Uncle Edward let him stay with him and your Aunt Margaret for the summer. Times were kinda hard, so your Uncle Edward enlisted in the Army reserve to make some extra money. He left for boot camp that same summer and while he was gone, your father began an affair with Aunt Margaret. By the time Uncle Edward returned, Aunt Margaret found out she was pregnant and too far along to abort the baby. Your Uncle Edward found out. At the time of the birth, your father was elected deacon of Mount Carmel Baptist Church in Mississippi under the late Bishop Caldwell. So, to keep from ruining your father's career, your Uncle Edward claimed Rodney as his own.

"He and your Aunt Margaret split up for almost a year, but ended up getting back together. Not only did your Uncle Edward love your Aunt Margaret enough to take her back, but he loved your father enough to endure this pain, but vowed never to have any dealings with him again. So everyone in the family kept it quiet."

"Franklyn, is what she's saying true?" My mother walked over toward my father as he stood there looking down. "*Franklyn, is this true?*" she repeated sharply.

"Is it?" Rodney asked.

My dad stared at us, breathing heavily as his chest moved in and out. Sweat began to form around the sides of his face. He looked over at my mother, then at Rodney, whose face was turning redder by the second. "Everyone, I'm not going to stand here and try to justify my actions from my past. Whatever indiscretions that occurred back then have been forgiven by God himself. And to sit here in front of such a sinful group of people would be an injustice to my faith in my Lord and Savior. So—"

Rodney jumped from his chair and grabbed my father and pushed him against the wall. "Answer the fucking question, man! Is all this shit true?"

My father looked into Rodney's eyes as they stared at each other for what seemed like minutes. "Answer me, mother—"

"Yesssssss, it's true!" my father shouted. "Is that what you want to hear? You are my son, the mistake, the disgrace of the family. I wish it had never happened, but it did. And look at you. Every time I see you, I get sick to my stomach. All my life I dreamed of having a son, someone that could follow in my footsteps and take over everything that I've worked so hard to build. But look at you, a-a-jailbird, with no education, no ambition, nothing going for you."

Rodney tightened his fist into a ball as tears ran down his face.

"Now what are you going to do?" my dad replied, seeing Rodney's anger.

Rodney yelled loudly. "Noooo . . ." As he pulled his arm back to throw a punch, Flip jumped between my father and Rodney as everyone at the table began to shout.

"Let me go," Rodney yelled.

"No, don't do this, Rodney. He's not worth it." Flip turned and looked at my father, who was in tears, leaning against the wall. "How could you tear apart my family like this, Bishop? I went against my own father for you. I believed in everything that you were teaching me, when all along you were nothing but a hypocrite using the Lord's name to get what you want. But you know what? As much as this hurts, I forgive you."

My father cried out loudly before turning and walking out the door. My mother ran upstairs to the guest bedroom, slamming the door behind her. My Grandma LeVeaux, along with Flip and Rodney, walked into the den. Everyone else was sitting at the dining room table in complete silence, stunned.

"Guys, I'm sorry this has spoiled everyone's Thanksgiving, and I apologize for the things my father said. If you'll excuse me, I'm going upstairs. I need to be alone," I said.

Stephanie and Mya came over to me. "Is there anything you need from us before we go?" Stephanie asked.

I shook my head slowly as I turned to walk upstairs.

CHAPTER 57

Stephanie

On our way home, as Brandon lay asleep in the backseat Curtis and I were in complete shock by the revelation that Rodney was Mya's brother by an affair her dad had with her Aunt Margaret. Not to mention Mya being pregnant by Angela's husband, Darryl. That was some straight-up Jerry Springer shit happening with her family. I tried calling Angela several times but she didn't answer her cell phone. In a way I didn't blame her. If I'd been embarrassed the way she was tonight, I wouldn't be in the mood to talk, either. The more I thought about it, the angrier I became, because this could very well have been me caught up in some shit with Reggie—or, better yet, Curtis and some other woman out in the street. I started giving Curtis dirty looks as my guilt began to set in about Reggie. "Curtis, don't you ever put me in a situation like the one we experienced tonight. If you have to cheat on me, leave me first," I snapped.

"What are you talking about? I'm not cheating on you," he replied with a confused look.

I turned and looked out the passenger-side window as he drove on. "You better not be. Because if you were and I found out, I would—"

"Baby, calm down. I'm not cheating on you. You think I'd risk losing you and my son over a piece of ass? Come on, baby, think about it. How dumb would that be?"

"Just know that I would never forgive you or take you back if you did," I replied, relieved at his response.

Curtis let out a deep breath, nodding simultaneously. My cell phone rang—I quickly picked it up, answering it before the first ring ended. "Hello?"

"Girl, what the fuck just happened?" It was Tangie. "I was just enjoying my damn turkey when all hell broke loose. And what were you thinking, bringing that girl Angela to Mya's house?"

"Hell, I didn't know Mya was sleeping with her husband," I replied defensively. "I didn't even know her husband's name. She never mentioned it."

"That was definitely a Thanksgiving to remember," Tangie continued.

"I know. We need to call Mya tomorrow. I can't imagine what she's feeling right about now."

"Get real, girl. When you find out your dad ain't shit, someone who you admired all your life, then to top it off you find out you're pregnant by the husband of the stranger sitting next to you, my guess is that she's feeling pretty fucked-up."

I let out a short laugh as Curtis drove past a Waffle House getting off on the Interstate. "Tangie, hold on one second. Curtis, can we stop and get something to eat? I'm starving."

Tangie laughed. "Girl, I just finished eating a damn Big Mac from McDonald's before I called you. I was so hungry, I wanted to snatch a turkey leg or something before I left, but it wouldn't have been appropriate."

We laughed in unison as Curtis pulled into the parking lot of the Waffle House. "Tangie, let me call you back later. We're about to get something to eat."

I tried calling Angela again once I got home. This time when she didn't answer I left her a message to call me when she was up to it. Curtis didn't say much about the evening until Brandon was in bed and we sat in the den watching TV.

"You know, I feel sorry for Mya. She didn't deserve to be embarrassed like that. I started to cuss her dad's ass out for his remarks about you and Brandon, but I just sat back and chilled for her sake. That's why I don't trust what these so-called preachers talk about 'cause they're the biggest hypocrites out there. Most of them are reformed playas, pimps, or thugs trying to get over by using the Lord's name. But I don't buy it," he said.

"I'm glad you were bigger than that, Curtis." I leaned over and kissed him. "It only would've escalated things."

"Are you going to check on Mya before you go to bed?" he asked.

"I'll call her in the morning, once she's had a chance to cool off some."

After breakfast, Tangie called me. "Have you talked to Mya yet?"

"No, not yet—you?"

"Let's call her," she suggested.

"What?"

"Let's call her," she repeated.

"I don't know, Tangie. She may still be asleep or in the middle of something with her family."

Tangie paused for a moment. "Hold on, I'll call her." Tangie clicked over to her three-way line and seconds later I heard the phone. "You still there?" Tangie asked.

"Uh, yeah, what are you—" I replied before being interrupted by a soft whisper.

"Hello," a voice answered.

"Mya?" Tangie asked. "Are you okay?"

Mya cleared her throat. "Yeah," she sighed.

"Hey, girl. Sorry to call you so early but we were just concerned," I said.

"No, I'm okay. Everyone left this morning except for Rodney and my mother. I'm sorry for the way my dad acted last night."

"Forget it, girl. We understand he was upset. I didn't take it personally," I said.

"Yeah, it's cool . . . Is there anything we can do?" Tangie asked. "I don't know *what*, but whatever it is, consider it done."

"No, I'm just tired. My family and I stayed up all last night talking. My dad apologized to everyone, but he is still having a hard time accepting the fact that I'm pregnant. He ranted and raved a little more before storming out the door and speeding down the street. Flip caught a flight back this morning, but my mother is so upset with my father for lying, she's still upstairs."

"Mya, I'm sorry for bringing Angela to your house. Had I known she was Darryl's wife, I never would have—"

"Stephanie, it's not your fault. Nobody knew . . . Well, guys, I'm still kind of tired so I'm going to get some sleep. Thanks for calling."

When Mya hung up, Tangie went off. "See? If it wasn't for Angela, none of this shit would've happened and things with Mya and her family would've been cool right about now."

"You can't blame her, Tangie. Mya's dad would have reacted the same way no matter when he found out about her pregnancy."

"Well, maybe things would've been different. I mean, with Mya finding out about her dad and all," Tangie continued.

"I'm glad it happened the way it did. Now maybe her father can stop being a hypocrite. Who knows? Maybe the Lord is giving him another chance to make up for his indiscretion by bringing another child into the family."

Tangie calmed down. "Well, I guess I didn't look at it like that."

Brandon came running in the kitchen toward me. "Girl, let me get Brandon some breakfast. I'll call you later."

Two days had passed when I finally talked to Angela. I was leaving the cleaners and decided to give her a call. Surprised that she finally answered the phone, I hesitated when I heard her voice. "Uh, Angela, I, uh, was just, you know, checking on you. Ever since Thanksgiving, I've been worried about you."

"I'm good, considering," she replied.

"I know. I feel so bad. I don't really know what to say. It's like everything is my fault."

"No, it was my soon-to-be-ex-husband's fault. Stephanie, I didn't run out because I was mad at you or Mya. I ran out because I was embarrassed. Darryl has subjected me to so much. I've had my cars keyed, smelled perfume on his shirt, found numbers in his pants pocket, just to name a few. When I left Mya's house the other night, I felt like a complete fool. I guess it was because it happened in the presence of other people—it made me come to my senses. I realized I can't be the victim anymore. It's time for me to get *my* shit together. Mya being pregnant by my husband has proven to me that his ass has been out there having unprotected sex, putting me at risk."

"Wow, I didn't think about that," I replied.

"There's no telling who else Darryl has gotten pregnant or what he's carrying, so I've scheduled an appointment with my doctor this week to have a complete physical. From there, I'm going to get my lawyer to expedite our divorce and take him for everything he's got. So instead of being mad, I'm grateful to you for inviting me over for Thanksgiving. He's going to find out soon enough that he fucked with the wrong bitch," she remarked.

A smile came over my face. It was like I felt Angela's transformation from a naïve little girl to a strong, independent woman.

"I'm glad to hear you say that. I know it's going to take time, but you know I'm here for you, girl."

"Thanks, Stephanie. I appreciate that. Well, I have to go and pick up my son."

"Well, let's do lunch or something when you're up to it," I suggested

"Okay, that sounds good. I'll keep in touch."

Although Angela was forgiving, I still felt like she held me responsible. In a way, who could blame her if she did? But, I've said my piece, so if she calls, fine, and if she doesn't, well, life goes on.

CHAPTER 58

Epilogue

My daughter, Jessica Michelle LeVeaux, was born on April 24 at six o'clock in the morning by C-section. She weighed six pounds and nine ounces with a head full of black hair. I was in labor for a day and a half before the doctors decided to operate.

My mother, who had been back and forth from New Orleans, was by my side from the time my water broke through the birth. I had her call my Grandma LeVeaux and give her the good news. Grandma LeVeaux was the one who suggested Jessica Michelle, after her mother.

My mother was still trying to cope with my father's deceit and was seeking spiritual counseling. In the meantime, she moved in with her younger sister, who lived outside of New Orleans in a small city called Slidell. Despite her personal problems with my dad, she still remained by his side during most of the Sunday services.

Although my dad and I hadn't spoken since the day after Thanksgiving, I still sent him a picture of Jessica a week after she was born. Since then, I received a card from him, wishing the two of us well. According to my mother, seeing Jessica's picture made him realize that God must be giving him another chance to make up for not being in Rodney's life. Last I heard, he plans to step down as the presiding bishop of the Full Gospel when his term ends in June.

Rodney and Flip call to check on Jessica and me regularly. Rodney got a job driving trucks, and when he has to make a delivery in or around the Atlanta area, he stops by or calls just to say hi. We are both still struggling with the fact that we are brother and sister, and often joke about it to lighten the impact of the truth. Nevertheless we remain closer than ever. Rodney and my mother have become closer over the past six months and they are starting to accept one another as immediate family.

The day Jessica and I were released from the hospital, Tangie drove us home. She volunteered to stay with me for a couple of weeks and help me out until I healed from my C-section. The doctor gave me strict orders not to lift anything heavy or do anything strenuous. Tangie had the time to spend with me because her social life pretty much slowed down after she decided to take a couple of classes in the evening at Georgia State University to get her master's to pursue a career as a student counselor.

Curtis surprised Stephanie at the grand opening of his new paint and body shop by getting down on one knee in the presence of family and friends and proposing marriage, which she tearfully accepted.

While Tangie was in class, Stephanie stopped by to see if I needed anything. Because I was running out of detergent, she agreed to go to the supermarket. While Jessica slept I slowly walked downstairs to the kitchen and made a sandwich and got some bottled water. On my way back upstairs, Tangie came walking through the door. "What are you doing home so early?" I asked.

"What are you doing up?"

I rolled my eyes at her. "I got hungry. Why are you back so early?"

"Well, we had a test tonight. Once I finished it, I was out the door."

She put her bags down and followed me upstairs as I sat in a chair, placing my sandwich and water on the tray next to my bed. Tangie walked over to Jessica, sleeping in her bed. "Oh, she looks like a little doll." She smiled.

"Yeah, I need to feed her once she awakes," I said and took a bite out of my sandwich.

"I hate to say it but I think I see some of Darryl in her." She stared with a frown.

"Oh God, I hope she doesn't have his lowdown ways," I joked.

"Well, now, wait a minute. You may want her to have some dog in her to fight these lowdown wanna-be players out there," Tangie laughed.

The doorbell rang. "Oh, that's Stephanie. She came over earlier and went to the store to get some detergent so I can do the wash. Can you let her in for me?"

Tangie went downstairs as I finished my sandwich. Minutes later, Jessica woke up, crying softly. I walked over to her bed, leaning over gently, stroking Jessica's arm as she began to calm down. Suddenly, Tangie came through the door in a rush.

"Girl, you won't believe who had the nerve to show her face in your house!"

"Who?" I replied, surprised.

"That girl, uh, you know, Darryl's wife Angela. She's downstairs right now with Stephanie."

My eyes opened wide in total shock as Stephanie came through the door. "Look, Mya, let me explain."

Tangie cut in. "Girl, what possessed you to bring her here? Not only is that disrespectful to Mya, but it's inconsiderate on your part."

"What? Look, Angela and Darryl are divorced. They have been for a couple of months now. She's moved on with her life. Jessica and Angela's son are siblings, whether we like it or not, and she wants them to have a relationship. She's only here to pay her respects."

"That's bullshit. I don't trust her ass," Tangie replied.

Jessica began crying loudly. "Tangie, can you put Jessica in the bed with me?" I asked.

Tangie picked Jessica up and walked toward my bed.

"If you don't feel comfortable, Mya, I'll go downstairs and tell her it's a bad time," Stephanie said.

Tangie looked over her shoulder. "Why couldn't you ask Mya if it was okay before you had Angela just show up unannounced?"

Stephanie looked at me. "I don't know. I just thought—"

"Look, I don't mind. It's just that I'm caught off guard, that's all. I've thought about this day in my mind over and over, and I *do* want Jessica to know her brother. I just didn't expect this day to come so soon."

"That's the same way Angela feels. She's not here for anything but to try and establish a relationship with you for the sake of the kids," Stephanie continued.

I nodded, looking at Stephanie. "That's fine. Tell her to come on up."

Stephanie left the room, and Tangie started in. "You sure you feel comfortable with this?"

"Yeah," I replied as I sat down in the bed next to Jessica.

My bedroom door slowly opened as Angela appeared with a small bag in her hand. "Hi, Mya. I'm sorry to show up like this, but I finally built up enough nerve to come over."

Stephanie cut in. "Well, I'm going to let you two talk. Tangie, let's go downstairs so they can be alone."

Tangie looked over at me as I nodded my approval. When they left, Angela placed the small bag on my dresser. "I got something for the baby. I understand her name is Jessica?"

"Yes, Jessica Michelle," I replied, smiling. "After my great grandmother . . . Have a seat, Angela." I pointed to the empty chair against the wall facing me.

Angela sat down, staring at Jessica. "She's adorable."

I smiled. "Angela, I appreciate you coming by. We never really discussed the situation about me and Darryl. I honestly didn't know he was married."

"Mya, I, uh, I don't want to spoil this moment by bringing him up. I've moved on. The only contact I have with him now is through our son DJ when he comes by to pick him up. Other than that, Darryl doesn't exist to me. Whatever he told you to get your attention is what he tells all of his women. I don't know, maybe that's why I made him pay during the divorce hearing."

"Really?" I cut in.

"Yeah . . . I got the house, my car, half of the bank account, custody of DJ, and he pays child support and alimony. Right now, Darryl is living in some hole-in-the-wall apartment in Clarkston, Georgia."

I looked away, shaking my head. "I don't feel sorry for him after what he did."

"And you shouldn't. I look at it like this—the only thing he did that's worth anything was to bring two beautiful kids into the world, and I just want them to be close some way or another."

"I'm glad you feel that way, Angela. You just don't know how that makes me feel. I don't want Jessica to have to find out she has a brother out there the way I did. As for Darryl, well, since he doesn't know Jessica exists, maybe I'll just keep it that way."

"Wait a minute—you're not going to take him to court for child support?" she asked, surprised.

"No, I'd rather just move on," I replied.

"Uh, um . . . I'm not trying to tell you what to do, but Jessica needs to know her father regardless of how we feel about him and he *should* have to share the burden of responsibility."

"I don't know," I replied. "I wouldn't know how to handle that. Right now, my concern is Jessica."

"Well, just think about it. It was tough for me, too, but I did it. I'll be glad to help you through it 'cause I have the perfect lawyer for you," she said.

"Let me think about it some more," I smiled.

Jessica started crying loudly. "Oh, can I hold her?" Angela asked.

I was hesitant at first but saw the love in Angela's eyes. "Sure," I replied.

Angela gently picked Jessica up and walked around the room with one hand holding her head and the other under her bottom. "Oooh, I can't wait for DJ to see her."

Instantly Jessica stopped crying.

"Wow, she likes you," I said.

Angela smiled. "Yeah, I'm good with babies."

Tangie came through the door. "I heard Jessica crying and thought maybe she needed changing." She stared at Angela.

Tangie smiled as Stephanie came in the room, then gently put Jessica on the bed as Tangie changed her diaper.

Later that evening, Stephanie cooked dinner. We all sat in the den and watched a movie with Jessica on the sofa next to me. As the hours passed, I felt more comfortable with Angela. Even Tangie started loosening up some as she and Angela conversed.

I took Angela's advice and got a lawyer, who served Darryl with papers for child support. After he disputed the whole idea of Jessica being his child, we went to court. When I walked in the courtroom, seeing Darryl again for the first time in several months terrified me. As I sat in the back waiting for the judge to call our case, Darryl looked over in my direction with an evil smirk. My lawyer leaned forward, blocking our view, after tears began to well in my eyes.

Thirty minutes passed before our names were called. The judge read through the petition filed by my lawyer and began asking Darryl about our relationship. I felt completely humiliated as Darryl explained all the details of our intimacy in front of a packed courtroom. He then began to lie about me stalking him and damaging his friend's home after he claimed he didn't want to see me anymore. There were people behind me laughing as Darryl continued to degrade me. My lawyer grabbed my hand and nodded, directing me to keep my attention on the judge as Darryl finished his lies about me. The judge read through some legal jargon before ordering a paternity test, after which a new court day would be set.

I ran out of the courtroom, crying alone in the elevator, reliving the bullshit Darryl had told everyone in the courtroom. When I got home, Tangie, who had taken off of work, was in the den with Jessica watching TV.

"How did it go?" she asked.

"It was humiliating. That dirty, lowdown bastard made me out to be some desperate tramp begging for his affection. He had the entire courtroom looking at me, laughing."

"Girl, don't worry about that. When his ass gets the results, he'll change his tune."

I stood there in silence as I thought for a moment. "You're right,"

"I know I asked you this before, but this *is* Darryl's baby, right?" Tangie joked.

I cut my eyes at Tangie before walking toward the kitchen. As pissed off as I was, that question didn't deserve an answer.

After I took the paternity test at North Lake Hospital's lab, a month went by before I received a letter from the courts with a court date to reveal the results.

The night before I was to appear in court, I was really scared. Crazy thoughts began to run through my mind. I've seen situations on TV where test results accidentally came back wrong. In my case, I couldn't afford such a mistake. Not only would this affect the way my friends would see me, but it would also have a great effect on the way my family would assess me and my character. Stephanie and Tangie tried to comfort me before I went to bed, but it didn't help because I tossed and turned the entire night. I got up and stood over Jessica, sleeping in her crib, and said a prayer.

The next morning, as I was about to leave my house with Jessica, I was met at my door by Stephanie, Tangie, and Angela.

"Mya, we just wanted you to know that we're here for you. Tangie has agreed to keep Jessica, and Angela and I will go down to the courthouse with you." We walked into the den.

I felt relieved and grateful as I looked at them. "Angela, are you sure you want to go? After all, this is your ex-husband," I said.

"That's why I want to go. I know this is wrong, but I want to see his ass suffer exactly the way he made you and me suffer. It will be my pleasure."

With the exception of Tangie, we left in my car, heading to the courthouse. When we walked in, Darryl was already sitting in front with his lawyer, his back to us. My lawyer came in a few minutes and gestured for me to sit with him. Angela and Stephanie sat in the back corner, out of Darryl's sight. Within minutes, the judge called out our case number. Darryl and I, with our lawyers, stood in front of the judge.

The judge cleared his throat. "This is case number 473552, LeVeaux versus Cooper for paternity, claiming the defendant, Darryl Cooper, is the father of Jessica Michelle LeVeaux. Do we have the results of paternity?" the judge asked the court clerk.

She nodded as she handed the judge a large yellow envelope. The judge opened it and began reading the results silently before looking up in my direction.

"It is determined by the results in front of me that the defendant in this case, Darryl Cooper, is in fact the father of Jessica Michelle LeVeaux by result of a 99.9 percentile."

I quickly looked over at Darryl, who was facing the judge, his eyes wide open in disbelief. "I will schedule another court date in which I will order child support for Jessica Michelle LeVeaux by her father, Darryl Cooper." I covered my mouth with both hands to keep from screaming out loud.

Suddenly the judge's emotions changed. He stared down at Darryl like he was going to jump from behind the bench and whip his ass. Without hesitation, the judge began yelling at Darryl at the top of his lungs about his remarks about me in the first hearing.

When the judge finished chewing his ass out, Darryl turned and found himself face-to-face with Angela as she walked toward me, wearing a huge smile. She glanced over at Darryl as his eyes shifted toward me and Angela simultaneously and we embraced. He stood there, stunned, before finally storming out of the courtroom.

"It's finally over," I said tearfully.

Before going home, I had built up an appetite, something I hadn't had for several weeks throughout this ordeal. We stopped by a restaurant and grabbed a quick bite before going home. When we got to my place I could hear Jessica screaming playfully in the background. "It's about time you all made it home. What took you so long? It's almost three o'clock. Don't tell me you were in court all this time—O. J.'s trial was shorter than this."

"We stopped to get something to eat," Stephanie said.

"What? And you hoes didn't get me anything?" Tangie snapped.

"We brought you some cheesecake." Stephanie handed Tangie a bag from the restaurant.

Tangie walked into the kitchen and grabbed a fork before coming back to the den as she opened her container, exposing the cheesecake. In the midst of taking her first bite, my home phone beside her rang. She chewed slowly, as if she was taking in the flavor, as the phone rang for a second time. "You think you can get that?" I asked Tangie.

"You see my mouth is full." She picked up the phone anyway. "Hello," she answered with a mouthful of food. "Uh—no, ma'am, this is her friend, Tangie. Yes, ma'am, she's right here." Tangie handed me the phone. "It's your mother," she whispered.

With a smile I grabbed the phone. "Hey, Ma,"

"Hey, baby, I have someone who wants to talk to you," she replied.

Confused, I held the phone. "Mya," my dad's voice sounded.

I didn't know having him back would bring happiness into my life the way it did that day. I walked upstairs, holding Jessica, and went into my bedroom, where my dad and I stayed on the phone for what seemed like hours . . .

PLAY THE GAME

DOUG DIXON

ABOUT THIS GUIDE

The suggested questions are intended to enhance your group's reading of *Play the Game*. We hope you have enjoyed this novel.

DISCUSSION QUESTIONS

1. What do you think of Mya? Do you think she was more influenced by Tangie or Stephanie? Why?

2. If you were Stephanie, would you have let Curtis live with you even though he was unemployed and you had his child?

3. What character do you admire the most? Tangie, Stephanie, or Mya, and why? What character did you admire the least and why?

4. What would you have done if you, like Mya, were in a relationship with Darryl and found out he was married?

5. Would you have stood by Curtis if you were Stephanie and found out he had been arrested again for drugs?

6. Did Mya make the right decision when she found out she was pregnant?

7. Did Tangie get what she deserved in the end? Why or why not?

8. What do you think of Bishop Franklyn LeVeaux?

9. Was Grandma LeVeaux right in revealing the bishop's secret?

10. Do you have friends like Tangie, Stephanie, or Mya in your inner circle?